IF I WERE YOU

Also by Joan Aiken

Mansfield Revisited
Foul Matter
The Girl from Paris
The Weeping Ash
The Smile of the Stranger
The Five-Minute Marriage
Last Movement
Voices in an Empty House

Midnight Is a Place
A Cluster of Separate Sparks
The Embroidered Sunset
The Crystal Crow
Dark Interval
Beware of the Bouquet
The Fortune Hunters
The Silence of Herondale

JUVENILES

The Stolen Lake
The Shadow Guests
A Touch of Chill and Other
   Tales
The Skin Spinners: Poems
Arabel and Mortimer
Not What You Expected
Go Saddle the Sea
Arabel's Raven
Street: A Play for Children
The Mooncusser's Daughter: A
   Play for Children
The Green Flash and Other
   Tales

Winterthing: A Children's Play
The Cuckoo Tree
Died on a Rainy Sunday
Night Fall
Smoke from Cromwell's Time
   and Other Stories
The Whispering Mountain
A Necklace of Raindrops
Armitage, Armitage Fly Away
   Home
Nightbirds on Nantucket
Black Hearts in Battersea
The Wolves of Willoughby Chase
The Kingdom and the Cave

IF I WERE YOU

Joan Aiken

DOUBLEDAY & COMPANY, INC.
GARDEN CITY, NEW YORK
1987

Library of Congress Cataloging-in-Publication Data
Aiken, Joan, 1924–
If I were you.
I. Title.
PR6051.I35I35   1987   823'.914   86-19766
ISBN 0-385-23964-5

To all female writers, past and present,
this trifle is affectionately
dedicated

IF I WERE YOU

I

On a hot June evening, two young ladies sat talking, with some intensity, in the gatehouse room of the Abbey School, Reading. This room, located over the arched gateway that led to the main entrance and the school quadrangle, was seldom used for lessons, being considered too noisy and distracting, as it had windows on both sides and any horseman or carriage arriving at the school must pass underneath; it was therefore generally relegated to minor uses: needlework, drawing, school preparation, and piano practice. A number of miscellaneous aids to these activities had found their way to the chamber: a pair of globes, a baize-covered dressmaker's dummy, a box of white chalk, a set of embroidery hoops, a couple of easels, two or three desks, and a pianoforte. Around the walls hung pictures of urns and weeping willows, embroidered in chenille by former pupils at the school.

It must be acknowledged, however, that the main predilection of the young ladies who repaired to the gatehouse room was gossip. Remote from the main current of scholastic occupation, the room was admirably suited for this purpose. Not that gossip was particularly discouraged in any area. The Abbey School was a comfortable, easygoing establishment, planned so as to place no undue burden on the most lethargic intelligence—though such pupils as did choose to apply themselves might pick up an excellent education from the masters who attended there every weekday morning. Mrs. Latournelle, the original founder, a motherly talkative lady with a cork leg and a past somehow relating to the theatre, had retired in 1805, ten years previously, to drink port and rest her cork leg on a sopha; but her place had been taken by her niece, Mrs. Camperdowne, of equally amiable and indulgent temperament. Under the aegis of the latter, the students, provided they were well mannered and did not quarrel, were allowed almost unlimited latitude to read novels, ramble in the garden, pick fruit, play games, chatter to one another, or pursue their studies in a leisurely manner, as the spirit moved them.

The two girls at present comfortably perched on the cushioned window seat of the gatehouse room were not pursuing any study, but one of them at least was very much in earnest.

"This is of *such* importance to me. I must, I *must* go now; don't you see? It may well be my only chance. If you do not help me to do it, you will be consigning me to a life of hopeless—narrow—provincial—"

"Oh, come, my dear Miss Winship! What grand language! *Consigning* you? Why, just tell me why, pray, should your future life be *my* responsibility?"

"You know why! You know perfectly well!"

"It is hardly to be blamed on me, is it, that your father refuses to let you go off and teach the heathen?" said the other reasonably.

"It will be your fault! It will be! Can't you see that this is all *meant?* The great battle against the French having been won at Brussels—the war being over—Mr. and Mrs. Tothill setting off for India next month—"

"You are suggesting," said the other girl rather drily, "that the Almighty settled the matter of the war against the French simply in order that Mr. and Mrs. Tothill could take you to India with them?"

"Oh, don't be satirical, Alvey! And—and blasphemous! You know perfectly well what I mean."

The two girls stared at one another with dislike. And there was reason for their antipathy. They were not close kin, not related in any way; one of them came from Northumberland, England, the other from New Bedford, Massachusetts—and yet they were so alike that they were continually being taken for sisters, not only sisters but identical twins.

Both had long oval faces, clear colouring, dark-brown hair with a slight natural wave, handsomely chiselled lips, and neat straight noses. Sarah Alvey Clement, from New Bedford, was perhaps the taller of the two by half an inch, but unless the pair stood back to back the difference was not discernible, especially as Louisa Winship took pains to dress her hair high on top of her head in a Quakerish coronet of plaits, disdaining the current mode for curls à la Grecque. And this was characteristic of Louisa, who frequently went out of her way to express her disdain for fine clothes or fashionable appearance, yet at bottom had an intensely competitive nature and could not bear to be outstripped in any particular, even the most unimportant.

It is a queer and somewhat shocking experience to meet your own double, your mirror image. How can you help resenting the fact that somebody else, a stranger, has taken the liberty of helping themselves to your personal appearance? To see another person wearing the same gown, the same pelisse, the same bonnet, can be bad enough—but to have them decked out in your own eyes and nose, your hair, teeth, and lips, is hardly to be borne. You are immediately devalued, made to seem simply an oddity, a duplicate.

For this reason, during the three years they had been fellow students at the Abbey School, the two girls had never been friends or intimates, but had remained sedulously aloof from one another. They had never been in the least amused by the ever-recurring ripple of jokes, astonishment, nonsense, and wonder which their identical likeness inevitably created, as other parlour boarders and day pupils came and went. Reluctantly, every now and then, they were forced into displeased partnership, obliged to play the roles of Viola and Sebastian, of Castor and Pollux, Antipholus or Dromio in school theatricals; but at all other times they kept as far distant from one another as the confines of the establishment permitted, since they possessed different tastes, different friends, different temperaments.

Miss Winship was a devout young lady. Her religion bordered on evangelism. She attended church three times on Sunday, and as often during the week as she could contrive. Her maternal grandfather had been a bishop, and she inherited his propensities. She was almost wholly lacking in sense of humour, but was a hard and dedicated worker, applying herself to all the subjects in the school curriculum, as well as various extras, with intelligence and fervour. Alone among the young ladies at the Abbey School she never read a novel, not even Miss Edgeworth, for she regarded with extreme suspicion all such frivolous and useless products of the imagination as stories, poems, or plays. Shakespeare must be endured, for he was on the school syllabus, but even the instructive volumes of Mr. Walter Scott were never opened by her, and as for Byron, whom the other girls read with passion, when they could get hold of his works, Miss Winship would have picked up a red-hot coal with her bare hand sooner than take the most fleeting glance at the pages of *Childe Harold.*

"My Father in heaven is calling me. I am *needed* out there among the heathen," she said now, clenching her fists and hammering them on the windowsill to give emphasis to her words. "I *know* that He wishes me to go."

"Don't you think that He is taking rather a roundabout way of getting you there? Making a great many people tell a great many lies?"

"Oh, don't, don't take such pleasure in being so—so unhelpful. So unsympathetic!"

"You mistake. I take no pleasure in thwarting you. Why should I? But are you absolutely certain that your father will never allow you to go?"

"It is wholly, wholly out of the question. Neither he nor my mother would countenance it for a single moment. Why, why do you think I was packed off to school, down here in the South, at the other end of England, as far from home as possible, but in hopes of forcing me to change my mind? As if a change of scene, or anything of such a slight nature, would make the least difference to *me,*" said Miss Winship, setting her chiselled lips together with the obstinate expression which had caused her nurse Phemie, regarding her at the age of three, to remark, "Ee, yin's a hunk o' the auld granite, if iver there wor!"

"You have written to your parents and suggested the plan again?"

"Of course! Any number of times. And the answer is always a flat negative. That is why they have never permitted me to return home at holiday time—Oh, they said it was because of the distance to Northumberland, because of the length and expense of the journey, but that is not their real reason. I know it was a punishment. From the age of six I have made no secret of my wishes—"

I'll wager you have not, thought her companion, regarding her with dispassionate interest. Miss Winship's eyes were flashing, her face was pale with the intensity of her feelings.

"You quite despair of talking them round, now you have reached the age of discretion?"

"Oh, completely. My mother is a very, very strong-willed character."

"Indeed? What a singular circumstance."

"Why should you say so? You have not met her," remarked Miss Winship, surprised, but did not wait for an answer. "And my father—he is indecisive, on the whole, but exceedingly obstinate. And he is in pain from a hunting accident—so my sister writes—must not be crossed or thwarted, for his temper is very unreliable. And his health is impaired; if he were angered it might cause a seizure, and his death."

"Well, that is very difficult, certainly. It puts him in a strong position. Yet, everybody must die sooner or later," Alvey said thoughtfully. "Are they very obnoxious to you, your parents—apart from forbidding you to go and preach to the heathen?"

"Oh, not in *themselves,* I suppose," said Miss Winship discontentedly. "But I am not close to them. How could I be? I have not seen them for four years. My mother and I have little in common—she has always been occupied with the little ones, or her garden—"

"How many of you altogether?"

"Nine."

"Nine. That is a family, indeed," observed her companion pensively. Alvey Clement, the other pupils knew, had no brothers or sisters; no relations of any kind to take an interest in her plans. Her school fees had been paid by an elderly cousin, now dead. "And all living at home?"

"James is with his regiment. I believe he was wounded in the recent engagement—we do not know how seriously. If God intends to take James, no doubt He will do so," said Miss Winship with a calm that suggested there was no particular love lost between her and her brother. "James is the eldest, my father's favourite, of course. Papa is only interested in the boys; his daughters are of no concern to him."

"Except insofar as they may not leave home to convert the heathen. Well—go on?" Despite her fixed resolve, Alvey began to find in herself a curiosity concerning this large unexplored family of Winships.

"James and Papa were at one time very close; the Third Scots were

Papa's old regiment. When James left Birkland, Papa tried to transfer
his attention to Tot—Thomas."

"Who is—how old?"

"Oh, I really forget." Louisa counted on her fingers. "Five, perhaps, when I came here—a puny, ailing little brat. He will now, I
suppose, be about nine; the only other boy in the family. He has
proved a disappointment, so Meg writes; will not share Papa's interests, prefers to slip away with Nish—"

"All the rest are girls?"

"Yes. Meg is twenty-one, a year older than I. She is to be married in
October—to John Chibburn, a neighbour—a red-faced, loud-voiced,
thick-skulled oaf," said Miss Winship bitterly, "who can only talk
about otter hunting and salmon, and the barley crop. Think of settling
down for the rest of your days with somebody like that!"

"Does Meg not like this person?"

Miss Winship sniffed.

"She is by far too good for him. She attended school here, when she
was sixteen—Mrs. Camperdowne thought her very clever—but she
grew homesick after six months and begged to go back to Birkland.
And they allowed her. She has been helping teach the younger ones.
When she marries you would take her place."

Miss Clement raised her brows at this, but made no comment, remarking merely, "Well, there is Meg disposed of. Go on."

"Then there is Isabel—Isa. She is not clever. She went to school in
Hexham for a little, but she never liked it. Miss Waskerley taught her
at home."

"Miss Waskerley—?"

"The governess. Oh, but she is about to leave—" in answer to
another inquiring lift of her companion's brows. "She is becoming
elderly and it seems the younger ones have grown too much for her."

"The younger ones being?"

"Tot, Parthie, and Nish."

"Parthie and Nish—those are strange names?"

"Parthie is short for Parthenope. She, I suppose, will be fourteen,
perhaps fifteen. Nish, short for Annis, will be eight. She and Tot had
become disgracefully uncontrolled under the rule of Miss Waskerley."

"Then I assume that it is just as well she is leaving."

"And then there is little Betsey, and the baby, Kate. I have never seen them. It is just as well that Miss Waskerley is leaving, certainly," said the single-minded Louisa, "for she might have been the one person who would penetrate the deception and think it her duty to inform my parents. She was never at all sympathetic to my ideals or ambitions—"

"Miss Winship. Louisa," said Miss Clement firmly. "I wish you to understand, once and for all, that there is going to be *no* deception, there will be *nothing* about which to inform your parents. This whole notion of yours is so rash—wild—fantastic—it is so absurdly inconceivable that I cannot imagine how such a sober person as yourself could ever have been brought to envisage it."

"It is because God put it into my head. He is calling me," said Miss Winship obstinately. "And I must go."

"Oh—! But what about the maids, the cook, the coachman, the gardener? The neighbours? How could such a substitution be—be so much as *thought* about—let alone carried out—for even so much as a single day?"

"Very, very easily." It was plain from Miss Winship's demeanour that not only had she been thinking about the details of the substitution, she had been giving the matter her entire attention, probably for many days, even weeks or months.

"I have been away from home now almost four years. Girls, young ladies of our age alter very considerably during such a period. *I* have done so. I am grown taller, my appearance has changed, my voice has changed. Who would guess, if you went to Birkland Hall in my place, that you were not Louisa Winship?"

"But there would be so many matters—both large and small—over which I should infallibly betray myself—details of family history—people, places, memories—"

"My sisters Meg and Isa would be vigilant to cover your mistakes. They would take care of you. Meg and Isa have always felt sincerely for me in my aspirations, although they do not share them. And the younger ones need not be told—they would simply follow the lead of their elders. If they accept you, why should my parents doubt? Especially since Papa has never taken the least interest; Mamma would be engaged with the baby—"

"The baby?"

"Little Kate. She is less than a year old. A disappointment to my father, who hoped for another boy; since Tot is of a sickly, unteachable disposition—or so Meg writes."

"But it would be wrong! I should be receiving care, comforts, affections, food, shelter—to which I have no shadow of right. And your sisters would be obliged to tell untruths on my account—"

"I doubt if that would trouble them one whit," said Miss Winship rather sourly. "They have light natures—they are not overburdened by moral scruples. As for the care, comforts, food, and so forth—they are mine by entitlement and I do not in the least want or value them. If I choose to bestow them on you, I have every right to do so."

This appeared such erratic and absurd unreason to Alvey that she saw no rational way in which to dispute it; besides, her companion was hurrying on vehemently: "Miss Clement, I have taken some pains to acquaint myself with your situation and prospects. I understand that you are an orphan, you were sent here by your guardian to obtain an English education so that you can return to America and teach there. But you wish—Harriet Utterley told me—to become an author, to write novels like Maria Edgeworth or Fanny Burney. It seems an odd, trifling kind of ambition to me, I must confess"—Miss Winship's voice indicated all too plainly her low opinion of it—"but if that is your wish, what better situation could you ask in which to do your writing than Birkland Hall? It is a large place, you will have ample solitude in which you may scribble to your heart's desire—"

"I thought you said I would be expected to teach the younger ones? Not and Tish and—and Parthie?"

"That need not occupy more than an hour or so in the mornings; Mamma does not concern herself about their education so long as they leave her in peace. As I say, I do not at all comprehend or enter into this wish to write works of a fictional nature—or, furthermore, what you will find to write *about*—but I conclude you must have some design in your own mind—"

Alvey nodded. She did not divulge that she had a novel already two-thirds written.

"The house is solitary, neighbours are too scattered to come calling. Whereas, if you returned to America, you would, I assume, be obliged

to teach in a school, your time would be governed by the requirements of your calling—I understand that you have no resources, no
income—"

All this was so unarguable that Alvey made haste to lead the discussion in another direction. "But suppose, when you arrive at the Indies,
that you find yourself mistaken? That you are homesick, disappointed?
That the life of a missionary does not, after all, please you? What
then?"

"Such an eventuality is quite impossible. Wholly, wholly out of the
question."

"Suppose you fall sick, are obliged to relinquish your plans and
come home? Suppose you find that you miss your parents, your family?"

Miss Winship's wooden expression conveyed her opinion as to the
utter unlikelihood of this.

"Well—suppose one or other of your parents were to fall sick—how
old are they?"

"My mother is approaching fifty—I do not know how closely; she is
in excellent health; Papa is some fifteen years older. She is not his first
wife," explained Miss Winship. "James's mother died in childbirth."

"So your Papa is in his mid-sixties—suppose he were to contract a
fatal illness? You might never see him again?"

"He would be in the hands of his Maker," said Miss Winship flatly.
Her face was set in a mask of unalterable intention; her eyes had a
fixed, fanatical stare.

Miss Clement studied her with a mixture of impatience and diffidence. How to breach that bastion of blind self-will?

She said, "There is another matter, Louisa, that must be taken into
account. Were you ever—did you—had you, before you left home,
any suitors? Did you ever consider marriage?"

"Of *course* not!" Louisa gave her an impatient glance. "Have I not
told you that from the age of—"

"Yes, yes, I know, I know, from the age of six you dedicated yourself to a missionary's career. You met an old lady who had heard John
Wesley give a stirring address at Felton forty years before; her one aim
was to go out to Serampore, and now it is yours. So you have never
entertained the thought of matrimony?"

"Never!"

"But still there might have been a suitor? You were—what—sixteen when you came away from home—were there no boys that you had played with as a child—lads, partners at country balls?"

Miss Winship curled her lip.

"We went to the Assemblies at Hexham—there were local young men. Red-faced boobies. One of them—John Chibburn—approached me before he put the question to Meg—and there was Robbie Carey —but I soon sent *him* about his business."

"I see. But suppose there should be others?"

"Others?" echoed Miss Winship. Her tone was vague. It was evidently almost impossible for her to stretch her imagination so far as to embrace another person's point of view. Devising this scheme must have cost her days of mental endeavour, weeks of sleepless nights. No wonder she looked so pale and racked. I daresay she will make an admirable missionary, thought Alvey Clement, it will be so easy for her to ignore any possible arguments on the side of the pagans.

"After all, Louisa, you and I—I may say this without vanity since the gift was administered with such impersonal equity—you and I share a certain degree of good looks. There may, probably will be other applicants for your hand. Your parents may—doubtless do—expect you to marry?"

"Certainly they have such expectations. But I have made plain to them repeatedly—on every occasion when the matter was canvassed— my unalterable resolution never to embark upon the married state. My life is dedicated to Another. So far as I am concerned, you are at liberty to refuse all such offers, if they should be repeated, during your sojourn at Birkland."

"I thank you! But suppose I should be minded to accept?"

At this, Miss Winship looked a little blank.

She said, "I thought your purpose was to be an authoress? Why should you wish to enter into matrimony?"

"The two conditions," Alvey suggested, "are not mutually incompatible. There have been married authoresses. There is Madame d'Arblay—Mrs. Radcliffe—"

"Oh—well—as to that, if you should care to contract such an alliance, you will, of course, suit yourself. I can have no concern, no implication in any such connection that you may resolve upon—though, I must say, I should have thought—"

"But do you not see," Alvey pointed out patiently, "that if I were to take such a step, if I were to enter into an engagement with some person, it would raise a whole host of problems, both moral and legal? Your father—should you marry—would, I daresay, endow you with a portion?"

"Meg is to have five thousand pounds when she weds John Chibburn; I think Papa intends the same for all of us."

Alvey reflected that Mr. Winship must be quite comfortably circumstanced.

Louisa went on: "But I renounce the money! Without the least hesitation. It is of no importance to me. Nor, I am glad to say, is it to my co-workers in the missionary field, who are prepared to take me without a penny."

"But don't you understand? I cannot possibly be receiving your father's money, on which I have not a shadow of a claim."

"If I don't want it, why should not you accept it?"

"Well," said Alvey, "let us simply say that I do not want it either. I will not argue with you on that head, Louisa. But if I enter into this gothick scheme of yours—which I have by no means definitely undertaken to do, mark you!—but if I do, then it must be for a term only."

"A term?"

Miss Winship's tone was one of strong displeasure, but Alvey repeated, "A term. Let us say a year—one year. At the end of that period I should feel myself at liberty to disclose the true state of affairs to your parents."

"You would be mad to do so!" Even Miss Winship's composure was shaken by the thought. "It would very likely kill Papa! And my mother—I—I really do not know what she would do. For a start, they would not believe you—you would possibly be consigned to Bedlam."

"Not if your sisters corroborated my story," Alvey pointed out.

"Oh." Louisa digested this in silence for a moment. She murmured, half to herself, "I would not put it past them to have my sisters set under medical restraint also in such a case—"

Good God, thought Alvey, what kind of an establishment am I

proposing to enter? But, after all, I have not the slightest intention of taking part in this crazy charade—how in the world could I have permitted the argument to go on as far as it has?

Curiosity, I suppose, to discover how far she has planned it.

Curiosity was indeed Alvey's besetting sin. Despite all her sober resolutions now, she could not prevent her mind from engaging in speculation about this unknown family of Winships—the proxy parents, sisters, brothers—the home in that faraway northern county, the whole unfamiliar region that she would be allowed to enter, as by right—how she might affect them, and they, her—

"Certainly no longer than a year," she repeated firmly. "At the end of such a period I must have succeeded in completing my novel, and I should therefore be able to discover whether I have the necessary talent to pursue a literary career." (Like all beginning writers, Alvey had not the least conception of the length of time that publishers frequently take to make up their minds about manuscripts.) "And you, by that time, would have come to a similar conclusion as to your eligibility for a missionary career."

"Oh, upon that head there can be no doubt whatsoever," pronounced Miss Winship. "My mind—as I have several times observed —is made up irrevocably on the matter—besides having already taken pains to acquire a great quantity of Hindustani grammar."

"Oh, have you indeed done so? Well, to be sure, that was quite a practical step." Alvey's tone may have betrayed some slight indication of doubt as to the other's actual ability to carry out her scheme; Miss Winship, with the acute sensitivity of the true egotist, fired up at once.

"*You* think this is all just a whim, a childish whim—do you not? A fairy-tale dream that will fade away when I first encounter the hot sun of Bengal! But you are mistaken—*quite* mistaken! You do not know so much about human nature as you fancy—sitting so quiet and poker-faced in your corner day after day, watching us all, thinking yourself so superior! Life at home—up there in Birkland Hall—should suit you well. There you can watch and watch to your heart's content, and make up as many stories as you please. And I hope that life there satisfies you—I can tell you, it would never satisfy *me!* One more month of it—one more week—and I should throw myself into the Hungry Water!"

She was half crying with indignation; Alvey had never seen the usually composed Louisa so agitated.

"Softly—softly! Don't fire up so—pray! Why in the world should you think that I feel myself superior? It is quite the other way round, I assure you. I sit silent because I have no confidence in my power to interest others in my conversation. All you English girls learn *that* from your governesses. I never had a governess."

"Oh well," said the other, still trembling and tearful. "Never mind! But you *will* help me—won't you? You can't—you cannot—having come so far—having raised my hopes—you *cannot* withdraw now! It would be too cruel and wicked—too monstrous and un-Christian!"

Her lip quivered, her eyes pleaded. She looked, suddenly, far younger than her twenty years . . .

II

The journey to the North of England lasted four days. It was taken by ship, and the leisurely pace of the passage was further retarded by calls at various ports along the way—Yarmouth, Grimsby, Hull, Whitby—and partly by early-autumn gales, which would have made the voyage almost unbearably disagreeable had it not been for the cheerfulness and good spirits of the Winship sisters.

Meg and Isa had travelled south, under the chaperonage of the departing Miss Waskerley, to meet their sister Louisa and return with her. Meg's secondary errand was to buy clothes in London for her wedding next month, Isa's to pay as many visits to museums and art exhibitions as their hostess, Lady Matfen, a cousin of Mrs. Winship, was prepared to countenance.

"Which would have been about three," said Isa with a chuckle, "but luckily my cousin's maid Brierley is of a more persuadable nature—"

"Bribable, you mean," said Meg.

"Well—I gave her two lace collars and three little drawings, one of herself, and for that I believe she would have accompanied me to the dungeons of the Bastille. She did not, I must say, care for the Elgin Marbles, but apart from that her taste was far superior to that of Cousin Caroline—"

"Who cares for nothing but fashion—luckily for me. I shall be able to lead the mode in Northumberland for the next three years." Meg glanced down with satisfaction at the new drab green pelisse, part of her trousseau which ought to have been packed away in her trunk, had not the sharpness of the wind furnished her with an excuse for putting it on.

"But now, attend to me!" said Isa.

The three girls were on the cluttered deck of the coastal freighter *Bethia,* watching the cliffs of Whitby disappear from view as the ship bounced through the choppy waters of the North Sea. Mrs. Girvan, their chaperone, a friend of Lady Matfen's on her way to Newcastle, was lying down in the cabin being ministered to by her maid with sal volatile and Tintagel water.

"It is fortunate that Mrs. Girvan is such a bad sailor," Isa went on, "for we have a most important matter to discuss. What can we call Alvey when we get back to Birkland? We really cannot address her as Louisa—I am sure she would not care for that—would you, Alvey?— and I myself would find it an uncomfortable reminder of our deception—"

"It is odd that you do not jib at the deception itself, yet scruple over such a small point as that," remarked Meg.

Alvey studied the older sister thoughtfully.

Meg was better-looking than either of her sisters: slighter than Louisa, and shorter, with the same dark hair and eyes, but a finer skin, a rounder face, a more feminine air and cast of countenance. She wore her glossy curls in a cluster on her brow, had a short, delicate nose and a coolly conspiratorial smile. Yet there was a touch of Louisa's resolution and trenchancy about her—which, in general, she managed to conceal, taking some pains over it, Alvey noticed. With such looks, it was not surprising that Meg would be the first of the Winship girls to marry. Poor Isa's chances of matrimony seemed slender indeed; she had said as much herself, with a rueful air.

"I am the plain one, you see, expected to remain at home and carry out the various tasks that Mamma has no time for. This is why I have been indulged with a London trip and a sum of money to purchase drawing materials—it is to be in lieu of matrimony."

Yet Isa, thought Alvey crossly, would not be so *very* plain—if something could be done about her complexion, which certainly was a disaster. And about her bunchy, round-shouldered figure—and if her hair were to be dressed in a different style— But her warm brown eyes had a direct and friendly regard; her voice was low, musical, and imbued with surprising humour and certainty—perhaps because her destiny lay so plain before her?

"It is easy for *you* to take a lofty moral tone about the deception— since you yourself are so soon to leave Birkland," she told Meg briskly. "In a month's time you can dismiss us and our consciences from your mind."

Alvey reflected that the discomfort and embarrassment of her situation was rendered far less acute by the dispassionate way in which the sisters were prepared to canvass it. They had accepted, without the slightest surprise, Louisa's disclosure that she planned an immediate departure on an East Indiaman with Mr. and Mrs. Tothill; had said a long, perhaps permanent goodbye to their sister and accepted Alvey in her place with the calm and temper of admirable breeding. Louisa must for some time, Alvey guessed, have been contriving to prepare them for such a development by hints in her letters.

"I do not receive the impression," Meg told Isa, "that *your* conscience troubles you too deeply on this matter."

"Oh! Well—no!—I weigh it in the balance against the benefit of Louisa set free to convert the heathen—and thus *my* conscience is made to seem a very trifling consideration. Besides, think what a pain Louisa would have been at home, cross and thwarted! I think we need not tell the younger ones about it at all, do you not agree? Nish and Betsey and little Kate can have no recollection of Louisa; and Parthie, if told, might fall into one of her sanctimonious, tale-bearing fits—"

"Like the time when her sense of duty impelled her to inform Mamma that James had gone to Blaydon Races. Well; we shall have to keep an eye on Parthie. Luckily she is greedy for notice and attention—"

"Having been ignored all her life by Mamma—"

"Like the rest of us; but she seems to have taken it harder. Perhaps because of her legs, poor child. Very likely a little notice paid her, a few opportunities to be in with 'the big ones,' will win her goodwill—"

Alvey listened with attention to these lights on her substitute family; she was a little startled by the detachment in gentle Isa's tone, and her expression showed it.

"Don't be alarmed, Alvey! I promise you that we are very happy to acquire a new sister." Isa tucked a friendly hand through Alvey's arm. "Only, what are we to call you?"

"Louisa's close friends at school called her Emily—I believe that is her middle name? You could call me Emily, perhaps? It was my mother's middle name, it would seem familiar."

"Why yes, that will do very well. Our mother's great-aunt was an Emily; I daresay Mamma will be pleased to hear the name brought back into use. Louisa's name came from my father's side of the family."

"Emmy, we shall call you," said Isa. "Names become abbreviated in our family."

At that moment Mrs. Girvan's maid clambered up the companion ladder, calling, "Miss Winship, Miss Winship, pray will you come down to Missus? She feels low and poorly and wants your company."

Sighing, Meg followed her below to the stuffy cabin.

"Poor Meg!" said Isa cheerfully. "Because she is so pretty, people believe she is good-natured as well."

"Is she not so?" Alvey was surprised. "She has been very amiable to me."

"Oh yes, because, finding herself the object of such expectations, she is obliged to take pains to fulfil them. But it does not come by nature."

While Alvey digested this, Isa, still holding her arm, gave it a little shake.

"Don't look so dejected! Louisa, in her selfish way, has thrust you into a most equivocal situation. You wonder, I daresay, why she did not just abscond with the Tothills. But then there would have been lawsuits—scandal—she would have been haled back with ignominy. That would not suit her book at all. But I assure you, we shall manage it all very well between us. And indeed I am delighted that you are coming to Birkland. Think how agreeable for me to have a new companion—Lou and I never agreed. But I think that you and I will become excellent friends, I feel it in my bones. You like to laugh at things, I fancy, do you not?"

How did you guess that? wondered Alvey.

"I had a sister Maria, who was closest to me in age, with whom I used to share a great many jokes, but she died of a typhus fever two years ago—there was an epidemic at the Hexham school." Isa spoke composedly, but it was plain that her composure came from resolution, not any lack of feeling. "Meg is always too busy for jokes—she takes after our mother; and Louisa—well, you have seen Louisa for yourself."

"High principles," murmured Alvey.

"So high that they perch everyone else on most uncomfortable pinnacles. She will do very well in Serampore, I don't doubt. It was certainly a piece of unexampled good fortune for her—your arrival at the Abbey School; your needs dovetailing so well with hers."

"My venality," murmured Alvey.

"Oh, fiddlestick! Louisa, of course, attributes the whole course of events to the direct intervention of Providence. I wish that *my* self-regard allowed me to believe that Providence would interest itself to such a degree in my affairs."

"Were your parents not surprised when they received Louisa's letter, informing them that they might expect to see her at the end of the school year, that they would hear no more about her wish to become a missionary?"

"No, not in the least. Neither of them ever took her wishes seriously. Mamma takes no interest in *anybody's* ambitions; and my father, of course, had thought all along that it was nothing but a foolish female whim, which would come to naught if treated firmly and ignored. — By the bye, that was a very cleverly worded letter; not a single untruth in it from first to last. I conclude that you composed it? Louisa could never be so ingenious."

"I composed it; I even wrote it," admitted Alvey. "Luckily Mrs. Camperdowne is so strict about ladylike penmanship that our handwriting is almost indistinguishable."

"And you really plan to become an author? Write novels? That is a grand ambition! But now I am coming to know you a little, I begin to think that you will succeed in it; you seem to be so observant, to have yourself so well in hand. Have you written a great deal already?"

"Nothing of any great length. I had little time at the Abbey School because I was teaching as well as learning; some poems, some stories and compositions—the kind of things that girls do write."

"Not in the Winship family," said Isa with a chuckle.

"Would your parents be very shocked if they discovered? Will it be as bad as Louisa's urge to convert the heathen?"

"Oh no, nothing like that. Ladies, after all, are known to write novels. There is Madame de Genlis, Miss Owenson, Miss Sykes, Hannah More—Miss Waskerley used to read a great quantity of novels from the Hexham circulating library—*Miseries of an Heiress, The Black Robber, The Mysterious Baron, The Chamber of Death, The German Sorceress, The Horrors of Oakendale Abbey*—and though Mamma did not read such things herself, and indeed dismissed them as frippery rubbish, she did not interdict us from reading them if we chose to waste our time so."

Alvey did not find herself encouraged by this; though she did feel a comfortable certainty that her own partially completed work was on a far superior level to any of Miss Waskerley's reading matter.

"But you do not think, if I had a novel accepted for publication, that your parents would be too greatly distressed and displeased?"

"Well," said Isa cautiously, "as to that I cannot say. To tell you the truth, such an idea, in our family, is so unheard-of that I find it impossible to predict how they would react. But of course you would be publishing your book under a nom de plume, would you not? So that no disgrace need attach to the Winship family?"

"Oh, of course," said Alvey laughing. "If I ever succeed in finding a publisher, that is."

"Thinking more about it," Isa went on, "I do not see why the fact need even become known to them. You could conduct your correspondence through Mr. Allgood at the library in Hexham—he has always been a friend to us, and indeed taught me more about good reading than Miss Waskerley ever did. Louisa sent letters to me and Meg in his care. But, Alvey, here have I been telling you so much about the Winship family, boring on, and I know nothing at all about you! Do, pray, tell me your history—I am sure it must be most exciting compared with our humdrum country life on the northern border. Louisa said that you came from New Bedford in Massachusetts. Have you always lived there? Is it a handsome town?"

Alvey thought of the little town on the hillside, the grassy streets, the wooden houses, some tarred, some simply left to weather, the tangle of masts in the harbour below. Even the biggest and finest dwelling there seemed small and plain compared with the English style of architecture, the houses of stone or brick, moss-grown and creeper-hung, snugly settled in the landscape for hundreds of years. She thought of the winding English roads, zigzagging between small, odd-shaped fields taking their shape from some series of ancient rights probably dating back to Saxon times, and the roadside banks rising six or ten feet high as the tracks sank deeper and deeper under the trudging feet of successive generations. "Why are your lanes dug so deep in the ground?" she had asked a fellow pupil when she first came to the English school, and at first she could hardly believe the explanation. "They are not dug, they have been worn that way." American corduroy roads were straight, flat, lay over the landscape like rules.

How to begin to describe the difference between old England and New England?

But Isa was going on: "And tell me about your parents? At what age did you lose them? Louisa told us that you had been brought up by a guardian who sent you to the Abbey School—was that a relation? Or a friend of your family?"

"I—I lost my parents at the age of ten." Alvey felt grateful that Isa's choice of words could dictate the form of her answer. This was a painful topic that she never discussed if she could avoid doing so.

"But you remember them clearly?"

"Certainly. They were—they were very austere. Very devout. They had been members of the Society of Friends, then Unitarians, then joined a sect known as the Universarians."

"A Christian sect?" Isa's tone was a little anxious.

"Oh, of course. They were deeply religious. Very gentle, unselfish people." Alvey paused and thought about this, then added, "But with that tremendous inner strength which comes from faith in one's own principles."

"Like Louisa," said Isa with a chuckle. "Which no doubt helped you to understand *her* character."

"Yes, I suppose that is true. It had not occurred to me."

No wonder Louisa had seemed in some way familiar. Yet Mother and Father—or, as they wanted her to call them, Sarah and Paul—had much more true feeling, true piety in them than Louisa, whose nature had always seemed to Alvey both shallow and selfish. How deeply,

desperately troubled they were—or, at least, Mother had been—
when—

"But I expect life in a missionary station will soon be teaching Louisa to modify her principles a trifle when necessity dictates," Isa went
on cheerfully. "I imagine she will be in for some surprises out there in
Serampore. Now tell me about your guardian, Alvey?"

"She was my cousin Hepzibah Babcock, a remote connection; both
my parents were only children and *their* parents died young, so I have
very few relatives. The Clements, my father's family, came from
Devon—an ancestor was that John Clement who was a protégé of Sir
Thomas More; he became president of the Royal College of Physi-
cians and later escaped into exile at Louvain, taking with him treatises
and letters by Sir Thomas—*A Dialogue of Comfort against Tribulation*
was one; he died in exile."

"An impressive ancestor! No wonder your parents were devout."

"My mother's family, the Alveys, came from Lincolnshire. But of
them I know nothing."

"And your cousin Hepzibah?"

"A formidable lady." Alvey smiled a little, remembering the icy
climate of disapproval in which she had grown up. It had taken her
three years to understand that the disapproval was directed, not at
herself, but at her parents. "But she meant very well by me; she
spared no pains to ensure that I had an excellent education."

"She was wealthy?"

"By no means. Her husband had been a feckless man who migrated
to the New World with great expectations, and squandered all his
capital on ill-fated ventures. When they were nearly destitute my aunt
invested the small remnant of their savings on a load of chandler's
stores which she sold from their house; my great-uncle was bitterly
mortified and died of the shame, but Cousin Hepzie prospered, and it
was on the proceeds of the store that she sent me to school. 'Never put
pride before learning, Sarah,' she used to tell me."

"Is she still alive?"

"No, she died two years after I came to the Abbey School. But my
fees were paid until the end of the year. And Mrs. Camperdowne was
so good as to say that I might remain there if I chose and earn my
place by teaching the younger ones."

"So you never saw your cousin Hepzie again," said Isa reflectively.
"No. And I was sorry for that. By the time I left for England we had
grown to be on very comfortable terms."

Alvey thought with sadness of that farewell; the indomitable old
lady, upright amid driving snow among the untidy casks and coils of
rope on the New Bedford quayside, frail but erect in rusty black,
protected by nothing but her old umbrella, her blue eyes blazing as
she called, "Mind thee learns enough so thee can be an independent
woman, Sarah!" before turning and trudging off into the blizzard. A
dock lad shouted something impertinent after her and she flashed back
such a withering reply that he turned scarlet and stood gaping after
her, openmouthed; Alvey wished she knew what Cousin Hepzie's
words had been.

She gave a long sigh, which turned to a shiver.

Isa said, "It grows cold; I believe we must go down to that odiously
stuffy cabin. We do not reach Tynemouth until after midnight."

"What do we do then?"

"Mrs. Girvan spends the rest of the night at the Dean Gate Hotel
before travelling on to Morpeth. So, I suppose, will we, if Papa has
not sent Archie with the coach to meet us. Papa does not always
remember details like that, when they relate only to us girls."

But Sir Aydon had remembered. When the passengers of the *Bethia*
had been rowed ashore, stiff, yawning, and half frozen (for the shoals
at the mouth of the Tyne were so dangerous that ships must anchor in
mid-channel; goods and passengers were ferried to land in flat-bot-
tomed barges), Meg, who was longer-sighted than Isa, cried out,
"There's Archie, I see him! Archie, Archie, here we are with Miss
Louisa and a whole coach load of luggage. Make haste, we are half
dead of cold!"

A figure shrouded in greatcoats stumped over to them and let loose
on Meg a torrent of grumbling admonition, not one word of which
could Alvey understand.

Mercy! she thought. If the servants all talk like that, how shall I ever
manage to communicate with them, or know what they are saying? I
never anticipated such a stumbling block. But what a dialect! It is
unlike any language I ever heard in my life.

Meg and Isa appeared to understand Archie's exhortations perfectly well, and to take little heed of them.

"He says he has been obliged to wait five hours; but after all, it is not our fault the ship was delayed. And he has not been wasting his time; he reeks of porter. Don't scold, Archie! Those are all our things, over there. Come and get in the coach Alv—Emmy, you must be half perished."

"What about Mrs. Girvan?"

"Oh, she is well enough; her manservant has found her a hackney coach. Thank heaven we have seen the last of the old misery. Meg will write a polite note of thanks to her when we are home, and we will all sign it. Quick, wrap yourself in this sheepskin; Archie will take care of the bags."

"How shall I *ever* understand what he says?"

Isa laughed.

"I forgot that little difficulty. They say it took the devil himself so long to learn Tyneside that he gave up in despair. You will have to explain that your years in the South have caused you to forget it. But you will soon pick it up. In any case, most of the servants don't talk so broad as Archie."

After a long and tedious interval, while the boxes were found and stowed, Archie climbed onto his seat, cracked the whip, and they were off, rumbling over cobbles. Alvey formed little impression of the city of Newcastle, save a black bulk of buildings, unlit at this bleak and early hour. They were soon away from the town, travelling between dark and silent fields. The air that penetrated, despite closed carriage windows, was biting cold, far colder than it had been in the South; Alvey was thankful for the thick sheepskin rug round her. Meg, in the far corner, seemed asleep, but Isa, in the middle, sat bolt upright and peered eagerly ahead into the darkness.

"I am so happy to be coming home!" she confessed. "How Louisa could bear to remain away all those years—and then travel to the Orient without ever seeing Birkland again! I could not endure to live anywhere but in Northumberland."

"Is it so very special? In what way?"

"Oh, you will see. In every possible way. The air, the trees, the landscape. Down there in the South," said Isa distastefully, "the landscape seems so woolly and shapeless. And the air is so dull and stuffy—as if it had been breathed already, a thousand times over. Whereas here in the North— But you are a writer, you will be able to describe the differences much better than I can, when you write about it. I shall look forward so eagerly to seeing it through your eyes, as you describe it. And our family—I suppose you will be making portraits of them all? That will amuse me very much. Shall you write stories about us?"

"Indeed I shall not!" returned Alvey, smiling inwardly at such simplicity. Ordinary people never seemed to understand that writers did not behave like jackdaws, picking up what was to hand, setting it whole and without embellishment into a story. How explain, without offence to Isa, that the delicious, funny, romantic narrative already shaped in her mind was, must be, wholly separate and different from any of the commonplace (though doubtless of great interest to themselves) activities of the Winship clan?

"Think how dangerous it would be if I were to describe you all so that you could be easily recognised," she added. *"Then* your parents would certainly have cause for grievance."

"But if not about us," said Isa, surprised, "what in the world *will* you write about?"

"Oh, I have plenty of ideas in my head . . ." Alvey thought affectionately of her hero, Wicked Lord Love. Her words ended in a yawn, and she leaned back in her corner, lulled by the sway of the coach and the steady plod of the horses' hoofs on the stony road. But Isa continued to sit upright, gazing eagerly forward, as behind them the eastern sky began slowly to pale and lighten, and a bony angular landscape revealed itself ahead.

Archie turned, as daylight grew, and flung back some grumbling, guttural morsel of information, like a bone to a trio of undeserving dogs.

"What does he say?" whispered Alvey.

Meg, without answering, gave a cross grunt and recomposed herself for sleep.

"Meg does not care; they always quarrelled. But *I* think it wonderful news!" exclaimed Isa in a joyful whisper, and she called through the open panel, "Is it really true, Archie? You wouldn't tease?"

"Noa, noa, hevvn't the measter a letter in his aan writing?"

"When does he come, Archie?"

"Saturday's a week."

"So soon! Oh, how happy I am!"

"Who is coming?" inquired Alvey.

"Of course *you* will have to pretend to dislike him, because he and Louisa were always at loggerheads. It would never do to be too friendly—everyone would think it most strange—and so, for that matter, would he—and he and my father are so close, I think he had best not be party to the deception. It would be too hard on him—"

"Who?"

"Our brother James. Half brother, in fact—his own mother died giving birth to him, and Papa married Mamma the following year, in order to provide a mother for him—but she has never been very fond of James."

"She preferred her own children?"

"She just is not interested in children at all, except when they are newborn, very tiny. And I suppose James was never that for her."

Ahead of them now, the landscape, viewed in full daylight, curved up into a series of wedge-shaped escarpments, like waves of hillside, rising gradually, then falling abruptly. The heights were crowned with spinneys of twisted, wind-battered trees, already denuded of leaves, and from hill crest to crest ran a high stone fortification, a palisade of crumbling grey granite, dropping behind each summit, then seen again, climbing at a crazy angle up almost sheer slopes.

"What in the world is *that?*" demanded Alvey.

"Hush! You *must* train yourself not to be so unguarded in your comments," Isa reproved her, gesturing towards the back of Archie's head.

"Oh, good God—so I must. And I thought myself so circumspect," murmured Alvey, pink with mortification.

"It's of no consequence! Archie is deaf as a post."

"But what is that astonishing structure?"

"Oh, it is the Roman Wall. Built, you know, by the Emperor Hadrian to keep out the Picts and Scots. It has been there for the past two thousand years."

III

Nish and Tot always woke early, but on the morning of the day when their sister Louisa was expected, they woke even earlier than usual, long before it was light.

Nish opened her eyes first and lay listening to the water of the Hungry Burn, always audible from Birkland Hall at night, when other sounds were stilled: a continuous hushing murmur, a never-ending natural harmony. Today it was extra loud, from rain in the night; the water would be up around the roots of the willows and alders, thought Nish, and all our islands will be half drowned; we shall have to build them up again. The water will be dark brown, darker than tea, and it will have brought down all kinds of branches and floating bits, and maybe a drowned sheep. And the grass along the banks of the Little Burn will be streaming sideways, and the stepping-stones will have only their tops above water.

She took out her diary from under the pillow and wrote in the entry for the preceding day:

"This Day was exelently well Spent in attending to our Estates. We worked hard all day long." Her spelling was extremely idiosyncratic.

Then she leaned across and poked her brother.

"Wake up!"

"I'm awake already," he said at once, opening his eyes.

"We must get up. Louisa's coming today."

"I know," he said. "That's why I was awake."

The two children shared a room at the end of the house, on the second floor. Conveniently for them, a servants' stair, just round the corner from their bedroom door, led down to a side entrance on the ground floor, which had enabled them on countless occasions to slip out early or creep in late.

They hurried on their clothes, Tot sometimes, with impatient kindness, helping his sister tie her petticoat strings at the back and fasten her tucker.

"*Don't* put on your shoes, they'll make such a row; carry them downstairs in your hand. Make haste—I can hear Annie already."

Barefoot, carrying their shoes, the two children stole down the scrubbed wooden stairs, along a stone-flagged passage past pantries and stillrooms, and so into the big, warm kitchen. One of its walls was entirely taken up with ranges, and two of the fires had been banked so as to burn all night. Somebody had been at work already: a batch of thin oatcakes had been baked and laid out on racks to dry and harden off. Round loaves of bread dough were set in pans to rise before the hearth. A warm smell of yeast and dough filled the room.

The children swallowed hungrily, but were too bent on escape to linger. They did, however, help themselves to a few crumbly corners of oatcake, which would not be missed.

"Quick!" hissed Tot. "Somebody coming along the passage!"

They scurried across to a door which led to a back entry, and so into the stable yard. In winter this would be a sea of mud; anybody who crossed it must wear knee boots or pattens. Just now, a network of summer weeds, tansy and dock and plantains, made a platform over the slime. Poultry pecked about, and pigeons fluttered and cooed on the stable roof. The children enjoyed the feeling of the slime on their bare feet, and took no pains to avoid it, though it was ice-cold from the night rain.

At the corner of the yard, where a gate and a track led into the pastures and down to the burn, they encountered red-headed Annie Herdman, their sister Katie's wet nurse.

"Hssst! Quick into the harness room!" whispered Tot, but Nish said, "Annie'll not tell on us," and went on confidently. Indeed Annie displayed no surprise at all at the sight of them up so early, only said, "Have ye na seen wee Geordie, hinny? Aa left him here, playin' in the horse trough. Aa was only gyen but a minute, fetching a pan o' milk—"

"Na, we hivvn't seen him, Annie," said Tot, falling naturally into her language.

"I'm feared he'll be gyen doon to the watter," said Annie worriedly. "He's fair mad on playin' wi' watter."

"If we see him we'll send him back," said Nish.

"Ay, fetch him back for me, hinny, he's ooer young to be oot alane."

They nodded and ran on, dismissing Annie and her son from their minds as soon as they had rounded the corner of the track. It was a well-worn cart road, leading between orchard and pasture. The children turned aside into the orchard, climbing stone steps set sideways in the drystone wall, and filled their pockets with small apples. Then they hurried on, down to a ford crossing the small stream that ran into the Hungry Water. Tall fawn-coloured grasses and dark-green broom bushes lined the rocky banks. By now the children were out of sight of the house, screened from it by the farm buildings and a spinney of ash and sycamore.

At the brook they found, as they had expected, that the stepping-stones alongside the cart ford were almost submerged; just their tops showed above the swift-flowing clear dark-brown water. Nish crossed by the stones, on principle, skipping nimbly from one to the next on her bare feet; but Tot splashed straight into the water, which reached to his calves. He paused a moment to hoist up his nankeen breeches and tighten the buckles.

"Is it cold?" called Nish, hopping in the silvery, dewy grass on the far bank.

"Not too bad—cold enough."

Crossing the triangle of land between the brook and the larger stream, they emerged into the sun, which had previously been cut off by a steep shoulder of heather-covered hillside above the Hall. At once the world seemed more cheerful; the soaked grass and bushes sparkled, one or two birds began to twitter soft autumn songs, they could hear the long, bubbling upward cry of a curlew.

"Wee Geordie can't have been down here," said Nish, looking at the black, noticeable tracks they left in the grass. "We'd have seen his trail."

"He's likely gone round to the Lion Pool,' said her brother. "I've seen him there before."

"Oh—*Mithras!*" Nish stopped in dismay.

"What's to do?"

"It's the first of the month—October. I meant to go round by the Lion Pool and get me a wish. I'd my bent pin all ready too, stuck in my collar."

"Well, you canna go back now," said her brother. "Mrs. Slaley or Surtees or Parthie would come out and catch us."

"But I meant to wish that Louisa would never come home!"

"Much good that would have done. I doubt they're in the coach already; I heard Papa tell Archie to start early yesterday evening—"

"Oh, I *wish* I hadn't forgotten! It was seeing Annie put it out of my head—bother Annie!"

" 'Twouldn't have helped," said Tot. "I reckon praying to Mithras is no more use than the other kind of praying."

"He does help! He helped when I lost my flowered ribbon. I prayed and prayed and put two bent pins in the Lion Pool and I found the ribbon the very next day in the harness room."

"Well, pray to him now, then," suggested her brother. "Pray at the wellspring and leave your bent pin there—I don't suppose Mithras minds where you put it."

"I suppose I may as well." But Nish sounded doubtful. "I suppose it's better than doing nothing at all."

She had been skipping at a rapid pace along the path, a narrow sheep track here between alder bushes and tufts of reedy grass, skirting the bank of the larger stream, the Hungry Water. But now she slowed, and began to look from side to side as she went, picking a few late flowers that had lingered in the Indian summer—a harebell or two, a purple head of scabious, yellow toadflax, a twig of scarlet rose hips and a spray of glossy haws, a red pimpernel and a tiny blue wild pansy. Having bound these into a posy with a reedy stem, she followed Tot over a narrow wooden footbridge that spanned the burn, which ran deep and chuckling among dark-grey tumbled rocks and small grassy islets. Both children bore right on the farther side, and soon came to a spring, which cascaded down out of a rocky cranny in the riverbank, and trickled, from a small natural basin below, into the main stream.

The children paused and drank from cupped hands here, ceremonially, as from long-established usage, standing to do so on a flat slab of rock evidently set there for the purpose. After drinking, Nish dropped her posy into the pool, as well as the bent pin which she took from her collar, meanwhile reciting in loud but reverent tones: "Oh, Lord Mithras, if it be thy will, accept these gifts from thy servant and grant that this day my brother and I may run into no danger, nor do anything to earn thy wrath. Also please prevent our sister Louisa from returning home. We ask this most earnestly. Also help Annie Herdman find wee Geordie and stop her father from being so nasty to him. With kind regards, Nish Winship."

"Amen," added her brother, but without her confidence; he spoke in a quick undertone, as if this were a needful, but embarrassing, social formality. Then he added, "I don't think you ought to bother Mithras about Annie and wee Geordie. Let Annie pray to Mithras for herself."

"She doesn't know about Mithras."

"Oh, come along," said Tot, suddenly tired of this. "We've a long way to go, to get to our last place. We'd best stay on the bank, as the burn's so deep; it'd take all day wading in the water." He pronounced this word *watter*, as Annie had done.

Nish looked disappointed, but submitted to his dictum.

"Only, what about our islands that have been spoiled by the spate? I can see three from here—Madagascar and Krakatoa and Great Isle. We need to mend them."

"No use mending till the spate's gone down. Then we'll have a great deal of new material, besides."

As they made their way along the uneven bank they looked assessingly at the rocky islands, most about the size of small card tables, some much smaller, which it was their continual self-imposed task to keep decorated with moss, flowers, twigs, shining lumps of quartz, and minute rock plants. About a mile of the burn's course had already been beautified in this way, and they were now obliged to travel farther and farther afield to colonise new territory. The spate overnight had washed a great deal of their work away.

"We shall have to do them all over," said Nish mournfully. But there was a certain satisfaction in her tone also, at the demands of the task that lay ahead. "It will take us days and days."

"We must finish Corsica and Sardinia first. We ought to get those done before we begin mending."

Tot preferred conquest and acquisition to the duties of maintenance.

He went on: "Besides, the nearer we are to the house, the more risk that we'll be spotted and sent back to be there when Louisa comes."

"How horrible was she?" asked Nish anxiously.

"*Very* horrible. You don't remember, you were only three. But I was four, and I remember a deal of things about her. She used to make a special face when I wouldn't do what she wanted—a furious, hateful face, showing all her teeth; it always made me cry. It wouldn't now, but I still remember it in dreams. And she used to pinch my arm in a special way when she was left in charge of me—and she told Mamma, if she saw you doing something forbidden—"

"What things did she want you to do?"

"I don't remember."

"Perhaps Mithras will arrange for the carriage to overturn and her to be thrown out and killed," suggested Nish, who had looked despondent at these recollections.

"But then Meg and Isa would be killed too; that wouldn't be fair."

"Mithras may not trouble about fairness."

They argued this point as they pursued their way along the riverbank, Tot maintaining that gods had to be fair, Nish contending that their notion of fairness might differ from that of humans.

Meanwhile the autumn sun rose higher and gilded them with warmth. A breeze, strong but not cold, tossed the osier branches and chased clouds across the sky. The stream at first zigzagged along a flat valley bottom, with level alluvial haughs on either side, and wide gravel beds on the inner side of each bend. Nish would have liked to stop and search these for new treasures the flood might have brought down or uncovered: worn pieces of wood, uprooted plants, or sparkling quartz stones, white, pink, and purple; but Tot impatiently urged her on. He was eager to arrive at the less explored reaches of upper water, where the valley closed in, the banks were steeper, and the rocks bigger.

"I'll tell you a story if you like," he suggested. "I'll tell you about

Captain Cook." Tot was in the middle of reading *A Voyage to the Pacific Ocean,* which he had discovered in his father's library.

"Very well." Nish agreed without enthusiasm. She found her brother's recitals intensely boring; he was a slow and laborious narrator, frequently forgetting points and being obliged to hark back—"Oh, I should have said that before this they unloaded all their stores from the boats." He told his story in a loud monotonous voice which made it hard not to listen. Nish continually annoyed him by asking awkward questions: "How big was the boat? How many men were there? You never said there had been a storm." "Don't interrupt, you make me forget things," he would exclaim impatiently. Nish much preferred invented stories, but these were not within her brother's capacity, though he, too, enjoyed them. Very occasionally Granny Winship could be persuaded to tell stories of the Black Douglas, who grabbed the woman's shoulder and startled her to death; or the Cauld Lad of Hylton, who wailed, "Wae's me, wae's me, the acorn is not yet fallen from the tree, that's to grow the wood, that's to make the cradle, that's to rock the bairn, that's to make the man, that'll lay me," or the bloodcurdling tale of Abigail Featherstonehaugh, who rode out as a bride "all gay with her ladies and the bridegroom and all his lords" but they never came back, only their ghosts, streaming with gore, at the cockcrow time. "Do, do tell that story again, Granny," Nish would beg, but the old lady was unreliable; on some days she would tell stories, on others not. Mrs. Slaley, the cook, if the spirit moved her and she was not too busy, might tell tales of gipsies or Scottish reivers, or the broomie huts where people were left to die in the Great Sickness. Her tales were gloomy, but interesting.

"Let's eat our apples," suddenly proposed Nish in the middle of a long and particularly dull passage about Captain Cook's division of rations. "It *must* be dinnertime by now."

"No, it isn't. Nothing like. Look at the sun," said Tot, who had a much more accurate sense of time.

"But the apples are heavy and I've got the most. And I have to carry them in my skirt."

"Oh, very well. We can sit on that rock."

They had reached a point where the burn narrowed to a miniature torrent between high, cliff-like banks, and the water divided in a roar of white and gold around a large central flat rock about the size of a grand piano. A gap of three or four feet separated the rock from the bank.

Tot leaped carelessly across the gap. Nish, burdened with a skirtful of apples, misjudged the jump, slipped, and gashed her leg. Worse, she dropped all her apples into the race of water. Tot grabbed her arm and hauled her to safety, then shook her crossly.

"*Look* what you've done! All right—don't cry so—I daresay I can get them back."

But she sat crying miserably on the rock, with her eyes tight shut, while he hopped nimbly down into the watercourse and pursued the bobbing apples among smaller rocks and inlets. When he came back, with most of them retrieved, she was still crouched, wailing, in the same position.

"All right, all right, you can open your eyes. I've got the apples."

"My *leg!* Is it very bad?" she asked fearfully, and extended it, still with her eyes shut. Tot inspected the wound with care.

"I'll wash it and tie my handkerchief round. Then you'll not notice it."

When the soaked linen was bound tightly round her leg, Nish at last consented to open her eyes.

"Thank you," she said on a last sob, then forgot the matter instantly. The sunshine was hot in the sheltered gully as they lolled on the flat-topped rock and ate their fruit.

"Louisa would never in the world come as far as this, would she?" Nish suggested, and Tot shook his head.

Up above the miniature ravine, heather-coloured hillsides blazed bright magenta colour in the noon sun, or darkened to slate when a cloud crossed the sky.

After they had eaten, the children resumed their journey, until they reached a point where a good-sized waterfall discharged itself into a deep pool of dark-brown water. This was Pike Force. At the pool's lower edge were two islands which had been christened Corsica and Sardinia. In the decoration of these, Nish and Tot proposed to spend their afternoon.

But after they had been working for an hour or so, Tot abruptly abandoned his task of carrying white quartz pebbles to pave the central square of Sardinia. He said, in a hoarse, deep voice, quite different from his usual tone, "Eh, Nish. I'm gyen to have one o' my turns."

"Oh, Tot!"

His sister instantly dropped the plants she held, and forged her way splashily across to him through water which, for her, was rather more than knee deep. She grabbed his arm with both hands, and glanced about her, assessing their position.

"Over there's best. On the little beach. Come along."

On one side of the pool lay a narrow gravel bed from which they had been quarrying their building materials.

"I have you quite safe," Nish said with authority. "Come along. Fast as you can."

Her brother followed without speaking as she pulled him along. His mouth had opened, his eyes looked blankly ahead, he had begun to tremble.

"It's all right; I've got you," Nish said again.

Reaching the little strand, she made him sit, then lie down and turn his head on one side. In a businesslike manner she poked a finger into his mouth to make sure that his tongue was free and would not choke him. His eyes were already closed. Now there was nothing more that Nish could do for him except to unfasten his shirt collar and see that, in his deep sleep, he did not roll over into the river. Matter-of-factly she settled down cross-legged beside him, with her skirt dipping in the water. He often slept after these turns for two, three, even four hours. Nish glanced at the sun and hoped he would wake before it set.

It was worrying his head about Louisa brought that one, she thought. Drat Louisa! Do, Mithras, do *please* help us. I gave you the pin and the posy, and you had some of our apples too. And a bit of my blood . . .

She dabbed a finger on her gory shin (the handkerchief had been washed away as she helped Tot across the pool) and marked a small circle of blood on a flat stone.

I do think, Mithras, that you might arrange for Louisa to be tossed by Coxon's bull?

She listened, but there was no sound to be heard above the roar of the waterfall. Mithras kept his own counsel.

Sighing, propping her chin on her fists, Nish took herself to the last point reached in the serial saga of which she told herself daily instalments.

"Then Nish and Tot rode on their white horses up the hillside to Sewingshields Castle, where King Arthur and all his court lie sleeping in the deep cave, waiting for a brave knight to blow the bugle horn and cut the white garter with the sword that hangs above. Nish tried her hardest to blow the bugle horn, but it was all choked up with sand, like the one Mr. Thropton dug up in his garden. Then Tot picked up the sword, but it was so heavy he could hardly lift it. So they had to look around for help. 'Who'll help me cut this garter?' shouted Tot, and a voice from the darkness shouted, 'Let ye wait, and I will!' "

Chewing on a pithy stem of reed grass, Nish meditated. Who was going to come out in answer to that call? Far ahead, in the distance, she could see the glowing culmination of her story, with King Arthur in splendour, restored to life and majesty on his golden throne, and the rescuers, Nish and Tot, reclining on velvet cushions at his feet, wearing cloth-of-silver, with ruby chains round their necks. But how to defer that ending as long as possible, until the sun set and Tot woke?

I need a subplot, Nish might have said if she had been a more sophisticated author. I'll help you, says the voice inside the cave, if in return you'll bring me—what? What might the voice want, what difficult thing? And, for that matter, who was the voice, wicked or good?

Frowning, chewing, Nish plaited away at her story and, like a chain attached to a ship's anchor, it flowed through her, unreeling; as fast as it took form it raced away from her again, out into darkness, and was lost.

At last, just after sunset, Tot woke, and they started home.

On their way, not far from Pike Force, they passed a shepherd's hut.

"Old Amos is getting dooms queer," said Nish, glancing up at the hut with a shiver. "Last time I saw him he was thrashing his dog dreadfully. And he yelled out, as I went by, that he'd as lief thrash *me*, or you, or wee Geordie, if he could get his hands on us."

"He *does* thrash wee Geordie—if ever he gets the chance. That's why Annie keeps Geordie at the Hall, not in the village."

"I know. Who's that coming up the burn?" Nish stared ahead, screwing up her eyes against the sunset light. "See—down there? Carrying something heavy."

Nish and Tot were extremely late home to supper.

IV

The old lady's room was kept scrupulously neat. This was not difficult to achieve, for she had very few possessions; as she grew older, and her propensity to mislay articles increased, she discarded more and more of her belongings. "I can't do with things that need dusting," she told Charlotte, her daughter-in-law, and so dresses and shawls were ruthlessly cut up for patchwork, feathers burned before the moths could get at them, and unwanted articles of furniture carted up to the attics. Charlotte would not have been above accepting some of the discarded garments if they had been offered—nor would Meg and Parthie—the materials were often sumptuous, and ample too, for Granny Winship had been a noted belle in her day, a day when skirts were so wide that ladies had to pass sidelong through doorways and cloaks contained enough stuff to cover a small sopha. Just *one* of her dresses would have cut up into two or three of the skimpy things they were wearing nowadays. But the offer was not made, and Duddy, the old lady's personal maid, chopped up the garments with a look of grim approval; Duddy was of a religious persuasion that held the wearing of finery in this world to be an almost insuperable barrier to eligibility for the next.

Despite its bare polished floor and emptiness, Parthie liked to visit the old lady's bedchamber. Her elder sisters never came here. Old Grizel was too sharp-tongued for Meg, too satirical for Isa. But Parthie rather enjoyed her grandmother's fierceness; so long as it was not directed too often at herself. And even when it was she endured it, letting most of the shafts pass over her head; Parthie was adept at disregarding unpleasant or inconvenient matters, and she greatly relished old Mrs. Winship's objurgations on other members of the family.

"Your sister Isa will never catch a husband if she walks about screwing up her eyes in that peering, shortsighted way that makes her look so ugly; she will have wrinkles before she is twenty-five. And her posture is scandalous; I do not know why Charlotte does not insist that she lie on a backboard every day. Or rather, I know quite well; Charlotte cannot be bothered to take the least pain about anything but her garden."

"My posture is good, ain't it, Grandma," said Parthie smugly, straightening her plump shoulders and eyeing herself in the old lady's cheval glass.

"Don't let me hear you say 'ain't,' child. And don't smirk at yourself in the glass. Once Meg is back I presume that mooncalf John Chibburn will come calling again every night; the man is little better than a bumpkin. How Aydon could permit the only one of his daughters with some looks to ally herself with a man who has nothing but his acres to recommend him—but that is Aydon all over. The wedding cannot take place too soon for me."

"Oh, I do wonder what kind of stuffs Meg will have brought back for the bridesmaids' dresses," sighed Parthie, for whom on the contrary the month to Meg's wedding seemed an eternity of waiting.

"As for the notion of Tot dressed up as a page—I'm sure I don't know how he and Nish will ever be made clean and tidy enough—let alone the fact that he will probably disgrace us by throwing a fit in the middle of the ceremony. Why your mother doesn't do something about that pair of young ones—allowing them to run wild over half the countryside, day after day! By the time I was Nish's age I had already embroidered three samplers. How will she ever learn if she don't start young?"

"But *you* must always have been a *wonderful* needlewoman, Grandma," enthused Parthie, turning to look with sycophantic admiration at the immense tapestry that hung on the inner wall. "How old were you when you began that—thirteen? And it took you twenty-three years to finish?"

"Don't soft-soap me, girl. Fetch my chamois and my orange stick;

you may as well be of some use while you are here. And bring the Madagascar liquid."

Granny Winship never especially favoured Parthie; but she was glad of a willing helper to run small errands about the house, for, these days, she seldom left her room before dinnertime, and Duddy was becoming more and more cross-grained. Parthie greatly enjoyed a chance to look into the old lady's drawers and shelves; besides the sense of importance and responsibility that her commissions conferred. She fetched the toilet things as requested, and a cloth dampened with rosewater. She always hoped for an excuse to visit the old lady's water closet. It was the only one in the house; Sir Aydon had had it installed five years ago for his mother, but, after that, parsimony or lack of interest caused him to suspend his improvements, and the rest of the family must make do, as they always had, with chamber pots and closestools. An ancient pele tower, used for defence in previous centuries when bellicose Scots might be expected at any moment, formed the northern end of Birkland Hall. It was next to Granny Winship's room, and part of its corner buttress had been ingeniously converted to this practical purpose. Past the door of the closet a spiral stair led on to the higher storeys of the tower; these rooms were thought to be slightly haunted, which caused Parthie to avoid them, though her younger siblings Nish and Tot used one of them as a schoolroom.

The brass and mahogany fittings of the water closet were what Parthie deeply admired, and she never entered it without the resolve that when she was grown and married she would have just such another. On one occasion she had incautiously let fall some hint of this intention to her grandmother; who, for once, did not snub her, but gave her a long, strange, dispassionate look and then murmured to herself an old country saying which Parthie did not understand: "Hoo dear's it, gin it costs yor life? Eh, hinny, it's dirt cheap."

In general the two got on well enough. "What like of day is it now?" the old lady asked—for Parthie had arrived at the same time as her grandmother's breakfast. "Draw back the curtains, child, and let me take a look at the sky."

The chintzes in this room had once been adorned with a splendid design of red, blue, and green Indian parrots, but they were now so faded as to be almost indistinguishable; it was with scorn that Parthie pulled them back. Hers, in the room she shared with little Betsey, were much prettier.

"It's a bonny day," she said, looking out. "A bonny day for my sister Louisa's homecoming."

The old woman sniffed. "Hech, sirs! I doubt there'll not be over-much rejoicing when that one's home again. Not if she's as stiff-necked and proud-stomached as when she went away. Which I'll lay she will be. She gets her obstinacy from Aydon; not that he'd admit it. — How old were you when she left, child?"

"Eleven, Grandma."

"Humph. So you remember her well enough."

"Oh yes. I used to sleep with her in those days. She said her prayers for an *hour*, morning and night. And never read anything but commentaries on the Bible."

"Affectation!" the old lady muttered impatiently. "Showing off. Better she should read the Bible itself." And she thumped a well-worn copy of the Testament which lay on her bed table, beside the bowl of salted porridge. "Pour my tea, child, and tell me what's doing out of doors. Can you see the carriage yet?"

Mrs. Winship's windows faced eastwards, to the wooded hillside above the house with the carriage drive curving down it, and the gravel sweep before the front door.

"No, Grandma, there's naught to be seen."

"Try the pele window, that shows more of the driveway."

Parthie obeyed, slipping into the water closet on the way, to rub her finger luxuriously on Grandmamma's rose-scented soap in the handbasin. Then she climbed a quarter spiral of the stair and stood on tiptoe to peer out of the pele window. This, being higher, commanded another stretch of the drive as it wound uphill among the pine trunks; also the fern-clustered stone basin at the foot of the bank which was known to the family as the Lion Pool.

"Well?" called Mrs. Winship. "Can you see the carriage?"

"No, I can't," replied Parthie in a puzzled voice. "But I can see Annie Herdman."

"Annie Herdman? What's she about, in front of the house, at this time? Why isn't she in the nursery?"

Old Grizel had run the house for forty years, before her son Aydon married, and in the interim between his first and second wives; she still knew where every member of the household should be, at any given hour of the day.

"She's taking something out of the Lion Pool," Parthie said. "But even if I stand on tiptoe I can't see what it is."

A grievous, keening cry broke the calm of the morning; even up here, behind thick walls and embrasured windows, the woe in it could be heard.

"Ah! Eh! My wean! My wean! My wee Geordie!"

"Save us! What's with the woman?" said Mrs. Winship sharply.

Soon other voices could be heard clamouring, and the sound of many feet running from the front entrance across the gravel. Dogs barked and from another part of the house a bell rang vigorously.

"That's Mamma's bell," said Parthie, listening. "She'll want to know what it's all about."

"What *is* it all about? — Is your mother still abed? When *I* was mistress of Birkland Hall I would have been up an hour past, and visited the stillroom and dairy—"

"Mamma *was* up, some time ago; I saw her going out to her garden—"

Parthie returned to the old lady's room and looked out of her window.

"Well? Well? What's to do?"

Parthie was seldom troubled by anything that did not concern herself, but at this moment, turning from the window, even she looked shaken.

"I think Annie fainted," she said slowly. "She's lying on the ground —they are trying to revive her. I think—I think it was wee Geordie— that she pulled from the pool—"

"*Drowned?*" Suddenly the old woman's shrunken lips were whiter than her mottled cheeks. The spoon fell back into her porridge bowl with a clatter. "Annie Herdman's baby? The one they said was fathered by your bro—" Belatedly remembering her companion's age, she snapped tight her lips as Parthie stared at her, round-eyed; then she broke out again. "I *told* Charlotte it was a piece of folly to employ that girl as a wet nurse. Surely there must have been some other body about the countryside that she could have found for little Katie? — Go away, child, go away, and send me Duddy; and find your mother and say that I must speak to her at once. Run—don't stand there gaping. Run!"

Shocked, pale beyond even her naturally colourless complexion, Parthie threw a last dismayed look at her grandmother, and ran stumblingly from the room on her thick, ugly legs.

The three girls seemed to have been travelling for an interminable time. Twice Archie had paused to rest the horses; on the first of these occasions he had produced a repast of oatcakes and cheese from a basket, and they had breakfasted perched on a bastion of the Roman Wall, which flowed away from them in either direction, seesawing up and down over the hilly landscape like a granite serpent.

The air in this land was like iced wine, thought Alvey, shivering; it braced and tingled, made your blood run faster and your thoughts whirl inside your head. Alvey had never drunk iced wine in her life but the simile struck her as so happy that she resolved to note it in her journal at the first opportunity, for future use.

"Does the wall really run from side to side of the whole kingdom?" she asked, munching oatcake.

"Certainly it does! Did you not learn Roman history at Mrs. Camperdowne's?"

Meg's reply held a coolly snubbing inflection. She looks down on me, thought Alvey unresentfully. I am a girl from nowhere who has stooped to this underhand trick, coming to live like a parasite among her family, and for what reason? In order to make up fictional romances. What a vulgar, trivial motive, she thinks. Meg is not going to betray me, because that would be equally to betray her sister Louisa, but she is not—ever—going to accept me as an equal, and she can't help making this plain. Well, thought Alvey, I don't care a pinch of snuff for Miss Meg Winship, who, in any case, is going to be out of Birkland Hall and off the scene by this time next month, and she answered composedly,

"Julius Caesar, why yes, of course we did. And Nero and Claudius. But somehow I had never imagined the Romans being up *here*. It seems so—so far from Rome."

"Not only were they here; they stayed for an immense time. Mr. Thropton, our rector, dug up an old Roman water tank in his garden (his house is thought to stand on the site of a Roman military encampment—he is always digging up bits of Roman pottery among his cabbages)," said Isa. "The tank must have begun leaking, he says, for they gave up using it as a reservoir and, instead, sharpened their swords on the stone sides. They sharpened their swords for *so long* that the sides are quite worn away. Imagine it! They were here nearly four hundred years."

"Four hundred years," Alvey repeated dreamily, gazing around her as the girls climbed back into the carriage. They were on a considerable height of land and could see for many miles, over many ranges of hills, hard and sharp in outline. "Where does Birkland Hall lie from here?"

"Over there—to the northwest." Meg pointed. "Close to the Scottish border. Our ancestors were continually being pillaged."

"Or pillaging," said Isa.

"What a lot of history has happened here!"

"History takes place everywhere," Meg informed Alvey.

"But more in border country," said Isa.

Their next stop was at a village inn, for a lunch of cold meat, buttermilk, and bowls of berries called "noops." The berries were more delicious than any fruit Alvey had ever tasted, and she asked where they came from.

"Oh, they are found up on the moor. They are just noops," Isa replied vaguely.

As they began the third stage of their journey, Isa fell more and more into a kind of bemused, adoring contemplation of the landscape. "Look at that," she would sometimes murmur to Alvey, gesturing at a black procession of wind-curved trees silhouetted along the sharp line of a ridge; "or those clouds," pointing to a dark-grey ragged mass over a pale rolling expanse of moorland, glittering with dry grass; "or the shape of that hill"—duplicating with her hand the long hog's-back curve which terminated in a sudden vertical drop. "All these shapes are so familiar—so much a part of our own country—I do not believe you would find anything quite like them anywhere else in the whole world. Poor, poor Louisa! How can she bear to live elsewhere? I never could."

"Louisa!" sniffed Meg. "Louisa would notice no difference between Newcastle and the Gobi Desert. Louisa is not interested in such things. But now, Alvey—I should say Emmy—we ought to be putting you to the question. We have left you idle far too long. What does my papa look like?"

"A red-faced gentleman of middle age, slightly balding, with gingery brows and whiskers turning white. He walks with two sticks because of a hunting accident. Why is he *Sir* Aydon, by the way? Is that a hereditary title?"

"No, it was bestowed on him for services to the Duke of York at Willemstad."

"And Mamma?"

"Tall and stoutly built with a handsome face, high colour, and grey eyes. Hair dark, with specks of grey. Generally to be found working in the garden in an old green cape and hat," promptly replied Alvey.

"Her maiden name?"

"Fenwick."

"She was an heiress from Yorkshire. Papa did well for himself when he married her," Isa remarked with detachment.

"Papa has the coal mine, however," said Meg, glancing at Alvey to see how this was received. "Grandmamma Winship?"

"An old lady, very pale, hook-nosed, bright black eyes. Beautifully cared-for lace caps. Has a maid called Duddy with a harelip."

"Grandmother's maiden name?"

"Armstrong."

"Parthie?"

"Age fifteen. Straight flaxen hair, pale complexion, china-blue eyes. Has an affection of the legs which makes them thick and unsightly."

"She is always asking when her skirts may be lengthened, poor child," put in Isa. "It is an hereditary condition from my mother's side of the family. Mamma suffers from it too, to a lesser degree."

"My father's dogs?"

"Batty, Roan, and Ginger; two spaniels and a pug."

"Grandmother's cat?"

"Maudge."

"Mrs. Slaley?"

"Ah—let me think. I know! The cook: no husband, never had one. Striped apron, round pink face, curly brown hair. She makes excellent hodgepodge and collops and tatie stovies."

"Amble?"

"The butler. Sir Aydon's batman in the siege of Dunkirk. Saved his life in the battle of—of Linselles. Face pockmarked all over with powder burns. Very devoted to your father."

"My brother James?"

"You never described him."

"No more we did. There seemed so little likelihood of his returning home. He and my mother do not—do not—"

"Do not like each other," gently, from Isa.

"Well! He is not her son, after all."

"What does he look like?"

"His hair is thick and very fair. Not tall—under six foot in height, but very active. Rides well, yet never shared Papa's passion for hunting."

"He likes to fish. And his favourite author is Sir Izaak Walton."

"Wounded at the battle of Waterloo. We do not know how badly. He is a very poor correspondent."

"He and Louisa always detested one another," Isa said bluntly.

"So," added Meg, "you have a good excuse for avoiding him."

Oho, thought Alvey, Meg is apprehensive that I shall fall in love with brother James. Well, and indeed that would be a complication! But I do not intend to become involved with the Winships in any way; why cannot Meg comprehend that I am strictly an observer, a detached onlooker?

Aloud she said, "And has your brother a sweetheart? Is there any local beauty whom he has escorted to balls—with whom he plighted his troth before he went off to battle?"

The sisters exchanged looks.

Meg said, "Oh, when he was sixteen or so he used to moon after Maria Chibburn, but she was two years older and paid no heed to him. Then, when he came down from Cambridge—"

"James is of a very reserved disposition," broke in Isa. "Since the calf love for Maria, he has never singled out any young lady for attentions, or worn his heart on his sleeve. In spring last year, when he was on furlough, we hardly saw him. Fishing, he said, up the Hungry Water. But after he had rejoined his regiment—seven months after—Annie Herdman, a girl from the village, came to Mamma and said she was expecting James's baby; she asked for money to go away and have her confinement in Alnwick, where she had cousins, as her father was being hard on her. He is a disagreeable, harsh old man, a widower—"

"Did your mother agree to this?"

"No, she did not. Papa would probably have done so, but Mamma was within three months of bearing her own latest child, little Katie. She was very displeased, of course," said Isa moderately.

Meg took up the tale. "She flew into a rare passion. She said that, since Annie had disgraced herself, the least she could do was come to Birkland Hall and make herself useful as a wet nurse, for Mamma has not been able to suckle her last three babies."

"So she moved into a loft over the stable and had her baby there. And now she looks after little Katie."

"What of her own child?"

"At first Mamma said that she could not keep him with her, that she must leave him with her father or some neighbour. But Annie was vehement that she would do no such thing—her father would ill-treat him, she said, and the neighbours would despise him as a love child; so in the end she was permitted to keep him. Of course, at first it was no great matter, for he slept in his crib all day. But then he learned to crawl and to walk—he is a forward little fellow and nearly a year old now. He learned how to scramble down the steps to the stable."

"Mamma will not allow him in the house," Meg said. "She ordered Annie to keep him locked up in the loft."

"But he had already encountered Papa in the stable, who said he was a fine fellow and should not be shut up," put in Isa.

"However, this was no great kindness to Annie, for she is occupied in little Katie's nursery all day, so the child roams about at will, getting into all kinds of mischief."

"Papa encourages him and gives him comfits."

Alvey found herself completely silenced by the oddness of this arrangement, and what seemed callous indifference on the part of Sir Aydon and Lady Winship to the feelings of the unfortunate Annie.

What a very extraordinary woman Lady Winship must be! Unable to find any appropriate comment, Alvey said at length, "Does your brother—is he aware of this arrangement?"

"We supposed so. Papa wrote him. But that was some months ago, when he was overseas. He has never replied to Papa's letter. Perhaps he never received it."

"And—and Annie? She complied with your mother's wishes?"

"What could she do? She had no other recourse. And at least she can have her boy with her. I fancy that Papa is truly attached to the little creature," Meg said remotely. "As we told you, Papa prefers boys; and his own sons have turned out a disappointment. James has never entered into his interests; Tot is always off on his own ploys, hand in glove with Nish—and he is delicate, also. Perhaps Annie hopes that Papa may provide for her child—"

"Of course," added Isa, "bastards were quite a commonplace in our family during the last century. It is said that our grandfather and great-uncles fathered dozens, about the countryside; wherever you see a long nose and a pair of bright blue eyes, it is probably a cousin sinister."

"So, when James returns to Birkland," Alvey said, pursuing her own line of thought, "supposing that by any mischance your father's letter never reached him—it may come as a considerable shock to find his child and his mistress boarded out in the stable loft. Unless Annie may have informed him?"

"Oh, Annie can neither read nor write," said Meg calmly. She then added, with more than a touch of malice, "All this would make a suitable theme for one of your romances, would it not, sister Emmy?"

Alvey decided that the best response to this would be an enigmatic smile, accompanied by a lift of the eyebrows. "Pray, Miss Winship, be under no apprehension; all my stories are constructed entirely out of my own head, they bear no relation whatever to real life."

And that was no more than the truth, she thought fondly, surveying in her mind's eye the outrageous escapades of Wicked Lord Love, who had, like Athene, sprung fully armed and accoutred from his creator's brain—with, perhaps, a little assistance from English literature in the persons of Mr. Walter Scott and Messrs. Fielding, Richardson, and Richard Brinsley Sheridan.

The carriage rolled on its way, going faster now, as the horses began to recognise familiar territory. Up, up, up great ridges of heather-covered hillside, the long straight road mounted, then, down, down, down the other side.

"It is like a switchback," Alvey murmured.

"This is a Roman road, of course," Isa replied absently, her eyes noting every clump of trees, every shade of cloud over the far landscape as they crested some high ridge. In the narrow tree-filled valleys they crossed tumbling, rock-studded water by ancient high stone bridges; then the passengers would leave the coach to ease the horses while yet another steep hill was tackled.

At a bare crossroads on a treeless summit, from which a further, blue, craggy range could be glimpsed ahead, Meg said with satisfaction, "Now we shall be home in half an hour. This is Worship Hill. Those are the Cheviots over there, and Scotland lies beyond them."

Alvey looked about the landscape with surprise. "I do not see any sign of a dwelling."

"Birkland is hidden in the valley."

And indeed, almost at once, the road began a precipitous descent, for which Archie made ready by putting the drag on the chain and himself walking by the horses to slow their pace and lead them, snorting and slipping, down the steep and peaty slope.

Alvey stared ahead eagerly, her heart beating rather fast. They had travelled so far to reach this place where she was to become a kind of voluntary prisoner. What kind of people would she find, what kind of haven would it prove? Suppose the family were repulsive, the location unendurable? But she comforted herself by remembering how detestable Louisa had found it, and how wholly dissimilar Louisa's tastes were from her own. Whatever Louisa disliked so heartily, Alvey thought, surely I am bound to find quite delightful?

Then it struck her, with a curious chill, how singular it was that, on the occasion of a daughter's return after more than four years of absence, neither parent had troubled to come, even as far as Newcastle, to meet her. Was not this rather cold-blooded? True, Louisa was not a very lovable person—I would not cross the street to meet her myself, reflected Alvey—but still, she is their daughter. What kind of parents can they be?

Perhaps Meg is right, Alvey thought, with a degree of irritation. Perhaps there will be doings and dealings at Birkland Hall which, as a writer, I shall find irresistible as a vein of fictional ore; but how I hope not! I don't want to be distracted; all I ask is peace and quiet in which to finish the tale of Wicked Lord Love.

Now the road swung sharply into a plantation of tall pines and sycamores.

"Papa planted these trees when he came into the property," said Isa. "They block any distant view of the house as one approaches, but shelter it from the north and east winds, which can be bitter."

Alvey imagined the place in winter, inaccessible under successive snows, and shivered.

Now the track passed between two high stone columns, topped by stone balls.

"The blocks of stone were taken from the Roman Wall. And the balls are cannonballs from some medieval war."

"How very thrifty. Everything put to use."

Passing between the gateposts, they continued to descend the curving drive and at last, across a gravel sweep, came in sight of the house. Set among beech trees, it was a large, rambling, three-storeyed building which had plainly been much altered and added to by successive generations; but the basic structure, of pale, yellowish-grey stone, was E-shaped with a central porch reaching halfway up the second storey. At the right, or northern, end of the house a square, battlemented stone tower rose to a height of forty feet.

"We told you about the pele tower," said Meg, noticing the direction of Alvey's gaze. "It was for protection against the Scots. The whole neighbourhood could take refuge, with their animals— But, good gracious, there is my mother! Positively coming out to greet us."

"How very singular," was Isa's pensive comment. "I have never known her bestir herself to such a degree. It must be in honour of Louisa's regeneration. You had best brace yourself, my friend."

To the best of her ability, Alvey did this, as the girls descended from the coach. She was no little daunted by the sight of Lady Winship, who had a tall, massive figure, robed in ample garments whose unfashionable appearance did nothing to lessen the formidable impression she created. Her face, large, flat, high-cheekboned and high-coloured, seemed set in a permanent expression of absentminded disapproval evinced by a straight, thin-lipped mouth and a pair of rather small grey eyes holding a curiously distant expression.

"Well, Mamma!" called Meg. "As you can see, we have brought back a grown-up young lady to gladden your heart. Would you recognise Louisa in this elegant person?"

Admiring the adroitness of this introduction, Alvey approached, to curtsey and submit to a formal kiss on the cheek. The other two girls were greeted without any greater degree of warmth, and Lady Winship at once proceeded to explain the reason for her taking the unprecedented step of coming out to meet her daughters.

"A most shocking occurrence—I stepped out expressly to warn you, so that you may say nothing to overset your Papa—he has been so distressed by the whole affair—"

"Why, what is it, ma'am?" cried Meg. "What can have happened? Nothing concerning John Chibburn, I hope?"

"Or my brother James?" said Isa.

"No, no—hush! Walk this way a moment."

A stocky, pasty-faced girl appeared in the doorway of the house. She had pale flaxen hair and was, Alvey judged, in her early teens. Parthie?

"Go inside!" called Lady Winship irritably. "I expressly forbade you to come out."

"But Papa wants you!"

"Tell him that I will be with him in a minute."

Beckoning the girls away from the immediate vicinity of the house, Lady Winship turned to order Archie: "Put the carriage away. And see the young ladies' luggage carried indoors. — It happened early this morning," she went on, in a lower voice. "A most deplorable business! How the miserable child could have got so far— But I should *never* have permitted her to keep him here. *That* was the mistake: a most foolish piece of indulgence. Aydon would have it so. He said old Herdman ill-treated the boy. Now it has led to this—"

Alvey perceived that Lady Winship was one of the kind who cannot tell a straight tale.

"What boy?" demanded Meg, but Isa, quicker-witted, exclaimed, "Why, has something happened to Annie? Or to her baby?"

Lady Winship wrung her hands together. They were all standing, now, on the far side of the gravel sweep, which curved round in a half-moon shape and was partly screened from the house by a bank of evergreens. Beside them, at the foot of the piney hillside, Alvey saw a charming small pool of deep, clear water, surrounded by hart's-tongue ferns, fed by a spring which gushed from the mouth of a stone lion's head. It was an attractive feature of the approach to the house, yet, looking at it, Alvey felt a premonitory shiver.

"Drowned himself this very morning," Lady Winship finally brought out, with a kind of strangled outrage. "Yes, Isa, Annie's boy. Saw something bright in the water perhaps—servants, ignorant people *will* drop in pins, nails, even coins—yes, I see something even now, though I told Carey to scour the pool—your father, in his passion, said it must be filled in, bricked over—"

"*Drowned?* Here, in this pool? Oh no! Oh, poor, poor Annie," whispered Isa. "How can she bear it? Where is she? Who is with her?"

"She was very distraught—naturally," said Lady Winship. "I believe Mrs. Slaley administered a tisane. Some such draught. But it is your father who—" She drew a sharp, angry breath. "Anyone would think— Well, I am sure *I* do my—"

She glared at the three girls who stood aghast and listening. In spite of being fatigued and crumpled from their journey they were all so fresh, blooming, glossy-haired, as yet unbruised by time. She surveyed them with exasperation.

"Oh, you all look so shocked and puzzled! Wait until you are my age! *Then* you will know more about what it is like to bear a child and lose it." With an angry laugh she added, "You think me heartless, I daresay. Eh, well—take your sister Louisa to her room, Meg—you will be wanting to change your clothes and freshen yourselves."

"Should we not greet my father? And the younger ones?"

"Not now. Papa is in his library. You may see him at dinnertime. The little ones? Betsey and little Kate are in the nursery with Tushie. They know nothing about all this. Best to keep them away—your father would not— As for Nish and Tot, they are who knows where? They have not been seen all day."

Lady Winship turned away abruptly and, instead of re-entering the house, walked off along a cobbled path and vanished round the side of the pele tower.

Meg and Isa looked doubtfully at one another, then Meg said, "Well, I suppose there is nothing we can do. We may as well go up, as she says. Archie or somebody will have carried up our bags."

They climbed three shallow circular steps and went through the front entrance into a stone-paved hall adorned with deer's antlers and pieces of marble statuary. Ahead of them a handsome stone staircase led up and branched to right and left; Meg, running in front, took the left-hand fork.

"You are to share with me at present, Emmy—but you will soon have the room to yourself when I am married and gone," she said, opening a door at the end of a short, wide passage. "Then you can remain up here all day and scribble to your heart's content. Ah, capital, the men have brought our things. And here is Grace; well—would you have recognised my sister, Grace?" Meg added with her naughty grin, evidently well satisfied by the success of this gambit.

"In course I would, Miss Meg." Grace, a weather-beaten woman in apron and stuff cap, made a sort of token bob to the young ladies; Alvey got the impression that she felt little joy at Louisa's return, though she dutifully added, "Welcome home, Miss Louisa."

"She's fallen into new ways at school, Grace; she wishes to be known as Miss Emily."

"Eh, I beg pardon; Miss Emily then."

Grace, Alvey was relieved to note, spoke with a much more intelligible accent than Archie the coachman. As the maid moved about, unpacking her young ladies' immediate necessities and pouring hot water for them to wash, Alvey glanced with deep interest around the room which, so soon, would be all her own. It was far larger than any bedchamber she had ever occupied before; she began to realise that the Winships must live more grandly than she had apprehended. Perhaps everybody did up here in the North of England?

The room was on a corner, with windows facing two ways. When Alvey approached the west window to look out she drew in her breath with surprised delight—the view was much more extensive than she had anticipated, judging from the tree-girt approach to the house. Remembering the presence of Grace, she caught back her exclamation of wonder and gazed out in silence over a grassy terrace, a spiked fence guarding a sunken ha-ha, and a rough pasture running down steeply to a rocky river. Beyond, at some distance, lay the blue Cheviot Hills. The approach to the house had given no hint of this wide prospect westwards. The river was so near that the sound of it could clearly be heard, murmuring among its rocks.

"You will notice the sound of the river at night," she remembered Isa saying.

"You need not trouble to remain, Grace. Miss Emmy and I will tie each other's ribbons. Isa may need you," Meg said carelessly, and Grace looked surprised.

"Are ye sure, Miss Meg, hinny? Very well, aa'll gan to Miss Isa— that one's always in a pickle."

"That was dreadful news about poor Annie's baby," Meg said slowly, and Grace gave her a quick, expressionless glance before pursing her lips together, frowningly shaking her head, and curtseying herself out of the room.

Meg was a slow and finicky dresser. She fiddled with her sash, her ribbons, her shoestrings, her curls; she made infinitesimal adjustments to her stockings, her tucker, and the hang of her gown. Alvey waited in patience, thinking how much she would have preferred to share quarters with Isa, who obviously never paid the least attention to her appearance—but Isa, being younger, occupied inferior space on the floor above. Alvey, soon ready, went on studying the room. As well as the two beds, and a faded but thick Turkey rug, there were slipper chairs covered in worn blue velvet, a pier glass, a roomy closet for their clothes, and shelves on either side of the fireplace which would accommodate Alvey's books. A writing table stood in the west-facing window; it contained two drawers with brass ring handles.

Oh, Wicked Lord Love, thought Alvey, you are going to be happy as a lark in this place; she looked gratefully at the comfortable chairs and the wide, chintz-covered window seats and wondered if the room would be freezingly cold in midwinter, and whether the young ladies were allowed fires in their bedrooms. Then she had a pang of guilt at her selfish light-mindedness, because here she was, rejoicing in her undeservedly comfortable circumstances, while somewhere close at hand the wretched nurse-girl—what was her name? Annie, that was it

—must be mourning her lost child. What would Annie do now? Could she possibly have the fortitude to go on suckling that other baby, Lady Winship's youngest, who must—how extremely strange—must be the aunt of the drowned boy? Supposing that the story Annie had told was true—that her lover had been James Winship; but no one seemed to doubt that aspect of the matter. Why? wondered Alvey. Nothing I have heard so far about this James particularly suggested that he was a womaniser.

Trying to ignore Meg, still absorbed and preoccupied in front of the glass, Alvey strolled across to the second window, and received another surprise. This window faced south, and instead of pasture a walled garden was revealed—but a most uncommon walled garden, of a long, narrow, and irregular shape, accommodating itself to the course of a rivulet which zigzagged down a little glen, doubtless joining the larger river below. Dusk was beginning to thicken, but Alvey could see all kinds of delights in the garden—clumps of tall flowers, bushes, spaces of lawn by the brook, a patch of rose garden, rockeries and terraces above, miniature islands set with growing plants and little bridges leading to them; low walls overgrown with creeper.

Among all this unexpected luxury of cultivation could be seen the shadowy shape of a person who stood motionless for a long period by the brook, then moved slowly away out of sight.

"Oh, the poor creature!" exclaimed Alvey, caught for a moment by the notion that this tragic-looking figure must be the luckless Annie, out there, all alone.

"What is it?" inquired Meg, her mouth full of hairpins.

"Somebody wandering in that beautiful garden. I wondered if it could be Annie—"

"Oh, good gracious, no! Servants are never allowed in Mamma's garden—except Carey, of course. In fact nobody is very welcome there. If you see anyone, it is probably my mother herself; she is nearly always late for meals, because her eye has lit on a weed that needs pulling, or a shoot that needs pruning. Ten to one she has even forgotten to change her dress."

Feeling snubbed, Alvey sat on the window seat and jotted down a few notes in a little leather-bound book.

"I suppose you are always putting together stories in your head?"

Meg inquired after a minute or two, pushing a last hairpin into place to support the cluster of small late roses she had taken from the dressing-table vase and pinned into her ringlets.

"Only one at a time. When that is finished, then I start another."

"How odd it must be! Do you never get bored, knowing what the end must be?"

"No, why? If you are working on a piece of embroidery, or—or playing a sonata on the pianoforte—you are not bored by knowing how you plan to finish the work, or how the music comes to its end?"

Meg looked a little put out. Doesn't care for argument, thought Alvey, she's like Louisa in that. Doesn't accept that her own point of view is not the only one possible.

"Shall we go down?" suggested Meg coldly, and dangled a shawl over her elbows.

The two girls left the room and walked along the wide passage.

Perched on a marble table at the head of the stairs, and gazing over the banister with lofty interest, was the largest cat Alvey had ever seen: a grey tabby, calm and dignified; it was almost as big as a small spaniel.

"Oh, you fine fellow!" Alvey exclaimed softly, and stretched out a coaxing hand, which the cat first inspected with caution; then, displaying a flattering acceptance, it rose and graciously rubbed its ear and jaw against Alvey's knuckles.

"Eh! B'gor!" exclaimed the maid Grace, chancing to pass at that moment, and she was so transfixed with astonishment that she dropped the freshly goffered tucker she was carrying and stood with open mouth. "Ah niver see owd Maudge tek to no one like thot afore! Paricular not ye, Miss Lou—tek thy thoomb off, more like, when thee wor yoonger."

"My sister has asked to be called Miss Emmy!" Meg said sharply. "And you have dropped Miss Isa's tucker."

"Beg pardon, I'm sure, Miss Meg, Miss Emmy." Grace seized the tucker and retreated.

But as they moved on they heard the miserable wail of a baby, coming from the opposite direction, and a second maid, coming from the right-hand passage, cried, "Eh, Miss Meg! Can you step this way a minute? Tushie's all of a do—and Missus not to be found—"

"You go on down, Emmy," said Meg. "I daresay you will find
Parthie down there—I will join you in a moment—" and she turned to
follow the second maid, a long-faced, dark-haired person who must,
Alvey decided after a moment's thought, be Ellen, Lady Winship's
maid.

How am I ever going to keep afloat in these waters? she thought,
continuing to descend the stairs rather slowly and reluctantly. Sooner
or later I am bound to expose myself by some piece of ignorance or
stupidity. Such as the cat! Fool that I was!

At the foot of the stairs she halted, confronted by four doors, all
closed. She knew what rooms they led to: Meg and Isa had drawn
plans for her, she had studied and learned them with care. Behind
those doors lay the library, breakfast room, drawing room, and dining
room; but the essential piece of information with which her tutors had
neglected to furnish her was: in which room, at this time of day, did
the family assemble, before the summons came to dinner?

Your father is in his library, Lady Winship had said. That would be
the first door on the right, at the foot of the stair. Ought she not—
would not Louisa, that dutiful soul, so full of rectitude and propriety—
would Lousia not consider it the correct course to go in, greet her
parent, and condole with him on the day's tragic event?

Not now, Lady Winship had cautioned. Louisa, though, never allowed herself to be deterred from what she felt to be the right
course . . .

But I don't know the man, Alvey argued internally with Louisa.
And what could I possibly say that would help him, in such a case? But
those considerations would cut little ice with Louisa, Louisa who was
always perfectly convinced of her own ability to say the needful thing.

I can't! Alvey cried in despair, but the invisible, inexorable Louisa
replied, You must; and, without in the least intending to do so, Alvey
found herself walking forward and opening the library door.

The room beyond was half in darkness, illuminated only by a pair of
small lamps on the mantel and central table. For a moment Alvey, with
surpassing relief, concluded no one was there; but then she saw the
bowed figure in the armchair by the fireplace.

"P-Papa?" she said timidly, all the carefully prepared equivocal phrases flying straight out of her head. He did not look up, and she tiptoed forward. "Papa?"

A wholly novel feeling had taken possession of her: looking at this elderly man, so bowed, so bent, so racked with grief, she was seized by pity; her heart felt almost ready to break in pieces. Moving closer, she ventured to take his hand in one of hers, laying the other on his stooped head, on his bristly hair. He said nothing, but silently grasped her hand in both of his, clutching and wrenching it so tightly that she was obliged to bite her lip.

Still neither of them said anything. What was there to say? Louisa, no doubt, would have had an appropriate morsel of religious consolation to offer; Alvey had nothing of the kind.

By and by he murmured some name, indistinguishable—Mary, Maria? She could not make out what he said, and would not disrupt the closeness and peace of the moment by any inquiry. She continued to stand by him and to stroke his head until the silence was abruptly shattered by voices in the hall, and by the sudden arrival of three persons, one of them bearing a larger lamp which brightly illuminated the room.

"Ah, there she is. And your Papa, too. Ay, put the lamp on the stand, Amble—don't tip it—see how it smokes! Now tell Slaley to make haste—I want my dinner. So there you are, Louisa! Well, let us have a look at you! Filled out, have you? Grown into a citified young lady, I daresay. *Grown* you certainly have—why, you must be half a head higher than Meg. You take after my side; the Armstrongs were always tall and rangy."

The old lady moved forward at a halting pace, scanning Alvey from head to foot with a pair of unnervingly bright dark eyes. Once she, too, had been tall, but was now stooped and shrunken; her face, narrow and paper-white, was dominated by a nose hooked like a peregrine's beak. Alvey had read tales of border wives in bygone days urging out their husbands on forays against the Scots, laying a pair of spurs on the breakfast platter as a gentle hint that the larder wanted replenishing; it would be easy to imagine old Mrs. Winship encouraging her menfolk on to battle in such a manner.

Alvey herself, swift as any lover surprised in dalliance, had stepped hastily away from Sir Aydon's chair, and now underwent old Grizel's scrutiny with what calm she could muster. Curtseying, she said, "Good evening, Grandmamma. I hope I see you well?" She dared not glance in the direction of Sir Aydon, but heard him murmur in a puzzled voice, "Louisa? _Louisa?_ I thought—I thought—"

What had he thought? Whom had he expected?

Alvey felt the blood sting in her cheeks as he stared up at her with what seemed astonished disappointment and dislike; but Amble was poking the fire, and a sudden bright blaze, throwing out heat, made it natural to step back even farther.

"Well, girl, well? So you have agreed to come home at last?" the old lady was inquiring tartly. "And are we to conclude that you have entirely relinquished those mawkish unseemly notions you used to cherish—that bee in your bonnet about converting the heathen? Eh? Eh? Thought better of all that nonsense, have you?"

How would Louisa reply to such a fusillade?

"Converting the heathen is hardly to be regarded as _nonsense,_ Grandmamma," replied Alvey with chilly dignity. "But I am, of course, bound to consider—to accede to my parents' wishes in the matter—"

"Foo! Foo! You don't impress me with your parliamentary language, girl. Prepared to consider! Very pretty talking! But are you prepared to match words with deeds—marry some decent neighbour and settle down as you ought? You have turned out a tolerable-looking gal—ay, ay, Meg won't love me for saying so, but your looks bid fair to equal hers—and what's more you give the appearance at least of having a brain or two in your head—"

Disconcerted, Alvey was wondering how to counter this when, to her relief, the unattractive, lumpy girl behind old Mrs. Winship—evidently dissatisfied with the lack of attention paid her—thrust herself forward and cried: "Well, sister? Do you know who _I_ am? Do you remember me?"

"Of course I do," replied Alvey in as cool and snubbing a manner as Louisa would undoubtedly have employed. "You are Parthie. How do you do, sister?" And she kissed the girl's pale cheek.

"Don't you think that I am grown a fine girl? Don't you agree it is time I should let my skirts down? Mamma says not until I am sixteen."

"Certainly not," said the old lady. "Schoolroom misses aping their elders is what I can't abide. Hold your tongue, child, and mind your manners. Who wishes to hear about *you?"*

Alvey felt deeply troubled because all this while the man in the armchair had neither moved nor spoken. Ignoring the arrival of his mother, he had turned his head away and sat staring into the flames. That strange moment just now, Alvey thought, that moment of close- ness and tenderness between us might never have taken place. In a way it did not. He took me for somebody else.

For whom did he take me? thought Alvey, perplexed and embar- rassed at her impulsive and blundering act, and for whom did *I* mis- take *him?* Not for my own father, certainly! I would never have rushed to embrace or comfort *him.* What can have come over me?

"Huts, tuts, Aydon," said the old lady, with a kind of rough, reluc- tant compassion, "pull yourself together, man! The world is not going to end because one bairn has left it. Look at me! Four I lost, one after the other, all under a year, before *you* were born. Did I sit down and repine? Did I fall into a melancholy? The little fellow was bonny and forward, I'll allow; but there will be others. Here's your daughter Louisa, home and cured of her megrims, we hope—she'll give you grandchildren—"

"*Quiet,* can't you! Leave me alone!" he burst out furiously. "Stop that infernal—complacent—gabble—"

Here Amble the butler, who had returned and in an unobtrusive manner had been occupying himself about the room, trimming the lamps, adjusting the fire irons, drawing the curtains further across, deftly intervened.

"I beg pardon, ma'am—I believe I hear her ladyship calling you in the hall." And, in an undertone, "Leave him to me, ma'am; he will come about in a little."

"Amble he *must* eat, he has taken nothing all day!"

"I'll see he takes something, ma'am; he will be better presently."

"Very well," said Mrs. Winship. "Come, Louisa, come, Parthie."

Amble had spoken no more than the truth: out in the hall, looking perturbed and distracted, her high colour even higher than it had been earlier, Lady Winship stood with Meg and the maid Ellen.

"Well, Charlotte? What's to do *now?"* demanded her mother-in-law rather impatiently. "Have we not sustained enough drama for one day?"

With a harassed, conspiratorial gesture, Lady Winship drew the older woman to the far side of the hall, much as, earlier, she had led the girls away from the house. Nodding, frowning in the direction of the library door, she laid a finger on her lips.

"Well? Well? Why all this secrecy?"

"The *girl* is missing now! She is not to be found! And poor little Katie upstairs hungry and crying her heart out!"

"What girl—oh, bless my soul!" Disturbed now, the old lady stared at her daughter-in-law. "You mean Annie H—?"

"Hush! Yes! She must have risen and gone out—nobody has seen her—and it is more than time for little Katie to be fed—"

"Well, for pity's sake!" exclaimed the old lady irritably. *"That* is no great matter! Give the child a feed of pap or milk gruel—"

"She will only suck, she is not used to be fed from a spoon!"

"Then let her suck through a piece of butter muslin. Let Mrs. Umfry be sent for, she will soon show one of the maids how it is managed. Lord bless us, do not make such a turmoil about a trifle, Charlotte! But where can the girl be? *That,* to be sure, is something to worry about, and my son had best not be told. Has one of the men been sent to find if she is at her father's house?"

"Yes, and she is not."

"Humph! Where else might she have wandered?"

As the two women stood conferring, with Meg and Ellen in anxious attendance, and Parthie fidgeting restlessly about the draughty flagged hall, Alvey could not avoid the reflection that this drama, as the old lady called it, fell rather conveniently for her. The child's death by drowning was a horrible occurrence—no wonder its poor mother was distraught; Alvey hoped that poor Annie would soon be located and cared for and comforted; but as she herself had met neither of them, she could have no personal feelings, only general ones; while the fact that the Winship family was so entirely concentrated on the tragedy made her own entry into the house pass off with much less attention than might otherwise have been the case.

It fell out fortunately for me, Alvey thought, with a troubled feeling of apology towards the missing Annie; and she stood politely aside while the two older women conferred together. I now have a first-class opportunity to sink unobtrusively under the surface of family life.

She glanced about the hall, thinking that, in spite of the present upset and trouble, this house breathed an unmistakable atmosphere of comfort and well-being. The furnishings, though not new, indeed somewhat shabby, were solid and of good quality; the air, though draughty, was warm; coal and wood must be cheap and plentiful in these parts, concluded Alvey, for the fire had been high-piled in the library, and another as bright could now be seen through the partly open dining-room door, casting gleams across a table spread with snowy linen, flashing cut glass, and heavy silverware; a pleasant scent of beeswax and dried petals hung in the air, besides that of wood-smoke, and, at a distance, the savour of roasting meat. Alvey swallowed, recalling that a good many hours had passed since that meal in the village alehouse. Servants came and went, elderly, unhurried, not rigged out in fancy livery or gold lace, but well and respectably dressed, clearly at ease in their duties and taking pride in their performance. It was all a great contrast to Mrs. Camperdowne's amiable, but somewhat spartan, establishment, or Cousin Hepzie's bare and frugal little house.

If I am not able to write well here, said Alvey to herself, then there is no hope for me as an author; and Wicked Lord Love sparkled at her, from a cranny in her mind: Feel no concern on that score, my duck! You and I will do very well in this place, very well indeed! Only take care not to become too enmeshed in the concerns of these Winships; you have to get away at the end of the year, remember that.

Suddenly, the end of the year presented a rather bleak aspect; like a door opening from a warm busy kitchen into a cold, frosty yard.

Parthie stole up close to Alvey and whispered, "Sister! Sister Louisa! Have you brought me something pretty from London? When you went away you promised that you would; do you remember?"

Oh, plague take the child, thought Alvey—she had already formed an adverse opinion of Parthie, who looked, she thought, like a pale pink pig, with her china complexion, lashless blue eyes, and straight flaxen hair. Would Louisa really have made her such a promise?

"Did I indeed?" she temporised.

"Oh *yes*, sister! Indeed you did!"

"Hold your tongue, Parthie!" ordered Lady Winship. "How often have I told you that it is very impolite to whisper while your elders are talking."

Parthie pouted and hung her head. At this moment an old, black-shawled woman arrived, panting and curtseying, who was greeted as Mrs. Umfry and led off upstairs to give counsel in the matter of the poor famished baby.

Parthie immediately started again.

"Sister Louisa!"

Fortunately by this time Alvey had remembered an amber necklace, the best piece among the modest collection of trinkets which Louisa had taken with her to school, and which she had insisted on leaving with Alvey when they parted.

"For I shall not want such adornments where I am going; and Mamma would certainly think it strange indeed if I did not return with Great-aunt Maria's locket and the corals and my christening ring and seed-pearl brooch."

So, with considerable reluctance, Alvey had taken charge of these articles, resolving to find some opportunity of returning them all into Winship keeping; this seemed just such a chance.

"After supper, perhaps," she murmured, and Parthie's eyes brightened.

Meg and Isa now ran down the stairs. Isa, despite Grace's assistance with her toilet, looked untidy and flushed; her hair had escaped from its ribbon and her white dress was bunchy and specked with damp. But she greeted Alvey with a friendly smile.

"There you are, Emmy! You must be as hungry as I am. Parthie, find Amble and tell him to ring the gong; Mamma and Grandmother will be down directly."

"But what about Nish and Tot? They haven't come in yet!" declared Parthie impressively; Alvey could not help feeling that she had delayed making this announcement until she could be sure of its maximum effect, for her mother and grandmother had appeared at the stairhead, and Sir Aydon had limped as far as the library doorway, supporting himself on two sticks.

But Amble, picking up the long-handled, felt-swathed drumstick, was able to deprive Parthie's statement of its impact by saying in a deflating manner, "Yes, they have, Miss Parthie, they've been in the kitchen these ten minutes past, getting out of their wet shoes and stockings by the grate," before beating a thunderous tattoo on the brass gong.

The family filed, with some ceremony, into the dining room, Sir Aydon in the lead, supported on either side by his wife and mother, then Meg and Alvey, then Isa, with Parthie a step behind her. Sir Aydon was helped by Amble into his massive chair at the head of the large table, and the rest seated themselves on either side. They all bowed their heads and for a moment kept silent; but as soon as the pause for grace was done, and Amble had begun serving soup from a china tureen on the sideboard, Lady Winship said sharply, "Did I hear you say, Amble, that Nish and Tot had but just come in?"

"Yes, ma'am."

"Where are they now?"

"Mrs. Slaley's giving them their supper in the kitchen, ma'am."

"At this hour? They should be sent supperless to bed," pronounced old Mrs. Winship in a tone of strong disapproval. "Coming home after dark? Disgraceful!"

Sir Aydon lifted his head and said with an effort, "No, not supperless. They should have something."

His wife and mother exchanged glances.

"Very well," conceded Lady Winship. "But tell Mrs. Slaley, Amble, to send them in here when they have had their supper."

"Yes, my lady."

Dinner proceeded, principally in silence. With Sir Aydon, speechless as a ghost at the head of the table, his head bowed, pushing away each plate after he had taken a couple of bites, the atmosphere was not conducive to light talk. Meg and Isa gave their mother some news of her cousin Lady Matfen, and all three girls supplied a few details about the journey on the ship.

The only person to ask Alvey anything about the Abbey School was old Mrs. Winship, who put one or two sharp questions regarding Mrs. Camperdowne's curriculum and regime; these Alvey answered composedly and concisely. A little embarrassed at her own appetite, she made an excellent meal, as courses of trout, roast mutton, vegetables, and some game bird, nature unknown, came and went, but she noticed with relief that Meg and Isa likewise ate heartily. When the cloth was removed, and silver dishes of nuts, apples, and dried plums set on the table, Amble withdrew.

Alvey, whose seat was nearest the door that led to the kitchen region, caught snatches of a low-voiced but vehement argument being conducted just outside the door, and sounds of a slight scuffle.

"Na, ye don't! Ye've to gan in and see your Ma and Pa. Her leddyship said so."

"But—"

"There's na buts aboot it. Gan along in wi' ye."

Two children appeared sidling round the door, their heads ducked apprehensively. That end of the room was in shadow, and Alvey received only an impression of smallness and skinniness. She remembered that Nish and Tot were eight and nine, respectively, but thought they looked smaller, and shabby, and undernourished, hardly like children belonging to this comfortable, prosperous household.

"Is that Nish and Tot? Come here!" ordered Lady Winship, and they approached her slowly, with reluctance, holding hands, bumping awkwardly against one another, and arrived at a point halfway between their father and mother, where they stood staring at the floor. The boy was darker, Alvey noted, with soft lustreless black hair and a pale oval face; the girl's face was rounder, and her tangle of hair nut brown, bleached in streaks from being so much out of doors; the colour of her eyes could not be seen, for she gazed fixedly at her feet, clutching her brother's hand for comfort.

"Hold your heads up! Turn out your toes!" ordered their grandmother, for Lady Winship said nothing. The sight of them seemed to have depressed her so much that she sighed profoundly and went into a kind of melancholy reverie; like Isa, thought Alvey.

"*Look* at you!" scolded old Mrs. Winship. "Your breeches wet—your skirts torn—you look like a pair of gipsy children. Barefoot, too! Where are your stockings, miss?" The girl murmured something inaudible.

"You do not *know?* How can that be?"

"Mrs. Slaley has them; she is washing them," put in the boy nervously.

"Speak when you are spoken to, sir! Not before."

Sir Aydon roused himself sufficiently to put the question "Where have you been all day?"

"Up the Hungry Water," muttered Tot.

"And who gave you leave to run off from your books?" demanded their grandmother.

Neither child replied, and as their parents did not seem inclined to pursue the matter, Mrs. Winship, shaking her finger at the pair, exclaimed, "Bread and water is what you deserve, and to be locked up until you promise better behaviour. If ever there was a pair of marred young ones—"

But now Lady Winship, rousing herself from her cheerless thoughts, whatever they were, sighed, and said, "Come! You have not greeted your sister, who has been away for so long. Have you nothing to say to her?"

At this apparently innocuous observation, Alvey noticed that the children huddled even closer against one another. They made no attempt to approach or greet her. Can they remember Louisa with such dislike? she wondered. Or fear? She was trying, without success, to think of some appropriate friendly remark—Alvey had had very few contacts with young children—when Sir Aydon, who appeared, in his state of grief and fatigue, to take several minutes before responding to any new piece of information, slowly inquired, "Did you see Annie Herdman while you were out of doors?"

Mutely, the children appeared to consult one another as to whether it would be politic to answer this question. Then, as if calculating that to do so might excuse them from the need to greet their returned sister, the boy said, "Yes. We did see her."

And the girl added softly, "Twice. We saw her twice."

"Twice?"

"This morning, early, she was out about the yard looking for wee Geordie," said Tot.

Do they know what has happened to the child? wondered Alvey.

"And where else did you see Annie?" demanded their grandmother. "And at what time?"

"Coming home this evening. When it was all but dark."

"Where did you see her then? What was she doing?"

"Along Blinkbonny Height. She was walking very fast, carrying a heavy bundle. We called to her, she saw us, but she wouldna stop. She was a fair way off, across the other side of the Hungry Water."

"Walking which way?"

"Up the track towards Pike's Force."

Nish opened her mouth to speak, changed her mind, and shut it again. No one seemed to be aware of this but Alvey, who wondered what the child had been about to say. Something this Annie had said to her then? Alvey's eyes met those of Nish, who looked down quickly. But it seemed that some spark of confidence had passed between them. Or had Alvey imagined that?

Sir Aydon had turned and was calling for Amble.

"May we go to bed, Mamma?" asked Tot in a voice little above a whisper. "We are very tired."

"Tired! I should think so! And it is no more than you deserve—rambling off like tinker children the livelong day," their grandmother scolded, but her daughter-in-law murmured, "Yes, yes, run along." Her voice was threadlike with fatigue. "Ellen is to see that you have a thorough wash. Tell her I ordered it. Say good night to your sisters now."

"Good night," muttered Nish and Tot, scuttling, like two small creatures released from a trap, past Meg, Isa, Alvey, and Parthie. Tot never lifted his eyes, but Nish, following him, clutching his hand, looked up and gave another quick, scared glance at Alvey, taking her in, it seemed, from head to foot; again, Alvey had a brief, odd sensation of mutual recognition.

As soon as the younger ones had left the room, Parthie exclaimed, "Mamma! It is unfair! If *I* had run off in such a way, at that age, I should have been whipped." Her voice trembled with injury.

"Hold your tongue, Parthie. Do not let me hear you address your mother with such liberty!" exploded Mrs. Winship. "Charlotte! How can you allow your children to be so ungovernable?" But Lady Winship, with a weary gesture, left her chair and walked stumblingly from the room.

Her husband roused himself to call after her.

"Charlotte! Will you tell Amble to have the men go up towards Pike's Force?"

"Yes; I am going to do so," her voice came back.

The old lady got up, stiff and grumbling, from her chair. "Come, girls, into the drawing room. We will leave your papa in peace. But do not stay here too long, Aydon," she said, tapping his shoulder with a clawlike hand. Alvey thought what she probably meant was: Do not drink too much port. But he shook his head irritably, flinching away from her touch.

As the four girls entered the drawing room, Alvey was impressed anew at Birkland Hall's handsome appointments. The room was low-ceilinged but spacious; oval mirrors in stucco garlands were set at either side of a marble fireplace; many family portraits hung on the walls; a large, if worn Turkey carpet covered an extensive area of floor; chintz-covered couches and ottomans were disposed around yet another blazing fire; a grand piano stood open, and pots of blooming indoor plants made the air fragrant.

Old Mrs. Winship had hobbled away with some murmured remark about little Kate and Mrs. Umfry; Parthie now seized the opportunity to twitch Meg's arm and demand: "Well? What of the bridesmaids' dresses, sister Meg? Were you able to get the stuff? Is it pretty? When can I see it?"

"Oh, Parthie! Do not be such a pest! Yes, yes, I bought it. But tomorrow will be time enough to see it. Grace has not unpacked all the boxes yet. What about John Chibburn? Is there no message, no note from him?"

"Oh yes. I forgot. He rid by this morning to say that he could not come in tonight; his aunt Clara is visiting them at Tinnis Hall."

"Well! I like that!" exclaimed Meg in tones of strong displeasure. "I *should* have thought that he would rate me above his *aunt,* on the night that I return from London!"

"Perhaps they think old Mrs. Forbes will leave John all her money," suggested Parthie shrewdly. "Have you brought back any new songs from London, Isa? Or did you spend *all* your time looking at pictures?"

"I brought some new songs. But I do not think Mamma would like us to be playing and singing tonight. You shall see them tomorrow."

"Tomorrow—everything is *tomorrow,*" said Parthie discontentedly. She gave a great yawn, and scrutinized herself in one of the oval mirrors, tugging at her stringy flaxen hair. "Do you think, Meg, that

Mamma would allow me to do my hair like yours? Is that a new London style?"

"Yes, it is. Cousin Matfen's maid taught me how. But I think Mamma might say it was too grown-up for you."

"Oh, psha!"

"Perhaps just for the wedding," Isa said kindly. "And Meg will ask if you can have your bridesmaid's skirts made down to the ground— won't you, Meg?"

"Only if you will leave off pestering and asking questions when we are all tired to death," snapped Meg, whose spirits had been greatly cast down by the absence of her betrothed. Frowningly, she picked up a book of engravings.

Parthie stuck out her lower lip in a grimace that made her look like a twelve-year-old.

"I declare I am sorry you and Isa and sister Lou are come home again, if there is to be no talking or singing, if we are all to sit like mutes after a funeral."

"Well, but, Parthie," said Isa reasonably, "our father is terribly distressed about poor Annie and her baby. We must respect his feelings—"

"Why?" demanded Parthie rebelliously. "When our sister Maria died he hardly seemed to notice. *Why* is he in such a taking?"

The sisters glanced at one another.

"It is not a suitable subject for your ears," Meg said.

"I am only three years younger than Isa. And in any case I know! I suppose," went on Parthie querulously, "it is because our brother James was said to be wee Geordie's father."

"*Parthie!* You are not to talk about such things."

"But why should Papa grieve so because James's baby died? He is not pleased with James," argued Parthie. "Last year when James was at home on furlough I remember how angry Papa was because James said he wanted to sell out of his regiment and Papa would not let him and said no Winship would do such a thing and that it would be the act of a base coward. *I* remember that if you do not. *I* don't believe Papa loves James above half. So why would he be in such a to-do about the baby?"

"Parthie, it is grossly indelicate to discuss such subjects—about which we can know *nothing*—and if you persist you must leave the room," began Meg, but at this moment Lady Winship reappeared in the doorway.

She gazed for a moment, vaguely, at the girls, without speaking, then wandered to a window table covered with pot plants and occupied herself in tending them, nipping off dead leaves and withered heads, using a small pair of gilt scissors which she carried on a chain attached to her belt. The girls fell silent. Absorbed in her task, their mother seemed, for a little time, dreamily content, away in some mental realm of her own. When Isa addressed her she started, and her expression at once grew dejected and harassed.

"There is still no word about Annie, Mamma?"

"No," sighed Lady Winship. "The men have gone up the track to Pike's Force. But the night is so dark . . ." Her voice trailed away.

Meg gave a great yawn, then apologised. "I think, if I may, that as soon as Amble has brought in the tea, I shall go to bed," she said. "I am very fatigued. Are not you, Emmy?" Alvey nodded. She was finding it hard to keep her eyes open; the day seemed to have lasted for a week.

"Shall I hurry Amble with the tea?" suggested Isa, and, taking her mother's inattentive half-nod as permission, rang the bell.

The perfunctory tea-drinking session was soon over; Mrs. Winship came in, but Sir Aydon did not, and the girls, directly after, went upstairs to bed.

"Good night, sister Emmy; I am glad we have you with us," said Isa cordially in the wide passageway, and really seemed to mean her friendly kiss, thought Alvey with gratitude.

Bearing their candles, Isa and Parthie set foot on the upper stair which led to their chambers on the next storey. At the shadowy turn of the stair Alvey heard a scuffle of feet; Isa gave a gasp.

"What in the *world* are you two doing still out of bed?"

No answer but the hasty patter of bare feet up the stairs.

"Little monkeys!" exclaimed Isa, laughing. "I suppose they wanted to take another look at Emmy!"

I wonder why, pondered Alvey, sleepily arranging her hair for the night. They did not seem so eager to greet me downstairs; on the contrary.

Accustomed, in the dormitory at school, to make a quick toilet, Alvey was in bed long before Meg had finished her lengthy operations and blown out her candle.

The bed was old, wide, and comfortable; the coverings thick and warm. In the distance, as Isa had promised, the voice of the river could be heard, murmuring among its rocks.

Nobody even bothered to take a second look at me, thought Alvey, sinking into sleep. Because of the trouble in the house they all accepted me without the least question.

And she drifted into unconsciousness, peacefully unaware that she was wrong.

V

"Grandma, do you think our sister Louisa is better than she used to be before?"

"Better? What do you mean by *better*, child? In health, in complexion, in spirits, in manners, in morals? You must learn to be exact in your speech. Pass me that orange-flower water, and a clean towel."

Parthie obeyed, making the second errand an excuse for a prolonged visit to the irresistible water closet.

"Make haste, miss! Give over dilly-dallying in there!"

"Grandmamma," said Parthie, returning at leisure with the towel, "why will Mr. Thropton not bury Annie in the churchyard?"

"Because she was a suicide, child. She took her own life, and the Bible tells us that is a sin. It is throwing away God's gift."

"So *she* has to be buried at Worship Hill crossroads, while wee Geordie is put in the churchyard," said Parthie pensively. "Annie would not be pleased if she knew that, would she? After she carried wee Geordie all that way up the moor to throw herself off Pike's Force."

"Better she thought of that before putting an end to herself," said the old lady curtly. "Although," she added, more to herself than to Parthie, "after all, what can it matter where our bones are deposited? I am sure I don't care what they do with mine."

"Oh, Grandma! How *can* you?" Parthie had very clear plans about the size and splendour of her own marble slab and the type of letters in which it should proclaim that PARTHENOPE, dearly beloved and deeply mourned wife, daughter, sister, mother, etc., etc., was laid below. She had frequently studied the stones in the graveyard at Birkland village and gazed in pity and disdain at that one which stated that John Surtees, his son Jack, his wife Hester, and *nine more* unnamed small children lay below. What a way to be dismissed from the world! Parthie intended her own obsequies and memory to be attended by as much pomp as possible.

"About Annie," she went on, hoping to extract from her grandmother the information that her sisters had refused. *"Why* was my father so very grieved? Anybody would think that wee Geordie was *his* child, I heard Mrs. Umfry say."

She stared at her grandmother with limpid, pale eyes.

"Then," said the latter, "Mrs. Umfry is a poison-tongued, hen-witted old woman, and you'd no business to be listening to servants' gossip."

"Mrs. Umfry isn't a servant."

"No, she is a spiteful old farm woman. I am glad that our servants have more sense and decency than to be talking so," said Mrs. Winship, resolving to tell Charlotte to send the woman about her business directly, now that little Kate had learned to take milk from a spoon.

"Your father was distressed because wee Geordie was the first child he had ever truly loved and taken notice of," the old lady went on, deciding that to be allowed a portion of the truth might satisfy Parthie and deflect her prying, probing mind. "At the time when James was a baby, your father's life was wholly given over to regimental duties, and when Tot was that age, Papa was entirely absorbed in hunting. So he never had the time or attention to spare for the boys that he has given to wee Geordie. And of course he never took interest in you girls—"

"I know that," said Parthie.

"Annie's boy chanced to come under his eye at a time when, because of his hunting accident and increasing gout, he did have time on his hands—so he developed a partiality for the child—"

"And Geordie *was* his grandson, after all, was he not, Grannie? Everybody says that grandparents dote on their grandchildren, much, much more, often, than they did on their own sons and daughters—just like you and me!" cried Parthie, taking up the idea with such suspicious alacrity that Mrs. Winship gave her an extremely narrow look before answering drily, "That's as may be! And that is quite enough on the subject!"

For the first few weeks of her sojourn at Birkland Hall, Alvey found herself in a continual state of confused rapture, shot through with anxiety and shame. How could she possibly allow herself so to fall in love with the place, when her own position in it was so invidious, so undeserved, so uncertain? The better she loved it, the more guilty she felt. How could she walk about, so bemused with delight, at a time when some other members of the household, it was plain, were so guilt-ridden, so wretchedly unhappy, so uncertain? Yet there was no way in which she could moderate her own feelings, or will herself out of love.

She had never before in her life been surrounded by beauty. New Bedford had been pleasant, the school at Reading homely and friendly; she had been unaware of any lack. But now she began to understand and sympathise with Isa's words: "How could Louisa bear to live away from all this? I never, never could."

The house itself was so pleasing, graceful, furnished with handsome, shabby articles—damask, mahogany, gilding, carving—that had been the best of their kind fifty or a hundred years ago, and with portraits of ancestors which, when no one was by, Alvey studied with deep interest and astonishment, because some of their faces were so like her own. For her the charm of the house lay not only in its appointments, or in its size and spaciousness or luxury, but in its tranquil animation, the human warmth of a large, active household, well governed, harmoniously composed, with all its members content and at ease in their stations. From whence, precisely, this harmony derived, she found it difficult to decide. For, taken separately, its elements were faulty enough: Sir Aydon was short-tempered and, at present, melancholy and morose; he thumped with his stick, bawled at the dogs, banged drawers and slammed doors. His wife was seldom to be seen within doors save at mealtimes when she wore a sad, perturbed expression and hardly spoke; if asked a question she would start as if roused from some unhappy trance. The old lady's remarks were usually of a dry and acrid character; the sharpness of her eye often made Alvey very uncomfortable. Yet somehow this odd triumvirate succeeded in creating a serenely cheerful efficient establishment around them.

And then, out of doors! Once she had surmounted the shock of cold —and each time she stepped out, it was like a dive into icy water— Alvey was in a continual state of enchantment with everything she saw about her. This is the place, the country for me, the land of my choice, she thought, over and over. The clean sweep of the high hills, the wind-carved outline of ragged thorn hedges, the stately slanting avenues of great beech trees, the grey walls round fields and along roadsides, massively built of loose granite stones, the dark purple curves of moorland, the rivers and brooks burling and flashing among rocks, the willows and clumps of rush and whin along their banks—all these things filled her with a deep, inexplicable delight. It was like being fed when she had been unaware of hunger. I belong here, she thought.

On the first morning Isa had said, "Come; you will want to look at everything. But first put on a warm pelisse."

Nothing owned by Alvey had been adequate. Isa had seized a cloak from the rack near the front door. "Here is an old one of Mamma's; it is too short but it will do."

"Won't she—?"

"No, she always wears her old green gown for gardening. And she goes nowhere. We shall have a task getting her respectably dressed for Meg's wedding. It's lucky that Strother, the Hexham tailor, is coming for a few days; he can make you a thick cloak."

"I can make one myself; Cousin Hepzie and I made all my things."

"You forget: Louisa would never do that."

The two girls followed the cobbled path around past the pele tower, the way Lady Winship had taken last night. It led them to the end of the terrace Alvey had seen from her window, which ran along the back of the house. At the distant end of the terrace was a wrought-iron gate in a wall. Isa hesitated.

"I think we will not go into Mamma's garden just yet. I will take you down to the Hungry Water." They bore right across an extensive stable yard, passed through a gate, and followed a cart track downhill past orchards and a meadow grazed by black-faced sheep and rough-coated horses.

"I never thought to ask," said Isa, chuckling a little. "But can you ride a horse?"

"After a fashion, yes. We sometimes borrowed horses and rode out to visit an old friend of my cousin's at West Point."

"Thank heaven for that! Your having forgotten how to ride *would* be hard to account for. And the only way to get about this country is on horseback."

"How far is it to the nearest town?"

"Hexham? About twenty miles. Southward. Over that way."

On the bank of the river Isa turned left.

"Another day I will take you a scramble up to the top of Blackshaw Crag." She gestured at the heather-crowned slope across the river, with its distinctive patch of dark forest. "But today you are tired, not in trim yet for a ten-mile walk. Also the servants will be wishing to talk to you; you have not seen Mrs. Slaley, or Carey, or Janet."

"What should I say to them?" asked Alvey nervously, looking at the bubbling dark-brown water, laced with coffee-coloured froth.

"Oh—ask how they are. Ask after Janet's aunt Alice. She used to make us treacle humbugs. But she died last winter."

They followed a zigzag sheep track along the riverbank. Alvey's anxiety at the forthcoming ordeal was lulled in some degree by the brilliance of the sun on the quilted water, by the cries of birds.

"What is that birdcall that goes up and up?"

"A curlew."

"It is the most beautiful sound! Like somebody crying out with joy."

Isa laughed.

"Keep those remarks for my ears. Louisa took no interest in birds."

"Isa! Look at those little islands, all covered with moss and flowers and shining stones. Why, one would think somebody had been carefully arranging them."

"Oh, they have. That is Tot and Nish's work. They spend half their time playing in this river."

"But what a labour!"

Alvey inspected the carefully adorned islands, her heart deeply touched. How much care, how much time had been spent on them!

"Why are they not here now?"

"Papa said they must be punished for playing truant yesterday. It was the day when they should have gone to Mr. Thropton for their Latin lesson. So they are to remain indoors and learn a hymn by heart."

"Poor little things! But should not I be teaching them?"

"Oh, not on your first day. See; here is the lower end of Mamma's walled garden. And there is my mother herself, working away."

Down the steeply sloping field from the house ran a wall, stopping at the river, crossing a tributary brook by means of a stone arch. A plank bridge crossed the brook and a wooden gate made an entrance to the garden, the one that Alvey had seen from her bedroom window. Lady Winship, wearing a shepherd's tweed hat, her old green gown kilted up, and a pair of stout fisherman's boots protecting her feet, stood up to her knees in water, planting bulbs along the banks of the stream. She looked up and briefly acknowledged the entrance of the girls by a jerk of her head.

"May we pass through your garden and return to the house this way, Mamma?" called Isa.

"Yes; you may." Lady Winship slowly straightened. Her large, flat face was flushed from stooping, but she looked more amiable than Alvey had seen her yet. "Find Carey on your way—he should be in the vegetable garden—tell him to come down here with a hand barrow for my weeds. And tell him to bring another hundred yellow iris corms." She rubbed her cheek with the back of a gloved hand, leaving an earthy smear. "How do you like that?" she said gruffly to Alvey, nodding at the sloping garden. "It is all new since you left home."

"Very beautiful," Alvey said truthfully.

The slope was smooth turf scattered with rocks cunningly set to look natural—perhaps they *were* natural; among these were clumps of flowers, blooming still, despite the lateness of the season, in this sheltered, south-facing gully: asters, small hardy roses, geranium, valerian, bellflowers and scented shrubs. Absently Isa pinched off a sprig from a low-growing, feathery bush and held it to Alvey's nose. It had a stinging, aromatic fragrance.

"Delicious! What is it?"

"You *must* remember Old Man? It used to be your favourite. Southernwood, Lad's Love?" Lady Winship frowned.

"Of course! It is—it was so long since I smelt it."

"What do they have in the Abbey School garden?"

"Not much. It is so trampled by the girls. A few roses and wallflowers—a medlar tree—Mrs. Camperdowne makes medlar jelly—" Here, at least, Alvey was on firm ground.

"Ah, a medlar. I've always wanted one. But they won't grow here. Well—tell Carey to make haste with those bulbs."

Dismissed, they strolled on up the winding path, which crossed and recrossed the tumbling brook by a series of small bridges, Alvey frequently exclaiming in pleasure at the sight of some tiny brilliant or tall handsome plant.

"No frosts here yet," said Isa. "But in another week or two—"

"Your mother can work here all winter?"

"Oh no. Autumn is her busiest time—until the snows begin. Then she does become frustrated."

It was interesting, thought Alvey, that this intense love of the outdoor world had been transmitted from Lady Winship to Isa, in the form of Isa's passion for landscape, and to the younger ones as an urge to decorate miniature islands.

She said something of this, and Isa laughed.

"There speaks the writer—always tracing out connections."

"But it is true."

"Oh, to be sure. And you will find it in my brother James—and in Papa, for that matter—we inherit it on both sides. Papa's lifelong addiction to hunting was because it gave him an excuse for galloping over the countryside six days a week."

"When did his accident take place?"

"A little over a year ago—at the very beginning of the season, poor man. He had a raw, half-schooled colt—it stumbled, jumping a wall, and fell on him. The horse was so badly injured it had to be shot, and both my father's legs were broken, and have not set as they should; so he is as you see."

"How terrible for him."

"Yes, it is terrible," said Isa moderately, "for he has no resignation, no strength of religion to uphold him, no mental resources, no indoor occupations. He is not a thinking man. And my mother is of no help to him. Indeed, one must admire him—somehow, despite these things, he contrives to live his life—"

They had reached the upper gate and left the garden; Isa turned right into a square, walled enclosure containing potato and cabbage beds, leeks, currant bushes, parsley, horseradish, celery, and cauliflower in neat rows. Against the high wall were glasshouses, and here they found a man in a sacking apron pricking out boxes of seedlings.

"Carey, my mother wants you and a hundred iris bulbs in double-quick time."

"Aathing her leddyship wants is double-quick," said Carey cheerfully, tugging his forelock to Alvey. "Welcome hyem, Miss Lou. Gud to see ye."

"Thank you, Carey. It's good to be here."

"We'll go in the kitchen way." Isa led Alvey along the broad terrace, into the stable yard, and through a back entrance past pantries and stillrooms into a large, lavishly appointed kitchen which seemed warm as a bakehouse after the tingling chill of the outside air.

Glancing round her, Alvey was able to take note of shining white-tiled walls, exquisitely whitened hearthstone, two long scrubbed tables, a whole wall of ovens and ranges, another hung with dazzling copper pots and pans, enough for an army, herbs and flitches dangling overhead and a pervasive scent of hot baking, before she was being greeted by a smiling round-faced woman, plainly Mrs. Slaley, the cook.

"Ee, Miss Lou, but ye've grown a likely and a bonny lass sin' ye've been awa'! Aa rackon yer mam and dad should be prood of ye! And is it gud to be back?"

"Good? I can't tell you how good!" said Alvey, and she was so touched by this friendly welcome, by far the warmest she had received so far, that, completely forgetting the unforthcoming character of Louisa, she stepped forward impulsively and gave the smiling woman a warm hug, which was returned as heartily.

"There! I said as ganning to school wud do ye a deal of gud. Didn't I, Becky? Didn't I, Janet?" Mrs. Slaley demanded of two maids who had been busy respectively beating eggs and grinding something in a quern.

"If kissing's i' fashion, aa'll hev a share," said the maid addressed as

Janet, laughing, and she too came forward and was hugged by Alvey, followed by Becky.

"Times change," said Janet. "Ye'd not have din that afore ye went, Miss Lou! Reet starchy and chill ye were in they days."

Alvey glanced guiltily at Isa, who raised her brows in mild reproof, though she was smiling too.

"Yoong Mester Chibburn's in to see Miss Meg," Becky told them then. "Ye'd best gan to the morning room; Miss Parthie's there wi' them and if aa knaw out o' the matter, she's driving them fair desprit."

"Oh, poor Meg! We'd better go at once. Come Al—Emmy."

"Umble pie for your dinner tonight, Miss Lou."

"Umble pie?" said Alvey, startled off her guard. "Why—?"

"Dyen't ye mind? Umble pie were elwis yer favourite. Aa've syeved the umbles a week sin we had a stag brought in—"

"Of *course* she remembers your umble pie, Mrs. Slaley, we were talking about it only yesterday in the carriage," cried Isa, giving Alvey a pinch, "with the oranges and lemon and Canary—she can't wait. Come along, Emmy."

As they left the kitchen the smiles were replaced by gravity behind them; the fate of Annie Herdman, Alvey guessed, had cast a shadow over the entire household.

"Heaven help me—how shall I ever maintain this charade?" she murmured, following Isa down yet another broad, stone-flagged passage. "My tongue continually betrays me."

"Oh, pho, pho! You are doing excellently well. What can such trifles matter? Nobody remarks them."

"But they may remember and add up. And sooner or later I shall perpetrate a major mistake. I find it so difficult to portray Louisa's character!"

"Oh, never mind that. Everybody is delighted to find Louisa humanised by school and the passage of time," said Isa shrewdly. "Now: do not be forgetting that John Chibburn was once *your* suitor. Some finesse, I grant you, *is* called for here."

Isa's meaning was plain to Alvey as soon as they entered the morning room. Meg, hitherto amiable and easy enough with her substitute sister, was all on edge, a mixture of assertiveness, conscious pride, and nervous watchfulness. While John Chibburn himself, a rosy, fresh-faced young man, with no pretension to looks, but a pleasant, simple manner, appeared, for the first few moments, a trifle confused, as if he hardly knew how to comport himself between the old love and the new. Though, to do Louisa justice, she had never encouraged him. "I soon sent him about his business," Alvey recalled her saying. An air of austere, lofty erudition, Alvey decided, would soon confirm the young man in the fitness of his choice; and she contrived without loss of time to be so extremely learned, to drop so many French and Latin and German tags into the conversation, to lard her remarks with so many literary and historical references, that Mr. Chibburn was soon looking quite aghast, and immensely relieved at the fate he had escaped, while Parthie, who had been driving the engaged pair mad with her fidgety and intrusive presence, began yawning uncontrollably and seized an early chance to slip away. Meg's relief and improvement in spirits, on the other hand, were instantly apparent.

Arrangements for the wedding were under discussion and, since Lady Winship was so wholly uninterested in the business as to be useless in the character of an adviser, they were awaiting the arrival of the old lady, who had, in her day, married off three younger sisters of Sir Aydon, and could claim to be an expert.

When she presently made her appearance her first task was to allay the anxieties of Meg, who had wondered if the wedding must be postponed because of the fatality in the house.

"No such thing, my child," she said with energy. "That would be to make altogether too much of the affair, and set the neighbourhood wondering. No: it will be better by far to continue with arrangements as planned. Of course, we are all greatly grieved about poor Annie and her bairn, that goes without saying, but it will be giving a wholesome and a fresh turn to everybody's thoughts, and especially your parents', if the ceremony goes on as planned."

Meg looked her satisfaction at this judgment, but said doubtfully, "Ma'am, what about my brother James? May he not be distressed?"

"Well! If he is, he must stay away."

"Oh, I hope he does not!" cried Isa, and added, "Besides, Papa wrote to him about the wedding some time since and he is supposed to be on his way; I do not see how he is to be warned—"

"Word flies about fast enough," said the old lady, frowning a little. "In any case, James must take his chance."

There was a ruthless streak in old Mrs. Winship, Alvey decided; she seemed to rate as of small consequence the shock the poor young man must receive, on his arrival home, at hearing that his sweetheart and his child had died untimely.

Appearing aware of this critical appraisal, the old lady glanced in Alvey's direction and remarked briskly, "By the bye, Louisa, the children, Tot and Nish, are awaiting your attentions in their schoolroom; Aydon wishes you to hear their hymn. Since you are become so learned you may as well outline a course of study for them to pursue. And high time too," she added sotto voce.

"Yes, Grandmamma; of course I will do that." Alvey, taken by surprise, had risen to her feet and was halfway to the door when she realised that she was uncertain where the schoolroom lay; but Isa came to the rescue, murmuring, "They still take their lessons in the pele tower, as we used with Miss Waskerley."

Alvey nodded gratefully. Only after leaving the morning room did she begin to wonder how to reach the pele tower; that it was at the northern end of the house she knew, but where was the entrance? She turned along a corridor that led in the right direction, hoping to find some helpful stairway, but found none, only a door that led out of doors. Here she was hesitating when accosted by a gardener's boy with a basket of logs.

"Looking for something, Miss Lou?"

This would never do.

"Yes—I dropped a pin," Alvey said, by good fortune spotting the gleam of one lying on the cobbled pathway; and she picked it up and stuck it nonchalantly into her collar, before adding, "Can you tell me where the children are, Master Tot and Miss Nish?"

He grinned. "Ay! Maister has 'em pint up in the pele room!" and he nodded to a door behind him. "I jist tyuk some wud for the old leddy's room, so I knaw that's whur they are," and he went on, with his basket, through the door from which Alvey had just come. Relieved, she opened the second door, and found that it gave on to a spiral stone stair. After climbing three turns of this she reached, first, a door that opened into a bedroom—from its antique furnishing, plainly that of the old lady; the next door revealed a well-appointed water closet; a third, another turn higher, led to a circular room, equipped with tables, books, and maps. Here she found the two children.

They looked up warily from their copybooks, and eyed her, she could not help feeling, as prisoners observe the approach of the torturer.

"Have you any use for a pin?" asked Alvey briskly. "I just picked up one from the path down below," and she took it from her collar and handed it to the little girl, who appeared as amazed and doubtful as if she had just been awarded the Holy Grail.

Since she was slow to take it—"I will pin it into your tucker," said Alvey, and did so; "it is odds but it will come in useful for something."

She was aware of the child's eyes trancedly following the motion of the pin, and her own hand carefully inserting it.

"Now, then!" said Alvey. "I am to hear your hymn; but I daresay you do not have it by heart yet?"

They shook their heads, agreeing; their eyes bored into her like woodpeckers' beaks. The boy's were dark-grey, almost black, narrowly set near the bridge of his nose. He would, Alvey thought, resemble his grandmother quite markedly when he was grown older. The girl's were several shades lighter, with a greenish tinge.

"Well, there is no use my hearing the hymn if you do not know it yet," Alvey went on matter-of-factly into the silence, which she found somewhat daunting, "so, instead, I will read you a poem which I think well of myself."

The four eyes consulted with each other; their looks, which had lightened just a little at the word "read," darkened with gloom again at the word "poem." Alvey drew a small leather-bound volume from her pocket. "Have you ever heard of Mr. Walter Scott?" They shook their heads. "What? And you live so near to his country? Well, listen to this. It is from a longer poem called *Marmion.*" And she began to read, " 'Oh, young Lochinvar is come out of the west—' "

They sat motionless, mouths ajar, utterly concentrated, hardly seeming even to take breath, until she reached the last line, " 'Have ye e'er heard of gallant like young Lochinvar?' " and shut the book.

A pause elapsed; then the boy asked, in a low, amazed tone, "Is that a true tale?"

"It *must* be!" exploded his sister excitedly. "For it's all around *here!* The Esk River—that's none so far off, at Longtown—and Canonbie—and the Solway—it is all about here! But who was young Lochinvar?"

Alvey was obliged to confess that she had not the least idea. "Perhaps your father would know?"

"I doubt he wouldn't; but Grannie might," said the boy.

"We'll ask her. She knows that kind of thing," agreed his sister.

Alvey was well pleased at the excitement the poem had generated. Gone were their looks of apathy and distrust. They begged for more, and she read them a portion from *The Lay of the Last Minstrel*. They were enchanted with Lord Cranstoun's Goblin Page, his fiendish supernatural habits, and propensity for yelling "Lost! Lost! Lost!" on every occasion. After his abduction of the Heir of Buccleuch she stopped.

"But what happened?" demanded Tot. "Did the boy get home?"

"What became of the Goblin Page? Who *was* he?"

"That you may find out for yourselves. I will leave the book here," said Alvey cordially. "Now I think you had better do some writing. I suppose you are very good at that, since you are so interested in reading?"

"No, we are not," said Tot flatly.

"Oh? Well, never mind. Write down for me a page of things you might need to make an island handsome in the river; and then draw a picture of that island."

No response. Their looks met again. "Have you paper?" inquired Alvey, turning to survey the room's resources. "Yes, I see some; and paints; but they look rather dry and dingy. Never mind, we shall just have to imagine the colours."

She furnished each child with paper, colours, and writing materials. A glum, hard-breathing silence fell. Alvey strolled to the window and looked out, over a hotchpotch of gabled slate roofs and massive stone chimneys, upward to the distant height which Isa had named Blackshaw Crag. It would be easy to imagine an armed lookout man posted here, on the watch for marauding Scots pouring over that hill . . .

"Does—" that stair lead onto the roof, Alvey was about to inquire, when she remembered that it did, and that she would be supposed to know; she changed her question to "Does Papa still allow us to go onto the roof?"

They nodded, and she mounted the stair, which wound around the circular room, to a door, which gave into a small, dim chamber above. From that, another door opened onto a leaded roof.

Here, the prospect was glorious: eastwards, to the wooded slope down which they had come yesterday; north, along a narrowing valley, the course of the Hungry Water, to enfolding blue hills; westwards, to Blackshaw Crag; south, to yet more hills. Not a roof, not a habitation in sight. Not a live creature to be seen, save some grazing sheep; not a sound to be heard but the cawing of rooks and the distant cry of a curlew. Oh, my dear Wicked Lord Love, thought Alvey, you are going to thrive in this place, though it is the last place in the world that you would choose to inhabit; and she reflected fondly on her creation's predilection for balls, gaming houses, soirees, and the delights of city life—delights which Alvey depicted with all the freedom of one who had never experienced or expected to experience them. Would the children downstairs, she wondered, be entertained by the adventures of Lord Love? His escapades were really of a very harmless nature, much more so than the libertines who figured in the romances issued by Minerva Press—tattered copies of which Alvey had observed on the shelves of the room downstairs, doubtless a relic of the departed Miss Waskerley. Alvey could not help adjudging Lord Love and his exploits far superior to *them*. And if that was all the children had in the way of reading matter, the poor things had been atrociously neglected. Really it was time somebody took them in hand.

With a sigh, feeling the icy air bite through her thin dress, she returned inside and fastened the door. After carefully descending the inside stair, which had no rail, she returned to the table and inspected the children's compositions.

"I plant iland wit plants," Tot had written, and Nish: "i paformed a grate meny tasx on knewmerous ilands, dekorating them al over with cort stones, bewtifle flars, mos an leves. i made a depe chanl an raste botes along it. i helpt tot with his iland an plantd litle treas on the damp sand. i made a hege of hasl twigz. i made a litil pule an gardn beds wit fethrs. the day as wel spent but wer rathr tard."

Both their pictures were excellent. "Who taught you to draw?" Alvey asked.

"Isa."

Alvey had observed, during the journey, Isa's dexterity at whipping off small sketches of the ship, the crew, the shoreline, the docks—anything that took her fancy.

"When you can write as well as you draw," Alvey told the children, "you shall each make an illustrated storybook. I shall show you how. Now, I have had enough schoolteaching for one day, and I am sure you have had enough learning. You may run outside, but take care to come home soon enough to learn that hymn, which I shall hear tomorrow."

"But Papa said—"

"Papa did not intend you to spend the whole day indoors," said Alvey, confident that Sir Aydon would neither know nor care how long their incarceration lasted. A cautious light brightened in their eyes.

"We can really go?" said Tot, and disappeared like a stone from a sling, in case she should rescind the permission. Nish remained behind for a moment, studying Alvey gravely.

"You are not really our sister Louisa, are you?" she said.

"What makes you think that?" asked Alvey, deeply startled.

"I *know* you cannot be she. So: who *are* you?"

"Well—shall we say—for the moment—that I am your fairy god-mother?" Alvey cautiously suggested.

Nish pressed her lips together, frowned, half nodded, then with a final, lingering, unsatisfied stare, left the room.

Alvey waited a while, until she had regained her composure. What to do? Tell Isa? Or wait and see what happened next?

Somehow she felt fairly certain that public exposure was not likely to result from the child's disbelief in her. Who would pay heed to a statement from such a source? If, that is, either of the children were inclined to make such a statement, which Alvey doubted; they seemed to lead a separate life of their own, without reference to their elders.

They have been amazingly neglected, thought Alvey. If *I* had written a composition like that when I was eight or nine, Mamma would have had something to say!

Still, they did enjoy Lochinvar and the Goblin Page.

Heartened by this thought, she left the room and descended the spiral stair. Observing Mrs. Winship's door open, and the room, so far as she could see, empty, she turned through it, reckoning that it must be a shortcut to the first floor of the house.

What was her dismay to find Parthie, scarlet-cheeked, half hidden in an alcove, turning over a bundle of papers tied with brown ribbon that lay in a small rosewood desk.

"Oh! S-sister Louisa!" stammered Parthie. "How—how you surprised me! I had not—I had not thought anybody was—that is, Grandmamma asked me to find her receipt for wedding cake—"

"I see," said Alvey calmly, and walked on through the other door. She was in haste to reach the room she shared with Meg; while on the leads she had been visited by a new and brilliant inspiration regarding the doings of Wicked Lord Love, and she was eager to make a note while it retained its first freshness and gloss.

The bedroom was tidy and empty; the beds were straightened, and somebody had given a stir to the great china bowl of dried rose petals and lavender that stood on the chiffonier. In the grate a peat fire gently smouldered.

Luxury! thought Alvey, and applied herself to work at the window table.

Only twenty minutes later did it occur to her that the bundle of papers which Parthie was inspecting looked much more like letters than household receipts—in fact, they looked remarkably like letters in Louisa's handwriting.

Bursting out of the tower door onto the cobbled path, Nish ran into her brother, who was waiting outside.

"Come quick!" said he. "Mrs. Slaley gave me some pepper cakes and a whole bundle of bannocks. And she says sister Lou has turned out a right gud 'un! Let's go up the Hungry Water."

"Bide a moment."

Nish darted round the corner and across the sweep to the Lion Pool. (No one had taken seriously Sir Aydon's order to fill it in, nor would they.) Nish tweaked the pin from her tucker, dropped it into the water, and whispered, "Dear Lord Mithras, thank you for answering my prayer. You are a great god! Yours to command, Annis Winship."

Then she followed her brother down the cart track. As she ran she half sang, half chanted:

"Are ye going to Whittingham Fair?
Parsley sage rosemary and thyme
Remember me to one that's there
For once he was a true love of mine . . .

Tell him I made him a cambric shirt
Parsley sage rosemary and thyme
Without any hem or needlework
For once he was a true love of mine . . ."

VI

Alvey had expected a summons, at some point, from Sir Aydon, to an interview in which he would admonish her about her past and lecture her about her future. But none came. Sir Aydon saw no need for it. His was neither a strong nor an optimistic nature; given agreeable circumstances, he could be as cheerful and active as any, but the recent fatality had thrown the whole framework of his being ajar, and it would be months before he recovered. Meanwhile Louisa was back at home, apparently behaving herself, making no trouble; all too well he remembered the stormy scenes of earlier years before she had been packed off to school in the South; he wished no repetition of those, and was glad that she appeared to have given over such ways. His daughters were of no interest to Sir Aydon. It was the part of girls to be biddable, industrious, and quiet; if they behaved otherwise, then there was something wrong with them, they were disordered, and he neither understood nor wished to have any dealings with them. Sir Aydon was good-natured up to a point; he could be generous, on his own terms; and he was possessed of physical courage, had led his brigade with considerable dash and earned the knighthood, to which none disputed his desert, in the battle of Willemstad under the Duke of York's command. Shortly afterwards being obliged to sell out on the death of his father, he had reluctantly left a military career to tend his estates, and passed the larger part of the ensuing twenty years in the hunting field. The estates were, in consequence, somewhat neglected, but still he had a respectable income from the coal that lay beneath a distant part of his land: enough to provide for his children and allow him to live as he chose. Marriage to Charlotte Fenwick, a

Yorkshire heiress, after the death of his first wife, Maria, had hand-somely augmented his fortune, and the girls would be respectably dowered. It was his sons who were the real affliction of his life and, since he detested affliction, and had no method of coping with it, he thought about his sons as little as possible. The imminent arrival home of his son James for Meg's wedding was an evil which there was no eluding; he felt it like a black cloud of gloom, already covering half the sky. He *could* not talk to the boy; had nothing to say to him; that was the end of the matter. Boy! James already had the age and stature of a man. Yet, since going away to school, and then to Cambridge, his views and tastes had diverged so far from those of his father that they seemed to belong to different species. And Tot bade fair to go the same way: sullen, sly, secretive, wilful, *odd:* God knows where the strain came from, not from the Winship side of the family, that was certain. The only one who had given him any joy, any joy at all, was the little fellow—but no use thinking about *that.* Indeed, thinking about that brought on such severe agony and terror, of a kind never before encountered, that a door must be instantly slammed in one's mind. Any, any distraction was preferable, even that of one's wife asking some trivial, irritating question.

They were assembled in the breakfast parlour, the hot dishes on the sideboard, Sir Aydon awkwardly walking about eating his oatmeal. This ritual he achieved with no little difficulty, because of the two sticks required for his support. Watching the ceremonial feat, every morning, for Alvey, was an entertainment shot through with appre-hension; yet his dexterity must certainly be applauded.

"Why *does* your father eat his porridge walking about?" she had inquired of Isa.

"Oh—from respect. Because oatmeal is the national dish of the north country. So men stand up while they eat it."

"Dear me! As when 'God Save the King' is played?"

"Precisely."

"Why must not women also stand?"

"I do not know," replied Isa after a moment's reflection, wrinkling her brow and screwing up her eyes. "I never gave the matter any thought. Women's observance of such a practice is not important, I conclude."

I wonder what Wicked Lord Love would think of that? reflected Alvey, watching Sir Aydon add cream and salt to his portion of oatmeal. The dish containing it was of frail Japanese porcelain, brought home in the last century by Lady Winship's grandfather, who had been an extensive traveller.

". . . Eh?" said Sir Aydon, abruptly coming out of his abstraction with the vague impression that his wife had addressed him several times. "I beg your pardon, my dear, what was that you said?"

He treats her with a heartrending, gentle courtesy, Alvey thought; as one would a person who is mortally ill and not aware of it. *Why? Is she mortally ill?*

"Mr. Thropton," said Lady Winship patiently for the third time, "is coming to see you again this morning about arrangements for Meg's wedding. And"—her voice shook and sank to a murmur—"about the little—about the child's—"

He made an angry, dismissive gesture with his hand. Amble walked swiftly from his station near the sideboard and received the empty oatmeal dish.

"Kidneys, Sir Aydon?"

"No, fish. No, a few eggs and a piece of ham. Can *you* not see the fellow, Charlotte? — Oh, I suppose I had better," he muttered. Sir Aydon liked to get out in the mornings and hoist himself painfully about the grounds, interviewing bailiff, steward, and gardeners, countermanding the orders he had given yesterday, looking into everything, and generally making his underlings long for the days when he would have been off a-hunting several hours before daylight. "What time does the fellow come?"

"At noon."

Mr. Thropton, Alvey recollected, was the vicar, who tutored James in Greek and Latin and now teaches Tot and Nish one day a week. He plainly has not taught them a great deal; they had acquired a few principal parts of verbs and declensions of nouns by rote, which they mumbled with no apparent understanding. Still, Miss Waskerley had not long been gone; perhaps Mr. Thropton's regime was of fairly recent duration.

"A slice of oatcake, Emmy?"

"Thank you; I will take a small portion."

Alvey had acquired a passion for the gritty, nutty oatcake, thin as a wafer, brittle as a biscuit, which was one of the staple foods of the household, served at every meal, sometimes as well as, sometimes in lieu of bread.

She spread honey on it and ate it with relish.

What a pleasant thing this breakfast ceremony is, she thought. So leisured. So civilised. Thick smooth damask on the table. Heavy silver. Asters in a cut-glass bowl. Amble presiding over the chafing dishes. Sparkle of pale sun on red leaves around the window. Cloudhaugh shining in the distance. (Alvey was learning the names of the hills.)

"You never *used* to like oatcake, sister?" said Parthie inquisitively. "I remember that you *detested* it."

"Tastes change," replied Alvey, raising her brows, looking coolly into the pale guileless eyes. "I have been deprived of oatcake four long years; now it tastes like ambrosia."

"What is ambrosia, sister?"

"Go to the dictionary and look it up."

I must not snub Parthie so often, she thought repentantly. I must find some means of gaining her liking. Or at least respect. But she is such a pest!

One of the dogs, Ginger the spaniel, came and flopped heavily against Alvey's leg, looking up at her with soulful liver-and-yellow eyes, hoping for a crumb. Alvey, who disliked dogs, surreptitiously jerked her leg to dislodge him, but he only leaned the more heavily.

"It is so sad that old Gelert died," Parthie said in a false tone of melancholy.

Nobody responded for some time until Isa, glancing up from a note she had been reading, said, kindly, "Why, Parthie? All dogs do die. And Gelert was seventeen years old. It was time he went."

"Gelert would have been *so* pleased to see sister Lou—sister Emmy back. He loved her dearly. He would have been so happy, if only he had lived to see her—"

"Well, he didn't," snapped Sir Aydon. "Don't talk so much, Parthie. Gels should be seen and not heard. Hold your tongue and eat your breakfast."

"I have finished. May I be excused, Mamma?"

"Yes."

Parthie said in a virtuous tone, "I will go and see if Grandmamma needs me," and skipped clumsily from the room, leaving Alvey to congratulate herself on the death of old Gelert, to whom her arrival must have been a bitter disappointment.

"Meg, you had best attend your father and Mr. Thropton also. There will be a great many things to consider and discuss," remarked Lady Winship, rising to leave the breakfast room.

"Oh, Mamma, must I? Is that necessary?" Meg came out of a pretty abstraction; to the uninformed eye she might have appeared to be thinking of her lover. In reality, Alvey knew, her thoughts were occupied with guimpes, frills, ruches, tucks, hemstitched handkerchiefs, and paper patterns. "Must I?" she pleaded again. "I have so much to do with Grace and Mrs. Galt."

"Yes, you must." Lady Winship's answer came with vague but inescapable authority as she herself escaped to go to her garden.

"Oh!" grumbled Meg, and then, "Well, I shall be in the sewing room; I will come down when Mr. Thropton is here. May I be excused, Papa?"

Isa said, "Fanny Beaumont has sent a note inviting Meg and Emmy and me to spend the night of the Hexham Assembly at her father's house. May we do so, Papa? It is very kind of the Canon to suggest it—"

Sir Aydon looked beleaguered. "You mean that you wish to *attend* the Hexham Assembly? Just *now?* And pass a night at Canon Beaumont's house?" He sounded as if a trip to the South Pacific were in question.

Isa replied patiently, "Meg and Fanny Beaumont are very fond of one another, Papa. And once Meg is married and living at Tinnis Hall, which is so very much farther from Hexham, they will have many fewer chances to meet. And it will be a chance for Emmy to meet—to renew old acquaintance with some of our neighbours. Also I am persuaded that our mother must have various commissions, relating to the wedding, which we could execute for her in Hexham."

Alvey plucked up her courage, remembering that Hexham boasted a circulating library and stationer's shop.

"I could purchase some books for the children," she suggested.

"Books?"

"Lesson books," she amended hastily. "They seem to have so few." And what there are, far too babyish and years out of date, she could have added.

"Books!" muttered Sir Aydon again, his red, weather-beaten countenance creased sideways in disgust, as if he had bitten a lemon. It was not so much the idea of the books themselves; simply that any innovation, the effort arising from any decision requiring to be made, irked him so severely that it was almost agony. Amble, refilling his master's cup, gave the young ladies a reproving look. "You must ask your mother," said Sir Aydon, and, ignoring the refilled cup, limped with speed from the room, adding, "When Mr. Thropton comes, Amble, I shall be somewhere about the stables."

Alvey said to Tot and Nish, who were about to slide from the breakfast room, "I shall be up in the Tower Room in ten minutes to hear your recitation." Their faces fell; they gave her melancholy, acquiescent nods and disappeared. Isa looked after them in mild surprise.

"They seem remarkably biddable. How in the world did you achieve that?"

Alvey replied after a moment's thought, "I believe it was a lucky chance."

Then she ran up to the room she shared with Meg. In her drawer of the window table she kept, as well as the manuscript of Wicked Lord Love, a small memorandum book in which she scribbled down her thoughts and impressions; she liked to do this as soon as possible after the occurrences that had given rise to them. Now she jotted down her thought about Sir Aydon, and added, "How *can* he have received a decoration for promptness and courage in battle? But that was twenty years ago. What has changed him since? *Was* it the hunting accident?"

Grace the maid, shaking Meg's coverlet, said, "Th' owd leddy was asking for ye, Miss Emmy, hinny. Bids ye gan in and hev a word wi' her on your way up to the childer."

That will save going all the way down and up the outer stair, Alvey thought. But she was not a little apprehensive, as she set off, at the prospect of the forthcoming interview. Old Mrs. Winship's pouched eye had a discomposing shrewdness in its gleam.

When Alvey knocked and entered she found the grandmother still in bed, wrapped in a woollen bedgown and a warm nightcap over her scanty white locks, tied under her chin, for the mornings were growing daily sharper; a thick white frost, today, rimed the gravel sweep, which was screened from sun by the piney hillside until midday. No footprint had as yet defaced the pure white, only the prints of birds, Alvey saw, as she stood by the old lady's window.

Parthie was bustling importantly about the large bare room with silver-topped toilet bottles, primrose vinegar and oil of almonds.

"Put those away, child, and bring me my spectacles. And be off with you," commanded the old lady. "You can go and help your sister Meg. I daresay she has plenty of seams that need sewing."

Parthie left, with a resentful look. The cat Maudge, which had been basking in a lozenge of sunshine on the polished floor, came and rubbed against Alvey's leg, and she scratched under its chin.

Old Grizel scrutinised her thoughtfully for a moment, and said, "Now, miss! Pay attention! You seem to have returned with a degree more sense than you took away. Which is no bad thing. Matters here —as you or any fool can see—are all at sixes and sevens. I daresay they will improve, but not without a push. A steady head is needed. Anything you can do to mend matters, to give your parents' thoughts a better turn—to take their minds off this sad business of Annie Herdman and her bairn—will be for the good of the whole household. — I treat you, you see, almost as if you were a stranger, an impartial bystander; because you have been away for so long."

"Oh, but—" began Alvey confusedly, taken by surprise. "That is, what can *I* possibly—?"

I am not here to mend matters for the Winships, she thought. I am here to write my book!

"Quiet, girl! Let's have no mawkish hypocrisy. I was pleased to see you come back with so little of that air of self-importance and superiority, and that morbid longing to distinguish yourself by martyrdom, which made you so detestable as a sixteen-year-old."

And as a twenty-year-old, thought Alvey. How well she knows Louisa.

"Don't spoil the improvement by false modesty," continued Mrs. Winship, giving Alvey another basilisk stare. Like many persons who are slightly deaf, she had a trenchant, resonant, commanding voice.

That, together with the effect of the very thick-lensed glasses she wore perched on her eagle's beak of a nose, and the paper-white pallor of her crumpled face, produced the effect of a statue giving utterance, some formidable oracle or Delphic Sibyl. Alvey stood mute and paralysed.

"Of course—in a way," said the old woman thoughtfully, "it is quite a pity you are *not* kicking up a dust and demanding to carry the Gospel to Sumeria, or wherever it was." She sniffed. "That would have caused a different kind of commotion; might have shaken them out of their melancholy."

"Well, I am afraid I have no such intentions," said Alvey firmly. A pretty kettle of fish it would be, she thought, if they suddenly agreed to permit me to go after all, and there were two of us out there converting the heathen. "In any case—when my brother James comes home, that is bound to stir up the tragedy all over again."

It seemed to her that the old woman gave her an especially glittering glance.

"Yes, miss! And that is what I am wishful to speak about. When James comes, there is sure to be trouble. And your sisters will be of precious little use, for they never are. Meg is too self-absorbed—"

"It *is* her wedding, after all."

"Don't interrupt. Certainly it is her wedding; and a good thing too. For all the use she is, she might as well be out of the house as in it; I wish that mutton-headed Chibburn joy of her. As for Isa, mooning on about Nature in some mystical way, her head's too far in the clouds to be any practical help."

"That isn't true!" objected Alvey, remembering Isa's kindness and timely interventions on many occasions.

"Yes, it is true. And don't contradict me. Nobody pays any heed to Parthie—fortunately!—and the young ones are too small. So that leaves *you*, miss."

"Ma'am, I do not fully comprehend your meaning."

"Pho, pho, girl, don't talk moonshine."

"What would you have me do, Grandmother?"

How odd! thought Alvey. I never had a grandmother to confide in. If Mother's mother—or Father's—had been living, had been there—matters might have been different . . .

"You know what I wish, girl, perfectly well. You don't lack for sense! I've been taking notice of you, these last few days; you sit there demure and mumchance enough, but you miss nothing, and you've a glib, canny tongue, too, when you please to speak. I want you to put your heart into this business: when James comes, to try and bring him and Aydon into some kind of accord—or at least avert any disastrous breach—"

But I don't even *know* this James! Alvey wanted to expostulate.

"Oh, I'm aware that you and James were never good friends in the past," Mrs. Winship went on, with another penetrating glance. "All the more reason he should turn to you now, if he finds you friendly, if he finds you ready to be his partisan and give him good advice. For a partisan he will certainly need!"

They may need one even more, reflected Alvey, picturing James's very probable disgust and outrage at the parents whose selfish, uncaring, and thoughtless usage had condemned his mistress and child to a needless death.

"The child—wee Geordie—"

"Oh, not only that affair. There will be other sources of friction. I have heard from James—he writes to me sometimes—" Her glance went to the little rosewood desk. "Which reminds me. Fetch me here those papers, child. The bundles tied with brown ribbon."

Alvey went to the desk and carried over several packets. One of them might have been the bundle which Parthie had been investigating the other day. On closer inspection, it was indubitably letters in Louisa's neat ladylike handwriting.

"Charlotte—your mother—has no patience with preserving correspondence. Indeed I sometimes think she scarcely reads through such letters as she does receive," observed Mrs. Winship tartly. "Ever since she married your father, it has fallen to me to maintain the links with other branches of the family."

Alvey remembered that it was always from her grandmother or her sisters that Louisa received news of home, never from her father or mother.

"Humph; those are from Cousin Matfen in London; those from your aunt Mary in Rome, those from your aunt Caroline in Shropshire —those were from your poor aunt Elinor in Bath—these are from

James; yes," she muttered, "I fear there will be a sad brew of trouble and discord when he is here, you must do all that is in your power to prevent it. But now, let me see, that reminds me—" With her twig-like, blotched fingers the old lady had untied the packet of Louisa's letters and was now glancing nearsightedly through the earlier ones, recognisable as such by the faded ink and more childish handwriting. She picked through the bundle once or twice in irritable puzzlement, then looked up, not at Alvey but past her, thinking hard, then said in tones of severe displeasure, "It is not here. The one I am looking for is not here."

"Which one is that, ma'am?"

Recollecting herself, the old woman glanced keenly at Alvey.

"No matter. You had best go up to those young ones and force a bit of knowledge into their heads. Ring the bell for Duddy."

And to the maid, who arrived in prompt response to this summons, she said, "Duddy, find Miss Parthie and send her to me directly."

Alvey read aloud to Tot and Nish the ballad of Christie's Will.

"Christie's Will was our ancestor, had you thought of that?" Tot interrupted her to say. "Gramdmamma told me so. He was her great-great-great-grandfather."

"Great-great-great-great," corrected Nish.

"Oh, what does it matter? Go on, Emmy."

"He thought the warlocks o' the rosy cross
Had fanged him i' their nets sae fast—"

"Who were the warlocks of the rosy cross, Emmy?"

"Oh, the warlocks? They were a set of German wizards called Rosicrucians." Alvey smiled a little, as she recalled her erudite father supplying her with this piece of knowledge, in what seemed another life, another century.

Grace knocked and said, "Sir Aydon asks will ye gan down, Miss Lou, hinny; he's wi' Mr. Thropton in the library."

The children made faces of disgust.

"Never mind," said Alvey. "I'll finish reading the poem later. Or you can read it to Nish, Tot. And True Thomas that comes next. And then write a story about a spider; one of those that live in holes in the riverbank. Then you can go out . . . Why do you pull a horrible face when Mr. Thropton is mentioned?"

"You'll see soon enough." Nish was always more ready to speak than her brother. "He wasn't here when Lou—when you were here before. It was old Mr. Newbury—I can just remember him. He used to give us peppermint sweeties after morning service on Sunday. Mr. Thropton is hateful. He teaches us Greek Delectus—"

"—and Latin declensions. He's *horrible,*" said Tot with feeling.

"I'll be the judge of that," said Alvey, and left them devouring Walter Scott.

Her first sight of Mr. Thropton inclined her immediately to the children's point of view. The rector was a tall, full-fleshed man in his early forties, with a balding brow, sparse reddish hair, several chins, and large protruding colourless eyes. Although plainly a gentleman he had an unfortunate manner, florid, consequential, yet ingratiating.

"Aha! Miss Louisa in person!" he said, rubbing his hands. "I have heard so many stories of the learned Miss Louisa that I am overjoyed to have my curiosity gratified at last."

He looks me over, thought Alvey indignantly, as if I were a tasty dish that he is inclined to sample.

Sir Aydon, meanwhile, sat plunged in glum abstraction, paying next to no heed to his clerical visitor.

Apparently having been informed of Louisa's religious proclivities, Mr. Thropton at once, to Alvey's alarm and dismay, began outlining a comprehensive programme of parish activities for her: sick visiting, the organisation of some ritual known as the Poor Basket, responsibility for a Sunday school, a Dame school, and arrangements for annual scholars' outings.

Her first self-protective impulse, which was to decline all these duties *in toto,* pleading that, between the instruction of Nish and Tot and work on her own book, there would be no time to spare, she reluctantly abandoned. This was not the moment to let fall in front of the unhappy Sir Aydon the news that she had embarked on a literary career. It would not do. He had enough already to distress him. In the meantime she countered every proposal with the calm answer that such plans must remain in abeyance until after Meg's wedding; she could give no undertakings at present; her time and labours were entirely at her sister's disposal.

Disappointed on this, Mr. Thropton made a comeback on another front.

"I have been told of Miss Louisa's erudition as a historian," he said archly, twinkling his eyes at her in what Alvey considered a most repulsive manner. "Word has come back of her excursions in the kingdom of Clio, of her wide explorations in that beauteous realm. I shall be delighted, Miss Louisa, *more* than delighted, to make you free of my own small share of lore, and the volumes in my modest library—which, though limited in extent, is, I flatter myself, choice in *quality*—quite choice! I have been at some pains to collect around me the utterances of mighty minds, the noble outpourings of the world's foremost thinkers."

And he turned a somewhat disparaging eye upon Sir Aydon's library, which contained, it was true, a fair number of ancient and mildewy volumes amassed by earlier generations of Winships, but remarkably few books collected by the present occupant, beyond various works on game preservation and a few county histories. Alvey had already surveyed it with considerable gloom, when its owner was occupied about the stables, and had come to the conclusion that some other means must be found of procuring for herself a supply of current literature. But certainly not through Mr. Thropton.

She made a polite but noncommittal reply, then excused herself on the pretext that she must return to supervise the children's studies.

Mr. Thropton beamed approval but detained her, taking hold of her arm.

"A moment more, Miss Louisa—a moment of your precious time." His voice on the adjective contrived to be both caressing and disbelieving. "Preciousss!" He drew the word out lingeringly, giving her what was evidently intended to be a winning smile. "I believe you may not have been informed of another enterprise of my own which—I am persuaded—must be of great and kindred interest—"

"Oh?" coldly responded Alvey, doing her best to extricate her arm from his damp clasp—but he only held it the tighter.

"I am—as you may not have been told—an amateur, an enthusiast of archaeology. One of my principal joys at being transferred to this interesting region was because of its abounding wealth in treasures of the past. My own garden—my very own plot—boasts, I have discovered, what bids fair to be one of the most important finds of recent times—a complete Mithraic temple, lying only two or three feet below the parsonage cabbage bed. Concealed there for two thousand years! Is not that remarkable?"

"Yes," Alvey could not help agreeing. "It is indeed." And she made another unsuccessful attempt to release her arm from his hold.

"So, my dear Miss Louisa, it is my hope that you—a fellow enthusiast, a fellow scholar—may, within the very near future, be persuaded to take your walk in the direction of the rectory—no great distance—and inspect my discoveries?"

Alvey made a vague rejoinder in which the phrases "so kind—time not her own to command just at present—perhaps later, after the wedding—" were intended to postpone this visit into the distant future. Despite the real curiosity aroused in her by his description of the Mithraic temple, she found herself disliking Mr. Thropton more and more, and was resolved to have as few dealings with him as might be managed.

"Ah, but—!" Mr. Thropton at last released his grip in order to wag a finger at her; much relieved, Alvey surreptitiously flexed her biceps, wishing that she could rub the damp spot with a handkerchief. "But my *very* dear Miss Louisa, I must constrain you to find a moment *before* the wedding—for your poor father here finds himself at this present quite unable to reach a conclusion about the trifling matter of the child's headstone. So I am going to ask you, Miss Louisa, to accompany the children when they come for their lesson tomorrow, and bring me at that time your papa's decision."

Alvey glanced at Sir Aydon, to gauge his response to this proposal, which, she guessed, formed what Mr. Thropton hoped would be a subtle species of pressure to oblige him to make up his mind. But Sir Aydon would require more powerful pressure than that, Alvey thought, feeling sorry for him. He appeared deeply sunk in lethargy and gloom; had taken little, if any, heed of the talk between the other two, but sat withdrawn and brooding, with his abstracted gaze roving through the windows which commanded the gravel sweep, the pine-clad hill, and the ferny pool where the small tragedy had taken place.

Mr. Thropton shook his head in reproval.

"Now, my dear sir, we must pull ourselves together, we must indeed! A useless repining is no part of the Almighty plan for us—you know that! I will bid you goodbye now, my dear sir, but shall hope that my words have not fallen on stony ground—"

Making no reply to this, Sir Aydon pulled the bell for Amble, who appeared at once.

"Amble, show Mr. Thropton out. And send Lumley to me with the papers relating to Shapely Dene."

Snubbed, Mr. Thropton bowed himself out of the library, but paused in the hall to adjure Alvey: "Now, Miss Louisa, I am depending on you to bring your father out of this dangerous melancholy—which, as you know, is a deadly sin. But I truly believe that, once the matter of the child's memorial has been settled and put behind him, his thoughts may take an onward turn. So—remember! I am relying on you."

With a last arch look, a last twinkle, he passed out through the main door and strode off. Alvey stared after him with a grain of unwilling respect. Repulsive as he might appear, shrewd he certainly was. His perception could not be denied.

Meg poked her head cautiously out of the breakfast room.

"Has that old horror taken his departure? Ugh! Thank heaven, once I am married, I need see him no more; mercifully the Chibburns at Tinnis have a very decent, gentlemanlike parson, only in his thirties, who hunts, and has a very fair cellar too, John says. But is not Mr. Thropton exactly like a toad?"

"Or a lizard?" Alvey suggested. "Those eyes, with their thick lower lids?"

"Or a crocodile! Some horrid reptile, anyway. He requires me to go to him for a short instructive talk before the wedding, about the responsibilities of matrimony. Ugh! Mind you come with me, Al—Emmy! I know Isa will not; she detests him. And I *will* not go alone. I dread the thought of such a talk. Perhaps John Chibburn will not allow it!" She giggled, but added more seriously, "You'll find you have to keep him at arm's length, Emmy. As soon as he arrived he began approaches to me and, finding I was bespoke, he immediately started making up to Isa; but *she* made it plain that she would have none of him. So now I daresay he has settled it that you shall be the one. The most shocking impertinence! Any other man than Papa would send him about his business, if he had any notion what was in the wind. But Papa cares not a straw what becomes of us or whom we marry; it would be all one to him if I took John Chibburn or Lumley, the bailiff."

And she ran up the stairs.

The following day, therefore, Alvey, despite her reluctance, found herself obliged to pay a call at Birkland Parsonage. Sir Aydon had finally been brought to agree that the words "Geordie, son of Annie Herdman" should be engraved on the tiny headstone. This message was to be taken, and Meg was insistent that she be chaperoned throughout the rector's counsellings on matrimonial behaviour. The two girls, therefore, set out midway through the morning of a tinglingly cold clear autumn day, with spangled cobwebs draped over every twig and leaf.

"Just imagine! In two weeks' time I shall be in Brighton," said Meg, leading the way at a brisk pace along a steep, narrow, pine-needle-carpeted path which slanted up from the carriage sweep, through the grove, and on upwards over a heather-covered shoulder of hill.

"This is the shortcut to the village. By road, it is full two miles; this way, barely three-quarters of a mile. But in winter, of course, it is not always passable. The wind blows the snow up over this hillside."

Meg chattered freely as they walked, giving the life histories of the villagers, foretelling the delights of her wedding trip to Brighton. Alvey was silent, absorbing with deep pleasure the expanding view down the valley of the Hungry Water, hummocks of distant lavender hills, and uneven stone-walled pastures closer at hand, running up the valley sides.

The village, really no more than a hamlet, was half a dozen grey stone cottages, snuggled into a fold of the hill where it met the valley floor, sheltered by ash and sycamore trees. The vicarage, a larger and newer building, stood separated from the rest among its own orchards and paddocks.

"That is where Mr. Thropton discovered the Roman ruins." Meg indicated an area of cleared ground, where rectangular excavations and low brick partitions could be seen. "He is forever boring on about

Roman customs and the cult of Mithras. Papa thinks it a most ungen-
tlemanly occupation."

"Clergymen have to do something with their time?" suggested Alvey. "The care of such a small parish cannot employ much of that?"

"Mr. Newbury used to hunt three days a week. Papa thought the
better of him for it. — Now, Alvey—Emmy: mind you do not leave
me alone with that man for a *single minute,*" urged Meg, pulling the
bell cord as they stood in the latticed porch.

Alvey made the promise, and was able to keep it, for, since the
parsonage boasted quite spacious rooms, it was possible for her to
establish herself at a far end of the drawing room while at the other
end the rector administered his homily on conjugal duty. She heard
snatches of the conversation: the rector putting his questions with unctuous deliberation, and Meg's replies coming very short, curt, and
bored.

"Now, my dear Miss Meg, you know that marriage is not designed
to satisfy man's carnal lusts, but for the procreation of children and to
avoid carnal urges; do you understand what that means?"

"Having eight brothers and sisters, sir, I should hope I do."

"Well, well; and you understand what is meant when the Gospel
instructs us that a man shall leave his father and mother and be joined
unto his wife, and they two shall be one flesh?"

"Yes, it means cohabiting," snapped Meg. The rector looked a little
crestfallen, as if he had hoped to explain this point in more detail.

"And you know that St. Paul, in the Epistle to the Ephesians,
ordains: 'Wives, submit yourselves unto your own husbands,' and St.
Peter tells you, 'Ye wives, be in subjection to your own husbands, and
let them behold your chaste conversation coupled with fear.' You
know what the saints *mean* by telling you to submit to your husbands?"

"Of course I do," said Meg crossly. "But anyone who expects me to
fear John Chibburn is a fool."

The rector looked displeased, and launched into a long lecture
about adorning and plaiting the hair and the wearing of gold and
putting on of apparel, in the midst of which Meg yawned very visibly.
Mr. Thropton appeared discouraged, and cut short his homily; Alvey
received the impression that it would have lasted considerably longer
without the constraint of her own presence. Then the young ladies

were offered a glass of wine and a biscuit, which they declined politely; then Meg said that they were instructed to fetch home the younger children from their Latin studies, since they were required for a fitting of their bridal costumes.

Mr. Thropton shook his head indulgently.

"My dear young ladies, how will these children ever learn their Delectus and their irregular verbs if they are to be removed from their lessons at every household whim?"

"My wedding is hardly a household whim," said Meg, but she made the retort under her breath, and the children were fetched from the dining room. They came with great alacrity. To them, it was plainly of small moment if the Delectus and the irregular verbs remained unlearned for the rest of their lives, and Alvey could not help but wonder, considering the poor state of their general education, what manner of use Mr. Thropton's instruction could possibly be to them.

The rector escorted the party as far as his excavations, and, pausing there, told them more than they wished to know about Roman religious customs. One of the men at work on the digging touched his forelock, and said, "Beg pardon, Yor Riverince, but we fund this—rackoned ye wud wish ti oppen it yersen"—and handed Mr. Thropton a dirt-encrusted object which might have been a small metal box or casket. The rector stopped his lecture in mid-sentence. He seemed to have forgotten what he was about to say.

"Well; we shall look forward to seeing you at the ceremony on Saturday, then, sir," suggested Meg, as he seemed to have become quite unmindful of his visitors.

"Yes, yes, Miss Winship," he replied absently. "Seven o'clock sharp at the church. That is—ahem, pardon me—ten o'clock."

"Goodbye, sir, and thank you for your kind instruction," said Meg prettily, but she might have saved her breath; Mr. Thropton's eyes were all for the casket, and he hardly spared a glance for the departing guests.

They lingered for fifteen minutes in the village, so that Alvey could be greeted by old Mrs. Colville, old Mrs. Thew, Mrs. Beall, Mr. and Mrs. Gill, Mr. Ruddock, Mr. Gibson, and Mrs. Leadbitter—who all told her how she had grown, how bonny she had become, and how they would have known her anywhere.

As they started for home past the churchyard, a raucous shout startled them.

Above the graveyard rose a kind of steep knoll, covered with thornbushes, which merged into a thicker wood of ash and sycamore rising up the side of the valley. Among the thornbushes could just be distinguished the figure of an old man, rangy and white-haired, who shook his fist at them and hurled out a stream of angry words, not one of which was intelligible to Alvey.

"Who is that?" she said, startled. "What is the matter with him? Is he mad?"

"No, not really. Come along," said Meg. "Take no notice of him." They hurried on, and were soon out of earshot.

"He looked like an Old Testament prophet," said Alvey. "Who was it?"

"Old Herdman—Annie's father. He has always had a bit of a grievance against our family—something to do with a ditch which was diverted and, he said, robbed him of a yard of his garden; and there was something else about his brother, I believe. And now I suppose it will be worse. He is a disagreeable old man. I hope he will not turn up and make a nuisance of himself at my wedding. — Ugh, is not Mr. Thropton a horrible hypocrite! I am glad that, after Saturday, I shall have seen the last of him."

Nish and Tot, as soon as they left the village, had bounded ahead up the footpath, and Meg went on, giggling: "Thropton told me that the only way to be a good wife was to obey my husband implicitly in all things—but it is said in Hexham that he caused the death of his own wife from ill-usage. He half starved her, the story goes; and she had to wear cotton and sit in a room without a fire. She died ever so many years ago. And he has been on the catch for another ever since, Fanny Beaumont says, one with money so as to pay for his diggings and delvings—but no one will have him."

"Why not?"

"Need you ask? Because his hands are like damp toadstools, because his breath stinks, because he sprays you with spittle when he talks—"

"I wonder what was in that box."

"So did he! He could hardly wait until we were gone to prise it open. I wish him joy of the dirty thing," said Meg.

VII

James Winship was travelling north in the company of his longtime school and army friend Major Guy Fenway. The major's final destination was Edinburgh, so it had not been difficult to persuade him to make the slight detour which would take in Birkland Hall; indeed he would have suggested the plan himself, had he not been a person of infinite tact. James, only just past the stage of convalescence and well enough to undertake such a long journey, was happy to have company on the way—skilled, sympathetic, and expert company too, for the major was a medical man; while his friend was unfeignedly curious to meet James's family.

"So many years as I have heard you talking about them all: Grandmamma, and the little ones, and all those sisters! But you were always so curmudgeonly about inviting me. I began to think I was not good enough for your friends, that you were ashamed of me."

"Oh, good God, no! It was just the other way round."

James came out of a gloomy reverie to meet the teasing smile of his friend, and smiled himself, reluctantly. "Well, you know how any boy is ashamed of his family. My father, interested in nothing but hunting—"

"Capital. He and I will find much in common."

"And my stepmother—"

"Ah yes. She must hate you, of course. And you, naturally, in return, detest her?"

James's fair brows came together in a frown. "No," he said after some thought. "I do not believe she hates me; though indubitably she does not love me. But then, she loves nobody—certainly none of her

own children. Except, perhaps, when they are very small, still babies
. . . And no, I do not detest her; how can you detest somebody who
is there so little? Her mind is in her garden; and so is she, most of the
time."

"Does she not love your father?"

"I doubt it. They rub along tolerably well, I suppose. But her true
devotion is for horticulture. Even when I was a boy she was always out
of doors, digging away, in her green gown and old hat. What kind of a
parent is that to present to one's school friends?"

"So you invited no one home."

"Besides, Northumberland is such a deuce of a journey."

"And your half sisters? Are they all beautiful and talented? But that
goes without saying. 'All very accomplished and pleasing, and *one* very
pretty.' Which one is that? To which shall I lose my heart?"

"They are uncommonly dull girls," said James. "I do not recommend that you lose your heart to any of them. Best wait until you can
sample the beauties of Edinburgh."

"Oh, come! There must be something to be said for the poor girls.
One of them is to be married, after all."

"Meg, yes, well, she is the prettiest. But bone selfish, and not two
ideas in her head—"

"Fie! I daresay she is as sensible a girl as ever wore shoe leather.
And the others—what are their names again?"

"Isa is good-natured enough, but so plain! And takes after her
mother; she is not interested in people, only in landscapes. Louisa I
have not seen for years, but she used to be insufferable—sanctimonious, priggish, conceited—"

"Her looks?"

"Well enough; nothing out of the common. And always an expression in her eyes as if you were an ignorant hobbledehoy, not fit to
black her boots—"

"I shall enjoy that," said his friend.

"Parthie—she is the one about whom you were inquiring—"

"Oh, the fourteen-year-old, yes," Guy said nodding.

"As insufferable as Louisa: pert, self-satisfied, meddlesome, always
thrusting herself into the middle of any group. As to the younger four,
Tot, Nish, Betsey, and little Kate, I know little; them I have hardly

seen. What chance can they have to be interesting? Nobody pays heed to them."

"*I* shall find them all exceedingly interesting," said Guy with vigour. "A whole family! And I with only one elder sister. It will be a new experience. But now: how are you feeling, old fellow? How is the leg? Does it pain you much?"

"No, no," said James impatiently. "I hardly feel it."

"I think you are lying. We had better spend the night at Durham."

"It is not my leg," said James. "If it were only that! I feel so lost—so empty—the whole of life suddenly so meaningless. Oh!" he cried out with furious impatience. "And to cap it all, I can only express what I wish to say in such trite language—the language of those trashy Minerva romances that the children's governess used to read."

"My dear old boy," said Guy with exemplary patience, for he had said the same thing perhaps twenty or thirty times during the journey, "believe me, you will feel better with the passing of time. I, who have broken my heart on at least a dozen occasions, can tell you this with confidence. Also you can at least comfort yourself with the reflection that you have behaved just as you ought. Moreover, in a little while, you will be able to cheer yourself further by thinking that if my wretched sister had had a grain of sense—if she had been at all worthy of you—she would not have released you, she would never have let you go, she would have clung to you all the tighter despite your altered prospects. So—take my word for it—you may congratulate yourself on a lucky escape. I daresay Meta herself may be sorry one of these days, when she is safely wed to her marquess—then, no doubt, she will look back and regret the pearl she has lost in you."

"But I love her so!" said James wretchedly. "And she said—she told me she herself would have made nothing of my altered prospects—but she was bound to respect your father's wishes in the matter—"

"Oh, in course!" said the other with irony. "A most dutiful daughter! Papa, I daresay, never said two words on the subject. He is very fond of you, old fellow—thinks you are worth a dozen of Alderney. Too good for her if the truth be told. She is sweet—and shallow—and you are better off without her. I am not even sorry to lose you as a brother, for we shall always be friends; whereas Meta would, by and by, have placed that relationship under severe strain. — Now I am sure you will be the better of a good dinner—and I know I shall, so let us put up here at the Three Tuns, and I will foment that leg of yours while dinner is preparing. My uncle Griswold, who used to be bishop here, told me they do an excellent saddle of mutton at the Three Tuns—"

The girls set off for Hexham early on the day of the Assembly, for, as Isa had predicted, there were a number of household errands to be executed, most of them in connection with Meg's wedding, now only a few days distant.

Parthie had begged and pleaded to be allowed to accompany them. "There would be room for me in the post chaise—indeed there would!"

"Indeed there would *not!*" said Meg. "What—four of us all crammed together with our bandboxes? Besides, you are too young to go to the Assembly—and, in any case, have not been invited to the Beaumonts'."

Lady Winship with vague but crushing authority confirmed this veto. Parthie was quelled, but deeply resentful.

"You are all hateful wretches. I hope that it snows, and that you get overturned in a drift."

The weather, after some days of rain and gale, had turned sharply cold, and, for their journey to Hexham, the travellers were obliged to wrap in many layers of capes and shawls.

"My hair will come out of curl," said Meg worriedly, pulling on a fur hood.

"Isa, sit *up,* and pull your shoulders *back,*" commanded Alvey, when they were packed into the carriage.

Isa laughed at her.

"Ever hopeful, sister Capability!"

For the last week, Alvey had been conducting a campaign to improve Isa's appearance; she had washed the lank hair with egg and rosemary water, and stiffened it by a preparation of bandoline, concocted, with the help of Mrs. Slaley, out of rum and gum tragacanth. She had enforced a daily hour on a backboard to straighten out the hunched, rounded shoulders, applied a paste of fuller's earth and lemon juice to clear the patchy complexion, and obliged Isa to endure numerous trying-on sessions, while Mrs. Galt, the sewing woman, with Alvey's counsel and assistance, constructed a ball dress for her, simpler and by far more elegant than the one she had been proposing to wear.

Isa had submitted good-naturedly to all this discipline, but the maid Grace had observed Alvey's regime with a grimly ironic eye.

"Hech, hinny, ye'll ne'er change Miss Isa; she's kittle cattle to drive."

"I fear that is true," sighed Isa. "I sincerely mean to comply, but I forget; so many other things seem so much more important."

"Fiddlededee! It is merely a question of acquiring good habits. Suck your breath *in,* girl, and stand straight up while I pin this. There! Now at least you look like a lady, which you certainly did not in that bunchy garment with the floss dangling about it."

"But," said Meg, as the carriage bore them towards Hexham, "what difference does it make? Isa's posture will not affect her chances of obtaining partners at the Assembly; her hand is bound to be solicited because she is Miss Winship of Birkland."

Meg spoke with the confidence based on knowledge of a London ball gown in the hamper and the awareness that as a forthcoming bride she must be the acknowledged belle of the evening. Alvey glanced at her in some irritation.

But Isa said, "It is exceedingly kind of you, sister Emmy (if a little out of character), to take all these pains over me, and I hereby vow at least to *try* and follow your precepts; not to put you out of countenance. — Why, look at the Tyne, how full it is—within four feet of the roadway! Let us hope that the water goes down, not up, tomorrow, or we shall be cut off in Hexham and Meg will have to postpone her wedding."

The Tyne was indeed high, dark as brown ale and roaring; they had heard the surge of it a quarter of a mile off.

"But I could get married in the abbey," Meg said quickly. "After all, John will be on that side too."

"Hexham bridge has been washed away twice in the last forty years," Isa told Alvey as they crossed it. "This one was built in '93. So far it has held firm. The town, fortunately, is up on the hill above flood level."

Alvey looked up with interest at the houses on the height above them, crowned with their handsome abbey. Hexham was a thriving, but not a large market town; within five minutes Archie had driven up a steep approach road to the main square alongside the abbey church, which was built of dark-brown stone.

In the square a lively cattle market was taking place: there were pens of beasts and poultry, stalls selling grain, eggs, butter, and meat, a few boxes of vegetables and fish, besides other commodities, leather, gloves, tools, cloth, crockery, and wooden shoes. The market stalls and activities leaked out of the abbey square into adjoining streets.

Among the pushing crowds the carriage made but slow progress, and Meg said, "You had best let us get out here, Archie, and you take on our things to the Canon's house, or we shall waste half the morning."

Rather reluctantly he agreed to do so, and the three girls descended eagerly into the bustle, and set about Lady Winship's various commissions.

When the household purchases had all been made, Meg undertook to carry the articles to the Canon's house and give them to Archie, who would be resting his horses before the return journey.

"Are you sure you can manage?" asked Isa.

"Oh yes. I am tired of the cold and the crowds. And I want to talk to Fanny."

Alvey and Isa therefore made their way to the circulating library. This consisted of two commodious rooms in a side street called Priestpopple. The proprietor was a pleasant, balding, studious-looking man aged forty or thereabouts who gazed at Isa with unmixed devotion in his brown eyes.

"Good day, Mr. Allgood! I am sure that you remember my sister Louisa," said Isa cheerfully.

He bowed and replied, "It would be an untruth to say that I recognise the elegant grown-up young lady whom I see before me, but I hope we shall continue as good friends as ever we were when at the age of thirteen you used to borrow the lives of the saints and journals of missionary voyages. I am happy to welcome you back, Miss Winship."

"Thank you," said Alvey. "I plan to be an even more persistent and demanding customer than the Louisa of bygone days. And, to make a beginning, I wish to purchase some lesson books for the children."

Eagerly he directed her to a round table piled with books at the rear of the inner room, where, happily browsing among the heaps, she soon came across copies of Moran's *Spelling Book,* Goldsmith's *History of England,* Rollin's *Ancient History,* Lindley Murray's *Grammar,* and Mrs. Chapone's *Letters on the Improvement of the Mind.* As a sweetener she also picked out Dorothy Kilner's *Life and Perambulations of a Mouse* and Sarah Trimmer's *History of the Robins*—books which a kindly neighbour had given her and which she had adored as a child. As well, she added copies of *Rokeby* and *Waverley,* paying for the large pile out of her own purse.

"You will think me dreadfully extravagant; but I am looking ahead to winter, when the children will need more entertainment than Blair's *Sermons* and Fordyce's *County History of Northumberland* are likely to provide," she told Mr. Allgood, who had been conversing with Isa in the front room, where the periodicals were laid out.

Wrapping the books in paper, he replied, "My dear Miss Louisa, why should I harbour such uncivil thoughts of such an excellent customer? If you wished to buy a dozen more volumes I should only think the better of you. Ah, by the bye, I have here a treatise on rock gardens which was ordered by Lady Winship. And there is also a letter for all you young ladies, which has come from overseas; I presume the sender was not sure of your direction, but trusted that such busy readers would receive it soon enough if it were sent to this address."

He handed Isa a yellow, sea-stained packet.

"Oh!" she cried, going a little pink. "How very kind of you! Why —why yes, a classmate of my sister's is travelling to the Indies—that is her hand—but we had not hoped to hear from her so soon! We are *very* much obliged to you, Mr. Allgood. If—if other letters should come from her—you will not object to putting them on one side until we can come for them?"

"Of course not, Miss Isa!" If this arrangement savoured of illicit romance, not a flicker of Mr. Allgood's benevolent demeanour suggested such a notion. "Any service that lies within my power, I shall be more than happy to render to you and your sisters."

But more to you yourself than to your sisters, thought Alvey, observing his wistfully intent gaze at Isa.

On an impulse she said, "I *do* have another favour to ask of you, Mr. Allgood—if I may? While at school I have—I have somewhat altered my ambitions. I have resolved upon a career of authorship—"

"Indeed, Miss Louisa?" he said with polite interest.

"—and have, in fact, half completed a story, a work of fiction. Isa informs me that you now have connections in the publishing world—"

"And you would like the benefit of my advice when your tale is finished. I shall be only too delighted, ma'am," he replied promptly. "And, as luck would have it, my cousin Malcolm has but lately obtained a position with the Caledonian Press in Edinburgh; he has even asked me to keep him informed of any interesting new material that might come my way. So this will be a pleasure combined with practical business."

"Of course, my work may be quite beneath anybody's serious notice," Alvey demurred modestly.

"In your heart of hearts you do not believe that," he surprised her by saying.

Isa flashed Mr. Allgood her unexpectedly conspiratorial smile and said, "We fully expect my sister to astonish the world by her creation, when it is completed. But in the meantime this matter is between ourselves, dear Mr. Allgood, if you will be so kind? Our parents are to know nothing of the business until they discover that they have brought forth a prodigy."

"You can rely on my entire discretion," he replied, bowing them out of the door.

"Is he not a dear man?" Isa said absently as they hurried up the hill. "Now what? Oh, I know—a ribbon for Parthie—" and turning aside into a draper's shop, she bought a broad white ribbon with a very pretty briar rose pattern, pink and green, all along its length. "It is better than she deserves—but she *was* so disappointed. Life is hard for her, falling, as she does, midway between us and the little ones. And her disability—"

"Have we time to turn aside into the churchyard and read Louisa's letter?" Alvey could take no interest in Parthie, whom she found a most dislikeable child.

"No, we had better not; the Beaumonts will be expecting us; also, we, the Winships I mean, are so well known in Hexham that anybody might stop and ask who our correspondent was."

Indeed this was true: Isa had been greeting people continuously ever since they came to the town—"Good day, Mrs. Coxon; how are you, Mr. MacDonald? Ah, Miss Ogle, my mother wished to thank you for the plants—you remember my sister Louisa, I am sure?" How shall I ever remember all these names? Alvey thought in dismay. Half the people encountered said they would have known Louisa anywhere, the other half said she had changed out of all recognition.

"Will all these people be at the Assembly?" Alvey asked.

"No, none of them. The Assemblies are *very* select: no townspeople, tradesmen or professionals, no infantry officers; to be admitted you have to belong to an unexceptionable county family with at least sixteen quarterings."

"Good God! I should probably be thrown into prison for outrageous presumption if my antecedents became known—"

Isa laughed as they strolled on to the Canon's house, a quiet, old-fashioned residence within a stone's throw of the abbey church. Its panelled parlours, small-paned casement windows, and wide expanses of polished floor put Alvey in mind of the Abbey School. She was introduced to the Canon, a frail, silent old man, evidently in poor health, and to his sister, Miss Beaumont, a gaunt lady in her mid-sixties whose principal occupation appeared to consist in tending her brother, placing a screen between him and any possible draught, adjusting the comforter for his neck, or the footstool for his feet. Satisfied on these points, she greeted Alvey cordially enough, and inquired after Mrs. Camperdowne; it was on Miss Beaumont's recommendation, Isa had informed Alvey, that Louisa had originally been sent to the Abbey School, for Miss Beaumont was an old acquaintance of Mrs. Latournelle, the original founder, and her niece Fanny had attended the school some twelve years previously. Miss Fanny Beaumont, now in her thirties, had, Alvey knew, been engaged to a young man who had sailed to India in the service of the East India Company, contracted a fever in Calcutta, and died there. Fanny was plain, kind-faced, and now resigned to spinsterhood, in a severe grey dress and muslin cap tied over her close-braided hair. But she was taking a lively interest in Meg's wedding preparations and had advice to offer on some nicety of the bridesmaids' equipment—"With white velvet it will be infinitely better, my love"—and she appeared to look forward to the evening's Assembly with unfeigned pleasure, though she had no intention of dancing herself. She greeted Alvey rather quietly; the latter received a strong impression that Louisa, of old, had been accustomed to snub and disparage Miss Beaumont as a person of no particular account.

But that shall be changed, thought Alvey militantly, responding to the unassuming kindness of Miss Fanny's greeting, and then caught herself up, as she did twenty times a day, with the thought: What right have I to revise Louisa's mode of behaviour to people? But yet she could not help doing it. In any case, she reflected, Louisa will very likely never return here, so the disparity between her manners and mine will not come under consideration; I shall be away from Birkland Hall soon enough, and what will it signify then whether I faithfully reproduced Louisa's ways, or behaved out of keeping? By the end of a year I shall be gone. The thought of this escape, which she had held out for so strongly once, now struck her with a singular chill.

Then, recollecting Louisa's letter, she became deeply impatient to learn what the contents might be; but that must wait until after dinner, when the girls retired to their rooms to dress for the ball.

Dinner—an early, frugal meal—was soon over, and the young ladies repaired to their respective chambers: Meg, as an old friend, was sleeping in Fanny's room, Isa and Alvey were together. Isa had the letter out of her reticule in a moment and carefully, with her scissors, prised up the wafer.

"Oh!" she said in disappointment. "It is sent from Cádiz! She had not yet reached India when it was dispatched."

"How could she possibly, goose? The journey takes months—and then the letter as long to come back."

"Very true—I had not thought." Her eyes skimmed over the closely written lines. "Seize this opportunity—send back by the packet boat—assure you that I am well and *very* happy—confidence that I am fulfilling my duty—Mr. & Mrs. Tothill exceedingly pleasant company full of proper attentions—truly devout—several friends on board with them of like mind—one or two excellent young clergymen—naval officers also most helpful and obliging—Captain Middlemass a truly respectable and God-fearing man—in haste, the boatman is calling—from your sister in God—L. Winship. P.S. I hope that my parents are in good health."

"She almost forgot that postscriptum," observed Alvey tartly, reading over Isa's shoulder. *The letter is like a child's,* she thought; *so full of her new adventure that she can spare no moment to remember anybody else.*

"She might have expressed a word of gratitude to you, for permitting her to enjoy this experience!" exclaimed Isa rather disgustedly, folding the paper and tucking it away among her clean handkerchiefs.

"Oh, she might be afraid the letter would fall into the wrong hands, so dare not be more explicit."

"*I do not believe she gave the matter one moment's thought.*"

"Had you not better destroy the letter, once Meg has read it?"

"No. Why? Who would come across it? And somehow—oh, I don't know—perhaps for legal reasons, I fancy it had best be preserved."

"Whatever you think. — *Isa!* You are not proposing to go to the Assembly with your hair like that?"

"Why, what in the world is the matter with it?"

"Everything! Come here—stand still!"

With skilled fingers Alvey rearranged Isa's hair, and embellished the knot of curls at the back with a couple of white geraniums taken from the *beau-pot* on the old-fashioned dresser. "There! Now you look more like a young lady of fashion. Do not forget to keep your shoulders *back*—don't slouch—and suck your breath *in!*"

"How can I possibly dance in such an unnatural posture?" grumbled Isa, as they ran down the shallow, slippery stairs, pulling shawls about their shoulders.

The Assembly rooms, adjacent to the Black Bull Inn, seemed well in keeping with the rural tranquillity of the town, with their high, lozenged ceiling, crimson velvet curtains, spindly, gilt Directoire chairs along the wall, and tiny gilt stage on which two fiddlers and a cellist could just be accommodated. There was a separate octagonal chamber for cards and chaperones, and an upstairs gallery, seldom visited because it was so draughty. Since the Black Bull was only two minutes' walk across the marketplace from the Canon's house, the young ladies walked to the rooms in shawls, calashes, and pattens, under the escort of the Canon's manservant, who would return for them, with a lantern, at eleven o'clock sharp.

"My brother sits up for us, you see, and would worry if we returned any later," Miss Beaumont explained.

Alvey was very fond of dancing—which, she found, was conducted very discreetly at the Hexham Assemblies: quadrilles, country dances, minuets being permitted, but waltzes still considered wholly unsuitable—and was happy to secure a partner for the first two dances. Meg and Isa were likewise paired off, Meg with John Chibburn. Quite a number of young men had approached Miss Beaumont and asked for the honour of the Miss Winships' hands. But the company was not large—there might have been twenty couples present; bearing in mind her strictures about "red-faced boobies," Alvey could not but admit that Louisa had some reason for her condemnation of the local society.

Alvey's first partner, a Mr. Fenwick, talked exclusively about hunting; her second, a Mr. Forster, talked entirely about fishing; and the third, a Mr. Clavering, appeared so terrified of her that he did not talk at all. He had evidently been ordered by his mamma to dance with the bluestocking Miss Louisa Winship and did not consider that his duty embraced the need for conversation as well. Since he was quite a passable dancer, Alvey was content to have it so. Isa's partners seemed equally unexciting; Alvey began to comprehend why she saw so little need to take pains with her appearance.

At supper they sat with Meg and John Chibburn; Meg, the queen of the occasion, was in high spirits and pouted rather when Miss Beaumont, not long afterwards, indicated that it was time for her young guests to leave. But since their self-sacrificing hostess had sat against the wall on a hard chaperone's seat all evening, with her niece beside her, Alvey could hardly blame the Beaumont ladies for retiring early; from their point of view the affair must, surely, have been tedious indeed. To her surprise she found that this was not so.

"That was *most* enjoyable!" sighed Fanny Beaumont. "I believe I could listen to the music and watch the dancing forever!"

And her aunt said, "Indeed it was a most agreeable occasion. I should not wonder, Fanny, if Captain Campbell were to offer for Hettie Musgrave; I observed that he was paying her very particular attention. And the younger Musgrave boy danced *twice* with Sophia Elliott; if *I* had been her mamma I should not have permitted it. And Tom Bamborough distinguished Mary Armstrong to an extent which should certainly not have been sanctioned by her aunt unless his intentions are serious."

It seemed that not a smile, not a gesture, not even the flip of a fan had escaped Miss Beaumont's scrutiny; she is like a kind of walking Record Office of behaviour, thought Alvey, not a little alarmed, and also greatly relieved that her own communications with her partners had been of such a trivial nature.

"I suppose you will be bringing Parthie with you to the Assemblies once Meg is married?" Miss Beaumont said to Isa.

"I suppose so, poor child; though dancing is not her forte, she of course longs to wear dresses down to her ankles and attend the balls."

"And what about you, Isa? When are we to hear of your engagement?" Miss Beaumont continued inquisitorially. "Now that your sister Louisa is come home, you must be looking about you. It is the duty of young ladies to get married."

But Isa only laughed and said that she had no such intention.

"Meg has made such a very respectable alliance that I can afford to remain single."

"My dear! That is no way for a young person to talk!" Miss Beaumont exclaimed reprovingly. "But I am sure you cannot be serious."

Then they were back in the Canon's house, where he was drowsily waiting up for them over a dying fire, by the light of a flickering candle, and they speedily retired to their ice-cold chambers; Alvey was quite glad that she and Isa were to share a bed, and reflected rather ruefully that she was growing dangerously accustomed to a life of comfort and ease; fires, even in bedrooms, were piled high at Birkland Hall.

Next morning, punctually at half past nine, Archie came to fetch the young ladies. A little snow had been falling for the last hour, and Meg shivered apprehensively.

"If only it does not snow so as to prevent our leaving on Saturday!"

"Na, na, Miss Meg, there'll be naught o' snow for a twa, three weeks yet."

Meg and John planned to take Isa with them, as company for her sister, on their wedding journey. This was very self-sacrificing of Isa, who was not at all attracted by the idea of a visit to Brighton, and hated leaving home again so soon after her last excursion; but Meg felt, possibly with reason, that her new husband, on his own, might prove rather uninspiriting company. Isa had agreed to the proposal only on condition that she might be allowed to view the Pavilion and see some notable beauty spots on the way back to Northumberland. They were to travel south by ship, remain some weeks in Brighton, then return northwards by slow stages, visiting relatives at Winchester and Warwick, pausing at Oxford, York, Matlock, Dovedale, and the Lake District. Only the thought of seeing these places had finally won Isa's reluctant consent to such a long absence from home. Alvey looked forward to the departure of the sisters with more than a little apprehension; up to now she had committed no major solecisms, but she still very frequently found it needful to apply to one or the other for information, and could not think how she would go on with neither of them at hand.

The cold was bitter as they drove homeward. Along the tops of the angular hills, snow lay streaked and skeined; against its pallor the grey stone walls and lines of wind-bent beeches divided the landscape like markings on a map. Isa said wistfully, "I shall miss the best of the winter here. Winter is such a beautiful time." And she sniffed the arctic air with keen pleasure.

Alvey shivered a little, imagining the seclusion of Birkland after a heavy snow.

"Heyday!" said Archie, as they passed the turn to Birkland village. "Here's folk ahead of us on th' road—" and he gestured with his whip to the tracks of carriage wheels leading onwards. "Rackon it'll be Mester James."

"Oh, mercy," muttered Meg under her breath. "*What* a to-do there is bound to be when James learns about Annie Herdman and her baby; I almost wish he had not agreed to come home for my wedding."

"Oh, come, Meg—you know he needs to rest at home for a while, to recover from his wound. How can you be so unfeeling?" objected Isa.

"And what about me? I shall only be married once! It is rather hard if the occasion is to be spoiled by these disagreeables."

Really, Meg is a selfish wretch, Alvey thought.

Archie turned the horses down into the Hall driveway, walking alongside them and holding their bridles to check their pace on the steep, icy track.

This had been Alvey's first night away from the house since her arrival, and she felt, with a slight twinge of guilt, how agreeable it was to be returning—even with the certainty of family dissensions ahead, even with the added problems presented by James's arrival, and the prospect of all the inquisitive strangers she was bound to meet at the wedding—despite this, she was startled at the feeling of homecoming aroused in her by the view, glimpsed between slender pine trunks, of grey walls and the massive bulk of the pele tower against the pale sky. The concern she felt for Sir Aydon and Lady Winship seemed almost akin to warmth. How dreadfully distressed they must have been, poor things, at the need to break such a piece of news to their son . . .

It occurred to Alvey that she was feeling, on behalf of these strangers, more solicitude than had ever been required of her for her own parents. This rather melancholy discovery kept her silent as the carriage drew to a halt on the gravel sweep and Archie came to pull down the step.

The moment they were inside the house, they were aware of the sound of raised voices, issuing from the library; Meg and Isa turned automatically in that direction; but Alvey, impelled by sudden diffidence, and scrupling to add her presence to the first family reunion, ran hastily up the stairs, murmuring that she had a packet for the old lady. This was true; she had bought Mrs. Winship a copy of Crabbe's poems. Depositing the other books in her bedroom, she bore the volume along the corridor to the old lady's chamber. Mrs. Winship was still there, making her slow toilet with Duddy's aid. The gift was received with gruff surprise.

"Very obliging of you to be sure—" Old Grizel darted one keen glance at Alvey, as if calculating whether the motive had been to purchase future favour. *"The Borough.* Hm. Tales of humble persons, I infer. I shall make Parthie read them aloud; very appropriate and salutary it will be for her." Alvey was left wondering whether *The*

Corsair by Lord Byron might not have been more suitable. "Parthie, of course, is below, dancing attendance, I've no doubt, on your brother and his friend, who arrived some half hour since; have you not seen them?"

Another keen glance.

"Oh?" said Alvey carelessly. "No, I came straight upstairs."

"I daresay they are all at cap-pulling, if not dagger-drawing, down there," said the old lady, not without relish. "Do you not wish to join them?"

"Not in the least. Who is James's friend? I did not know that anyone else was expected."

"Hah! *That* whets your curiosity! He is an army surgeon, a major. He and James have known each other since school days, and latterly, I understand, they met again, in Brussels, and have become very close; I believe there was talk of an attachment between James and Major Fenway's sister."

"Indeed? But I thought James—"

"Well, we shall see, we shall see," said the old lady impatiently, as if she found the tangled affairs of the young too tiresome a subject for close consideration. "Come, Duddy, make haste, woman; I had better go down and join the gathering before blood is shed. Not that anyone pays *me* any heed. Run along, girl, run along; doubtless you will be eager to discover what kind of favoured man the major may be."

Obediently, Alvey left, but not to join the group in the library. What would Louisa do at such a moment? she wondered. Louisa, feeling herself superior, would remain elsewhere; Louisa never favoured her brother James, she would certainly display no particular eagerness to greet the returned hero.

Wrapping herself in an old pelisse, Alvey ran quietly down the back stairs and out into the tingling grey chill of the day. She turned along the cobbled way, noticing with pleasure that a coating of ice had turned the moss between the cobbles to a netted pattern of glistening emeralds; she skirted the slippery stable yard and took her way along the broad terrace that lay on the south side of the house. No one would see her here; they were all in the library, which faced the other way. Here she could walk undisturbed, and think about Lord Love, and look out across the valley at the blue-and-white Cheviot Hills.

Down below her the Hungry Water ran full and vociferous; she could hear it very clearly, and the cry of a curlew, and the lonely sound of sheep bleating. This time next week, she thought, they will all be gone, the wedding will be over; and now even the prospect of Meg and Isa's departure came as a satisfaction.

Sniffing the sharp air, with its scent of grass and woodsmoke, Alvey thought, I am growing like Isa; even one night in a town, encircled by other people, leaves me with a feeling of restraint and confinement.

She began to walk fast, to and fro along the terrace, with her arms folded inside the pelisse, planning the next adventure of her hero, who had been somewhat neglected this last week. What nonsense it is! she thought, and how I enjoy it. How can people endure the monotony of daily life when they do not have a story to plan?

Engrossed in her story, she had taken half a dozen turns when she became aware, with no inconsiderable surprise, of a person emerging from the iron gate that gave on to Lady Winship's private garden. It was a man—a stranger—hatless, but wearing a caped greatcoat. Alvey was too far advanced along the terrace to retreat without positive ill manners; she therefore bowed to the newcomer in a distant, haughty manner, as Louisa might, but without speaking.

He, however, approached and addressed her with politeness.

"Good morning! I am obliged to introduce myself: I am James's friend, Guy Fenway. I have already met Sir Aydon and Lady Winship and the younger children, so I guess that you must be Miss Meg, Miss Isabel, or Miss Louisa. I believe"—studying her—"from James's description, that you must be Miss Louisa. Have I guessed correctly?"

"Yes; you are perfectly correct," said Alvey coolly. "How do you do, sir?"

She had already half turned away from him, and hoped he would take this as a hint that his company was not welcome to her; but with a total lack of sensitivity he turned and walked along the terrace beside her.

"You will be wondering, I daresay, how I come to be visiting Lady Winship's garden—which I am well aware is an honour restricted to a very few," he went on sociably. "But I must explain that my own mother is just such another enthusiastic gardener, and she had entrusted me with a gift of some hellebore roots for your mamma, and a most vehement demand for a minute description of her ladyship's garden. In case an early fall of snow should frustrate my purpose by concealing its features, I requested permission to inspect it without delay."

"I see," said Alvey calmly. "I understand that no considerable fall of snow is expected for some weeks yet. And I wonder that my mother did not wish to escort you in person."

Covertly she studied this easy-spoken individual who walked beside her so imperturbably, as if they were the oldest of acquaintances. He was not particularly tall, no taller than Alvey herself; his hair was a nondescript colour, between dull brown and fair, cut short in military fashion; he was clean-shaven and far from handsome, having a pale complexion and an undistinguished, though animated countenance; what redeemed him from the commonplace was a pair of pale, remarkably intelligent, green-blue eyes; they were as clear as glass, Alvey thought, clear as ice; and then she scolded herself for a pair of hideously trite similes while endeavouring to find a less hidebound description for Major Fenway's unusually piercing glance. This man should get on excellently with old Mrs. Winship, she thought; he is certainly no fool. She could not help contrasting his air and manner very favourably with those of her partners at last night's Hexham Assembly.

"Ah," he said, smiling. "I see how it is. You marvel at my impertinence in walking out of doors and making myself so much at home not half an hour after my arrival in a completely strange house."

"Not in the slightest, sir; why should I do so?"

"The truth is," he went on confidentially, "that—added to my wish to visit the garden—there was also a family scene being enacted in which I felt that I, as an outsider, had no part; so it seemed proper to withdraw."

"I am sure that your feelings did you credit, sir." Alvey delivered these words with a cold composure worthy of Louisa at her most supercilious, but at that moment she had the misfortune to slip on a patch of ice coating a hollow in one of the flagstones; if Major Fenway had not caught her elbow she must have fallen ignominiously.

"Take care! That is the danger of these flags. They seem dry, but many of them are coated with ice."

"I thank you, sir; I am perfectly all right. In no danger whatsoever." Ignoring this hint, he persisted in holding her arm as he guided her along the terrace and the cobbled path, until they were safely arrived on the gravel sweep in front of the house.

"I am obliged to you, sir," Alvey said again, coldly, shaking herself free of his clasp. "And I will leave you here. Amble has, I trust, shown you your chamber?"

"Oh yes. But I shall take another turn outside."

Retreating indoors, Alvey could feel him looking after her with an amused and slightly puzzled stare. Had he not been taken in by her performance?

The scene in the library still continued. Wishing no part in it, and dismissing James's friend from her mind, Alvey ran upstairs, and, returning to her and Meg's room, where a new-lit fire crackled pleasantly on the hearth, flung open the table drawer where she kept her Lord Love notebook, and pulled out pen and paper. Several admirable ideas had occurred to her during that ten-minute walk on the terrace; this was often, she found, how the creative process worked, new material emerging in a sudden spate after a period of enforced inactivity. She could feel her story unfold, like a great tent above her as she hauled on the guy rope, swaying about, crumpling a little, then rising higher and taking its angular shape. Eager to note her new plot elements down as fast as possible, before she set to writing the next scene, she began to scribble at speed, ignoring the slight rearrangement of articles in the drawer, pencils, wax, notebooks, and sandbox in unaccustomed places. Had Grace been tidying? But Grace never touched the drawer, had strict instructions to leave it undisturbed. Never mind, it was of no consequence. Here was Lord Love, face to face with the scheming pair, the Duchess of Smithfield, author of a shady plot to discredit him but herself an imposter, and the fraudulent nun, Sister Lutilla, who was really an assassin in disguise—

There came a timid tap at the door.

"Who is it?" Alvey said crossly, scribbling down: "Mother Superior goes every night to Quincey's Gaming Rooms—"

But the tap had been *very* timid and supplicating and was not repeated; with immense impatience Alvey rose, walked swiftly to the door, and pulled it open.

Outside stood Nish and Tot.

"You two?" Alvey said, astonished. "Why, I thought you would be downstairs welcoming your—our brother James."

"We were," Tot said forlornly. "But Mamma sent us and Parthie out of the room. Matters were being discussed that weren't suitable for our ears, she said—"

"All about Annie Herdman and her baby, you know," supplemented Nish.

"Papa told us to go up to the Tower Room and study our Latin. But we saw you come in—"

"We thought—"

"We hoped you might read to us."

Their eyes fell, almost with incredulity, on the window table, heaped with new books. They stood silent, staring.

"Oh," Alvey sighed. *"That* was what you thought, was it? Well—" She paused, and drew a long, resigned breath. "Oh—very well. But only for half an hour, mind!"

Their eyes began to sparkle. Nish jigged up and down a little.

"Shall we stay here?" she said hopefully. "The fire here is better than the one in the Tower Room; that went out while we were downstairs."

VIII

Meg and Isa, like their younger siblings, had been dismissed from the library, and Sir Aydon was saying heavily, for perhaps the tenth time,

"But Annie Herdman herself *said*—"

"Sir, it is not of the least consequence to me what she said. If she—"

"James! The poor girl is dead!"

"Ma'am, *would* you be so obliging as not to interrupt me?"

"Aydon! Would you do me the kindness to request your son not to address me in that tone of voice, if you please?"

"Oh, for pity's sake!" Sir Aydon, goaded, thrust a whole pile of papers relating to estate business off his desk and onto the floor. Both father and son were ashy pale, in signal contrast to Lady Winship, whose customary high colour was even higher than usual.

"Charlotte, you did interrupt James, you know. It would be better, in my opinion, if you took less part in this discussion. Since you—"

"As to that, sir, I cannot agree," said James stormily. "Since Lady Winship seems to have initiated the step—the *disastrous* step—entirely for her own convenience—of introducing this unhappy girl into the house—I regard it as perfectly germane that she should be included in the discussion and hear what I have to say. If Lady Winship will occasionally permit me to speak, that is all I ask."

"Oh!" ejaculated his stepmother in tones of outrage, but her husband held up a silencing hand.

"Well, James?"

"Sir, I am as sorry as can be that the poor girl and her child are dead. I have said so before and I say so again. But I can only assure you again that at no time did I have anything to do with her—that the child was none of mine. How, how can I convince you of this?" he cried wildly, staring into their shocked and disbelieving faces. Lady Winship, that is, with her lips pressed tight together, looked wholly sceptical and disgusted; Sir Aydon, his son thought, grieved and haggard, seemed to have aged ten years in as many minutes.

"It is rather cowardly behaviour to deny an accusation when your accuser is no longer here to refute you."

"I would deny it equally, ma'am, if she *were* here. Annie Herdman! Good God, I hardly knew the girl by sight. I suppose she selected me for a father because I was far away and not likely to return and contradict her story. Or because—" Because of the proclivities of my grandfather and great-uncles, he might have been about to say, but Lady Winship interrupted again.

"I regret, James, but I fear we see no reason to believe you. I remember, all too clearly, that occasion when, as a boy, you played such an unkind trick on your poor sister Louisa—with the pail of water —you might have injured her severely—and then obstinately refused to own up and apologise. You told a falsehood then. How can you expect us to believe you now?"

"What? You bring *that* up again—a stupid prank when I was no more than fourteen years old? For heaven's sake, ma'am!"

"As the shoot grows, so does the tree."

"I can see I have my sister Louisa to thank for your part in this," muttered James, disregarding his stepmother's horticultural dictum. "Coming home, losing no time in raking up old scores—I wonder I do not see her here, adding her sanctimonious voice to the chorus."

"We may as well terminate this discussion, if you are so stubborn and rancorous over old grudges that you cannot bring yourself to admit your culpability," said the lady. "It is shockingly distressing to your father—and all to no purpose, apparently. But if you are so resolved—what more can be said?"

Lady Winship left the room, slowly and with dignity.

James clenched his fists as if he could only just restrain himself from flinging a book after her erect, retreating back. He had stood up, out of an automatic courtesy, as she withdrew; but then, turning even whiter than before, he was obliged to lower himself to a sitting position once more, grasping convulsively at the edge of the table.

"You are far from well yet, my boy," said his father concernedly. "Your leg—"

"Oh, it is nothing, Father."

"It is all a bad business, a dreadfully bad business," muttered Sir Aydon. "If only you could have acknowledged that—"

"My dear sir, I have not the slightest intention of owning to an act I did not perform, however convenient that might be for Lady Winship and yourself. — Oh, I am sorry, Father—" Racked and sick as he felt himself, by no means equal to support this painfully distressing scene, James could not but feel considerable pity for his father, who seemed, he thought, to have suffered grave physical deterioration since his last visit home. And there was another piece of news which must be broken to him—

"I am truly sorry for you, sir," James added in a gentler tone. "I know—Lady Winship said—how particularly attached you were, yourself, to the little lad—"

Sir Aydon waved a dismissing hand.

"Never mind. Never mind that. The thing is—it is all so—Charlotte herself—oh, it has all been so very dreadful!" he cried out in a shaking voice to his dismayed son. "Much, much more dreadful than you can conceive! And now you come home—and with only one *leg*—and all this dissension begins at once—oh, how am I supposed to endure it?"

And, before James's aghast eyes, Sir Aydon bowed his grey head in his hands and fairly burst out crying. Sobs shook him. Tears spurted between his fingers.

"*Don't* be like this, sir—pray don't do so! Matters will come about in time—to be sure they will, they must." Though not for poor Annie Herdman, James thought, uttering these platitudes. Nor, perhaps, for my insensitive stepmother, whose callous treatment indirectly brought about these deaths; if the girl had been permitted to keep her child by her, none of this need have happened. I daresay Lady Winship may be haunted by that thought for a good few years to come. As may this wretched old man.

It was the first time James had considered his father as an old man. Good God, he thought, the poor devil's life is almost over. And then came a corollary to the thought: Father has aged so very suddenly. He has felt so violently about the child's death. Could the child have been his?

Was that why he was so anxious for me to admit paternity?

Was that why *she* was so anxious?

Apart from my father, perhaps, thought James, I am the only person who knows for sure that wee Geordie was not my child. But I am not going to tell a lie about that, even if it would relieve my father and his wife of anxiety.

Do I have the heart, at this juncture, to go on and break my next piece of news?

Indecisively, he stood up and limped on his crutches to the window, where he stood with his back turned on Sir Aydon, looking out.

After a while the distressful sounds behind him diminished. Sir Aydon sat up, shook his head as if to clear it, and blew his nose.

"Try not to think about it any more, sir. Try not to grieve. What's done is done. And we have Meg's wedding upon us, and we are all supposed to rejoice and be jolly."

James did his best at an encouraging smile, meeting his father's reddened eyes, and thought: No, I cannot tell him yet. After the wedding. That will be time enough.

Sir Aydon made some kind of indescribable noise, denoting, his son hoped, an attempt to respond to this encouragement. Then the door opened; James turned in relief, welcoming the distraction, whoever it might be.

It was his grandmother, unwontedly resplendent in black satin of antique mode, Mechlin lace, and a Paisley shawl.

"Well, James!" she jerked out in her gruff voice as he limped to embrace her. "So you left a leg behind at Waterloo? That is certainly a bad misfortune, but still, a great deal better than leaving *yourself.* We are very happy to have you home, even deficient of a leg. I daresay Carey can soon fettle you up another one, made out of yew wood; I understand yew is the most durable."

"Trust you, Grandmother, to have the matter at your fingers' ends." James looked at his grandmother with affection. "I will apply to Carey without delay."

"Where are your sisters?" demanded the old lady, who, after one swift scrutiny of her son, had ignored him, leaving him to gather himself together as best he might. "Have the girls not greeted you?"

"Meg and Isa and Parthie did. And the little ones. But Mrs. Galt called them off; something to do with bridesmaids' dresses."

Sir Aydon rose and tottered towards the door. From it he faintly said, "Make what arrangements you wish, James, for your friend's comfort. Major Fenway seems a very pleasant, gentlemanlike fellow— I suppose he is from the Leicestershire branch of the family?"

Then he left the room.

"Grandmamma," murmured James, softly and urgently, "was the child his? The child who died?"

"Humph! That would not wholly surprise me. But I have no information." The old lady's words were brusque; it was an admission she disliked being obliged to make. "I think it possible that *she* believed so."

"My stepmother?"

She nodded.

He whistled silently, in dismay, comprehension, pity.

"I see. Then—"

"Hush!"

The door, which Sir Aydon had left only half closed, opened wider, and Parthie minced into the room. She was rigged out in a bridesmaid's dress of white velvet with crimson ribbon trimmings. The colour scheme, designed to offset Meg's dark piquant prettiness, had a disastrously opposite effect when contrasted with her younger sister's lank fair hair, pallor, and lashless no-colour eyes; the pretty costume hung on her like a bedizened shroud. She, fortunately, appeared unaware of this and announced joyously, "Look, Grandmamma! Look, James! Am I not fine! *Look!*"

Proudly she shook out her long skirts.

"Very handsome," said her grandmother drily. "How came Mrs. Galt to let you escape from the sewing room?"

"I tiptoed away in my bare feet while her back was turned, pinning up Isa. They never heard me leave."

"You deserve to catch your death of cold before the wedding. And you had best tiptoe back again without loss of time, put on your shoes and stockings, and take off that fine dress before you crumple or soil it. Make haste now!"

Slowly and with great reluctance, Parthie moved towards the door, casting several disappointed glances at James, from whom she had hoped to elicit some admiring comment. But he was looking out of the window again, across the gravel sweep to the rise of the pine-clad hill and the ferny grotto enclosing the Lion Pool.

A trio of persons had just emerged from the path by the pele tower and were making for the pool; now they clustered round it, apparently in performance of some ritual. They had flowers and branches of berries in their hands. Two were children, the third was older.

"Who is that with Nish and Tot?" James demanded in a startled tone.

"Where?"

Old Mrs. Winship limped across the room to stand by him and look out. Then she let out a sudden cackle of laughter.

"Why, that is nobody. No stranger, I should say. Whom did you think it was? That is your sister Louisa."

"What are they doing with those flowers?" James asked curiously, still intent on the group.

"Oh, I have seen the children do that before. It is some ceremony they have; I think it is a kind of mourning. For the little lost one, you know. Earlier in the day I recall they were searching for some toy of his—"

"But were they so strongly attached to him?"

"Not to my knowledge. But I fancy they feel," said the old lady detachedly, "that, although such a dust has been kicked up about the matter, the more tragic aspect of it has gone unregarded. And so they are fulfilling that part themselves."

Parthie gave a loud peevish sniff and left the room. Nobody heeded her departure.

"And Louisa?" said James perplexedly. "Was *she* so very devoted to wee Geordie?"

"Gracious me, no! *She* was not even here when the event took place."

Parthie, back in her everyday clothes, went in search of her younger siblings and found them in the harness room.

Fewer horses were kept, latterly, than had been in Sir Aydon's hunting days, and this roomy place, next to the coach house, was now the repository for various discarded playthings, archery targets, croquet mallets, and wooden bats, as well as the coach mops, wheel jacks, dandy brushes, stable forks, horse cloths, boot levers, and lanterns which, with all the harness hanging on hooks, were its normal furniture.

There was a fireplace, and a boiler for cooking bran mash; wall cupboards and shelves held jars of harness paste, blacking, guttapercha, sal ammonia, and saddle soap. The room was comfortably warm and smelt of linseed and tar.

"Look," said Tot, rummaging in a capacious broom closet, "I found the sledge that Sim made for us. Poor Sim. It is too bad that he never came back. If he had done so, things might have been different—"

"Here is the hobbyhorse!" cried Nish in triumph. "It was lying under the saddle tree all the time. I made sure I had seen him bring it in here—"

Then they both fell silent, realising that their sister Parthie stood in the doorway regarding them with her usual blend of hostility and contempt.

"What are you doing with that hobbyhorse?" she demanded, walking forward. "Give it to me!"

"It's not yours." Ignoring Parthie's extended hand, Nish stepped back a couple of paces.

The hobbyhorse in question was a homemade but handsome toy, with a carved beechwood head attached to a short shaft terminating in a small pair of solid wooden wheels. Small red leather reins were fastened to a painted snaffle.

"Give it here!" repeated Parthie.

"Why? It's not yours. Papa had Surtees make it for wee Geordie."

"And so, as Geordie is dead, *you* are taking possession of it," said Parthie disagreeably. "Greedy little monsters. Jealous of a baby! Because Papa loved him better than you!"

"We weren't!"

"Why have you taken it, then?"

"We're going to burn it," said Tot coldly. "So Papa shan't be upset by seeing it if he comes to the harness room."

"A likely tale!" Parthie made a determined pounce, but Nish eluded her, being much quicker and lighter on her feet.

"Why should you have it?" she panted, tossing the hobbyhorse to Tot, over the top of the saddle tree. *"You* can't ride on it." And she looked pointedly at Parthie's thick, unshapely ankles and legs.

Parthie slowly reddened with rage.

"I was going to give it to Mr. Thropton for some poor child in the village," she said. "And I shall, too. Just because you have big sister Emmy to take your part now, you think you can be as impertinent to me as you please. But you are very wrong! Emmy won't be at Birkland for long."

"Why not?"

"You do realise, don't you, that she's not your real sister at all?"

"Of course we do," said Tot coolly and quenchingly, but Nish, with less discretion, cried, "Who is she, then?"

"Very likely a witch who will suck the marrow out of your bones one night."

"I don't believe you," said Tot with sturdy scepticism. "That's just a tale to frighten us."

"What were you doing with those flowers in the Lion Pool?"

"None of your business. A thing we do with Emmy."

"It's witchcraft. It's blasphemy. You'll go to hell."

"Emmy says there's no such place."

"Oh! You'll be sorry for those words when you are screaming out, and writhing, and burning and frizzling."

Parthie made another snatch, but Tot vaulted over the saddle tree and raced out of the door before she could catch him.

She ran after him, fast and clumsily, but he had vanished among the bushes of the shrubbery before she turned the corner of the house; meanwhile Nish made her escape in a different direction.

Later, when they were burning the hobbyhorse ceremonially over a fire of thorn trimmings, Tot said to Nish, "Why do you think Parthie really wanted the hobbyhorse?"

He often deferred to his younger sister's opinion about people; she had much more certainty in such matters.

Nish said without hesitation, "To curry favour with Mr. Thropton. Or just because she is a thief. She often steals from Grandma. And because—" Nish wrinkled her brow. "Because *she* was jealous of wee Geordie. It made her angry that Papa loved him so. Those things she said about us were true about *her.*"

"Parthie said once to me that Papa was wee Geordie's father," observed Tot, carefully raking up the fire with a stick. "Do you think that was true?"

"No."

"Why?"

"Papa didn't like Annie. I heard him say once that she was sonsy, but pigheaded obstinate."

"Umn. Parthie believed what she said. I think."

"Parthie *likes* to believe bad things about people."

As the flame swept up, and the little horse's head began to blacken and char, both children bowed deeply, murmuring together: "Oh, Mithras, as we offer you this sacrifice, take into your kind keeping our young brother Geordie and Annie his mother. Watch over their steps in the underworld, lead them to your bright courts. With kind regards from Nish and Tot. Amen."

Meg and Isa had retreated to Isa's bedchamber, where Meg was anointing her locks with the bandoline mixed up for her sister by Alvey and the cook.

"You are a simpleton not to use this preparation more; it makes one's hair feel so thick and luxurious."

"Oh," said Isa impatiently, "I hate to feel my hair all clogged with some artificial paste. And to what end? Who will look at it twice?"

"Major Fenway! He is rather puny and ill-looking, I grant you, but a sensible, gentlemanlike man, far superior to those Forsters and Musgraves and Fenwicks. I daresay he would talk to you for hours on end about books and landscapes. And it seemed to me that *you* were not uninterested in *him.*" Meg gave her sister a shrewd look.

Isa slowly reddened.

"I wish you would not talk so, Meg. It is vulgar. And—and not to the purpose. You know my views about men and matrimony. I shall not change them."

"Up to now, I grant, you have had no occasion to. But in the next few months, I assure you, you will encounter a vast deal of new persons—new experiences—it is absurd to make up your mind so adamantly before you have seen anything outside Birkland. Oh well, if you don't want it, I shall finish up the bandoline. — To think that this day week we shall be in Brighthelmstone—"

"Listen, Meg. Never mind Brighthelmstone for the moment. What are we to do about James and Alvey?"

"About James and Alvey?" Meg's tone was inattentive; peering into Isa's small mirror, she was twisting her dark hair into ringlets.

"Whether to tell him about the deception. He is our brother, after all; should we not let him into the secret?"

"Why?" replied Meg carelessly. "He tells us little, if anything at all, about *his* affairs."

"Well, but suppose—suppose anything were to befall us while we were away—our ship founder, for instance—or there might be a carriage accident—"

"Goose! Why should such things occur? And even if they did, even if we were both dispatched into the next world—Louisa is still in this one, to cry rope on Alvey if she chooses to. But for my part, Alvey is very welcome to remain here until she is as old as Grandmamma. I see no need to tell James."

"Oh well—if that is how you feel—" Isa's expression lightened. "Poor James; it was not that I wished to burden him with the information. He has enough troubles—with the loss of his leg—and all the agitation about Annie's baby—"

"Annie's baby, Annie's baby," said Meg irritably. "I wish our mother had never introduced that wretched girl into the house. Thank heaven by next week we need never hear her name again."

"I will tell Alvey, then," said Isa, "that we think it best James is not undeceived."

The complete party did not assemble together until the hour of dinner, by which time Sir Aydon had succeeded, to some degree, in regaining his composure. His wife bore her usual aspect, stern, vague, and *distraite*. As the gong sounded, Meg, Isa, and Alvey all came down the stairs together, with Parthie trailing behind. James and his friend, with Sir Aydon, were in the hall with John Chibburn, who had ridden over for dinner.

"James, have you made your friend Major Fenway known to the girls?" demanded his father, who liked things done in proper form.

"Yes, sir; that is, I introduced him to Meg and Isa—"

"And I introduced myself, in the most forward manner, to Miss Louisa Winship," said Major Fenway, with a little formal bow, as the girls reached the bottom step.

"How d'ye do, Louisa? I fancy it must be some five years at least since we last met," James remarked coolly, making no attempt to salute Alvey.

And she replied, as coolly, "Oh yes, James, at least that. I declare, we meet quite as strangers."

Isa gave Alvey a puzzled, anxious glance, and then tucked her arm through that of her brother, saying with warmth, "Well, I trust that you will not continue as strangers. Do take me in, James dear. Your friend the major will look after Emmy, as we have taken to calling Louisa."

At the table, Alvey was placed almost opposite James, and was often able to study him unobserved, for he kept his eyes down and sat, sometimes for several minutes together, heedless of what was going on about him, silently plaiting and replaiting his napkin. Poor boy, thought Alvey, her heart wrung with pity. What a homecoming for him. And now for three days he must pretend high spirits, act as a good son and brother, do the civil to the neighbours, and say all the proper things at Meg's wedding.

There was something about his looks that she found deeply touching and full of forlorn appeal. Like Parthie, he was fair, but his hair was much thicker and brighter than Parthie's. He had a narrow gentle face, though his mouth and chin bore promise of firmness, even obstinacy. Just now his dark-grey eyes were filled with so much suffering that Alvey could hardly bear their expression, but they were large, beautiful, and well set. I wonder if Sir Aydon could have looked like that when he was James's age, mused Alvey, glancing towards the head of the table. Perhaps; it is possible; the bone structure is the same, but James certainly has more intelligence than his father; and he looks as if he possessed imagination as well. Which I am very sure Sir Aydon does not.

"What are you thinking of, Miss Louisa?" inquired her neighbour, and she replied absently, "I was thinking that James looks as if he suffered from imagination."

"You are right; he suffers from it severely. But what a singular remark for a sister to make!" remarked the major. Alvey blushed.

"Oh well, you must remember we saw very little of one another when we were younger. Our—our natures did not accord. So—as James said—we are virtual strangers to one another. Poor James: he does not look at all well."

"Nor is he. He has borne his sufferings gallantly, but a long period of peace and care in this pleasant house is what he needs to put him back on his feet. — Oh, perdition take it! How one's tongue does continually trip one up! Forgive me, Miss Louisa. James himself would laugh at such a blunder, fortunately. But it is no laughing matter."

"No, I can see that," replied Alvey, frowning. "And I am afraid that the situation in this house is no laughing matter; I very much doubt if a prolonged sojourn here will be so beneficial to James as you hope—"

"Indeed?" The major's pale brows flew up; he gave Alvey a very penetrating look and said, "I assume that present circumstances prevent your enlarging on this topic, but, perhaps, on a future, more private occasion—"

"Oh—well—as to that—" Alvey, disconcerted, hardly knew how to respond. Was this man proposing to make her his confidante in regard to James's problems?

However, at this moment old Mrs. Winship broke in, questioning the young men about their military campaigns, and about the city of Brussels, which she had visited on her wedding journey. "And Paris, too; but that was forty years ago, when the king and queen were on the throne—before all these shocking upheavals. And is the man Buonaparte safely stowed away now, pray? Well I recall the alarm—twelve years ago it must be now—when it was rumoured he had landed on the Scottish coast, and they lit the beacon on the castle in Chillingham Park."

"Yes, he is safely stowed away, ma'am, and all of us military men are at a stay, wondering how we shall fare for promotion now that our superior officers are in no danger of being carried off in battle."

"Yes, that is so; the peace comes as no boon to serving officers," agreed Sir Aydon heavily, relieved to find a topic into which he could enter. "Who wants to kick his heels in barracks? That is no life for a soldier."

James opened his mouth to contribute some remark, then hastily closed it again.

"So how do you intend to tie up your loose ends, Major Fenway?" inquired the old lady.

"Why, ma'am, my regiment—an infantry one—is soon to be ordered abroad, to assist in the pacification of central India. But before I embark, I wish to enlarge my knowledge of medicine and surgery. While at Cambridge I interested myself to quite a degree in medical studies, and the lore that I acquired then, scanty though it was in all conscience, stood me in good stead during the recent campaigns—"

"Stood *me* in good stead," interpolated James. "Without Guy's expert care I should have died—"

"Then Major Fenway is doubly welcome to this house," said Sir Aydon. But he spoke in a flat, puzzled tone. Medical studies? he seemed to be asking himself. What kind of an occupation is that for a gentleman? What kind of a man is this?

"You are an anomaly, Major Fenway," remarked old Mrs. Winship. "A soldier *and* a medical man. With one hand you take away life, with the other you restore it."

"Ma'am, I have observed so much needless suffering on the battlefield; men dying from loss of blood whose lives could have been saved; wounds turning putrid when a few elementary precautions might have enabled them to heal cleanly. — But I fear I distress the young ladies."

"Indeed you *do*, Major!" cried Meg with pretty vehemence. "Keep those topics until after we have left you to your wine, if you please! And in the meantime, tell us about the balls in Brussels, and about the Duke of Wellington—is he as abrupt and strange in his manner as they say?"

Politely, the major changed the subject, and talked instead of balls and diversions. Alvey was rather sorry; she would have been interested to hear more of his plans, and where he intended to continue his medical studies; but she had noticed that James—who came to the meal looking fatigued, ate next to nothing, and contributed hardly more to the conversation—had turned deathly white during his friend's mention of the battlefield; indeed James looked so extremely ill that she wondered his family did not notice his state; and for his sake she felt it was fortunate the topic had been abandoned.

Shortly after, Lady Winship rose, nodded with vague authority to her daughters and mother-in-law, and trailed away, like a ship governed by an uncertain wind, towards the drawing room. Old Mrs. Winship limped briskly after her, and the girls followed.

What can have taken place during that long, evidently painful scene in the library? Alvey wondered, settling herself in a corner and taking up a volume about the rivers of England, to which she paid no heed. Clearly, nothing to anybody's satisfaction.

She was soon to discover. Taking advantage of a loud, staccato Italian sonata, which Meg rattled off on the piano to relieve her impatience while the males finished their wine, Isa came to sit beside Alvey and said, in a low voice, "Well, it seems that all our conjectures were at fault. James has entirely denied any connection with the unfortunate Annie, and refuses to have her child fathered upon him."

"Isa! Do, pray, moderate your voice!" Startled at such rashness, Alvey glanced about the room; but it was true that both older ladies were at a considerable distance, occupied in a low-toned dialogue; while Parthie dangled around Meg and the piano, turning Meg's pages and demanding a favourite air.

Isa was angry and perturbed. "Poor James! It is dreadfully hard on him. And he with only one leg, and so thin and pulled-down as he looks. If that kindhearted Major Fenway had not looked after him so solicitously, I am very sure he would not have survived. And then to come home and have false accusations flung at him— And it seems that, also, poor James had been betrothed to the major's sister, but felt obliged to release her from the engagement because of his disability—"

"The major's sister? And she let him *go?* She can hardly have loved him!"

"No; that was what I thought. Anyone who could part from James for such a reason must have a heart of flint."

"He is better off without her," stated Alvey.

"Yes; perhaps; but only consider his position at present. Oh, Alvey, he is so very miserable! He came to my room and told me all about it."

Much to her own surprised and embarrassed annoyance, Alvey felt a distinct jealous pang. But was the jealousy owing to Isa or to James? How absurd, how shameful, to feel aggrieved and left out because of a brother's natural wish to confide in a favourite sister. You are a great fool, Alvey told herself; a fool and an ill-natured wretch. How can you entertain such greedy, unkind feelings towards Isa—friendly, helpful Isa—and a man whom you have only just met, with whom you have exchanged no more than half a dozen words? It is childish—humiliating—silly—and disgusting.

"What was her name—the major's sister?"

"Meta—Lady Meta Fenway—the major is a younger son of Lord Farne. And, having thrown over our poor James, she has now allied herself with the Marquess of Alderney."

"It all sounds very grand," said Alvey shakily. "I don't doubt that James will by and by come to be much relieved that she gave him the go-by. Such a connection would present many problems, surely?"

"Oh yes. The Fenways are decidedly above our touch. Though the major does not behave as if he felt so; do you not find him a very pleasant, easy person to talk to?"

"We have spoken very little. He has a good deal of self-assurance. But very gentlemanlike, I grant you."

"He has been so *good* to James—escorted him all the way from Ghent, looked after him on the journey, like a brother, James says." Isa's eyes shone, her plain face was quite transfigured. "I *wish* I could be certain that Papa and Mamma had thanked him as they ought— their minds are so taken up with this affair of Annie's baby—"

"They were so determined on James being the scapegoat," Alvey said slowly. "They must be enraged with him for refusing to accept the role. I suppose now they are sorry that he ever came home to disprove that supposition. If he had remained at a distance, the affair would have remained inconclusive."

"Poor James. It is all sad and horrible. And I do not see how it will all end."

The gentlemen now entered the drawing room, John Chibburn striding ahead, eager to be reunited with his love, James and his friend walking slowly and conversing quietly, Sir Aydon in the rear, frowning and silent.

No, thought Alvey, I cannot imagine either how it will all end. She sighed, watching as Isa moved to welcome her brother and find him a comfortable seat. Real life is so untidy and sad, compared with my dear cheerful story. People's actions are performed for obscure reasons, they reject the roles offered them, they behave out of character. Here is this James, refusing to be set down as a rake and libertine, commanding instead one's helpless pity, looking like a bewildered, brokenhearted boy—

Major Fenway made his way to Alvey and sat down beside her, in the place that Isa had vacated.

"You are interested in the rivers of England?" he inquired, taking up the volume that lay beside her.

"No, not in the least."

"You are not a bookish lady, I infer?"

You quite mistake me! the affronted Alvey would have exclaimed, but he continued without waiting for her to speak.

"You prefer the study of human nature, I conclude; and you are very wise, since it is presented here before us in such lavish and diverse plenty. Now I want you to tell me about some of your family, for I have it on your brother's authority that you are an extremely clever and well-informed young lady. I am told by James that you had intended to devote yourself to missionary work but have been thwarted in that aim by parental authority. I must commiserate with you"—he did not sound in the least commiserating—"but let us hope the ban may be of merely temporary duration. In the meantime it is a piece of good fortune for me; I am sure that your sagacity can furnish me with the answers to many questions about your interesting relations."

These words were uttered with such smooth rapidity of locution that Alvey found it impossible to decide whether he intended to mock her. His face and the clear eyes engaging hers were simple, open, and inquiring, apparently eager for any facts she might vouchsafe.

Alvey replied with caution.

"I will tell you what I can, sir, though—since I have only recently returned from a four-year absence at school—I may claim to be less well informed about this group than almost anybody else you might have chosen. You should rather apply to my sister Isa."

"And so I have done," he promptly replied, "but she is at present applying much-needed solace to your brother, and furthermore I find that your sister Isa takes less interest in humans than she does in geological formations; whereas you, she tells me, are a shrewd student of society and its peculiarities."

Oh, she does, does she? Alvey thought; but only said, "Well, ask me what you will, sir, and if I do not know the answer I will tell you directly."

"Good. First, then, about your father. I observe in him a strong resemblance to his son James. He seems to me a good and simple man who finds great difficulty in dealing with any situation at all out of the ordinary. Would you agree?"

"Why—why yes! *Well-intentioned,* he is, certainly—I think he finds it hard to reach a decision about any but humdrum affairs—though I am sure he sincerely intends to do right—"

"Just so. Would you say this tendency had been exacerbated by his hunting mishap—that when he was a whole, strong man he found his life less complicated, saw his way plainer before him?"

Now Alvey found herself in a dilemma. How could she pretend to information about what Sir Aydon was like before she knew him? But, recalling various remarks that Isa had let fall, she deliberated and replied: "I do not think he has *ever* found it either easy or agreeable to take any but the simplest decisions. Before his accident he devoted the largest possible amount of his time to military affairs—and then to hunting—"

"As an escape from his personal anxieties?"

"Well, I suppose," said Alvey thoughtfully, "that was how it fell out. And yet when problems did come his way, I do not believe he avoided them. The estate—the tenants in the village—the household —these responsibilities are not evaded, and he is a respected master and landlord; more than respected. He commands the devotion of his tenants and servants."

"Ah! Does he—?"

"Furthermore," Alvey went on firmly—it was her turn to hold the floor, she decided—"he is, at present, I am fairly certain, in considerable pain at all times. I have noticed his face when he thought himself unobserved—his expression is not that of a well man. I am sure that he suffers far more than he would be prepared to admit."

And receives remarkably little sympathy or assistance from his wife, she might have added, but checked herself.

Fenway nodded thoughtfully.

"It is plain to see that whoever had the job of setting his bones after that fall—"

"It was a local apothecary and surgeon named Tarset, who died earlier this year of drink."

Alvey had discovered this fact with some relief; since the aforementioned Tarset had brought Louisa into the world and tended her through various childhood ailments such as mumps and chicken pox, he would have been a hazardous and awkward neighbour.

"I doubt if he was much loss to the district. It's plain that he made a shocking botched job of your father's legs. I am not surprised that Sir Aydon is in constant pain."

"Oh, that is dreadful. You mean it could—ought to have been done better?"

"I certainly do. These country bonesetters—no better than carpenters—"

The major drummed with his fingers on *The Rivers of England,* directing a frowning stare at his host, who sat, for once, peacefully absorbed in the perusal of a bundle of London newspapers the young men had brought with them.

Alvey said, "What else did you wish to ask me, Major Fenway?"

"Ah yes. I am interested in your young brother—he was not at supper, by the bye?"

"No. In general he and the sister nearest with him in age *do* eat with us, but as there was company—"

"The boy—Thomas is his name?"

"Yes, but known as Tot."

"He is of an epileptic habit?"

"Now, how did you guess that?" said Alvey, startled. "Or did James tell you?"

"No, I am not sure that James is aware of it. But I am right?"

"I am not sure that anybody is aware of it. And I have been wondering very much what I ought to do—"

Alvey had in fact discovered the case herself only that day when excitement brought on by the return of his admired elder brother had induced one of Tot's convulsive attacks. She had found him in the Tower Room, being competently ministered to by Nish, and had become aware of the almost fanatical pains which the pair took to prevent the rest of the family realising the nature of Tot's disability.

"They are so terrified of being forbidden to lead the lives they prefer, going out on the moors for hours on end—also the poor boy is in mortal dread of being derided, stigmatised as being lunatic or feebleminded, and perhaps dosed with laudanum or some similar medicine. He told me of the parson's child, the incumbent before this one, a poor little creature much subject to fits, who was dosed daily with opium until her brain was quite dulled and she died under the treatment. They begged me not to tell Sir Aydon. And I promised I would not, at least until I had reflected on the matter. As it is, Sir Aydon rather despises the boy for his frailty and backwardness—and if he were to be told—"

"You doubt if he would take any useful action?"

"Well—yes. Also, at present, his mind is so troubled that I would hesitate to distress him further—"

"You are perfectly right. It would serve no practical purpose."

"But how in the world did you guess about the boy?"

"Oh, there is a look about the eyes, the skin, the manner of response. It was only a conjecture. I wonder if there have been other examples in the family—it can be hereditary—"

Alvey had heard of none. "My grandmother would be the one to ask," she said, rather doubtfully. "But what should be done about the poor child?"

"He may outgrow the disability. On the whole, at present, I would advise leaving well alone. See that he eats well—meat, good brown bread, fresh vegetables, fruit—rests well—and, in general, leads a sensible, well-conducted life. You yourself teach those children, I understand?"

"Yes; and besides that, they learn Latin and Greek from the rector."

"Is the boy intelligent? Does he work well at his books?"

"He *had* been rather slow and backward for his age—but I attribute that principally to the bad teaching of an elderly governess who has recently departed. Both children had been rendered apathetic, learned very little from her, and were convinced that lessons must be boring. But I must confess that I have been quite astonished at their rapid growth of interest and alertness—"

He looks less acute and inquisitorial when he smiles, Alvey now decided of the major.

"When the boy is due to go off to school will be the time to think more deeply about the problem," he said. "I wonder if his mother is entirely unaware of it?"

His eye dwelt speculatively on Lady Winship, who had risen to her feet and was glancing about in her usual vague way for scissors, work bag, and thimble: articles only brought into use when company prevented her retreat into glasshouses or garden.

Not at all wishful to attempt an analysis of the workings of Lady Winship's mind, Alvey stood up.

"I will bid you good night, Major Fenway. I hope my answers have been of some use to you."

"Indeed they have. My motives are not simple inquisitiveness, I would have you know, Miss Louisa; rather, I hope, by extending my knowledge of his father and brother, to increase my ability to be of service to James."

"Poor James," said Alvey, thinking of the major's sister. "He does look so wretched. But now that his leg is in a way to heal—"

"I imagine you are aware that he has other problems beside that."

Not a little disconcerted at the major's apparent ability to read her thoughts, Alvey left him and walked upstairs with Isa, who said, "I saw how absorbed you were in talk with Major Fenway. Is he not a clever, well-informed man?"

"Rather too inquisitive," said Alvey.

"Oh, I do not at all agree. I think he must be an excellent friend for James."

IX

The remaining days before Meg's wedding passed quietly. Meg occupied herself in packing her clothes and belongings, Isa in visiting various well-loved locations that she would not see again for many months. The longer of these expeditions were performed on old Phantom, a discarded hunter of Sir Aydon's, too stiff and sober to have been thought worth selling; on the shorter excursions Alvey, and sometimes Nish and Tot, accompanied her. But much of Alvey's time at present was occupied in helping and taking counsel with Mrs. Slaley about arrangements for the wedding breakfast; for, as that lady said, "Missus is so moithered and put-about these days, there's naught useful to be had from her," while the old lady was closeted for many hours together with James, evidently giving him good advice or comfort. So Alvey, who had never imagined herself engaged in such occupations, became involved in the making of a Plumb cake containing six pounds of currants, twenty eggs, a quart of brandy, and three pounds of butter; she learned the mysteries of "quaking puddings," the plucking and trussing of teal, wild duck, turkey, pigeon, and green goose, and the skinning of hares. The pigeons were made into a vast pie, the hares were jugged. Tot and Nish sometimes came and hung about the kitchens, big-eyed, as delicacies such as Carolina Snowballs and Lemon Sponge were concocted. "Gan awa' wi' ye, hinnies, there's no place for childer here," said Mrs. Slaley, but she sweetened the edict with handfuls of hunting nuts. Alvey, remembering her mother and Cousin Hepzie, wished they could have seen this big, warm, dazzling kitchen with its cheer and plenty. There was to be a breakfast for the gentry, after the wedding ceremony, and a feast for the villagers, held in the rectory barn. Mrs. Slaley and her staff were in charge of both events, and there was much to-and-fro with hampers and wagonloads of napery and benches between Hall and village.

" 'Deed an' ye've a heid on your shoulders, Miss Emmy," said Mrs. Slaley. "I knaw Miss Meg and Miss Isa's got ither things to concern them, but ye'd think Miss Parthie'd lend a hand now and now. Not she! She's nae more use than a broken striddle."

Parthie, it was evident, had taken a huge fancy to Major Fenway, and placed herself in his vicinity at every possible opportunity. He was extremely patient and kind with her—far kinder than she deserved, Alvey privately considered; allowed her to show him over the house and grounds, listened with apparent interest to her long, self-laudatory monologues.

James took little part in the family activities and was seldom to be seen. Sometimes he watched his friend knock a ball about in the billiard room; he listened to Meg if she chose to play and sing, or spent hours with Isa, poring over her drawings and sketches. "That's Haughton Mains, is it not?" "Yes; and this is Green Law, and that's Thrang Stones." "I wonder when I shall get up there again?" mused James wistfully, and Isa said, "Oh, you will be riding again very soon. You could try old Phantom. He has such an easy pace," but Alvey saw her press her hands together with a convulsive gesture. Once or twice, to Alvey's surprise and pleasure, James made his way on from the old lady's chamber up to the Tower Room, where he expressed astonishment at the number of new books and increased extent of the children's activities.

"We had nothing like this in the days of Miss Waskerley," he remarked with a faint smile.

"Look! Brother James, look at our journals! Emmy has given us a proper book each to keep them in, and we may draw pictures or do anything we like, but she says we must write at least ten lines every day. Emmy is writing a book of her own too, a story, but we may not see it until it is finished. And Nish is writing a story about King Arthur and Emmy helps her."

"These are capital. I like Tot's picture of a trout. And when will sister Emmy's book be finished?" James inquired politely.

"Not until some considerable time after the wedding." Alvey

smiled too, wondering a little what James's notion of her literary labours might be. She did not enlighten him.

Some protective impulse urged her to quit the room, leaving James alone with his younger siblings. She thought their devoted company must be good for him. It was plain that something weighed deeply on his mind. He was restless and preoccupied, wandered about his home, inside and out, with a wistful yearning expression as if bidding good-bye to it.

"James loves this place as I do," Isa said to Alvey, who was helping her to pack. "I think men have a harder time of it than women do. They must leave their homes and go out into the world—"

"*No, Isa!* You do *not* place a whole heap of sketching books on top of a gauze dress! Here, let me do it. — But why must a man go out into the world? Why cannot James stay at home and help your father take care of the estate?"

"Well," Isa said vaguely, "the Winships have always been soldiers. It is a family tradition going back for centuries. — You will write to me, Alvey, will you not? And tell me how all goes on at home?"

"Of course I will, goose! Provided you send me your direction well in advance. I wonder when we shall next hear from Louisa."

"Oh," said Isa, with one of her flashes of cynicism, "it is odds that she is so deeply engaged in her new existence she will not find time to write again."

The simple wedding ceremony was soon over. Mr. Thropton offici-ated, at his most unctuous; his fish-mouth opened and shut like a trout snapping at flies, Alvey thought, as he droned his way through the homily. Meg looked remarkably pleased with herself in her wedding finery, John Chibburn stiff, uncomfortable, and rather sober. The elder Winships maintained an unbroken gravity which hardly ac-corded with the nature of the occasion.

In the churchyard, after the ceremony, there was much standing about, handshaking, kissing, and greeting of neighbours and guests from more distant parts; this was because, if they were to catch the tide at Newcastle, the married pair could not return to Birkland Hall for their own wedding breakfast, but must set off on their journey without delay. A room in the rectory had been prepared for the bride to remove her wedding gown, helped by her sisters. Parthie and Nish were there, even little Betsey, so there was no chance for last-minute admonitions.

"I—I do hope all goes well with you, Emmy dear," said Isa at the carriage step, looking suddenly stricken at the prospect of the months that lay ahead. "Take—pray take care of Mamma and Papa. And of James too!"

Assisted by John, she vanished inside. Meg, all smiles, was fluttering her handkerchief at the window, as the crowd pressed close and a few handfuls of rice and late rose petals were flung.

The coachman cracked his whip and the eager horses broke into a canter.

At that moment a raucous shout was heard, and a stone, hurled from the back of the crowd, missed the carriage, apparently its intended target, and struck Parthie in the face. There were shrieks, oaths, and a general commotion. No one had seen who threw the stone; it had been discharged from the bushes above the churchyard. Guests and spectators ran about vainly, exclaiming and shouting; as for Parthie herself, she stood half dazed, sobbing hysterically, with a cut and bleeding cheek and a great smear of earth down her white velvet dress, until Major Fenway took command of the situation and had her carried into the rectory. The bridal equipage had long gone, its occupants quite unaware of anything amiss.

The rest of the crowd dispersed slowly, chattering feverishly in the aftermath of amazement and shock, the gentry to the Hall, the villagers to the barn.

"Who could a took and done such an orra thing?"

"Perfectly scandalous—outrageous—disgraceful. The perpetrator should be flogged!"

"Who could have done it? Some poacher, perhaps, who bears a grudge against Sir Aydon," the gentry said to one another. "What a regrettable mishap to take place at the poor girl's wedding."

Alvey reflected, as she worked hard at being civil to several dozens of guests, that, in fact, Meg, as usual, had succeeded in avoiding the unpleasantness; it was her unfortunate younger sister who, with a chipped tooth and what promised to be a notable black eye, was missing the party and being ministered to with hartshorn and spirits of ammonia.

How furious Parthie will be, poor child, at missing a treat she has looked forward to for months, thought Alvey, trying to remember which was Lady Edmondbyers, which Brigadier Henshawe, and which Colonel Espershields. "Thank you, ma'am, yes indeed, I am very happy to be back at Birkland. Yes, it was a most shocking occurrence —some boy, perhaps, who had been beaten for trespass. How do you do, Colonel, no, I have quite given up the wish to be a missionary in India—Mamma and Papa were not at all in favour of the idea—"

Glancing at Sir Aydon and Lady Winship, both surrounded by guests, she wondered how they found the stamina to meet the demands made on them by the occasion. Both looked startled and distressed; Sir Aydon kept rubbing his forehead; his wife's cheeks were a dark, mottled red.

Alvey felt a deep sympathy, too, for James, subject to the same ordeal, doggedly parrying the same remarks, answering the same questions. He was even paler than usual, a jerking muscle in his cheek betrayed his tribulation and fatigue. Yet at least, poor devil, thought Alvey, he elicits everybody's sympathy for his leg; and at least he *knows* these people.

"Ah, Louisa, my dear! How pleasant to see you back at home. You must come over to Robinsrock very soon, before winter settles in—"

"Why, thank you, that is very kind, but I do not believe I can leave Mamma and Papa just at present. Having just lost both Meg and Isa, you see—"

Who *are* these people?

"Ah yes, just so. Well—as soon as you can—" A kind nod, and thank heaven they had moved on.

Or, worse still: *"Well,* Louisa! Do you remember us?"

"I fear, dear ma'am, you must hold me excused—such a long absence—"

"Tut, do you not recall how you used to come to Simonburn as a child and play with our Polly—who sends all kinds of messages—but within a week of her lying-in—"

Mercifully, many of the guests had come long distances, some from right across the county, and the early-autumn darkfall dictated early departures. By slow degrees they all took their leave. At last only Mr. Thropton was left, lamenting over Parthie's injuries.

"The poor, poor child! I was never so shocked. Who, Sir Aydon, who do you think it can possibly have been?"

"Oh, how can I tell?" Sir Aydon, like his wife, looked wearied to death. "It is of no great consequence, I daresay. Some disaffected tinker or besom maker. Is the girl being properly tended?"

"Yes, sir, she has been put to bed with a soothing draught, and the maid Tushie is with her."

Major Fenway had overseen the transfer of Parthie from the rectory to the Hall.

"We are much indebted to you, Major."

Plainly Mr. Thropton would have liked to linger and discuss the incident at length, but Major Fenway managed to get rid of the rector by exerting his authority as a medical man and saying firmly that Sir Aydon appeared shockingly fatigued and should retire to rest. With evident deep gratitude his host obeyed this recommendation and took himself off. Mr. Thropton reluctantly said his farewells, but, bowing extremely low over Alvey's hand, added that he looked forward to seeing her in church the following morning. Then at last he departed. Lady Winship had slipped away long before. Tot and Nish had collected a bundle of broken meats and done likewise, probably to the moor. "Mind you take your good clothes off before you go anywhere!" Alvey called after them, and they gave her hasty, preoccupied nods.

All of a sudden Alvey found herself in the big empty room, among dirty plates, champagne glasses, and discarded napkins, alone with James and the major.

"Well. Thank the Lord *that's* over," said James. "Another fifteen minutes and I'd have foundered."

"What? And you with another six sisters to marry off? How can you be so poor-spirited?"

"Six? Can it really be *six?* Well, no one is likely ever to take Parthie off Father's hands."

"I had better go and see how the poor child is doing," exclaimed Alvey, recalled to a sense of her continuing duties.

"You need not trouble yourself. She is sound asleep. Don't run away and leave us," Major Fenway urged her. "Let me help you to some champagne. You took none all afternoon—not a single drop. I have been keeping an eye on you, you see."

"Thank you, you are very kind. No, I did not dare to take any wine; I needed to keep my wits about me." With a wan smile, Alvey received the glass and sipped.

"You had better eat something with that," James roused himself out of his stupor of melancholy and fatigue to say, "or, so tired as you look, it will go straight to your head."

"Will it? I have never drunk champagne before."

"Good God, yes, you have. On any number of occasions. Do you not remember Cousin Patrick's coming-of-age celebrations?"

"Oh—oh yes. Yes, of course." Alvey felt the major's amused eyes on her. He must think me a hen-witted fool, she thought, as he handed her a plate of ham and turkey.

Amble and a couple of the maids came in and began quietly clearing away the used plates and glasses. Stridge, the footman, made up the fire.

"Well, Miss Emmy, I reckon that passed off as it should," Amble said to Alvey. "Not above seven glasses broke, and over three dozen of Master's best champagne left. Mrs. Slaley's cake got ate up to the last crumb."

"That was *my* cake, Amble, not Mrs. Slaley's," Alvey told him. "But will you please tell her that the hare patties were quite excellent, and so was the pigeon pie. I heard many of the guests remarking on them, and Lady Edmondbyers asked me for the recipe, which I promised to send her. I shall be coming to congratulate Mrs. Slaley on everything myself by and by, but just now I find myself a little tired."

"I should just about think so, Miss Emmy, seeing you was on your feet since six this morning. I'll tell her, right enow."

Alvey sank down on a sofa, listening without paying too much heed while, in a pleasant, desultory fashion, the two young men talked over the occasion. How agreeable this is, she thought drowsily. If I had had brothers, I suppose this is what life might have been like. If I had had brothers . . .

Almost asleep, she became aware that Major Fenway was playing the piano; not in Meg's self-conscious tinkling style, but with mastery and power. She opened her eyes and watched James's fair, incisive profile outlined against the faint glow of the dying fire.

What a pity it is, thought Alvey regretfully, that I made Wicked Lord Love into a dark, saturnine hero. A fair aquiline man is so much more interesting and distinguished!

But it is too late to change now.

Suddenly becoming aware of the lateness of the hour, she rose, rather uncertainly, to her feet, bade a friendly good-night to the two young men, and made her sleepy way upstairs to the bedroom which from now on would be all her own undisputed territory.

The house next morning seemed strangely hushed after the bustle and excitement of the wedding. And we are a smaller household, thought Alvey, brushing her hair. Not that Meg and Isa were obtrusive housemates . . . But what a luxury to be able to rise in silence, to be free to think her own thoughts as she fastened her laces and put on her collar, without the constraint of a second presence in the room.

Before going downstairs she walked along to visit Parthie in the room the latter shared with little Betsey. Parthie, surprisingly, was not seizing the chance to remain in bed and be looked after, but was already up, in a dressing gown, submitting to the ministrations of Tushie, the smaller children's nurse, who had removed yesterday's bandage and was carefully placing a court plaster on her cheek.

"How do you feel?" Alvey asked. "It was shockingly bad luck that you were obliged to miss the wedding breakfast; but I think you might have found it very dull; most of the guests seemed to be in their sixties."

Parthie shot her a resentful, disbelieving glance and said that she felt atrociously stiff and sore, and her head ached abominably. "But Major Fenway promised me a draught and said that I would notice the pain less if I busied myself about my usual employments."

Aha, thought Alvey, there is the reason for this unexpectedly stoic behaviour.

She soon discovered, from the broken eggshells and ham bones in the breakfast parlour, that the two young men had already eaten and gone out. Alvey made a rapid breakfast herself, for a multiplicity of tasks lay ahead of her, tidying-up operations and saying the proper things to the servants, the children's lessons, and a number of letters that she had promised to write for Meg. "As you are such a writer," Meg had said lightly, leaving her the list.

"How is Lady Winship?" Alvey asked Amble.

"Her ladyship keeps abed this morning. She is worn to a bone. But Sir Aydon is coming down this minute."

Sir Aydon entered and consumed his porridge in his accustomed morose silence. But Alvey was not disturbed by that; in fact, she was engrossed in perusal of a letter from Mr. Allgood at the Hexham circulating library, which had arrived along with a parcel of books.

"I send these things by hand," wrote Mr. Allgood, "for Whin Bob the clock mender informed me that he will pass Birkland today and I know him to be a reliable messenger. I am happy to inform you that the handwriting copybooks ordered by you have come in; and I also enclose another communication from your correspondent in the tropics. Knowing that matters relating to your sister's wedding may prevent your visiting Hexham in the near future, I thought it best . . ."

Another letter from Louisa was in the packet.

What a pity Meg and Isa missed it by so short a time, reflected Alvey, cutting open the sea-stained paper. However, she was soon bound to admit that Louisa's second letter, dated from Cape Town, was hardly more exciting than her first had been. Many of the details were the same—the sobriety and godliness of Mr. and Mrs. Tothill, the respectability of Captain Middlemass, the obligingness of the crew. Then there were animadversions on the beauty of Cape Town— where, unfortunately, they had not been able to pause above a day and a half because of favouring winds. There were allusions to the virtue and helpfulness of some of the officers, especially of a Lieutenant Dunnifage, and the convenience of the ship's accommodations; though it began, confessed Louisa, to be a little confining, housed in such a small vessel week after week. She would be glad when their destination was in sight. She hoped her parents were in continuing health and was their affct. sister Louisa Winship.

Parthie entered the room with a wan and suffering air, and cast a disappointed glance at the evidence of the young men's departure.

"Oh, it hurts so dreadfully to chew," she sighed, taking a large bite of bread and butter.

"Fiddlestick, girl!" growled Sir Aydon. "Folk get worse injuries every day in the hunting field and never give them a thought. Eat your breakfast and don't mope."

"Papa is right," agreed Alvey. "Food will do you good." And she handed Parthie a cup of coffee, giving her a commiserating smile, which was received stonily. Plainly, Parthie considered that she had been dealt utterly unfair treatment by fate.

At this moment James and Major Fenway re-entered the breakfast parlour looking extremely perturbed.

"Sir," said James, "I fear we bring you a piece of most disquieting news."

"Eh? Ha? Well? What is it?"

"My stepmother's garden has been—has been damaged in a very unpleasant way—"

"Laid waste," said the major more bluntly.

"Plants pulled up, cut down, *savaged*—"

"What is this you tell me?"

"I think you had better come and see, sir."

"Amble! Fetch me my greatcoat!"

The three men went out. Alvey followed them, wishing to see for herself.

In Lady Winship's enclosed garden the scene was as James had described it. Plants had been torn up, shrubs hacked to pieces, rocks and stones tossed from their beds and used to smash glass cloches protecting delicate growths; the whole charming dell had been mutilated and ravaged in, as James said, a very unpleasant manner. Not just senseless vandalism but real hate seemed to have been expressed by the kind of damage performed.

"Good Gad!" said Sir Aydon, aghast, gazing about him at the devastation. "This is malice—*barbarism*. Charlotte must on no account see this—it might kill her."

Carey, the gardener, was there, gloomily inspecting the wreckage. He and Sir Aydon conferred together in low tones.

"Have you any idea who might have committed such an act of mayhem?" Fenway said to James. "I thought your father was so popular, so greatly respected in the countryside?"

"So I would have said—this is something quite untoward. I have never seen anything like it. My wretched stepmother—this garden is her whole *raison d'être*—"

Tot and Nish had arrived with solemn faces and stared around them, awestruck.

"This took somebody a long time to do," said Tot.

Alvey had had the same thought. Some person must have been in the garden, hacking, slashing, and smashing, with undiminishing malevolence, for a number of hours. The idea was both unpleasant and frightening.

"It is unfortunate the garden is situated so far from the house."

"That is why Mamma likes it; because she is safe from being bothered."

Nish began to cry, gazing at a clump of saxifrage that had been kicked and stamped to pieces.

"It is like a murder!" she sobbed.

"Come indoors, children," said Alvey concernedly. "We can do nothing here."

She led the children back into the house. "Come, I have some new copybooks for you, we may as well go up to the Tower Room and you can do an exercise from them. That will settle you, and give you an occupation for your thoughts."

Up in the schoolroom she trimmed their pens, ruled their lines, and set them to work. Both children rather enjoyed copying, and applied themselves with goodwill, Tot only breaking off to say, "Who will tell my mother about the garden?"

"I expect your father will do that."

They continued working peacefully, but Alvey's thoughts could not be peaceful. The image of the ravaged garden was still before her eyes. Who could have done it? The same person who had thrown the stone at the wedding party? And how could the wrongdoer be discovered? Or, Alvey wondered, would it be best if the perpetrator were not discovered? An uneasy suspicion flitted across her mind, but was hastily banished—no, no, the idea was impossible! But suppose the family were to be the target for more disturbing acts of malice?

"I must leave you for a while," she said to the children. "I have several other tasks—letters to write, and I promised to help Mrs.

Slaley put away the silver. But I will come back later and read you about the Princes in the Tower."

The value of horrific episodes in the past, she thought, is that they distract us from our own terrors.

Then, for the first time, she recalled Louisa's letter, which she had left tucked among the children's copybooks. She sorted through the pile, but the letter was not there.

"Have you seen a letter—on rather sea-stained, crumpled paper?"

They shook their heads.

"Could I have left it on the breakfast table?"

Alvey ran downstairs. But the table had been cleared and polished; and Amble, when asked, disclaimed any knowledge of the letter. So did the maid Janet, now engaged in sweeping the room and putting it to rights.

Alvey revisited the Tower Room for a second and more careful search among the children's books but with no more success; the letter was not to be found.

Duddy entered the schoolroom while Alvey was still engaged in a fruitless search.

"Missus 'ud like a word wi' ye, Miss Emmy."

"Missus" in Duddy's case referred to the old lady, so Alvey followed the maid through the door from the spiral stair. Old Mrs. Winship was still in bed, propped against pillows, bundled up in her cashmere shawl. She peered at Alvey over her thick spectacles.

"What's this I hear about Charlotte's garden? I sent for James, I sent for Aydon, but they are out of doors; or they don't come, they don't heed me. I am of no account in this house any more. Go away, Duddy, go away, and see if you cannot make one of them come."

It must be hard, Alvey thought, when you grow old, to feel the threads of command slackening and slipping from your hands. Especially when you have been used to govern. Sometime, she thought, I must ask the old lady about her past; about her youth, and the years when she was in command of this house. She must have many stories to tell. But not just at this time.

Mrs. Winship did not look at all well today; her ghostly pallor was even more pronounced than usual, and a slight tremor was visible in her head and hands. The wedding breakfast must have been a fearful ordeal for her too, though she had seemed to enjoy it more than her son and his wife.

As Alvey described the wreckage in the garden, old Grizel listened with pursed lips, her glasses in her hand, her eyes fixed myopically on vacancy.

"Somebody hates my daughter-in-law," she remarked, in a matter-of-fact tone, at the end of the account.

She is like Tot and Nish, Alvey thought. Straight to the heart of the affair; no needless exclamations.

"Who do you think could have done it, ma'am?"

Old Grizel did not answer that question. She murmured to herself, "This will be a bad blow to Charlotte. When you possess nothing but a garden—and that is taken from you—you are singularly ill equipped to sustain the misfortune. Other people mean nothing to you; so you can receive no comfort from them."

"Does *nobody* in this house mean anything to her, Grandmother?"

Mrs. Winship put the glasses back on her nose and then peered at Alvey over the top of them. Still she did not reply.

"Where is Parthie?" she presently demanded querulously.

"I think it possible that she has returned to bed. She is in low spirits, with her black eye and bruised cheek; she complained of a headache."

Or, Alvey thought, it was possible that Parthie was dogging the footsteps of Major Fenway.

The old lady echoed her thought.

"Dangling round that friend of James's, more like. A clever, well-conducted man. Pity he's such an ugly, unimpressive stick of a fellow. — No, I'll not rise from my bed today. Find me the Crabbe poems, girl, and the spermaceti and the hazel oil and my little ivory mirror and my Bible. Oh, and the letters from your poor aunt Elinor in Bath —I wish to reread them."

Occupied on these errands, Alvey wondered if there would be any purpose in asking old Mrs. Winship if she had seen the letter from Louisa. Could Parthie have removed it from the breakfast table? She had been the only person in the room when Alvey left it—apart from Amble. Or had one of the servants merely assumed it to be wastepaper and thrown it on the fire?

"I don't seem to be able to find the Crabbe poems, Grandmother.

Did you take them downstairs? Nor can I lay my hand on the spermaceti oil."

"Have you looked in all the drawers, child?"

"Every one. And I have searched in all the other places I can think
of."

There were not so many possible repositories in the bare room.

"I do not know how it is," said the old lady fretfully, "but I seem to
lose more and more articles every day. And when I make lists of
where I put things, then I lose the lists. I think God does not mean me
to have possessions. He is reminding me that it is high time I set out
on my last journey, and there are no porters and no boxes for travellers on *that* road . . . You had better put a linseed poultice on
Parthie's face; that will reduce the inflammation. And send Aydon to
me if you see him; and James."

Thus dismissed, Alvey went about her other duties. Parthie was
discovered back in her room, wrapped in shawls and self-pity. When
Alvey knocked and entered she hastily thrust some object under her
pile of pillows, and then threw herself back against them with a
martyred sigh and a die-away expression. Offered a linseed poultice,
she resentfully declined it, saying that the wound was well enough
under Tushie's court plaster.

"How about the chipped tooth? Does it pain you very greatly? I
suppose you should see a dentist. Is there one in Hexham?"

"Oh no! It is not— I do not wish that at all."

"Then can I do anything else for you? Fetch you a warm drink?
Read to you?"

"*Read* to me? I thank you, no!" With a theatrical sob, Parthie slid
farther down the pillows, muttering, "Nobody in the house cares
whether I live or die, and you offer to *read* to me!"

"Well," Alvey said reasonably, "there are several people here in
worse case than you, after all. Poor James with his leg, and your
grandmother gravely overtired, and your mother having sustained
such a dreadful calamity—how is she, by the bye?"

"Mamma? Oh, she fainted." Parthie imparted this news without the
least sympathy in her tone. "When my father informed her that her
garden had been destroyed she fell into such a deep faint that Major
Fenway gave orders for her to be carried to bed and her stay laces cut.

He is with her now, administering soothing draughts; has been this hour."

"Oh, my gracious! Poor Lady—poor Mamma." Wisely deciding to take no notice of a glance full of malice and animosity from Parthie's pale eyes, Alvey reflected: And that is why *you* have taken to your bed, my girl, and are lying here in hopes of a similar medical visit from the major.

"Well, I will send up Tushie by and by with a nuncheon for you," she said kindly, and went out, closing the door.

Now I suppose I ought to go along to Lady Winship's room and offer my services, she thought, with some reluctance.

So exiguous was the bond between Lady Winship and her grown daughters that neither Meg nor Isa ever thought of setting foot in their mother's bedchamber, and Alvey was not even certain of its exact whereabouts, though she knew that it lay among the suite of rooms that ran along the east front of the house, above the drawing room. Hesitating outside the row of doors, she was relieved to see the maid Ellen emerge from one of them.

"How is she—how is my mother? May I go in to her?"

"Reckon she's still in a swound, Miss Emmy. Reet nasty one it was, wi' convulsions an' all. The major's given her a dram—he's a-watching over her yet, in yonder"—she nodded to the door from which she had appeared. "He said as how there's naught more to be done for her noo. Ye can gan in, miss, if ye will—ye can do no harm, that's for sure."

"Where is Sir Aydon?"

"Took hisself off to his library, the poor maister did. Mebbe Mester James is with him."

Encouraged by this qualified permission, Alvey entered the bedroom, walking on tiptoe.

Major Fenway, sitting on the bed, rose and laid a finger to his lips, then drew Alvey over to the window, which commanded a wholly uninteresting prospect over the shrubbery that lay beside the front carriage sweep. How strange, thought Alvey, that of all the possible rooms with commanding views from their windows in this house, the mistress of it should occupy a chamber with no view at all.

It was true that the room was large and handsome, amply furnished and richly decorated. Perhaps it had always been the master bedroom and Lady Winship was given no choice in the matter. Doors on either side led to dressing rooms or powdering closets.

"How is she?" murmured Alvey. "Is there any way in which I can be of use?"

"No, I thank you," he returned in the same tone, but with a very kind look. "It is an exceedingly bad faint; it seems to me highly possible that the boy Thomas may have inherited his epileptic proclivity from his mother's side of the family; I do not expect that she will come out of it for several hours yet. I think I had best be at hand when she does—I have some little experience with this kind of collapse. But there is no occasion for you to remain also; I am sure you have many duties that call you—"

"Principally keeping those poor children occupied—"

"If you can likewise find some distraction for your brother James it would be a good deed," Fenway said softly. "He is in dreadfully low spirits."

"I am not certain that he will accept distraction at my hands. But I will do my best."

Alvey smiled at the major, threw a quick, nervous glance at the great bed, where Lady Winship's massive body lay totally inert, motionless, like a carved figure on a tomb. It was strange and rather frightening to see that usually high-coloured face so pale and grey, to see the large vague staring eyes now closed and lightless. Fenway must be right, she thought. This seemed no ordinary faint.

Casting one more quick, inquisitive scrutiny round the room, Alvey silently withdrew.

It was rather tantalising, she thought, with a touch of self-pity, that, just when she was made free of a room all to herself, in which she might sit writing all day long without interruption—just when she had acquired this unheard-of luxury—so very many misfortunes and distractions supervened to prevent her making full use of her privilege. And she had such a quantity of new escapades in mind for Lord Love! But there was Mrs. Slaley waiting for the silver to be counted—and she had promised to read about the Princes in the Tower to the children—and now Major Fenway had saddled her with the additional responsibility of James—besides which, the thought of Sir Aydon, forlorn and solitary in his library, lay like a shadow at the back of her mind—

Bracing herself, Alvey ran briskly down the stairs.

X

"Go away, child," said Mrs. Winship irritably to Parthie. "You look a *sight!* I don't desire to have you about me until you are more pleasing to the eye."

"But, Grandmamma, I want to *tell* you something—"

"Not now, miss! I have been told by far too many things already this day—I do not wish to hear any more scandal or disaster. Be off with you—go and pester Major Fenway—I daresay he will be prepared to listen to you with more complaisance."

Scarlet-cheeked, Parthie closed her grandmother's door with something of a slam. For it was no use going in search of the major, she knew full well; he was still with Lady Winship.

"What shall you do, sir, about searching for the villain who did the damage to my stepmother's garden?" James was saying, downstairs in the library.

"Oh? Ha, humph. Precious little that *can* be done, I fancy. Why, what d'ye expect me to do? Summon the Bow Street Runners? No, no, there's not a deal that can be effected—only supply poor Charlotte with the funds to put the place to rights again; I don't see my way to do anything more than that—"

"But, sir, surely you wish to bring the fellow to book?"

Sir Aydon's face closed up—like an oyster, Alvey would have thought, if she had been there to note down the simile.

"That would only be to prolong the whole scandal; I am persuaded it is the *last* thing Madam would wish. Of course," he mentioned as an afterthought, "naturally I shall consult her wishes when she is—when she is more herself. We are fortunate in having your friend Fenway here at this juncture. Not that I consider such medical activities lie within the province of a gentleman—hmn, ha!—damned peculiar sort of propensity—comes from a decent family too, can't understand it—lucky *you* ain't by way of having such tastes—still it certainly falls well for us in the present circumstances—"

"Sir—"

"Which brings me to another matter, my boy. When do the leeches and bloodletters consider that you may be ready to rejoin your regiment? Not that we ain't happy to see you here for a spell, of course," he added hurriedly, "but I daresay you won't be wishing to kick your heels at home a day longer than you need, ha, hm?"

"Well, sir, in respect of that, I—"

Luckily, or unluckily, for James, at this moment Mr. Thropton was announced.

The rector bustled in, all concern and commiseration.

"Seeing not one of the family present at matins—being apprised, later this morning, of the new and shocking occurrence that has afflicted you—felt it my duty to come in person—"

He hopes to be invited to dinner and take a share of the cold pigeon pie, thought James sourly, though he was aware in himself of a certain guilty and shamed relief at the rector's arrival.

"Ha! Mr. Thropton. Good morning; you find us at sixes and sevens, I fear—"

And we wish you at the devil, Sir Aydon's expression said, so plainly that Amble, still hovering, murmured, "Would you wish me to send for Miss Louisa, Sir Aydon?"

"Do so, Amble, will you? I cannot remain with you just at present, Mr. Thropton, I fear; I have to discover how my poor wife goes on; quite prostrated, you know, utterly cut up by this last catastrophe. By the bye, Amble, could you tell the servants to look sharp for Lady Winship's ring—noticed, when she was laid out on her bed, that it was missing from her finger. Knocked off when she fainted, perhaps; she'll be sorry to come to and find it missing."

Amble murmured a promise that the ring should be sought; though he ventured to think that the ring had been missing before today; he could not recollect seeing it on my lady's finger of late.

Sir Aydon hurried off to escape from Mr. Thropton, going upstairs, not to his wife's bedchamber but to the dressing room adjacent, which he had occupied, on and off, since his hunting accident.

Alvey, descending the stairs, heard Mr. Thropton's unctuous tones issuing from the library and hesitated—but she also heard the voice of James, sharp with strain and reserve.

"—Excessively hard on my parents: my father still not himself—the child's death—"

James is doing his best to make it plain, thought Alvey, that he himself has no personal interest in the matter of the child's death.

Amble intercepted her and whispered in her ear, "Sir Aydon asked, Miss Emmy, as how you'd entertain the reverend gentleman, for he finds himself a touch overset—"

Their eyes met with perfect comprehension. Alvey nodded resignedly.

"Bring a bottle of Madeira to the library, Amble."

"Oh, and Miss Emmy, have you seen Madam's ring anywhere—her signet ring?"

Alvey had not; she could not even recollect seeing a signet on Lady Winship's finger. What a lot of things seem to be lost in this house, she thought; that is certainly one disadvantage of living in a mansion. Nothing could be lost for long in Cousin Hepzie's house . . .

"Aha, what do I see! The lovely Miss Louisa! But how truly distressed I was, dear Miss Louisa, to see none of you at divine service—"

Oh, good God, thought Alvey, what a scandalous thing. It is Sunday, of course!

She said, smoothly: "I am sure you will comprehend how it was, Mr. Thropton. My mother and grandmother so fatigued by the events of yesterday—my father too, indeed—and then this new horrifying outrage. But I had proposed coming down, later, to the rectory, to thank you for your most important part in yesterday's ceremony."

And thank goodness I don't have to do that now, she thought, disengaging her hand from his clammy clasp. Past his shoulder she noticed James's expression of strain lifted by a faint relief at her arrival; he gave her a look of gratitude and her heart rose, absurdly.

Amble brought the wine and poured it, while Mr. Thropton continued to discourse about the wedding, which, he flattered himself, had gone off in the most elegant possible style—due to the eminence of the family, and the superiority of their connections, and the dignity and respectability of the congregation, the charming looks of the bride— Here he waited for one of his auditors to compliment him on the eloquence of his sermon but as neither of them did so he himself mentioned a very touching tribute paid to it "by my old friend Lady Edmondbyers"—and the pleasing air of naturalness contributed by the youthful attendants. He means when Tot tripped over Meg's train, thought Alvey, plying Mr. Thropton with Madeira. From the wedding he went on to talk about his Roman excavations. "I flatter myself that you would not be uninterested in them, Mr. Winship—I believe I am right in saying that you pursued the study of history at the university? Any time that you care to come and inspect them I shall be greatly honoured—Miss Louisa knows that she is always a welcome guest—" and from the excavations he somehow managed to lead the conversation back to the subject of Annie Herdman's baby.

"Such an exceedingly regrettable pair of fatalities—especially occurring in such a small and remote community—arousing a not unnatural hostility, I fear, towards your family—"

"Oh," said James, cutting through the flow (rather like, thought Alvey, a person with a pair of sharp shears chopping through an unwieldy thicket of brambles, as she had seen Carey doing two days before). "Oh, you are suggesting, are you, Mr. Thropton, that the two acts of aggression, the thrown rock and the damage to my stepmother's garden, are intended as an act of retaliation for those two unhappy deaths? I suppose it might be possible; if, that is to say, my father, in his capacity as Justice of the Peace, has not recently had any poachers transported or flogged?"

He spoke with an assumed air of cold composure which plainly irritated Mr. Thropton. His already florid complexion reddened even more deeply.

James ought to try to be a little conciliating, thought Alvey; but I can't find it in my heart to blame him. Mr. Thropton is such an odious man.

"Do you yourself, Mr. Thropton, hold any particular suspicion as to the perpetrator? Birkland is a very small village, after all."

"Some friend, relation, or past suitor, you mean, of the unfortunate girl?" Mr. Thropton said delicately. "She is not known to have had any such suitor; and her only relative, her father (a most disagreeable, uncouth fellow, and otherwise a likely candidate for the part of villain), is known to be away at present, visiting, I understand, a brother at Riding Mill. — But of course all these village families are connected and interconnected, not only with each other but by ties crisscrossing over the whole county. I must confess I always thought it a *most* injudicious move to receive that girl into the house here; condoning her fault, almost rewarding it, you might say."

"Annie must have had some suitor," James remarked, "or she could not have borne a child."

"*Mr. Winship!* Pray! Remember that you are in the presence of your sister!"

The eyes of James and Alvey met. Their faces remained carefully expressionless. But Alvey said, "You forget, Mr. Thropton, how often in this house I have heard the subject canvassed. You may, if you please, consider me unshockable."

Mr. Thropton's eyes bulged with outrage. He said, "Nonetheless, Miss Louisa, I must consider it a wholly improper remark, wholly unsuitable for the ears of a pure and unblemished young lady such as yourself." And, so saying, he cast her a look of so lingering, meaningful, and lascivious a nature that Alvey, startled to death, had the sudden thought: Could *Mr. Thropton* have been the father of wee Geordie? I would not at all have put it past him to seduce a village girl, now that I consider the matter. And then he would have told her to say that the child was James's—since he himself could never acknowledge paternity or support her—but if she could get her story accepted at the Hall, then they would both be secure enough—

"It is certainly a pity that old Herdman was away," remarked James thoughtfully. "For he is, as you say, a very likely suspect." And that is about the only sensible thing that you have said, his tone suggested.

Mr. Thropton, having put down four glasses of Madeira and seeing no likelihood of being invited to dinner, at last stood up to go.

"Should I, perhaps, pay a visit to the sickbed of your mamma?" he offered.

"To the best of my knowledge, she is still unconscious. My medical friend Major Fenway is watching over her. There would be little purpose in such a visit. At a later date, perhaps." James's tone was uncompromising, and Alvey said firmly, "My brother is right, Mr. Thropton."

"But there is another member of the family who stands in need of my consolation and solace—poor little Miss Parthenope, subject of such a rude and shocking assault. May I not take her some pastoral comfort?"

Again the eyes of James and Alvey met. His, this time, were inquiring.

"Well, I do not see why not," Alvey said thoughtfully. "She might well be glad of the attention." In default of the major, she added internally.

"Oh, by all means visit Parthie if you wish to," agreed James. "The wretched girl's spirits were quite cut up by missing the party; I daresay she will be very much obliged to you. Amble: have one of the maids show Mr. Thropton to Miss Parthie's room."

As Mr. Thropton's portly form disappeared upstairs in the wake of Tushie, James brushed a hand over his forehead and let out a long breath of relief.

"What a pestilential fellow," he murmured. "No wonder my father beat a strategic retreat."

And he gave Alvey what almost amounted to a smile.

Major Fenway had been sitting by Lady Winship's bed for more than three hours when she stirred slightly and let out a faint moan. He held a bottle of smelling salts to her nostrils, sprinkled her face with a few drops of cold water, and when she finally opened her eyes, gave her a spoonful of sal volatile.

Turning his head, he softly called the maid Ellen, who had been sitting in a corner and came swiftly to the bedside.

"Oh, ma'am! Are you feeling better? What a dreadful fright you gave us! Is there owt you'd fancy? Some wine? Or tea?"

"No—no—nothing. Only to be left in peace."

"Her extremities are very cold," said Fenway. "Fetch some hot bottles. And a hot brick for her feet."

These were brought, and Lady Winship submitted to having her hands chafed, a pillow placed beneath her head, and a comforter wrapped more warmly round her. But then she began to sob and said again, "Leave me alone! Only leave me in peace!"

"But, ma'am, all we want is to help you."

"Well—you can't. Go away. No—not you"—to the major. *"You* stay here. You saw my garden. You know what I have lost. Be off, Ellen! Shut the door as you go."

"Oh, ma'am—" But Fenway gave Ellen a nod, and she did as she was bid.

"You are anxious to talk about the garden, Lady Winship?" said Fenway. "I believe that to do so might relieve your feelings."

"No—yes—not about the garden. I deserved to lose it. I know I did."

"Why so?" he asked gently.

She sobbed suddenly. "Oh, I have been very wicked. Listen—"

Going in search of the children, Alvey found the Tower Room empty. They had, however, carefully completed their tasks, which they must have tackled with unusual speed. Glancing out of the spiral-stair window, as she went down again, she saw them beside the Lion Pool, conducting one of their ceremonies. Their heads were bowed and they were chanting.

Alvey fought a short internal battle with herself. On the one hand, Lord Love beckoned, more insistently than ever. The stress and trouble in the household, displayed in one way or another by almost all its inmates, made her long more than ever to escape to her private well-organised world; but, somehow, she had come to consider this pair of children as her own particular charge, and she felt specially responsible for them in the present situation. Duty won; sighing, she went on down and crossed the carriage sweep to the pool.

They had collected a basketful of the bruised and broken flower heads from Lady Winship's garden, and were sprinkling them on the surface of the water, meanwhile quietly muttering a kind of litany.

"Deliver us from ourselves, O Mithras, god of crops, enemy of evil spirits, master of light, champion of armies, protector of souls."

"And accept our sacrifice."

"Deliver us from other people, also."

"And accept our sacrifice."

"Deliver us from people who seem to hate our family."
"And accept our sacrifice."
"Deliver us specially from Mr. Thropton."
"And accept our sacrifice."
"Deliver us from ourselves, in case we offend thee."
"And accept our sacrifice."

Alvey waited until they had finished. Then Nish said to her, "Mamma won't be cross, will she, that we took the flowers from her garden? They were all broken in any case; they would only have died."

"No, I am sure she would not object. And she is very ill, hardly conscious. Major Fenway is still with her."

"We thought she would not mind," said Tot. And he added gruffly, "Perhaps Mithras will help her to make a new garden."

"*Why* did somebody *do* it?" cried Nish. "Do you think it was because of Annie and wee Geordie?" She gazed fearfully at Alvey. "Will they do it again?"

"We must hope not," said Alvey, as calmly as she could. "We must hope that whoever it was now feels that they have avenged what— whatever wrong was done to them."

The children were silent, obviously pondering over the savage act of reprisal, if reprisal it had been.

Nish said, "Suppose the person had done it to our islands! We never mind if the river rises and washes them away; that's one thing; but if some person were to come and smash them all on *purpose—*"

To turn their thoughts in a less menacing direction, Alvey said, "Tell me some more about Mithras. You seem on very good terms with him. How did you know the Lion Pool belonged to him? And where did you acquire all your knowledge of Mithraic practises?"

"Oh, it was a Latin exercise that Mr. Thropton gave us. All about the underground temple, you know, and what the people said at their services—"

"And the bulls," put in Tot.

"There are seven classes of people who serve Mithras."

"The raven, the ghost, the soldier, the lion, the Persian—"

"The sun's messenger, and the father."

"Nish is a ghost, and I'm a soldier. You can be a raven, sister
Emmy, if you wish—"

Alvey wondered what Mr. Thropton's attitude would be to this
enthusiastic adoption by his pupils of the Mithraic religion.

"Have you talked to Mr. Thropton about it?"

"Oh *no!*" said Tot in disgust.

"Hush, there he comes," said Nish. "Don't let him see what we are
about. Besides, Emmy, I want to ask you about my story. I'm stuck
where the seals come out of the water and I don't know what to make
them say—"

They caught Alvey's hands and pulled her away from the pool, to
the cobbled path that ran beside the pele tower.

Mr. Thropton saw them, but said nothing. Alvey had half expected
that he would wish to speak to her again, but, to her relief, he neither
paused nor beckoned, only threw towards her one very singular
glance—hostile, it seemed, doubtful, suspicious, *angry*—before striding off homewards through the pine trees.

What had Parthie been saying to him?

I suppose Father would consider, thought Alvey, that I am encouraging these children in idolatry; that I should give them a severe
talking-to and make them promise not to worship Mithras any more.
But, firstly, I am quite sure they would take not the least notice of
my order; it would only impair the good understanding which is growing up between us; and, secondly, if the observances comfort them, I
believe it is better they should continue; no doubt it will die away
naturally as they grow older.

Heaven knows there is little enough comfort in this house at present.

Nish has a remarkable faculty for story weaving, thought Alvey; and
stifled a faint, envious twinge. Would this untaught, spontaneous gift
one day excel that of her teacher?

Rather to Alvey's surprise, the old lady came down to dinner. But
she hardly appeared her usual self; she was vague, inattentive, her
clothes were untidy, she spoke little, and ate practically nothing.

Sir Aydon had decreed that Nish and Tot should have their supper before the adults, in the kitchen, and retire early to bed; he was weary, he said, and did not wish to be bothered by the chatter and clatter of children. Parthie would have been insulted and furious at such an order, but dining-room dinner, to which they had only recently been promoted, was no treat to her younger siblings, and they obeyed without apparent regret. "Mrs. Slaley gives us much better supper in the kitchen," said Nish.

Parthie herself still kept to her room and sent down a plaintive request to the kitchen for "something light."

"I tuk her oop a big basin o' hodgepodge, Miss Emmy, an' three lemon cheesecakes, an' she et the lot; there's naught amiss wi' her appetite. But yon black eye's turning all manner o' colours—green, yaller, an' orange; racken she divvn't want the major to see it," said Ellen.

The party around the dinner table, thus reduced in number, ate, for the most part, in silence, and talk was confined to perfunctory and trivial topics. Alvey felt it no part of the duty of a daughter of the house to make light conversation at such a time; she meditated about her story, and replied civilly but briefly to Major Fenway's one or two polite inquiries about her own school days and the children's lessons.

Sir Aydon's mood was perturbed and gloomy; even for him, unusually so, even considering the distressing circumstances.

Informed kindly and carefully by the major that his wife had recovered consciousness, had accepted a little sal volatile followed by a brandy posset with a sedative in it, had talked for a while in a rational manner but expressed a wish not to be troubled by seeing any members of her family just at present, Sir Aydon merely grunted. Whether this response denoted belief or disbelief, approval or disapproval, Alvey was unable to decide; really he is very uncivil to the major, who, merely a guest after all, is taking such good care of his wife, she thought, and pitied James, obliged to be embarrassed by his parent's uncouth behaviour. But James, crumbling untasted bread, appeared absorbed in his own thoughts, hardly aware of what took place at the table.

"Ah; errh; humph," said Sir Aydon presently. "Great pity you had the ill fortune to visit my house at such a time, Major Fenway."

"Pray, sir, don't regard it. I am only glad if I have been able to be of any assistance."

"Harrumph. Appreciate what you have done. Don't recall—that is —forget when you said you required to reach Edinburgh. I have sent off for Madam's own medical adviser from Newcastle—Dr. Cunningham—fellow should be here tomorrow, I trust. Don't wish to detain you unduly—presume you have business of your own to transact—"

Good God, thought Alvey, outraged, now Sir Aydon wants to get rid of the major. He is hinting that Fenway has outstayed his welcome, and in no very subtle or delicate way!

Pink with indignation, she opened her mouth to speak; but then she noticed the two young men exchange significant and wary looks. Well, it is no affair of mine, she decided; let James deal with the matter. Major Fenway is his friend, after all.

"Why, sir, the sooner I am embarked on my course of study in that town, the better it will be," Fenway answered calmly. "Once assured of James's well-being—and satisfied that Lady Winship is in a fair way to recover and under professional care—"

"Quite. Quite, quite, quite. She will do well enough now—persuaded of that. Sad, shocking business about the garden—can't be helped. Hope to replace it in due course. Think it best for all if the matter is alluded to as little as possible—less to remind her—"

No! thought Alvey in protest. That is not at all the way to deal with it. — And yet she felt a flicker of sympathy with Sir Aydon, recalling her strange flash of response on first seeing him, which had died away almost entirely as she grew to know him better. He wants his son, his house to himself, at this time of crisis he is irked by the presence of strangers, especially this friend of James's, whom he perhaps believes to be secretly in league with his son against him—poor man, he longs for his household to return to its old orderliness. Yet how can it? A household is a growing, changing organism like any other.

"Ma'am," said Alvey in the drawing room after dinner, "are you sure you would not prefer to retire?" For the old lady looked so troubled and restless, so shaky and frail; she made one or two ineffectual attempts to work at her embroidery, then put it away and, instead, drew a paper out of her reticule, on which she jotted down a couple of words with a trembling hand.

"Go to bed? No, no. I am better here. I am better here," she repeated. "In case—" But she did not finish her sentence.

When the gentlemen came into the drawing room, Mrs. Winship beckoned her son to come and sit by her, which he rather reluctantly did.

The young men sat near Alvey, and their talk ranged over a number of topics, from the tumbling prices of corn, riots, frame breaking, and the activities of Orator Hunt, on the one hand, to the poetry of Lord Byron and various plays to be seen at Drury Lane and Covent Garden, on the other. Both James and Fenway had seen Kean several times and agreed with the poet Coleridge that his acting was terrific—demonic—like flashes of lightning. Alvey had read about him, and longed to hear descriptions of his performances as Shylock, Richard III, or Iago. She listened intently and said little.

"You have never been to the London theatre, Miss Louisa?" Fenway asked.

"Oh no," she sighed. "If only it were possible—"

She had a tiny income bequeathed her by Cousin Hepzie, and a small stock of savings accrued from private teaching at the Abbey School; but, looking ahead to her precarious future, she had felt that visits to London theatres would be an unwarrantable extravagance.

"Well, Kean will not be there much longer. He is going to New York," Fenway remarked, and added, to Alvey's great surprise, "I should think the New Yorkers will worship him. When I was in that city there was only the most paltry stuff to be seen on the stage."

"When were you there, Guy?" James asked.

"Humph! It will be about five years ago—before that foolish war with the Americans. My father wished me to go over and study their ways of mining and transporting coal; I was among some devilish little mining towns in Pennsylvania, and then took a bolt to the city to get the taste of coal dust and sourdough bread out of my mouth. — Though Philadelphia was a pleasant town enough—brick houses and lilac trees; it quite put me in mind of Ramsgate or Deal."

Alvey found herself much tantalised; she longed to ask the major about his experiences in America and opinions on that land—whether he had been farther north than New York, had visited any towns in Massachusetts; but feared to do so lest by some slip of the tongue she might betray more knowledge herself than she might be expected to possess. But his mention of her birthland aroused in her homesick feelings of which she had hardly been aware.

James asked about the coal mining. Alvey had already learned from his daughters that Sir Aydon, like Major Fenway's father, owned land on which coal was worked; which fact, with his wife's holdings, rather than his somewhat mismanaged estates, enabled him to dower his daughters with five thousand apiece.

"I believe my father would be interested to hear this—" James was saying, when raised voices on the opposite side of the room caused him to look that way with a nervous frown.

"—You live in the past, Aydon, it is not right, it is cowardly," the old lady stated in her resonant, harsh voice. In her displeasure she appeared to have shaken off the confused, tremulous mood of earlier in the evening.

Her son muttered something inaudible by way of reply, glancing at the young people.

"Fiddlestick, Aydon! Every generation says so; but that is not true. You must not allow the past to become more important to you than the present, you are by no means old enough for such a habit. Why, man, look at me! Twenty-two years your senior, and I can still find diversion enough in what I see around me. It is wrong to make the past your only good; that is like allowing parts of yourself, your limbs, to become dried up, corrupt, gangrenous—"

Beside her, Alvey felt James shiver.

"You have to make something useful of the world around you, which means endowing it with a portion of yourself. If you neglect to do this, you are betraying your trust—"

Alvey had never heard the old woman speak so vehemently; was it the absence of her daughter-in-law that liberated and galvanised her? If I had a grandmother to speak like this to my father, to my mother, thought Alvey, would it have influenced their actions, would matters have fallen out differently? *Do* people ever influence the actions of others? I suspect the old lady is not making much impression on Sir Aydon.

She noticed that Guy Fenway was listening with absorbed interest to the dialogue between Mrs. Winship and her son.

"Trust, trust!" grumbled Sir Aydon. *"What* trust? Did I ever ask for a parcel of chattering girls? Or a sulky, seedy lad who can't even pull a fish out of a brook?"

Alvey stood up. Delicacy, she felt, forbade that such a personal discussion should have auditors; she could not play the piano like Meg and she was in no mood to start a counter-theme.

"It has been a tiring, distressing day," she said to James. "I shall go up and see if Parthie needs anything; and—and poor Mamma; then I shall retire—"

James nodded without any particular interest. It was Guy Fenway's eyes which followed her, Guy who seemed disappointed in her early retreat. Alvey curtseyed to the old lady, who acknowledged this with an abstracted nod, and to Sir Aydon, who hardly seemed to observe her.

"Ma'am, you dropped your paper." Alvey picked up the crumpled sheet from the floor and handed it back to Mrs. Winship. After visiting Parthie, who was asleep (or sulking), and Lady Winship, also asleep, she hurried to her own refuge and, as usual, experienced an extraordinary lift of the heart the moment she stepped inside its sheltering door. To have a room of her very own! What a rare privilege. Even Lady Winship, Alvey reflected, was not so lucky; Sir Aydon might invade her territory, disturb her train of thought, at any moment he chose; she had no retreat, poor woman, but her garden. Her garden . . .

Soberly, Alvey made her toilet. She jotted down a few notes, with a curious little pang recalling the old lady's memorandum sheet. Upon it were written the same two words, over and over: "Make lists, make lists, make lists . . ." What a paradoxical creature old Grizel was, one moment so confused, the next so clear and forthright.

Alvey blew out her candle. In the screening darkness—as it had done for several nights past—a face came to beguile her from sleep: not the familiar satirical countenance of Wicked Lord Love, but the face of James, haggard, unhappy, with its wide sensitive mouth and searching eyes.

Alvey was engaged with the children and their lessons next morning when Guy Fenway found his way to the Tower Room.

"So this is where the Goddess of Learning has her temple," he remarked, inspecting the globes, the maps, the books, and the drawings of flowers and animals with which Alvey had allowed the children to enliven the walls.

"How is La—my mother this morning?" Alvey asked him, knowing he had been to visit Lady Winship after breakfast.

"Her temperature is down."

"Temperature?"

"I have a thermometer for measuring degrees of fever." He produced the instrument in its little leather case and displayed it to the interested children. "You have not seen one before? It was invented by a Dr. Currie of Liverpool, some twenty years ago, but the use of them is not widespread as yet."

"Dr. Cunningham, who looks after Mamma, does not have one," said Tot. "All *he* does is feel your head with his hand."

"And if he is an experienced physician, his deductions are probably just as accurate as those of a medical beginner like myself," said Guy cheerfully. "May I go up and look at the view from your roof? James has told me that it is very fine. But I do not wish to interrupt your studies."

Naturally the children were only too anxious to accompany him and impart information relating to features of the landscape visible from the tower: Hammerton Crag, 576 feet high, from which Scots raiders had thrown down various members of the Winship family to their death; Crampton Cleugh, down which other members of the Winship family had rushed in retaliation on the Scots, uttering their battle cry of "Yet, yet, yet!" and dispatching seventeen Scots in the ensuing battle; the little wood on the far side of the valley known as Michael Scott's wood.

"Who is Michael Scott?"

"Oh, he is a wizard, a friend of the Evil One. He built the Roman Wall, you know, sir."

"I had thought the Romans built it?"

"Oh well, you can believe what you choose, I suppose."

"I quite prefer your version," Guy said. "I wish you could show me some of these places? Your brother is having his wooden leg fitted this morning"—Alvey flinched a little, but the children received this piece of information as calmly as it was imparted—"so he will not be able to take me about the policies; and tomorrow I must leave and go on my way to Edinburgh. What do you say, Miss Louisa? Might they have a half holiday—may I beg your indulgence?"

"I am sure you can see that I would get little work out of them after that," Alvey said, smiling. "In point of fact I do not usually keep them in after the hour of noon. And I am sure that you will enliven the excursion with instructive and improving conversation."

"Will you not accompany us?" he asked in a disappointed tone, as the children ran off to find jackets and hats, for the weather grew daily colder.

"I? Oh no, I fear I have too many duties within doors. And the children will be much better guides." Ignoring his look of protest, she left him, for Duddy, the old lady's maid, had come tapping at the Tower Room door, asking if Alvey could spare Mrs. Winship a moment.

"She's no' feeling so grand this morn, Miss Emmy; aa wish ye'd come and tek a luk at her."

Duddy's attitude towards Alvey had modified during the last weeks from a dour distrust to a grudging respect; this request was quite the highest mark of esteem yet shown by her, and Alvey felt proportionately pleased, but also apprehensive; what kind of state could old Grizel be in to cause such disquiet in Duddy, who was generally equal to any crisis?

"I will see you later, at dinnertime," she said absently to the major. "Don't let the children lead you into a bog. There are many, and quite dangerous—" as she followed Duddy down the winding stair.

Old Mrs. Winship was very tremulous and confused. She lay in bed turning a couple of velvet patches over and over in her thin fingers. Evidently she had reverted to her mood of yesterday evening before the sudden vigorous hortatory address to her son after dinner.

"Nothing more can be done about it now," she said querulously to Alvey. "What is the use of recrimination? The deed was done, and was avenged."

"What deed, Grandmother?"

"There is no sense in carrying matters further; and so I told Aydon.

An eye for an eye, a tooth for a tooth—a body has only two eyes, after all . . ."

"I do not perfectly follow you, ma'am—"

"Oh, don't be a fool, girl," said the old lady crossly. "Has *no* one about me any sense at *all?* James, utterly set on his course—Aydon, refusing to value what he has—and as for Charlotte, heaven only knows what can be done about *her*—"

"Oh, ma'am, won't you tell me what you would wish me to do?"

The blazing, shortsighted eyes finally focussed on Alvey.

"Oh yes—you," she remarked feebly. "You, the grit in the oyster. Is it because of you that all this has come about?"

"No, no, Grandmother. Me? What can you possibly mean?" queried Alvey, with a sudden hollow feeling of apprehension.

"No matter, no matter. I have made my dispositions. They are not much. Oh, but you had best—in case—before I forget anything else— I lose so many articles these days—and what I don't lose I overlook— Duddy, give it to her: you know what."

"The ring, ma'am?" Duddy, during this discourse, had stood with a grim face at the foot of the bed, her arms folded in her apron.

"Of course the ring, what else, woman?"

Duddy threw a look of doubt, of disagreement at Mrs. Winship, but in obedience to her mistress's vigorous, repeated nods, finally crossed to the fireplace and, to Alvey's considerable surprise, rummaged in the wood basket under the pine logs in it, and came up with a little packet, wrapped in yet another velvet patch, and tied with thread.

Alvey received it perplexedly.

"What is this? Should I undo it?"

The old woman nodded again, and she broke the thread. Inside the velvet wrapping she found a gold signet ring with a dark jade seal containing what she recognised as the Winship crest: a pinnace under sail.

"But this—can it be—Lady Win—my mother's signet ring that was missing? I heard Sir Aydon speak of it—"

"Just be sure she has it back. That is all. Don't make a stir about it."

"I will take it to her directly."

"No *talking*—" said the old lady, and suddenly curled herself up, huddling down in the bed like a child worn out with effort.

Duddy gave a slight, gloomy nod.

"That'll be a weight off her mind, ony road, Miss Emmy."

Alvey went, as she had promised, directly to Lady Winship's chamber. What a contrast it presented, she thought, with its carpets and furnishings, to the old lady's spare, austere retreat. And yet the younger woman probably ascribed as little value to those things as the older; very likely she would not have cared whether they were there or not. They were there because it was the custom, that was all.

Dr. Cunningham, the physician from Newcastle, had arrived, and was in low-voiced consultation with Sir Aydon, who looked, as so often, wretched and grey with indecision.

"Her ladyship has been reduced low—very low—by these shocks. I would, my dear Sir Aydon, recommend bleeding and cupping, and perhaps a clyster."

"You do not think," suggested Sir Aydon doubtfully, "that such treatments will reduce her even lower?"

"My lady is of the stoutly built, high-complexioned habit of persons who can only *benefit* from such treatment," replied the doctor patiently. Alvey conceived an instant dislike for him: he was a small, stout, black-haired personage, himself so high-complexioned as to suggest a heavy intake of alcohol. However, he had an air of confidence which evidently impressed Sir Aydon.

Alvey stole apart from the conference and approached the bed, where Lady Winship lay with a strange, dull look of suffering and passivity, similar to, and yet very different from, her customary vague and absent expression. Alvey pitied her deeply, bereft of her precious garden, and now, it seemed, due to undergo such a rigorous programme of medical discipline.

"Ma'am," she murmured, "I have brought you back this—I was asked to give it to you—" and, gently lifting the left hand, which lay nearest to her, she slipped the signet ring onto the fourth finger. It went on very easily. Lady Winship raised the hand with a puzzled look and stared at the ring.

"My ring!" she murmured. "How very—how very singular." A brighter look came into her face. "Thank you, Louisa," she said faintly to Alvey. "I am very happy to have it back again. But that finger won't do—it is too loose—that must have been how it came to slip off before." She transferred the ring carefully to the middle finger. "Now it will be safe enough. I shall take care not to lose it again."

"Indeed you must, ma'am. I hope you will soon be better. We—we miss you downstairs."

The roaming, puzzled eyes met hers again. Lady Winship did not ask how Alvey had come by the ring; she did not ask any questions at all. She sighed deeply, moved her hands so that the bedclothes covered them, and then, with a faint frown, closed her eyes, as if she could find no useful purpose in keeping them open.

Alvey went away to visit Parthie. What a houseful of invalids this place has become, she thought, and how queer that is, considering the abundant food, the healthy situation, the comfort and warmth. Is the old lady right, am I the grit in the oyster, was it my arrival that precipitated this change? But no, that was pure coincidence, the whole chain of events was set in motion long ago. What a mixed metaphor! How can you set a chain in motion? I must mind my language.

Parthie was languid and irritable, bored in bed, yet not prepared to rise and resume her normal duties and activities. Her black eye had reached the orange-and-green stage; it was still strikingly visible.

"Can I bring you books? Your work basket? Writing materials?" suggested Alvey.

Parthie gave her a scowl of pure hostility.

"I thank you, no! Books and writing materials may do well enough for some people, but I am not bookish. I find books a dead bore."

"Well, how would you like to amuse yourself? Playing cards, perhaps?"

"*Some* of us, sister Emmy, wish to do more than merely *amuse* ourselves. I am not a child, remember! I am a woman grown, just as capable of running a household as yourself."

"In that case," said Alvey with acerbity, "I should think you might get up, instead of lying there playing at being ill," and she left the room and went downstairs to order a nuncheon for the doctor, who, after having bled and cupped his patient, proposed to set out immediately on the first part of his journey back to Newcastle. Parthie at times is remarkably like her sister Louisa, Alvey thought; I wonder where that priggish streak comes from. It is not particularly noticeable in either of the parents. And certainly not in old Mrs. Winship.

Major Fenway and the children returned from their excursion in high spirits. He does seem to have a way of winning people's confidence, thought Alvey, remembering how warmly and spontaneously Isa had chattered away to him, and the evident devoted attachment that James bore to his friend. Nish and Tot appeared immensely the better for the outing; they were pink-cheeked and bright-eyed at dinner, and plainly had many things they would have liked to communicate, though they stayed silent in deference to Sir Aydon's injunction. He remained gloomy and for the most part speechless. The old lady, greatly to Alvey's surprise, had again taken the trouble to rise, dress, and come down for the meal; but she, too, preserved almost unbroken silence, and made no pretence of doing more than pick at her food while her eyes, behind their thick lenses, moved slowly from James to his father and back again.

After the children had gone off to bed and the rest of the party had transferred to the drawing room: "At what hour in the morning do you propose to set forward, Major Fenway?" inquired Sir Aydon.

Can't wait to get him out of the house, Alvey thought. And makes no secret of it.

"At about eight, sir, if not earlier," replied his guest. "My horses are well rested, thanks to your excellent stable man, and with good roads and fair weather I shall hope to reach Edinburgh by tomorrow evening."

James, who had turned very white, now cleared his throat with an effort, as if it had almost closed, and said, "Ahem. I intend to travel to Edinburgh with Guy tomorrow, Father."

"Eh? How? What freak is this? Edinburgh? Why the devil would you wish to go there? You are in no case to travel yet—only fitted with your leg today. No, no, no, my boy; put such an absurd notion out of your head. Home is the place for you, at present. Your best course by far is to remain quietly here until it is time to rejoin your regiment."

"But, Father—I am not going to rejoin my regiment."

"*What?*"

"I am not going to rejoin my regiment."

"I *hope* that my ears deceive me," said Sir Aydon, after drawing an immensely long breath.

"No, sir; they do not."

"I trust this is some sick, crazy fancy . . . *no?* Why—what in the world has come over you?" Sir Aydon's voice was rising in dangerous jerks.

"I—"

"Do you think you are the only soldier who has ever lost a leg?"

"I know I am not that," said James, whiter still. "Why—on that field —along by that hedge where Picton's Fifth routed d'Erlon's corps— you could see arms and legs lying about like—like branches after a gale. The—the bodies were piled six feet high . . ." He gave a violent shudder; so did Alvey. Guy Fenway, she noticed, had set himself more squarely in his chair, like a person who expects an earthquake.

"I wish to hear *no more* of this," said Sir Aydon. "Hateful—abominable—distempered rubbish! But I can see how it is. You are still sick —feverish—not back in full health yet. I shall be happy to ignore— forget what you have said. It is very fortunate that your mother is not present."

"Lady Winship is my stepmother," said James, pale and pinched about the nostrils.

"I meant Maria," surprisingly shouted Sir Aydon. "*She* came of a line of fighters."

James drew a sharp furious breath and stood up, holding the arm of his chair.

Sir Aydon went on, "Good Gad, sir, your grandfather served under Clive—he fought in the battle of Plassey—your great-uncle Charles was at Malplaquet—I myself knew what it is to be wounded—I still carry shrapnel from the French guns at Willemstad—and a bayonet scar from the assault at Linselles—"

"That was medieval warfare," said James scornfully. "Fists and daggers!"

"Bayonets, sir, bayonets! As gallant a charge as you could ever hope to see. Those men of the shires were heroes, sir, heroes! And in the siege of Dunkirk—"

"Where the Duke of York had to retire! He was nothing but a

young fop—an amateur—up against a professional. Carnot knew more about warfare than the Duke could ever—"

"Be silent, sir!" thundered Sir Aydon, now thoroughly incensed.

"Wait. You are going the wrong way about it," said Major Fenway quietly to his friend. "There is no point in exacerbating your father."

But James, now as enraged as his parent, shouted, "What do *you* know about modern warfare? You left the army in '94—they were still using *bows and arrows* then! What do you know about the effects of a bombardment of cannon? Do you realise—have you ever thought—what the losses were at Brussels? *Thirty thousand men killed*—ours and theirs. Have you ever seen thirty thousand men lying smashed to pieces against the hedge? Or wounded—maimed and dying? The roads were so choked with them—groaning and bleeding and crying —on the ground, or on carts—that we had to walk—we had to go at a walking pace all those twelve long miles into Brussels—at first Guy wheeled me in a hand barrow he found, until we were lucky enough to come up with a transport wagon. If Guy had not seen me—I should not be here now—and I wish I were not!—I should be lying among that heap of men by the hedge—"

He stared ahead of him as if he saw it still.

"You utterly disgust me," said his father. "But once you are back with your regiment I shall endeavour to erase this conversation from my mind—I shall do my possible to forget it—"

"Then you will have to wait a precious long time. I am not going back to my regiment. In fact I have already sold out—"

"What did I hear you say?"

"I have sold out," repeated James. "I am never going back. I have no fancy for blowing men to pieces and mangling them to bloody pulp. I intend rather to try and mend them. In that shambles after the battle there was one surgeon for every five hundred men—for all I know to the contrary, one to every thousand. I am going to follow Guy's example and pursue a medical training; then at least I shall be some use in the world, instead of being fit only for butcher's work."

"Medical training? Did I understand you?"

"Yes, sir, you heard me. I am sorry if it does not suit your standards of how a gentleman should occupy himself. But I am quite resolved. My mind is made up."

Alvey could have clapped her hands. James still looked white, sick, and shattered, but his eyes blazed with a light that had not been in them since he had come to Birkland. Sir Aydon, on the other hand, looked as if he had fallen over a cliff and were still falling. Alvey wondered with detachment if he would have a stroke; his eyes bulged, his face was the dark colour of Burgundy wine.

"Then," he said hoarsely, "not a penny of my money do you receive from now on for this—this piece of outrageous foolery—not a penny, not a penny—"

"Don't put yourself about, sir, I shall not ask you for a penny—"

"You can starve, for all the help you'll get from me—you shall be cut off—"

Here, greatly startling everybody, old Mrs. Winship spoke up.

"No, he will not starve, Aydon, so pray do not be so gothick. There is no need for all this melodrama! I have told the boy I intend to let him have money for his needs; so let that be an end of the matter. I do not consider his plans to be outrageous foolery; quite the converse. I only wish that anybody else in this family owned to such a practical ambition."

Sir Aydon swung round and stared at his mother, mouth agape.

"*You* have announced your intention of financing him, ma'am?"

He looks like the lame Vulcan about to swing his hammer, thought Alvey.

In front of Sir Aydon the old woman seemed to shrink and shrivel in size, like a dead leaf in a blazing bonfire.

"Yes, I do, Aydon! Don't glower at me like that—don't—"

Her mouth hung ajar, she slipped and sagged sideways in her chair; she would have fallen to the floor had not Major Fenway leapt forward and caught her.

"We must get her to bed; I fear she may have suffered a stroke," he said.

"*Now* see what you have done, sir," said Sir Aydon to his son.

XI

"It distresses me to go off like this, leaving you with the cares of such a stricken household falling chiefly on your shoulders," said Guy Fenway to Alvey, early next morning.

They were standing in the chamber of old Mrs. Winship, who lay mute, unmoving in the bed; her eyes were open, but whether she saw her visitors, who could say? Besides, Alvey remembered, without her spectacles on her nose, it was probable that anything she saw beyond the range of four feet was nothing but a blur.

"You are very kind to feel anxiety for me," Alvey told the major. "But I don't doubt I shall manage. The servants here are wonderfully experienced, helpful, and kind." Really, she thought, it is James who ought to be feeling brotherly solicitude for me. But he, not surprisingly, was so engulfed with relief at having finally delivered his ultimatum to his father, mingled with horror at its consequences to his grandmother, that he had no attention left to spare for other members of the household.

"Do you think she will recover?" Alvey looked down at the bloodless old face on the pillow, at the small blotched hands resting idly on the patchwork quilt which, long ago, for weeks and months on end, they had busily stitched together.

Guy surprised her by answering, "Yes; I think she has a good chance of recovery. I have examined her carefully, she has a remarkably strong constitution. Her heart is sound. I know she has been under excessive strain these last few days. James had of course informed her of his intentions and enlisted her sympathy. And then, wretched fellow, he kept postponing the announcement until the last possible opportunity—"

"He is like his—my father in that," Alvey said. "Sir Aydon never will come to a decision or take any action until he is positively pushed into it by circumstances."

"Just so." The major gave her a keen, scrutinising look. "What can we do for my grandmother?"

"Keep her nourished. Light food, broths, eggnogs, brandy. Rub her, warm her, keep her limbs moving. Encourage any signs of intelligence or activity. If she begins to speak, give her plenty of practise. The mental and motor faculties are like a machine that requires regular oiling and use to keep in working order."

"And my mother?"

He shrugged. "Another strong constitution. If she can survive Dr. Cunningham's treatment, she must be an Amazon. But I think she will do well enough."

"She *is* very strong," Alvey said thoughtfully. "The result of all those hours each day spent in the open air, working in her garden . . . poor thing."

Major Fenway walked across to Mrs. Winship's window and stood looking out, drumming his fingers on the sill. He seemed to be staring across the carriage sweep towards the Lion Pool, but there was a perplexed, inward-looking expression on his face. Alvey joined him at the window and he gave her another of his intent, measuring glances.

"I think your mother will be up and about again, to some degree, in a week or so. Then she is going to need as much sympathy and companionship as you are able to give her."

"Indeed?" Alvey was no little daunted by this suggestion. Rubbing the old lady's hands and encouraging her to resume the faculty of speech would be a labour of affection and interest; but there would be little recompense, she feared, in cultivating Lady Winship's arid company. "Mamma has never seemed to take pleasure in my companionship," she said doubtfully.

"Could your sister Isa perhaps be persuaded to forgo her travels and return home?" Guy suggested.

"Isa? Oh no, I do not think that would be right or fair. This may probably be the only time she will ever escape from home." Alvey was surprised to discover how strongly she felt on this point; Isa, she knew, would agree to come home like a bird, might be only too glad of the chance to do so; yet she should not be encouraged to sacrifice her one glimpse of the outside world. At the end of a year I shall be gone, who knows where? Alvey thought. I have the whole world at my disposal. No, no, Isa must have her journey, must make the most of it.

She said, "We shall manage well enough. I can enlist the help of Nish and Tot in the care of their grandmother; they are good children; if their interest is engaged they will devote a great deal of energy and ingenuity to the project. And as for La—for my mother; well, of course I promise to do all I can."

"Your own work will suffer?" Another probing look. "Your sister Isa told me that you are engaged in writing a book."

Oh, did she, indeed? thought Alvey. And who gave sister Isa leave to tell that? She said, "My book is in good train at the moment; I see my way clear to the end, and, in the meantime, it makes a very enjoyable diversion to go back to it after dealing with household matters."

"Ah! That accounts for your air of—"

"Air of—"

"Of—of having other resources to draw upon. You are fortunate!"

"Oh yes. I am. I know I am." Alvey went on thoughtfully: "If only Sir Ay—if only my father could be brought to involve himself more in his family's affairs. His state of mind is very bad at present—low, despondent, irritable—the least thing aggravates him, and lately, poor man, he has had no small troubles to contend with. This last declaration by my brother—of course, James was quite right to take his decision, naturally I applaud his courage and good sense, but it has been and will be a *terrible* blow to his father; a shame, a mortification, a grief; especially just at this time; I hardly know how he is going to sustain it."

"I have been thinking very much about that matter," Major Fenway surprised her by saying. "In fact, I have at the back of my mind a plan with regard to Sir Aydon. But it is so wild—so mad, I believe you might consider it—that I will not speak of it more explicitly at present, not until I have at least some slight hope, some expectation of its achievement."

"Good God, sir! What can you possibly have in mind?"

All manner of implausible notions chased each other through Alvey's head; but none of them accorded with what she knew either of Sir Aydon or of the major. "I fear that Sir Aydon rather dislikes you," she mentioned diffidently. "I doubt—after last night—whether he would with complaisance accept *any* suggestion from you regarding his future manner of life."

Fenway laughed. "I doubt so too! He cannot wait to see the back of me—and that is a salutary reminder that I must hurry James with his packing and set forward."

Duddy came into the room with a stone hot-water bottle, which she carefully placed at her mistress's feet.

"That is right," said Guy. "Keep her well warmed at all times. But I know you will. I can see you tend her far more skilfully than I ever could."

Duddy gave him a wintry smile. "Eh, lad, nivver fash thisen buttering me oop."

"I won't." He smiled back at her. "You do it for love. That is the difference." Turning to Alvey, he said, "One last thing. When I was out yesterday with the children—we were up on a part of the moor called, I believe, Gilcastle Fell—we encountered an old shepherd who seemed very ill disposed to them—indeed to your whole family. He shouted a lot of abuse. I myself found his language almost impenetrable, I confess; but they understood what he said well enough, they told me he was uttering various vague threats—"

"Who can it have been?" said Alvey, disquieted, but Duddy exclaimed, "Eh, that'll be owd Herdman, sartin sure! Gurt owd critter with a white beard?"

"That's the man. Yes, Herdman, that was the name. I think Sir Aydon should be warned about him, I fancy he will bear watching."

"Can it have been he who was responsible for the garden? But no," Alvey recollected, "he was supposed to have been away from the neighbourhood at that time. But perhaps a friend of his—"

"He has nivver a friend," said Duddy. "He's a bitter, sullen owd weasel. That's why he bides oop i' the hut on the fells wi' his sheep all summer long, for none in the village can abide him."

And that was why Annie couldn't leave her baby at home, Alvey thought. Lady Winship certainly made a bad mistake when she commanded his daughter and grandson into the household. But I suppose somebody who spends all her days in a garden cannot be expected to have a very shrewd judgment of human nature.

Major Fenwick's carriage drew up down below on the sweep, the horses led by Archie.

"Good heavens, here it is half past seven already, and I have been boring on at you, Miss Winship, as if—as if I were your Reverend Thropton. Forgive me! I have no right to lay duties on you—and no need, I am sure; I—I have a great esteem for your abilities. Allow me to bid you farewell."

Before the impassive eyes of Mrs. Winship and the neutral ones of Duddy, the major took Alvey's hand, pressed it, and raised it momentarily to his lips.

"Oh, but I will come down with you and say goodbye to James," said Alvey quickly.

Nish and Tot, and even little Betsey, were out on the sweep, hopping around and getting in the way as Amble and Stridge, the footman, carried out the young gentlemen's bags.

"Goodbye, goodbye, Major Fenway, goodbye, brother James," they chorused sadly. Nish and Tot in particular had a profound admiration for their grown-up brother, increased to hero worship by the flinching gallantry with which he jerked himself about on his newly acquired wooden leg.

"You had best travel inside the chaise, old fellow," said Fenway.

"Gammon! I'm coming on the box with you."

The major shook his head, but did not dispute the matter any further.

"Goodbye, James," said Alvey. "I—I wish you the very best of luck with your studies."

"Oh, halloo, Louisa—are you up at this hour? Goodbye, then," said James, and just brushed her cheek with his. "I—I say—you will keep me posted as to how they all go on, will you not?"

"Of course I will, if you send me your direction."

"Yes, yes," he said impatiently, and with Amble's help was assisted onto the box. The well-rested team started off briskly up the hill.

"He's a champion whip, that Major Fenway," commented Amble, as Alvey turned indoors. At the library window she thought she saw a face, quickly withdrawn. Sir Aydon had not emerged to say goodbye to the young men. Nor had Parthie. But, unlike Sir Aydon, she appeared later in the dining room and consumed a large breakfast. Alvey took this opportunity to pass on to her Major Fenway's injunctions regarding old Mrs. Winship.

"We must be with her a great deal, and encourage her faculties as much as possible."

"Why?" said Parthie sulkily. "What is the value of that?"

"Why, to bring her back to a normal way of living, of course. I should think you would be anxious to do that, as you are so fond of her."

"It seems a great waste of time, if she is only to be like a baby from now on, drooling and stupid. That's what Ellen says is likely to happen. So why take the trouble?"

"Major Fenway thinks there is an excellent chance of her making a good recovery," said Alvey, rather astonished. But Parthie did not seem at all rejoiced at this forecast. She hung her head over her plate and muttered something about James and money.

"You begrudge the allowance your grandmother is making to James while he learns how to be a doctor? That is not very generous."

"It is because she thinks there may not be enough left for Grandmamma to leave Parthie in her will," said Nish dispassionately. Parthie scowled at her younger sister.

"In any case, you are in no position to make comments or lay down rules for our behaviour," Parthie said to Alvey with spiteful temerity.

"Come, that is enough talk about money and wills," announced Alvey, deciding to ignore this. "It is not a proper subject for any of us. We are all upset and worried—all the more reason for doing our best to look after the invalids, until they are better and the household is itself again. Nish and Tot, go and sit with your grandmother for half an hour before our lessons—see if you can engage her attention in any way—while I go to find out how—how Mamma is doing today."

Parthie is like an unexploded train of gunpowder, Alvey thought, climbing the stair. Sooner or later, something will touch it off. But really, just now, I have too many other concerns pressing on me to be very troubled about her.

What could Major Fenway conceivably be planning in regard to his friend's father? Try as she would, her imagination completely failed to come up with any scheme for the amelioration of Sir Aydon's nature. People do not change, she thought. How could such an alteration possibly be achieved? And yet, it was true, he had changed, for the worse; once, by all accounts, he had been an active, cheerful, vigorous army officer, and then an intrepid, tireless huntsman. That was why he was so angry and disappointed with James, with Tot—

You have to face the facts, Alvey told herself at this point. You have fallen miserably in love with James. His face haunts you. You continually hear the inflections of his voice in your mind's ear. If nobody were about, you would even go back into the dining room and moon dismally over the broken eggshells on his plate, just because it was he who left them, he who sat in that particular chair. You are in the throes of a fit of lamentable, ignominious calf love. You, my poor girl, are smitten with the greensickness, and the only consolation to be found is that, apart from yourself, nobody knows it. Except, possibly, James's friend the major, who gave you that strange, heedful, pitying look, as James said his hasty farewell.

James will never take the least notice of me. To him, I am his half sister Louisa, a disagreeable and priggish relative, too close to be considered as a person. And if he knew that I was *not* his sister—if he knew that, I do not believe that matters would be in any way helped. I would still be tinted with the disagreeable hue of Louisa; and, still worse, smeared with the stigma of an imposter, some kind of creeping, sneaking parasite who has invaded the family stronghold. He would repulse me as a deceiver, as a charlatan; he would utterly despise me.

I have to put his image out of my mind.

Easier said than done.

What would Wicked Lord Love do in such circumstances?

Lord Love's creator knew very well what her story-child would do: he would call for his boots, tie his cravat in some unsurpassable manner, and go off to Watier's, or the Cocoa Tree; he would watch a match between the Putney Pet and the Battersea Bruiser; he would wager a pony on a prime bit of blood at White's, ride out with the

Abingdon, or post down to Newmarket, where his mare was the favourite; he would—but why continue? None of these resources were open to his progenitor.

Instead she tapped on Lady Winship's door and walked quietly into the large, gloomy, well-furnished room.

Lady Winship was lying propped against a heap of pillows. Her aspect was more alert and wakeful than that of her mother-in-law; it was plain that she could think, remember, and look forward; it was equally plain that she was doing all these things, and deriving no pleasure from the process.

"How do you find yourself, ma'am, this morning?" asked Alvey quietly, moving forward.

"She's wishful to go out, Miss Emmy, already," said Ellen, the maid, who was plaiting the frills of nightcaps on a table near the window.

"Out of doors? Already? Did Dr. Cunningham give you leave to do so, ma'am?"

Lady Winship shook her head slowly. She was still unusually pale; but that was probably due to the bloodletting. Dr. Cunningham had drained her of several pints.

"Air," she said. "Must have air. Too close in here. Like a grave."

Alvey surveyed her doubtfully. The poor lady was in possession of her faculties, had sense, and knew what suited her best; why should she be deprived of what she felt would do her good?

"Ma'am, it is very cold outdoors this morning—really too cold, I think, for someone as enfeebled by shock and—and severe treatments as you have been. But if the sun shines tomorrow, I do not see why you should be immured in the house. Is there a wheelchair or basket chair somewhere about the place?" she asked Ellen, forgetting that she might be expected to know such a thing. But the maid replied,

"Yes, Miss Emmy, there's the basket chair that Master first used after he broke his legs and Amble used to push him about the grounds."

"That will do capitally. I will engage to push you in that, ma'am, as far as you wish; if you, in the meantime, will resign yourself to another day in your chamber. Can I bring you anything to while away the hours?"

"You are a good girl," said Lady Winship vaguely. The large, absent grey eyes lifted and met those of Alvey with, for the first time, something approaching acknowledgment. Come, we are making progress, thought Alvey.

"It is a kind thought," Lady Winship went on. "But no—I wish for nothing. Yet perhaps—you might bring me paper and pencil. And the works of Sir Thomas Browne, which you may find in the library—I recall he wrote something about a quincunx—"

Already, it seemed, she was planning the renewal of her destroyed kingdom. But then she seemed to reconsider.

"No, it will not do. No, no, it will not do. Give me my Testament."

But when handed the Testament she made no effort to open it.

Lessons with the children passed off quietly. Alvey had undertaken to have little Betsey as well as the elder two, since Tushie, the maid who generally cared for the two smallest children, was sharing with Duddy and Grace the nursing of old Mrs. Winship. Betsey was a docile, calm-natured child, quite happy to sit for an hour at a time with a small pot of paint, colouring the trees and houses, ducks and hens, sheep and horses, that her elders kindly drew for her. In view of this nursery atmosphere, Alvey did not attempt to embark on studies at any serious level, but read aloud some chapters of history and some of *Waverley.* She reflected on the fact that neither Nish nor Tot alluded to Parthie's parting shot at the breakfast table; this, she felt certain, was due not at all to lack of curiosity, but to a strangely adult innate tact and consideration which underlay much of their behaviour to herself.

On the subject of James they were unaffectedly inquisitive, and Alvey saw no reason not to gratify this curiosity.

"*Why* is Papa so angry with James?"

"Because, instead of going back into the army, he wishes to learn to be a doctor, like Major Fenway. Instead of shooting people, he wants to find out how to mend them."

"Well, I think he is right to do that," said Nish. "Besides, how could he be a soldier with only one leg?"

"Nelson had only one arm," argued Tot. "And one eye."

"He was a sailor. They don't have to march, or ride on horseback."

"They have to climb rigging."

"Admirals don't. And Nelson was an admiral."

"Never mind that!" said Alvey, who could see this argument going on for hours. "Your papa was angry because of course he has been a soldier himself—and so had *his* father—and I daresay he hoped that James might become a general or distinguish himself and win a medal. He was just very disappointed. Still, I daresay in time he will come about. It was foolish of James to wait so long before telling Papa what he planned to do. It gave Sir Aydon no time to grow accustomed to the idea. And so he just exploded with rage. And that upset your grandmother and caused her to have an attack."

"Will she get better from it?"

"Major Fenway thinks she will. If we take a lot of pains with her. I am going to her now, to rub her hands for a while, and talk to her. Will you keep an eye on Betsey until Grace comes for her."

"We'll read her young Lochinvar," said Nish. "She'll like that, won't you, Bet?"

In the afternoon of the following day an unwontedly warm sun shone out, and Alvey, with the help of Ellen, half led, half carried Lady Winship downstairs, wrapped her in half a dozen layers of pelisses and shawls, and tucked her into the basket chair.

"I will push her back and forth along the terrace, Ellen, for half an hour," said Alvey. "Then you come out and help me in with her again."

"Half an hour is not nearly long enough," asserted Lady Winship.

"If you still feel so at the end of that time, ma'am, you may stay out longer. But the chill settles down quickly these afternoons."

To and fro along the terrace Alvey walked, wheeling the wicker chariot. The gate to Lady Winship's garden faced them each time they came to the southern end of the walk, but Lady Winship did not ask to go through it; perhaps she dared not. To Alvey this was a great relief. Too many scalding emotions had been let loose during the last week; too many shattering scenes had taken place. She approved the stoic forbearance with which Lady Winship eyed the gate each time they approached it, and then deliberately turned her head away. It was not lack of courage; Charlotte was no coward; she was merely waiting until she had her strength gathered together again.

"Did you *see* the garden, after it happened?" she asked once, and Alvey simply answered, "Yes."

"Major Fenway is a good man," Lady Winship observed, with apparent inconsequence, after a while.

"Yes, I believe so," Alvey answered quietly.

"James is lucky to have him for a friend."

"He is, indeed. I hope they remain friends in Edinburgh," Alvey agreed, very ready to carry on with any conversation that related to James.

"I should be pleased to entertain the major at Birkland again. It is a great pity that James put his father in such a passion. Aydon will not wish either of them to come now, I daresay. I am sorry for that." Lady Winship did not express any opinion as to the rights and wrongs of the dispute; she spoke as dispassionately as if she were canvassing the merits of two different kinds of grass seed. "How does your grandmother go on? It is unfortunate that Dr. Cunningham had left already when she took her seizure."

Alvey was not so sure about that. She felt that the old lady probably had a better chance of regaining her strength without the doctor's drastic purgings and bleedings.

"Major Fenway thinks she has a good chance of recovery."

Lady Winship sighed deeply. "How strong some of us are. How we hang on to our life."

Unlike that unhappy pair, thought Alvey, unlike that girl and her baby. She felt sure that Lady Winship's thoughts were running in the same direction. How very queer this is, thought Alvey. I never had the care of my own mother in a situation such as this; I hardly know this odd woman, yet, in a way, I knew my own mother even less. I never had the chance . . .

"I think, ma'am, it is time we went in," she said gently. "The sun has almost left the flagstones. And look, here is Ellen, come to help you indoors."

As they skirted the side of the stable yard, which was the quickest way into the house, they encountered Sir Aydon, limping painfully along the cobbled way with the help of his two sticks. To Alvey's astonishment, he did not pause to greet his wife, nor ask how she did; he had no comment to make, even, on seeing her out of doors. Alvey had been prepared for a scold, for some kind of admonition, but not for the total silence in which he passed them, with head bent forward and red face set in a bitter scowl. It felt just as if a wintry cloud had drifted by. *Now* what is he punishing her for? wondered Alvey indignantly. It is not as if she were James's mother, after all!

"Would you like to sit for a little in the drawing room, ma'am?" she asked Lady Winship. "Or shall we take you back to your bedchamber?"

"I will go back to bed. The air did me good," said Lady Winship in a quenched voice, "but I do find myself quite fatigued. It is very strange—just from being wheeled to and fro!"

When Alvey had said to Isa, "I shall miss you," she had by no means anticipated a situation like this. She had expected the usual family occasions, family meals, with the younger children, Parthie, the old lady, Sir Aydon and Lady Winship: normal domestic routine. She could not possibly have envisaged sitting at table *à trois* with Sir Aydon and Parthie and a chilly expanse of gleaming white linen stretching empty away on either side.

"Send the younger ones to have their meal in the kitchen," said Sir Aydon. "I can't be bothered with 'em," and the younger ones had been glad to go. Now Sir Aydon chomped on his mutton in brooding silence, and Parthie cut up her food and pushed it about her plate without eating it.

"I wonder when we shall hear from Meg and Isa," Alvey remarked.

Neither of her companions troubled to reply. But, after a longish pause, Sir Aydon said, "You had best write to inform your sisters of—of the misfortunes that have overtaken their mother and grandmother. Isa may wish to return home."

"I am sure she will not," said Parthie pertly.

"Hold your tongue, miss!"

"Would you not wish to write to Meg yourself, sir?"

"Certainly not! Why should I want to do that?"

"Very well; I will write," Alvey said quietly.

After the meal she made no pretence of lingering in the drawing room; let Parthie pour Sir Aydon's tea, if tea he required, and she chose to play the lady of the house; but Sir Aydon's tendency of late had been to remain in the dining room with his decanter of port until the decanter was empty, and then limp off, somewhat unsteadily, to the library, where he snored in an armchair until Amble and Stridge more or less carried him up to bed.

He is in a bad way, thought Alvey; but I do not see what can be done about it.

She almost ran up the stairs to her room, and Lord Love.

The outings with Lady Winship in a wheelchair proved such a success that, rather to Alvey's surprise, they became a regular daily habit. Between the two participants it developed into a kind of conspiracy; Lady Winship was well enough, after a week or so, to get up, walk, and resume some of her household duties; she herself knew this, Ellen knew it, Alvey knew it, but the return to normal routine was somehow continually postponed. The time had not come yet; when it would come, who could say?

Meanwhile Alvey, unexpectedly, found herself enjoying the odd, quite unanticipated communication that was growing up, on these daily walks, between herself and the older woman.

Pushing somebody in a wheelchair is an especial situation. It has about it a touch of the relationship between priest and penitent in the confessional; the two persons concerned cannot see one another's faces, it is an interchange of voices only; and the dialogue, furthermore, is aided, eased, and encouraged by the accompaniment of steady motion, the passage of fresh air, and continually changing scenery. Though, to be sure, all the pair did was promenade back and forth along the terrace. Going up the drive or down to the river was not to be attempted; both these ways were too steep to allow the propulsion of the heavy chair and its heavier occupant.

Yet these walks, to and fro, to and fro, over the same ground, with the wide prospect of the Hungry Water valley and the Cheviot Hills, appeared to unloose some long-standing constriction in Lady Winship. She began to talk. And Alvey, listening, wondering, unjudging, curious, was content to play a passive part, merely prompting the flow by an occasional question.

"When I first married your father . . . oh, twenty-five years ago . . . James is twenty-six . . . I knew perfectly well that he did not love me as he had loved Maria. In fact," said Lady Winship simply, "he did not love me at all. He wanted a mother for the boy."

"Did you love him?"

"I thought so, yes, of course. What does a girl of that age know about love? Nothing in the world. I had read a few novels—as girls do. I thought that marriage was the end of the tale. It never occurred to me that there would be life after marriage; apart, that is, from having my own carriage and being able to order what I liked for dinner."

Slowly, with divagations and backtrackings, but, it seemed, very few concealments, no hesitations, no apologies, Lady Winship meandered through the history of her married life. "Childbirth is very bad. Let no one tell you otherwise. If Isa wishes to remain unmarried and avoid it, I cannot truly say that she has chosen the worser part. Childbirth is a pain that men cannot at all comprehend. They lay down rules for it, to their own satisfaction . . . Perhaps they feel contrition in their own way? I do not know. I have suffered it fourteen times—"

"*Fourteen*, ma'am?"

It was fortunate, Alvey thought, that Lady Winship could not see her face of shock as she received this information. Meg, Louisa, Isa, Parthie, Tot, Nish, little Betsey, Kate . . . where were the other six?

"Many of you died at birth. My first three did so, before Meg was born. And one after, between Meg and yourself. Aydon was very displeased at that. And then, to have four girls in succession . . . he began to think I would never have a boy. And when Tot *was* born, he was so puny and ailing; was not expected to live; Aydon was very aggrieved about that too, especially as it was not long after he had sold out of the service; he was missing the military life and companionship. That made him impatient and he did not care to be thwarted.

"That was when I began making my garden . . . It gave me something else to think about . . ."

"I wonder, ma'am, that you were able to do so much in the garden —to achieve all that you have. For—so much of the time—you must have been increasing—"

"Yes, it was often difficult. For, unlike some women, I do not feel at all well when I am breeding. Some say it is the best time for them. That was never so in my case. The first four or five months I was always sick and wretched; could not eat, almost any food nauseated me; my head ached, I vomited continually; then, at a later stage, I always suffer from congestion of the—of the lower extremities—which makes walking any distance exceedingly painful. And sitting down, also," she added detachedly, after some thought. "And then, of course, one's back aches so wretchedly."

Alvey felt a chill down her own back. Fourteen babies: that meant a hundred and twenty-six months of pregnancy: almost ten years of nausea, backache, and inability to walk or sit down with the least degree of comfort.

"I wonder you did not take to your bed, ma'am."

"Oh no; I preferred to be out in the garden; in the fresh air. While I was out of doors I did not feel so likely to vomit."

"But the backache? The—the congestion? How could you stoop or work?"

"Well," said Lady Winship practically, "that was the reason why I had my garden planned on a slope, do you see? So there was not so far to stoop. That was Carey's father's notion; he was my gardener until his death. You remember him? You would have been eight or nine when he died; a wonderfully canny old man. In a way he was the greatest friend of my life. I missed him severely . . . But Carey is a very good gardener."

"And Sir Aydon never objected to your gardening activities?"

"Oh yes, he did at first. Yes, very much. So did his mother. They thought it would impair my ability to give birth. I believe Mrs. Winship still thinks so. But Aydon could see, at least, that the being out of doors was healthy and helped to reduce my sick spasms . . . So it was permitted. But, at first, with considerable reluctance."

Lady Winship went on reminiscing happily, dreamily, about her garden.

"You cannot permit small children in the garden, of course. They trample on the seedlings, they pick the heads off the flowers; in their ignorance they often do untold damage. And, of course, you cannot spare the time to be continually following and correcting them, or nothing gets done. So the children were forbidden entry until they reached an age of sense. And then, later, when they were older, and might have been of some use, they did not seem to want to come. I remember asking you once if you would like to weed out the witch-grass from among the lilies; you said no. Of course you can only give children the routine jobs, which they find tedious; the skilled ones are beyond their powers. No, none of you have ever shown the least interest in gardening."

Alvey thought of Nish and Tot, their exquisitely planned little island kingdoms.

"It is a pity," Lady Winship went on pensively. "A garden is so much more rewarding than people are. It does not dispute . . . or fly into rages . . . or go into sulks. It works *with* you, not against . . ."

"The six children who died," said Alvey with diffidence. "Did you grieve very much, ma'am? Did Sir—my father grieve?"

"Oh well, over the ones who were boys, yes, he did grieve. Yes, he grieved very much. Three of those who died were boys. Yes, that did make him very low-spirited. And the little boy who lived to the age of one: Jasper. The croup carried him off. That was when you were five. I suppose you do not remember. His death was highly distressing for Aydon."

"But you, ma'am? What did you feel?"

"Of course I was distressed," said Lady Winship brusquely. "You cannot carry a child within you for nine months, and have all that trouble, and then lose it, without feeling the loss and waste. But you have to try to protect yourself against feeling too deeply. Or else you would go mad. I believe some women do go mad when they lose children."

Her voice had become faraway, dispassionate.

"I used to wonder if I would go mad," she remarked after a moment or two. "Sometimes I felt strangely removed from everything about me. And often I used to feel angry with Aydon; even hated him. Sometimes I do still. But what is the use of that? He is as nature made him. — When the pains began, I would think: Is this I? Am I really here? Is it indeed all beginning again? Often I felt like a bystander, watching it all from the other side of the room, and I wondered if perhaps one day I would become that bystander forever."

"I believe I can understand that frame of mind," said Alvey, who, at Birkland, had sometimes been overtaken by the same kind of feeling. Am I really here? Where is *here?* Who is *I?* She added, "But did you never think it wrong, ma'am, that you should be obliged to bear so many children?"

"Wrong? Why? Other women do so. And lose them likewise. What would be the use of thinking it wrong? It is not to be avoided." But, after a moment's thought, she added remotely, "It is true that, after Aydon's accident, when he was in great pain for some months, I *was* glad to think I might have a respite from childbearing. During that time he seldom wished to cohabit with me, and was so restless at night that he required to sleep in a bed by himself. I did hope that might free me . . . But it did not. And then I conceived little Carrie, if you recall, who died at two months. She was the last before Katie. And Kate *is* the last." She spoke with triumph.

"You mean, ma'am—"

"Aydon does not know it yet. He still, perhaps, hopes for another son. Some women, I have heard, do continue bearing into their fifties. There was Sarah, and Isaac—but I thank God I do not seem to be of that breed. Aydon will be displeased, I daresay, when he discovers. He may perhaps attribute the cause to all my gardening work—in which case he will think me justly punished. And perhaps—perhaps I am . . ." The detached voice lost a little of its detachment.

She resumed.

"You have been away for so long, Louisa, that I look on you more as an acquaintance, a person from outside, than my own daughter. I talk to you more freely than I would to Meg or Isa. Perhaps the loss of my garden was visited on me as a reminder that I have not paid sufficient heed to Aydon and the children; that I have neglected them; what do you think?"

"Oh, ma'am, I cannot believe that. You have suffered your share of trouble already. What has happened here—" They had reached the wrought-iron gate once more; Alvey quickly turned and pushed the wheelchair in the other direction. "What happened here is wicked human malice, and whoever did it deserves to be soundly punished."

"That will not bring my garden back," said the voice from the wheelchair.

"No. I suppose that is true. It won't. But—so long as we do not know who did it—surely we are in danger of another, similar act? A repetition. That is what worries me."

A mad suspicion had been lurking in the corners of her mind. Suppose that Sir Aydon himself had destroyed the garden? In some fit of ungovernable resentment against his wife? Could such a thing be possible?

"Oh," said Lady Winship calmly, as if plucking the thought like a splinter from Alvey's consciousness, "I don't doubt old Amos Herdman did it. And I doubt he would find the energy to do more, vindictive as he is. Besides, what more could he do? No, I daresay he has shot his bolt. He had only one grandchild. And I had only one garden."

"But why, ma'am, *why?* Besides—they said he was not here, was away visiting his brother."

"Easy to say so. No doubt his brother would speak for him."

"But I thought he hated his grandchild—ill-treated the boy. And was angry with his daughter for having borne a bastard."

"Nonetheless his daughter *was his property.* And so was the child. Annie brought him her wages every week—"

"And that would be enough?"

"Oh yes, it would. It would be enough."

Some hours later, making notes in her bedroom, it occurred to Alvey that Lady Winship had spoken about the actions of Sir Aydon and of old Mr. Herdman in exactly the same tone—philosophical, uncomplaining—that she might use of drought, or late frosts, or severe winter weather.

Not to be wondered at, really, in somebody who had spent so much of her life in a garden.

XII

About two weeks after the departure of James and his friend, a letter arrived in James's handwriting, addressed to Lady Winship.

The long siege of winter had almost begun. An iron cold gripped the countryside; the mornings were quiet and dark, and no birds sang; the last leaves had blown from the deciduous trees, and a ring of white ice encircled the Lion Pool. Already a little snow had fallen, but the roads were still open; for how much longer they would remain so was in question. Nish and Tot had reluctantly abandoned their ploys in the Hungry Water, which was icy, full, and roaring, no longer their friendly summer playmate, but unpredictable, dangerous, possibly lethal. Instead they took Alvey on long expeditions over the moors, for the ground, now hard with frost, made for easier walking. Or sometimes, now that she was learning the landmarks for ten miles around, she rode out alone on old Phantom, who, if she lost her sense of direction, could be relied upon to find his way home.

She had also, before winter conditions threatened to cut off Birkland entirely, made another excursion to Hexham. Rubbing liniments and essences were needed for the old lady. Mrs. Slaley had a list of stillroom requirements and there were winter supplies to be put in hand for stable and storeroom.

Alvey invited Parthie to accompany her on this trip, hoping that the shared errand might improve the relations between them, but it did not. Parthie was a slow, inefficient, forgetful shopper, requiring constant advice and reminders, incapable of making practical decisions; Alvey was soon heartily tired of the younger girl's company and felt that she could have completed the various commissions quite as fast, if not faster, on her own.

When the main tasks were accomplished she left Parthie, with relief, at a draper's shop, to buy herself some ribbons, and made her way to Mr. Allgood's circulating library, proposing to buy more books and more drawing materials for the children, who seemed to have developed a devouring thirst for education. With the books, Mr. Allgood handed her another letter from Louisa, this one dispatched from Port Elizabeth, and, to her surprise and pleasure, a letter from Isa.

Containing her impatience to read these, she tucked them safely into her reticule, to await the privacy of her own room at home, and went in search of Parthie, who was discovered in the marketplace, absorbedly studying a sign on a wall which said:

> Andrew Lyon begs respectfully to intimate that he can be found at his residence, Coxon's Lane adjoining Walken Gate, Larriston, any time his services may be required by any person visiting the hymeneal Shrine on the Scottish border. Ginger beer also sold.

"Are you thinking of getting married?" Alvey asked lightly, as they climbed into the carriage with their bundles.

Parthie gave her a glance of surpassing scorn.

"A scrambled border marriage, performed by a blacksmith? I thank you, no! Where would be the pleasure in that? No bridesmaids, no fine dresses, no attendants, no cake, no lace, no veils, no wine—it would be a most pitiful way to get married. I suppose it might please *you*, sister Emmy—it would be like something out of a romance—"

"Well, I should certainly enjoy the ginger beer," said Alvey, and retired into her own thoughts, deciding, as she did ten times a day, that it was useless to try to conciliate Parthie, who was determined to be hostile.

Louisa's third letter did no more than reiterate the delights of shipboard life and the gallantry of Captain Middlemass and Lieutenant Dunnifage, dwelling, perhaps, a little more on the meritorious qualities of the latter.

Isa's letter contained more substance.

"I cannot write freely to you at Birkland," she wrote, "for well I know the family inquisitions, the reading-aloud and passing from hand to hand of all correspondence received. So I confide this to the faithful Mr. Allgood. But tell me truly, Alvey, would you not wish me to return home? Meg and I were terribly distressed by your account of the various occurrences after our departure—the dreadful destruction of my poor mother's garden, and then my father's breach with James and the shocking effect of this upon my grandmother; I do not feel it right that you, a stranger, should be obliged to grapple with these afflictions unassisted, and I am very certain that neither Parthie nor my father make the least push to cheer or comfort the other members of the family . . ."

Another letter, jointly from Meg and Isa, was received direct at Birkland Hall, merely detailing the sights and delights of Brighton.

"Just imagine!" wrote Meg. "Ladies still take to the water in flannel gowns and oilskin caps. Only fancy! At this time of year! But it is thought very healthy, and of course it is warmer by far, here, than in Northumberland. We have seen the Prince Regent, driving a phaeton; he is exceedingly fat and wears a blue jacket and a cocked hat; Isa said he was not at all her idea of a prince. But everybody cheered him and he took off his hat and was very civil." No mention was made of Meg's husband except at the end. "John is well, and joins me in all kinds of wishes . . ."

Alvey wrote back to Isa at Winchester, which was to be their next stopping point, paying a visit to some Chibburn cousins. "On no account should you feel obliged to curtail your journey and come home. Your mamma is making an excellent recovery and bears her loss with remarkable fortitude. We have every hope of your grandmother's improvement. The children are wonderfully good with her and take great pains. As to your papa and the breach with James: the latter has written home making a proposal about which I shall not attempt to particularise at the present time in case nothing comes of it, which would lead to great disappointment . . . I hope to tell you more of this in my next communication. *Pray* do not concern yourself as to my part in all these events; I am truly glad there is a little I can do to help the family that is sheltering me so kindly . . ."

The letter from James, delivered one afternoon by Whin Bob the clock mender and carried immediately by Alvey to Lady Winship in her chamber, had said:

My dear Stepmamma: I write to you rather than to my father lest he is still so enraged with me that he is tempted to destroy the communication unread. My purpose in writing is to enlist your cooperation in a scheme to help him. My good friend Guy Fenway has become acquainted with a very expert surgeon here in Edinburgh, a Mr. Phineas Harle, who is skilled in the practice of breaking and resetting bones that have been ill-set and so mended badly. From Guy's descriptions to him, and his drawings of my father's gait and posture, Mr. Harle is confident that it would be possible for him greatly to ameliorate my father's sufferings, and also restore him to far more facility in walking. His fee is £50. The operation need not take more than two or three days, and there would then be needed three or four weeks of recuperation. If my father could only be persuaded to this step, I am very sure both he and the whole household would benefit from his improved health and spirits. But if this treatment is to be undertaken, the plan should, of course, be initiated without delay, before the roads between Birkland and Edinburgh are blocked by snow. (It would be necessary for my father to remain in Mr. Harle's care here during the treatment.) Both Guy and Mr. Harle are of the opinion that the operation *should* be undertaken as soon as possible, for so long as my father is walking on the incorrectly set bones, he is impairing his own chances of improvement.

I most deeply hope that with your goodwill and assistance in the matter, my father may be persuaded to a step so necessary and important to the benefit of his health and spirits and prolongation of his active life.

Your respectful Stepson, James Armstrong Winship.

Below were appended a few lines in another handwriting:

This Postscriptum is simply to endorse and confirm what Mr. Winship has stated above. Mr. Harle is wholly confident that he can help Sir Aydon and bring him back to greater freedom of movement and alleviation of pain. In the profound hope that Sir Aydon—to whom I extend my respectful good wishes—may be prepared to undergo this operation, I subscribe myself,

your friend and humble servant, G. Fenway.

Pray give my kind remembrances to Miss Louisa Winship.

The perusal, re-perusal, and digestion of this letter and note occupied the whole of a morning for Lady Winship and Alvey.

"Could it really be so? *Could* there be a possibility of such improvement, after so long a period?" was the first doubtful reaction of Lady Winship.

Alvey, from the start, was more sanguine. "Only think, ma'am, what a sensible, responsible man Major Fenway is; I am very sure he knows what he is talking about; he would not extol the work of this Mr. Harle unless he had satisfied himself of the truth of his claims by visiting many persons who had been helped in this manner. And then, both he and James know Sir—know my father, know how exceedingly hard to convince he is, how suspicious of change, how reluctant to embark on any new course; they *must* have the greatest confidence in the treatment, or they would never think it worth while to make the suggestion."

"Yes; that is so," said Lady Winship, in a doubtful, pondering tone.

Does she—perhaps—not *want* Sir Aydon to be helped in this way? Alvey wondered unhappily, remembering a good many of their conversations on the terrace. (One feature of these conversations, and, Alvey thought, a most important one, was that indoors they were never alluded to by either of the participants. They might have taken place between two different people. No reference was ever made by Alvey, during her humdum household consultations with Lady Winship, to any of the information imparted through the latter's quiet, meditative, confessional utterances. As, for instance, the fact that Sir Aydon had quitted the conjugal bed during the period of his worst pain and incapacity, and had made only intermittent returns to it since that time. Would his wife perhaps prefer that this severance became permanent?)

Would Lady Winship prefer her husband's physical condition to remain unchanged?

"Aydon was riding a young, unschooled colt on the day of his accident," his wife had related, on another of those promenades. "I ought to have dissuaded him from going out on it. I knew that I ought to; I did not."

Setting aside the basic improbability of anybody's ever being able to dissuade Sir Aydon from a course on which he had determined, Alvey could not help wondering if his wife had secretly hoped, on that occasion, for some kind of disabling accident; perhaps even for her husband's death? When we lightly wish misfortune upon those close to us, and our curses come home to roost, we learn to bitter effect what the long-term results can prove to be, where we had looked no further than the immediate outcome.

I must note down that idea, reflected Alvey; though I do not quite see how it can apply to Wicked Lord Love, who never plans ahead at all.

Meanwhile, to her great relief, Lady Winship seemed to be overcoming her doubts and prepared to think favourably of the proposal.

"Only, how shall I ever broach such a suggestion to your father?" was her next difficulty. "What time of day do you think would be most propitious?"

Alvey could think of no time that was better than any other. An added impediment to the success of James's proposal was the circumstance that, since the recent train of misfortunes, for some reason only known to himself, Sir Aydon appeared to entertain hard, angry, hostile feelings towards his wife. He seldom spoke to her unless it was absolutely necessary to do so; never looked in her direction; spent as little time in her company as possible. Alvey feared that the very fact of James's communication having been addressed to Lady Winship in the first place might render it unacceptable to his father.

"Perhaps at noon, when he takes his glass of Malmsey in the library?" Alvey suggested doubtfully. "I do *not* think at breakfast; and then, by dinnertime, he is always fatigued and—and in pain—" And tries to drown it all in wine, without success, she thought.

"He is never pleased to see me enter his library," Lady Winship said simply.

"Perhaps it would be best to ask some third party to make the proposal? Mr. Thropton, for example? Or even Amble? Sir—my father is so fond of Amble."

"*Amble?* We could hardly apply to *him* in the matter."

"Then it had better be Mr. Thropton. Shall I ask Parthie to step down with a note?"

Parthie no longer made the least attempt to cultivate Alvey's good opinion or court her company. She was rude, hostile, and disobliging. But since the wedding and Mr. Thropton's attention to her when she was hurt by the stone, she had on several occasions made excuses to see him, and brought his name into the conversation whenever possible.

"Parthie is sweet on Mr. Thropton," Tot had remarked bluntly one day.

"No, she isn't," said Nish. "She just hopes that he will dig up a treasure in his garden and that she will be there when he does so, so that he will be obliged to give it to her. Why, the rector of Corbridge dug up a whole *jugful* of gold coins and precious jewels in *his* garden; I daresay Mr. Thropton expects to do likewise. Remember how disappointed he was when that little box the men found turned out to have nothing in it but ashes."

"He did give a jet bead to Parthie."

"Much she cared about that! She was hoping for gold or rubies. She said it was a dirty little object."

Alvey had little doubt that Parthie would not refuse the chance of a visit to the rectory.

"Very well," said Lady Winship after another long, thoughtful pause. "Send for Mr. Thropton. I fancy that will be best."

But she sighed again, as if she did not have high hopes of the outcome.

Mr. Thropton was all eagerness to serve Lady Winship in any particular. He came hasting up to the Hall, his ruddy colour flushed to an even deeper shade by the rapidity of his pace. Lady Winship, who now spent the larger part of the day downstairs, received him in the drawing room and disclosed to him the contents of James's letter.

To her dismay, he was not at all enthusiastic as to the desirability of performing this operation upon her husband.

"Dear ma'am, how can we be sure that this is God's will? We know that suffering brings purification and strength—if our Maker had intended Sir Aydon to live without suffering, He would not have caused the accident in the first place."

This seemed to Alvey very suspect reasoning. She could not resist intervention, for Lady Winship was looking beleaguered and might, by this unexpected rebuff, be persuaded to change her mind.

"But, Mr. Thropton—firstly, anybody can see that suffering *hasn't* purified or strengthened my father; quite the reverse, it has only made him bad-tempered and miserable; secondly, why should not this suggestion from James and his friend be another evidence of God's will— just as much as the accident was in the first place?"

Mr. Thropton gave her a very wintry look. Up to this moment he had been studiously ignoring her presence. He said, "I do not believe, Miss—Miss Louisa—that this matter is *any* proper concern of yours. It is entirely a matter for Sir Aydon to decide—with the help of prayer and the advice of myself and Lady Winship."

Lady Winship said, "I asked Louisa to advise me. And I am sure that she has been most sensible and helpful."

At this, Mr. Thropton seemed a little put out of countenance.

"Well—then—in that case, ma'am, what would you have me do?"

"If you could just broach the matter to my husband," faintly urged Lady Winship. "And—and lay before him the advantages of the operation."

He was still not pleased, but could not help preening himself on this important role of intermediary.

"Very well, ma'am. Shall I do so directly?"

Lady Winship rang the bell for Amble, who came in and told her that Sir Aydon had just returned from the stables and gone to his library.

"But he's in a twitty mood, my leddy, and no' wishful for company, I doubt."

"Never mind, Amble. Just tell him that Mr. Thropton is here, with an important communication to make to him."

Amble retreated, shaking his head, and presently from the direction of the library could be heard the sounds of Sir Aydon thumping with his sticks and shouting in an enraged tone which boded most unpromisingly for Mr. Thropton's mission. Even the rector's rubicund countenance paled a little at the prospect before him.

"Perhaps—some other day?" he suggested.

"No, no, my stepson insists on the need for haste. Pray, do go now, Mr. Thropton, and get it over."

"Very well, ma'am."

Mr. Thropton went off nervously on his errand. Soon the sounds of Sir Aydon's disapprobation became considerably louder. Alvey, moving unashamedly out into the hall, heard through the open library door his voice roaring: "What? Go and have my bones broken *again,* by some damned horse leech in Scotland? I thank you, no! I'd as soon offer my carcass to the body snatchers straightaway and have done with it. And I'll thank my puling whining coward of a son to attend to his own business—he and that friend of his. *I* can endure an injured leg—*two* injured legs—better than he can, seemingly!"

This speech made Alvey so indignant on James's behalf that she walked into the library, uninvited, bent on speaking her mind, for once, to Sir Aydon.

She arrived at a moment of crisis. The footman, Stridge, had been on the point of handing Mr. Thropton a glass of Marsala, but it was evident that Sir Aydon, waving his sticks in furious endorsement of his argument, had accidentally dashed the glass from the salver on which it was presented, and straight into the unfortunate footman's face. Now the man was bleeding copiously from a severe gash on his cheekbone.

"Quick—lay him flat!" exclaimed Alvey. "Amble—do you run and fetch some linen while I hold the cut together to stop the bleeding."

Amble gave her a rather odd look, she thought. But he only said, "Yes, Miss Emmy," and departed at speed, while Sir Aydon and Mr. Thropton, almost equally disconcerted, stared at each other over the recumbent body of Stridge.

"What a—what a shockingly unfortunate mishap!" ventured the rector after a moment or two. "Are you all right, my man?"—to Stridge. He himself had turned quite pale at the sight of all the blood.

"Damned careless idiot," growled Sir Aydon; it was not clear whether he referred to himself or to the footman.

"Did any of the glass go into your eyes?" Alvey anxiously asked the young man. "Do you feel any pain in them? Can you blink?"

"I—I think they're all reet, Miss Emmy, I feel naught i' them. But my heid fair swims!"

"Just lie still then, don't talk," said Alvey, and stanched the blood with her wadded handkerchief, pressing it hard against the cut. Amble hurried back with a handful of linen table napkins, one of which Alvey swathed round the boy's head, tying it over her handkerchief as tightly as possible. By this time Mrs. Slaley and a couple of the maids were in the hall, hovering distressfully.

Alvey said, "It would be best if he could be carried to a bed."

"Allow me to assist!" exclaimed Mr. Thropton, springing into activity.

He and Amble and Mrs. Slaley raised Stridge and carried him away to the servants' hall; and Mrs. Slaley could be heard bidding Janet to fetch a stoup of water from the Lion Pool and Becky to rin awa' to the stables for a good thick hank of cobweb. Then the green baize door closed on them.

Sir Aydon and Alvey stared at one another in a silence bursting with unspoken hostility. He was breathing hard, obviously furious at having put himself so signally in the wrong, and uncertain how to extricate himself from the situation.

At this moment his wife entered the room, wide-eyed and pale, looking about her apprehensively.

"What is it, Aydon?" At the sight of a bloodstained napkin she gasped with fright. "Mercy! What happened?"

"Don't distress yourself, ma'am," Alvey said quickly. "It is nothing —merely an accident—no great harm has been done."

"You have blood all down your gown!"

"Well, it is none of mine—it is poor Stridge's blood. And he is taken care of. I will go and change."

Alvey took herself off, thinking that, on the whole, it was just as well that her impulse to burst out into an indignant tirade had been frustrated. If, now, Lady Winship and Mr. Thropton could only employ a little guile, a touch of diplomacy, perhaps Sir Aydon might be brought to admit the merits of James's proposal. He was in a poor position to argue, and must know it.

She changed her gown, handed the bloodstained one over to Grace, and explained the cause of the excitement to the interested children, who, from as far as his mother's room, had heard Sir Aydon shouting, and had come out to hang over the banister rail as Stridge's recumbent form was carried away.

"Is Stridge dead?"

"Did Papa mean to strike him?" said Nish, awestruck.

"No, no, I am sure that it was a complete accident. And he is not badly hurt. How is Grandmamma?"

"Oh, she is still just the same. She did open her eyes once, but she did not seem to recognise us."

Grace, taking the blood-spattered gown, said of Stridge, "Faith, Miss Emmy, the lad's jist head-ower-heels grateful to ye. He thowt his eye was knocked oot for sure, till ye wiped the blood awa' and set his mind at rest."

"It was a most unfortunate mishap," said Alvey. "I am very glad he is no worse."

"Ay, he's took no great hurt. But," said Grace with a grim chuckle, "in the village they'll be saying this is a hoose o' misfortune. There's enow rumours rinning roond a'ready. This'll add tae them."

"Why, what do they say in the village?"

"Ah, 'tis nowt but blethers. I'd best pit this i' cowd watter, Miss Emmy, afore it sets i' the cloth and won't budge," and she hurried off with the dress over her arm.

When Alvey next went downstairs, Sir Aydon was nowhere to be seen. Nor was Mr. Thropton. Lady Winship was in the drawing room, snipping dead heads off geraniums in a desultory fashion. She looked to be in very low spirits.

"Would you care to be wheeled out in your chair now, ma'am?"

"He will not be persuaded, Louisa! Indeed he declared that it was all a plot to make him even more lame than he is now—if not to do away with him entirely!"

"Oh dear; I am very sorry for that," said Alvey. She spoke no more than the truth. She had been thinking, rather guiltily, how very pleasant it would be to have a month's respite from Sir Aydon, whose personality in the house was tiring, and always to be felt, like a nagging wind. And yet he was a good man, a well-meaning, high-principled man; it was sad . . .

"What a terrible pity that my grandmother is—is not herself. I believe *she* might have been able to persuade him, if anybody could."

Lady Winship shrugged. "And Aydon has written to James—himself!—already—bidding James mind his own business and not meddle in family affairs, since, by his choice of career, he has voluntarily cut himself off, and can expect no sympathy or support from his father."

Alvey knew that for Sir Aydon voluntarily to bestir himself to write a letter was a very remarkable occurrence; usually he delegated all correspondence to a daughter—Isa had undertaken the task in the past —or to his bailiff, Lumley. She was inclined to think this quite a good sign. In her view, it meant that Sir Aydon still loved James—or he would not be so anxious to keep in touch with him, to quarrel with him.

"You do not think—if James were to come home in person, to remonstrate with his father—?"

"No, I do not," said Lady Winship with unusual firmness. "I think that would only make bad worse."

It was not James who came in person, but Guy Fenway, turning up unexpectedly, quite early one morning. Alvey and the children had taken a walk down to the river, to exclaim over the marvellous ice formations made by frozen spray glazed over the rocks and mosses; they were returning by a roundabout route when they were surprised to see a carriage carefully descending the slippery hill.

"It is Major Fenway! Hurrah!" shouted Tot, who had taken a great liking to his brother's friend; and the children raced through the pines and then alongside the carriage, shouting and capering. Its driver pulled his team to a halt, then dismounted from the box. He seemed delighted with the meeting.

"Major Fenway! This is wholly unexpected!"

"Good morning, Miss Louisa! And you are afraid that it will be wholly unwelcome. It is not so to you personally, I do hope?"

"Oh no, not in the least. But I am afraid that—that my father will not be pleased."

"Papa was in a great rage with James when his letter came," explained Tot, "and said that he was a meddlesome milksop."

"Well, that is a great pity, to be sure, and we must see if matters cannot be mended. Can you," the major said to Tot, "can you, do you think, lead my horses down the hill and into the stable yard, and give them into the charge of Blackett?"

"Oh yes, sir, I am quite sure I can," said Tot, joyfully proud of the trust reposed in him.

"Excellent! I am sure your sister will help you. And I shall look forward to a long talk with you later. Now I wish to have a short talk with Miss Louisa here—if she will permit?"

"Of course," said Alvey. "Though if you can come up with any scheme to persuade Sir—to persuade my father to this course of treatment, you are a great deal cleverer than anybody in this house, Major Fenway, and must have the tongue of Demosthenes! But indeed we are all very much obliged to you for the kind consideration that prompted you to make the inquiry and to inform us about the skill of Mr. Harle."

"The thing is," said Major Fenway, as they turned in tacit consent and took a path leading upwards through the pine grove, "the thing is that I have the greatest possible dislike of *ineffectuality*. I do not like to see objects put to wrong uses, or human beings consigned to pain or inconvenience which they need not suffer. In fact it enrages me. The things that I saw and heard at Birkland Hall set me quite in a passion."

Alvey could not help smiling: his calm and even cheerful demeanour seemed so at odds with what he said. But he went on earnestly: "It was really so, I do assure you. Oh, not *you*, or your part in the household—though we will come on to you presently—but the relations between Sir Aydon and his lady are so bad, so twisted, that they are plainly beginning to have an injurious effect upon the rest of the establishment. And much of this is due to the circumstance that Sir Aydon is not a well man. I am interested, Miss Louisa, in the link between a man's physical health and that of his mind; I intend, later, to make this my study; I am sure there is a strong connection between the two."

"Of course there must be!" cried Alvey. "I have noticed so often, myself, how hard I find it to apply myself, to use my mind, when I am fatigued, or in pain."

"Just so," he said, giving her one of his intent looks. "And in Sir Aydon there is little question but that the wrong functioning of one part has begun to impair the whole."

"But how can you ever persuade him to agree—?"

"Well," he said, smiling, "as to that I have a scheme in mind, but perhaps I had better keep it to myself at present so that afterwards, if any blame is flying about, you will be able to say truthfully that you had no hand in it, or any knowledge of it. I am aware, you see, of *your* somewhat equivocal position in the house; your sister Isa—if I may call her so—explained to me, when I was here before, about your situation; I refer to your entirely commendable and disinterested substitution—or exchange, should I say?—with the *other* Miss Louisa."

Alvey's heart gave a great thump. She stood still and stared at him, aghast.

"You *know?* Isa *told* you? You have known, all the time?"

"Well, not all the time. But since her disclosure, yes, I have. We went for a walk, the day before the wedding, and she told me the whole."

"*Isa* did? Without any reference to me? How *could* she? Good heavens," gasped Alvey, "I shall go clean distracted."

What shocked her so deeply was not that the major was party to her secret—that was bad enough, in all conscience, but somehow she instinctively felt certain that he would not betray her; no, what shook her to the roots of her being was the fact that the revelation had been made by Isa—by Isa, whose loyalty, she would have thought, was utterly to be relied upon. *Isa,* of all people!

Was no one what they seemed?

Major Fenway said, smiling, "You must not blame Isa too severely. I had already gone some way towards guessing the truth—and I do have what you might describe as a professional skill in cultivating people's confidence—persuading them to let down their guard; it is my métier, after all. I hope to make it my life work."

"Well!" said Alvey. "Just the same I would *never* have thought it of Isa!"

Privately she felt that, besides the professional skill on which he plumed himself, quite rightly no doubt, Major Fenway had in this particular case an advantage of which he may or may not have been aware: the fact that Isa had, from the start, been clearly predisposed to like him, enjoy his company, and place considerable trust in him. In fact, Alvey had wondered once or twice if Isa were not falling a little in love with the major; and had thought, also, what a very good and suitable match it would be, between two people of warm kindly temperament, considerable intelligence, and not a little sense of humour. Neither had anything to boast of in looks, to be sure, but that might also endear them to each other.

"What a dangerous man you are, sir!" she said, regarding the major with a satirical eye. "How shall I ever dare to have a conversation with you again, after all the falsities that you must have detected in me, over and over? It was really too bad of Isa!"

"On the contrary," he said cheerfully, "I hope that my disclosure may place our intercourse on a new and easier footing. Will it not be some relief to you to know that there is *one* person with whom you have no need to be on your guard, now that Meg and Isa are no longer at home?"

"Humph! I am not so sure as to that. In general I find that the safest way to maintain the pretence is to be equally on guard at all times, regardless of where I am or who is with me, even when I am by myself."

"Was that the reason why James was never told?" he asked inquisitively.

"Partly . . . No: Meg and Isa thought it best. Otherwise there might have tended to be some delicacy—some constraint between James and myself," Alvey explained in a constricted tone which seemed to prove her point. "And I myself had far rather he remain in ignorance. — You have not told *him?*" she cried in a sudden fright. "I really would far prefer him not to know—he would think so very badly of me!"

"No, no—set your mind at rest! He shall not hear the story from me, I promise you. But do, pray, tell me all about yourself; I confess I am immensely curious to hear your history. That you are an author I know already; Isa told me that you are at work on a novel. And that you come from America. But beyond that I am in complete ignorance."

"And your professional wish to acquire information is whetted to fever point? You long to discover what makes an apparently well-brought-up, well-educated female, in full possession of her faculties, engage in such an underhand, reprehensible scheme?"

"You do *not* take the words out of my mouth. I pass no such judgment. But I *am* greatly interested in the powerful creative impulse—in the urge to express, communicate, to generate original work—which must have impelled you to such a step; I should like to know about your past, your forbears, your background, in a word."

Such a request is, of course, irresistible. Alvey said, "Well—I suppose there is no reason why I should not tell you. But should you not be going down to the house, to make yourself known?"

"By no means," he said. "My intention is not to appear at the house until the dinner hour, when Sir Aydon cannot so far depart from the tenets of northern hospitality as to drive me from his door. *I* am quite unprincipled, you see, and have my scheme carefully set out."

"Why, then, arrive so early?"

"First, because I wanted to talk to you!"

"I am not in the least flattered—being aware that your interest is all in the way of business. And your second reason?"

"Why," he said, "I plan to leave exceedingly early tomorrow—at about six if not before—with Sir Aydon, of course, if my mission has been successful—so I wished my horses to have a good rest."

"Very practical! But I fear I cannot imagine *any* way in which your mission can prove successful—even I, with my fertile writer's mind, cannot at all fathom how you will set about it. But we shall see! In the meantime, ask me what you will."

"First, then, tell me about Louisa. I have had descriptions of her from Isa, from James, and from Meg, but I should be interested to learn how she persuaded *you* to this switch—for I am certain the plan did not originate with you."

"No indeed! I was wholly reluctant—"

Alvey described her discussions with Louisa, and that young lady's amazing, single-minded perseverance. "She is so very forcible! Rather like you, Major Fenway. She has a way of achieving her ends. I am persuaded she will make a most effective missionary. In the end I suppose she just wore me down."

"Now tell me about your parents. Are they dead? Who were they? What were they?"

"Well," said Alvey, "there, in a way, you come to the nub of the matter. At least I daresay you will think so. No, my parents are not dead. But they are lost to me."

"In what way? Describe them to me."

"They lived in New Bedford. My mother's people, the Alveys, were from Lincolnshire, my father's, the Clements, from Devon. He was a teacher, and a preacher. But when I was ten—I suppose my parents had, for some time, felt constricted by the life in New Bedford; they found the people there narrow, prejudiced, bigoted; my father came under the influence of a German preacher from Westphalia, Friedrich Müller, who invited him to join a religious community in a town he had founded in Union County, Indiana. It was called Unison."

"A monastic community?"

"Not exactly. But celibate. Married couples lived separately, and children, if any, were brought up in a different compound, parted from their parents, except at certain times. All lived as brothers and sisters in God."

"This was when you were ten? Did you join the community?"

"No," said Alvey, "I could not tolerate the prospect. I could not endure the idea of being deemed a—a somewhat discreditable product of my parents' union. I loved them; I had believed in their love for each other; to have all this, as it were, *nullified,* was entirely abhorrent to me. I disliked Herr Müller very much and resented his attitude to me. If I must lose my parents, I said, I would rather lose them entirely. I would rather go to an orphanage than exist beside them in a kind of prison where we must all pretend to be other than we were."

"A strong-minded view for a child of ten!"

"I suppose. But my parents had always insisted, as soon as I could read, that I must learn to judge and think for myself. They were, both of them, deeply religious—dedicated—detached. That, I suppose, may have made the parting easier. Though it was *not* easy. Fortunately for me, as matters fell out, I was not obliged to enter an orphanage; an elderly cousin took me in and completed my education. It was she who sent me to school in England, for she intended that I should be able to earn my living as a teacher. But before I had finished at the Abbey School she died; so, for the last two years there, I combined the role of pupil and teacher. Have I told you enough?"

"Indeed no! What about your parents? Do you hear from them?"

"No, never. That was another of the commitments at Unison—that there should be no communication, by members of the group, with the connections they had severed when they joined it. The only way in which I could reunite with them would be by joining the community myself."

"Which you have no intention of doing?"

"None."

"It is an interesting reversal," he said. "Instead of the child running away from home, the parents decamp."

"*Very* interesting," Alvey said so drily that he laughed.

"You are a formidable young lady, miss—may I call you Alvey? Good heavens—you call *me* dangerous? I regard you as far more so."

"Why, pray?"

"Because you have seen the damage that high principles can effect, and immunised yourself against it. Now I see why Louisa Winship's call to the missionary life touched a sympathetic chord in you."

"I am not sure that it did," Alvey said seriously. "What I mostly felt was impatience with her pretensions. I was almost sure that they were based on affectation—that if she were given her way, they would dissolve and vanish overnight."

"Was that why you were prepared to indulge her and fall in with her wishes?"

"Perhaps. To see—to see—"

"To see if her resolve would fail?"

"No—yes; a little. To see how she would behave. I must admit that up to now she has not justified my doubts. And of course also I was curious to see what her sisters were like—and her family. To find out."

"Just so. To find out. You and I," he said, "have a great deal in common. I shall be most curious to read this work of fiction that you are engaged on. Does it go well?"

Alvey began to laugh. "Oh yes, it goes well. But *you* would think nothing of it, Major Fenway! It is the most frivolous piece of work possible. A fribble! Quite beneath your notice. Gentlemen, I am per-

suaded, do not read such things; gentlemen read philosophical treatises or the works of Samuel Johnson."

"I myself prefer Shakespeare."

"There you are! You will not like my hero."

"It surprises me that you find the atmosphere of Birkland Hall sympathetic to such work; especially as so many household responsibilities
have lately come to rest upon your shoulders."

"Yes; and if you succeed in removing Sir Aydon, I am sure that even
more will devolve on me. My—Lady Winship is in a rather curious
frame of mind at present, far from showing any wish to resume her
functions and authority as head of the household."

"Well," he said, "poor woman. It is not to be expected. Not after
what has been happening to her."

He gazed at Alvey thoughtfully, as if he were on the point of making some communication, then, evidently changing his mind, inquired, "And do you hear from the real Louisa? Does the life come up
to her expectations?"

"Oh, she is not yet arrived at her destination. The next letter, I
suppose, will come from Madagascar; but she certainly seems like a
creature liberated; there is no doubt that the choice of a missionary's
career was the right course for her. So, there, I was mistaken. — But, I
pray you, sir, do tell me about James. Is he happy in his studies? Was
he greatly overset by Sir Aydon's angry letter? Has he managed to
accustom himself to the wooden leg? Has he recovered from the distress of those unjust accusations regarding the dead child?"

"You take a keen interest in James."

"Oh—why no—no more than in other members of the family. They
all interest me," returned Alvey coolly, though colouring somewhat
under his gaze. All except Meg and Parthie, she thought.

"Well, I will answer your questions. Yes: James is exceedingly
happy in his studies. He has a good intelligence and a true interest in
the subject; the auguries are excellent for his progress. No: he was not
greatly surprised by his father's letter—he had expected something of
the kind; but he has good hopes of my errand. Yes, he hobbles about
gaily enough on his wooden leg, and is already, with his good looks
and interesting situation, turning the heads of several pretty profes-
sor's daughters."

"Oh," said Alvey.

"I think it my duty to warn you, Miss Alvey, lest you take too deep an interest in James, that he is almost never heart-whole; since I have known him he has tumbled in and out of love half a dozen times, the last occasion being with my almost equally volatile sister. Fortunately, that came to nothing! James is one of my dearest friends, he is a dear clever fellow, but not such material as husbands are made of."

"You are not suggesting that he *was* the father of Annie Herdman's baby?" said Alvey indignantly.

"No, I am not. Do not ruffle up! The history of that poor child is a sad tangle which only time will unravel . . . it is to be hoped. No, I am perfectly sure that James had no part in that tragedy—"

"But you think it proper to warn me against him. I cannot imagine why! You need feel no responsibility for me, after all. And—and in any case, I daresay James and I will never meet again, if his father takes such a censorious view of his medical studies that he forbids him the house. — Besides, James has not the slightest interest in *me.*"

Alvey studied the watch at her waistband, consequently missing the look of rueful sympathy she received from her companion. She said, "It grows late. I must return and take my mother—Lady Winship—for her airing in the basket chair. It is a daily habit we have fallen into. What will you do with yourself, Major, until it is time to throw yourself upon Sir Aydon's hospitality?"

"I shall take a walk down to the village," he said. "James told me that he has an old nurse down there, a Mrs. Claver, to whom he asked to be remembered. Perhaps she may have some information to impart about the baby."

"I rather doubt that. Or it would have come to light by now. Well, I will see you later, sir," said Alvey briskly, and turned back towards the house. He looked after her, still with the air of wistful sympathy.

Alvey thought it best to waylay Amble during the afternoon, and warn him of Major Fenway's intention. Amble, she knew, was sincerely attached to Sir Aydon, and she had privately felt that he would have been a far better choice than Mr. Thropton to urge the merits of Mr. Harle's course of treatment.

She found him in the pantry, polishing plate with new milk and hartshorn powder. He rose and greeted her with his usual civility, to which a new warmth of liking and respect had been added.

"How does Stridge go on, Amble?"

"Well enow, Miss Emmy; the lad's got nowt but a bit of court plaister on his cheek, and that'll be off in a twa, three days. He's frit of Sir Aydon, though, an' won't come into the Rooms if he can help it."

"Well," said Alvey, "that is what I have come to talk to you about. Major Fenway has returned, as I expect you know."

"Ay, Blackett towd me his carriage was i' the stable and he himself walked doon to the village."

Nothing takes place that is not known, thought Alvey. It is almost impossible to believe that *somebody* does not know who was the father of Annie's baby.

"The major will be here to dinner, and spend the night. I fear Sir Aydon will not be pleased but—but I do not suppose he will raise any objections."

"Nay, he wilna. He thought the major a decent body enough; and he's taken his bread and salt, he canna fling him fra the hoose."

"Just so. The major tells me he has some new scheme to persuade Sir Aydon to change his mind and agree to travel to Edinburgh and undergo this treatment to mend his legs."

Amble sighed deeply.

" 'Deed, Miss Emmy, 'tis what he *should* do. Time and again I've said so. But you know Sir Aydon, he's neither to hold nor to bind. Stubborn as a stirk. If the major can wheedle him into a different mind, that'll be the best day's work he ever did."

"Well, that is what he intends, Amble, and if you can help him, I hope you will."

"I'll do owt I can, Miss Emmy, and blyth to."

XIII

Dinner that evening was quite as uncomfortable a meal as Alvey had expected.

Sir Aydon showed civility to the uninvited guest, but no more; he made no reference to his son, but talked long and pertinaciously of Helvoetsluys, Flanders, and the siege of Dunkirk. "Ah, those were gallant days," he kept saying, firmly ignoring the Peninsular War and any later battles such as Waterloo. "Abercromby, now. *There* was a general for you!"

Lady Winship, perhaps embarrassed to recall how very confidential she had been with James's friend while in her first distraught and stricken state after the rape of her garden, sat silent and withdrawn, making no contribution to the talk. Alvey, knowing her imposture discovered by the major, felt equally constrained, but did her best, nonetheless, to keep some kind of conversational current running. Parthie made her usual excellent meal but remained for the most part speechless and sulky; evidently she had not forgiven the major for failing to attend her when she took to bed with her black eye; and although he asked her kindly whether she were now quite recovered, she apparently refused to be mollified and merely muttered a monosyllabic reply. Nish and Tot inquired eagerly after their brother but were instantly commanded to be silent by their father, who then added, looking at Fenway:

"If you, sir, are come here in expectation of persuading me to that nonsensical scheme of James's, I may as well tell you straight away that you are wasting your time. Good God! I have twenty better ways of spending my money than to be laying out fifty pounds on such a harebrained venture. Fifty pounds! Such a sum would pay the tax on my coach and horses for an entire year, and the coachman's wage as well. So pray put any such notion quite out of your mind. And if you are come to plead James's cause, you may spare your breath. I will listen to nothing."

"I do not ask you to do so, sir." Major Fenway then succeeded in turning the talk to fox hunting, with much happier results; Sir Aydon, now that he no longer rode out himself, had lost touch with his hunting acquaintances and had nobody to reminisce with over notable runs and cunning foxes. He was soon in highly nostalgic vein. "Ay, they say the foxes of Simonside are superior in clever wiles to any in the whole country," he said proudly, and told at great length of one terrific run when a tailless fox led the hounds from Croppie's Hole on Simonside right down the valley of the Coquet to Amble Sands.

"A matter of twenty mile and more. Heigh-ho, they don't breed foxes like that any more."

"Oh, the poor fox!" exclaimed Nish incautiously. "Imagine dying like that—in the sea, so many miles from home." She turned pale and her eyes filled with tears at the thought.

Tot also had gone white and was swallowing hard, looking down at his plate.

"Hold your tongue, miss!" thundered their father. "And be off to bed with the pair of you."

They were happy to escape.

Lady Winship, Alvey, and Parthie likewise beat an early retreat to the drawing room, but Alvey, as she left, glanced doubtfully back at Major Fenway, who had courteously risen to his feet as the ladies left the table. He gave her a reassuring smile, and turned to sit down again as Amble placed a couple of decanters by his master.

Alvey heard the major say, "I believe you have a troop of volunteer cavalry hereabouts, sir, do you not? How many do they number?"

"Oh, aye, the Coquetdale Rangers; aye, aye, they are a decent body of men enough, and none so badly mounted or equipped. Before my disability I used to have command of 'em, but that's all gone by now; in any case, since Boney's laid by the leg, they are not required any more and I believe the troop has been disbanded; though, faith, considering what we hear of riots and rick burning in the South, the presence of such a body of men in the district is no bad thing . . ."

The ladies sat long and late in the drawing room, not a little apprehensive, expecting to hear shouts, thumps, or crashes; but the steady murmur of voices from the dining room went on and on, never raising its pitch; when Lady Winship finally rang for Amble and the tea tray, she said to him, "Will the gentlemen be coming soon, do you think, Amble?" and he replied, "Not for a while, I'm thinking, my lady; Sir Aydon just called for another bottle—but he's no' fretted nor moithered; the major talks so quiet and canny it's a pleasure to listen to him."

The ladies drank their tea in silence, and Parthie presently took herself away, yawning, to bed. A considerable time later, Major Fenway walked silently into the drawing room.

"I know it is disgracefully late now to ask your indulgence, ma'am," he said, "but if there is one thing in the world that I long for, it is a cup of tea."

He appeared sober, cheerful, and quite relaxed.

"Is my husband—is he not coming in?" asked Lady Winship, nervously handing the major his cup.

"He finds himself somewhat sleepy—so much talk of hunting! Amble is helping him to bed. I may say," disclosed the major, after taking his tea at a gulp and returning the cup to the tray, "that I have succeeded in my errand; I have persuaded him to accompany me to Edinburgh tomorrow and submit himself to the ministrations of Mr. Harle."

"*What?*"

"You *have?*" burst out of the ladies simultaneously. The major favoured them with a benevolent smile.

"I have: Amble will bear witness. But—just in case Sir Aydon changes his mind during the night—or, waking, forgets his decision—I intend to set out *very* early tomorrow; to be precise, at about half past four. Amble entirely concurs with me in this decision; and I am glad to say he will accompany his master on the journey, and remain in Edinburgh to take care of him while Sir Aydon is undergoing the treatment."

"Oh," faintly replied Lady Winship. "How very—yes, that is an excellent plan; Amble is so attached to his master; that will—but, are you *sure,* Major Fenway? Are you quite sure that you are not mistaken?"

"Perfectly sure," he said, smiling. "You must give me credit for a *very* persuasive tongue. Now—if you will excuse me—since I have to make such an early start—"

"Yes—yes—of course. Well! I must say, I was never so surprised in my life!"

"Are you telling the truth?" murmured Alvey to Fenway as she accompanied him into the hall, on the pretence of lighting bedroom candles. "Is there nothing underhand about this sudden reversal?"

"As Amble is my witness!" he replied, virtuously. "All I did was ply him with some excellent claret I had brought with me, and encourage him to talk of horsemanship. By the end of the evening he was so anxious to get back into the saddle that a trip to Edinburgh seemed as nothing if it would achieve that object; I believe he would gladly have accompanied me to Land's End. Still, as I said, I intend to whistle him off early, while he is still drowsy—just in case of any afterthoughts or backsliding."

"Ah. What was in the claret?"

"Now there I see the writer's imagination at work—always detecting subtle schemes and evil designs! Good night, and pleasant slumbers—"

Taking his candle, he ran lightly up the stairs.

Alvey had intended to rise in time to see the travellers depart, but overslept and missed them; she came down at five to find the major's carriage gone, and Stridge thoughtfully tidying away a few breakfast dishes.

"Amble ganned off wi' th' maister," he told Alvey.

"And Sir Aydon was still quite willing to go? He was not—had not changed his mind?"

They did not actually tie him up and bundle him into the carriage? was what she would have liked to ask.

Stridge grinned, the scar crinkling his smooth young cheek.

"He seemed a bit dazed-like, I'd say, miss, but he took a cup o' coffee and went off very biddably; yon Major Fenway has a wonderful

soothing manner o' talking. He'd be a grand chap wi' the horses if he
warn't a gentleman an' a doctor!"

Alvey ate a little breakfast and, as soon as it became light, went for a
stroll in the silent frosty pine grove, as neither Lady Winship nor the
children were down yet.
The air tingled with cold, no sounds of birds could be heard save
the cluck of a pheasant. How far will the coach have gone by now?
wondered Alvey. What time will they reach Edinburgh? What in the
world will James and his father have to say to one another? But perhaps they will not meet, perhaps Guy will take Sir Aydon direct to the
house of this Phineas Harle.
When had she begun to think of the major as Guy? Perhaps when
she learned that he shared her secret. He is a strange man, thought
Alvey; I suppose talking to people, persuading them of his trustworthi-
ness, extracting their secrets from them, is his preferred occupation;
rather a questionable one! Though very probably he believes that he
docs it for their good. I wonder, though, if that is really the case.
Yet she had to admit that she herself felt wonderfully eased, solaced,
almost lighthearted after divulging the story of her parents to this
interested and intelligent listener. That couple had been locked inside
her for so long; it was a great comfort just to be able to speak of them
to a third party, a dispassionate third party. Cousin Hepzie had been
far from dispassionate, she had been so violently prejudiced against
Herr Müller and his community that only regret and distress ensued
after any talk with her on the matter. If Mr. Thropton had been a
different kind of parson, mused Alvey, I could have talked to him; but
unfortunately his comments would be totally unhelpful, and, furthermore, I suspect that he is not a reliable confidant. I would not be
surprised if he spread gossip; I would never trust him with a secret.
Turning homewards—for by now the children must be up—she was
not a little surprised to see Mr. Thropton himself, as if conjured from
the ground by her thought, marching down at a hasty, blundering
pace through the pine grove; she was approaching the entrance from a
different angle, and they met beside the Lion Pool, fringed, now, with
icicles that dangled from the ferns and from the lion's head itself.

What in the wide world brings the rector out so early? wondered Alvey as she wished him a civil good-morning.

He seemed decidedly put about by the meeting.

"Ah—good morning, miss—er—that is—I wonder to see you out so early! I am come because—I understood—that is—word reached me that—er—Mr. James Winship's friend Major Fenway intends to try to persuade Sir Aydon—"

"Oh, how very kind of you," said Alvey. "You came to add your voice to the general chorus of persuasion. That was the act of a good neighbour, Mr. Thropton."

She was amused to see that he found himself greatly embarrassed in her presence.

"No—that is—well—I did not think it in the smallest degree likely that Sir Aydon *would* allow himself to be persuaded—but it was being said, in the village, that Major Fenway intended setting off this morning again quite early—and there was a matter on which I greatly wished to speak to Sir Aydon—"

"Oh, how very unfortunate," said Alvey sympathetically. "I am afraid you have missed him, Mr. Thropton. Major Fenway was anxious to reach Edinburgh quite early in the day, so they set off long before daylight."

"You mean—they are *gone?* Sir Aydon as well? He has left Birkland?"

Mr. Thropton was really dumbfounded at this news.

"Yes, that is the case, I fear."

If Mr. Thropton were not a clergyman, he would obviously have let out a heartfelt oath. His eyes bulged, his florid complexion turned a duskier red.

"Absolutely *gone?*"

Alvey nodded. He held, she observed, a folded paper in his hand. It had a vaguely familiar appearance.

"When," Mr. Thropton asked, collecting himself with a visible effort, "when do you expect Sir Aydon back again?"

"That is rather a matter for conjecture. Major Fenway told me that Mr. Harle will, if he can, perform the operation at once—within the next couple of days; but that, of course, is not the lengthy part of the business. As you are probably aware, it is the recovery that takes time,

since my father is now in his sixties, his bones will not mend so
quickly; it may be a matter of several months, perhaps—"

Mr. Thropton directed at Alvey a look of extreme dislike, almost
hatred.

"Miss—I do not know your real name—let me inform you without
delay that I am apprised of the disgraceful—the *utterly* disgraceful circumstance—that you are an imposter—a *deceiver*—that you have no
more right to refer to Sir Aydon as your father than—than—" He
fumbled for words.

"Than that lion's head, shall we say?" suggested Alvey. "Was that
what you came to tell Sir Aydon? Then I cannot help thinking that it
was very fortunate that he had left before you arrived. Such a piece of
information, received just before undergoing a difficult and painful
operation, would almost certainly have impaired his chances of a
speedy recovery."

She smiled at the rector and thought: What will he do now? Will he
demand to see Lady Winship? Or would she not serve his purpose? Of
course, he must have had the information from Parthie—I am sure she
has had her suspicions for some time past—

Now suddenly Alvey realised why the paper in his hand looked
familiar. It was the missing letter from Louisa. She extended her own
hand, gently twitching it from his grasp before he could put it in his
pocket.

"Ah, this is my property, I believe? Yes, Louisa's letter. She seems
very happy in her chosen avocation. But I wonder how you came by
this private letter, Mr. Thropton?"

He made a snatch to reclaim it, and the paper tore in half, both
pieces falling into the Lion Pool.

"Dear me, what a pity. Now the ink is all washed off. But there was
no address upon it, only Port Elizabeth, so I could not have written
back to her. This pool is supposed to have certain magical properties,
is it not? I do hope they will not adversely affect Louisa's chances of
success in the missionary field. The children think this pool belongs to
Mithras. You are an expert on Mithraic lore, I believe, Mr. Thropton?
Was it you who told them about it?"

It is rather unkind to tease him, she thought. But then, he certainly
came here with no good intentions regarding me. What *were* his inten-

tions? What did he hope to achieve by his disclosure? Or was it prompted solely by love of the truth?

"Would you wish to go in and see Lady Winship? I am afraid she will not be leaving her chamber for some time yet; we were up quite late last night—"

"No, no," he muttered. "That would serve no useful purpose."

"I believe you are right. I rather doubt if she would be equal to such a disclosure, or know how to deal with it."

What would Lady Winship do? Alvey wondered. Faint again? Refuse to believe the story? Temporise and say the whole issue must await the return of Sir Aydon?

Perhaps all three.

"It is too bad that your evidence is destroyed," she sympathised.

Mr. Thropton said crossly, "That is by no means the only—that is to say, Parthenope tells me she had seen notes, memoranda written by you—of such a nature as to show, most conclusively, that you are not what you say—"

Oh, the little toad, thought Alvey. I did think somebody had been rummaging in my writing-table drawer. Well, listeners never hear good. She will have read some fairly severe dissections of her own character.

"Well, Mr. Thropton: you must of course do just as you think best. At the present time I will bid you good morning, for I find it chilly out here and the children will be waiting for me."

And, giving him a formal smile, she turned indoors.

A pale face behind the library window had been watching their colloquy; as soon as Alvey walked into the hall Parthie came hurrying out of the library, robed very fine, in a Sunday dress instead of a weekday one, with her hair dressed high in a Grecian knot, and the hem of her skirt let down to hide her unsightly ankles.

"Was not that Mr. Thropton I saw you talking to outside just now? Why did he not come in? Where has he gone?"

"When he learned that Sir Aydon had left four hours ago, he said his visit would serve no purpose. It was Sir Aydon he wished to see. So I fancy he has gone home again."

"*Gone?* My father is *gone?*" Parthie was as staggered by the news as the rector had been.

"Yes, I suppose they may be almost halfway to Edinburgh by now. It seems Mr. Thropton had some letter that he wished to show your father. But unfortunately it fell into the Lion Pool—very annoying for the poor man—so he has changed his mind," said Alvey with an expressionless face and voice.

Parthie turned bright pink, bit her lip, hesitated a moment, then ran up the stairs. The distant slam of a door could be heard as she retired to her room.

Nish and Tot were with their grandmother. Alvey had encouraged them to spend a portion of their mornings and evenings in this room, the time that was customarily given over to reading, or painting, or working by themselves. The voices of the children, and their activities in the room, would, Alvey hoped, in time stir the old lady into some kind of awareness, or interest. While one child read aloud, or recited, the other sat on the bed, carefully rubbing and manipulating the old, cold hands, warming and chafing them.

"So she'll remember it is us," said Nish, "even if she can't see us."

For the piercing, shortsighted eyes, though they were open, seemed to stare at nothing.

Duddy, who entirely approved this arrangement, had persuaded Stridge and Surtees to fetch a worktable from one of the pantries, on which the children could spread out their books and drawing materials. And Tot had had another good idea. He suggested bringing in a variety of interesting objects for the old lady to look at—"to give her something out of the common to think on."

"We don't know that she thinks," said Nish.

"Well, to look at, any road."

One of the upstairs rooms had, in the previous century, been turned into a kind of minor museum by a bygone Winship lady with a much-travelled husband and time on her hands; from this chilly, dusty, and little-visited place the children fetched various treasures: a model of a bridge made from cork, a narwhal's tusk, an enormous bees' nest from Brazil, fortunately divested of its bees, a gorgeous silk hanging showing Indian gods and goddesses in lively attitudes, and a large stuffed prickly monster from Borneo.

Duddy was a good deal less enthusiastic about these imports. "They're no' hygienic," she said. "And they take a deal of dusting." "You *can't* dust the prickly monster. And I'm sure Grandma likes looking at them."

After a few days of this regime, the old lady's room began to resemble a souk.

"Ye'll have tae stop them bringing in any more objects, Miss Emmy. Say a word. They'll mind *you.*"

"Very well, Duddy. But I do think, don't you, that Grandmother looks a little better for their company? And they take *great* pains with her."

"Aye, they're good childer," agreed Duddy; and her grim face approached as near as it ever came to a smile these days.

"You don't think we should fetch back Dr. Cunningham from Newcastle?"

"Na, na, the farther he's awa', the better she'll fare. I don't howd wi' all that bleedin' and purgin'; 'tis flat against nature. Major Fenway said we were dae'in the very best for her when he looked in—"

"It seems very quiet in the house without Papa," said Nish, gently working over her grandmother's fingers, bending and straightening them, kneading them as if they were bread dough. "I do wonder how long he will be gone?"

"Emmy said Major Fenway thought it might take two months at least for his legs to mend."

"Poor Papa; it is hard that he has to go through all that pain again."

"Well," said Tot, "at least this time he has a better chance. In a way it serves him right for letting that old bonesetter from High Haugh mend his legs the other time; if he had had the sense to send for a proper surgeon, think what a lot of trouble would have been saved."

"I miss him. It is queer, I thought I should be glad when he went, for he is always cross nowadays, but I am not glad. I feel safer when he is in the house."

"*Safer?* What danger is there to be afraid of, little spoony?" said her brother with scorn.

"Well, there must be some danger. There is the person who threw the stone that hit Parthie; and did the damage to Mamma's garden."

"That is old Amos Herdman for sure; and I do not suppose he will do anything more. Smashing up the garden would be revenge enough. Anyway, I am not at all afraid of *him*."

"I am," said Nish with a shiver.

"You are only a girl."

"I wonder if Mamma will ever make another garden. We could help her, perhaps."

"She will not be able to start till next April," Tot observed. "Look, it is snowing quite hard."

"If the roads are blocked, Papa will not be able to come back, even when his legs are mended. Winter is a hateful time, when we can't go up the Hungry Water."

"Still—this winter will be better than last."

Nish nodded. Then she exclaimed, "Oh, Tot! Only see! Grandmamma is looking at you!"

Indubitably, the old lady's eyes had turned in his direction.

"Come closer," whispered Nish. "Come by the bed. Take her other hand."

He did so, holding it between both of his, and said, "Can you see me, Grandma?"

The eyes in their hollows rested on his; shut; opened again.

"I'm sure she sees me," he said. "Grandma: can you blink twice if you hear what I am saying?"

A pause; then two slow blinks.

"She does hear! She understands!" cried Nish joyfully, and kissed the paper-white cheek. "Soon you'll be talking to us again, Grandma, won't you?"

"And scolding us," said Tot.

The eyes blinked again, and a cheek muscle twitched.

"Should I fetch Duddy, do you think, or Emmy?" Tot asked his sister.

"No, no, they'll be here by and by. Granny doesn't want a lot of noise or fuss, or to be hurried. Do you, Grandma? Why don't you show her some things, Tot? Slowly; so she can have a good look at them."

So, one after the other, he fetched to the bedside and exhibited the cork bridge, the narwhal's horn, the wooden carvings from Bohemia, the Greek pot, and the prickly monster. The eyes accepted and studied them. The cheek muscle twitched again, more noticeably, at the prickly monster.

"In a week's time you'll be talking, Granny," said Nish. "Now listen and I'll sing you a song."

She sang:

> "Are ye going to Whittingham Fair?
> Parsley sage rosemary and thyme
> Remember me to one that's there
> For once he was a true love of mine . . ."

"You always sing that song," said Tot.

"Of course. It's because of Annie," said Nish.

It was agony to drag herself away from Lord Love, now that the climax of his story was so near, the shape of it all spread out before her; Alvey felt an absolute contradiction of impulses, she wanted to write and write and write, scribbling, skipping, condensing, abbreviating, because the exhilaration and joy of shooting down the last breakneck slope was so very intense; on the other hand, she did not know how she was going to bear the parting from her loved characters, and she could see this severance approaching with fearful speed. Still, she thought, I'll at least have the pleasure of working through it again, making a fair copy, and improving as I go; in a way, that will be almost the best part, for then the *worry* of creation, and the pain, will be over, it will be just embellishment and improvement.

Firmly she clapped her pages together, folded them inside a sheet of blotting paper, and locked them into the worktable drawer, sliding the little brass key into the reticule she wore at her belt; nobody but Parthie, she felt sure, would pry into the drawer, and there remained nothing there now of a suspect nature, but she could not endure the idea of Parthie being the first person to read her story, turning the pages with her fat, clumsy fingers and ploughing uncomprehendingly through the delicate witticisms.

Since Sir Aydon left Birkland, Parthie had fallen almost completely silent; she occupied herself with needlework in her own room or in the sewing room, making clothes for herself; practised on the piano

with commendable diligence; and looked at Alvey with a stony glare
when their glances happened to meet. Long may such a state of affairs
continue, thought Alvey, and went up to the pele tower to give the
children a Latin lesson.

Mr. Thropton had sent word by a garden boy that he had a severe
cold and must discontinue their instruction for the present.

Arrived in the Tower Room, Alvey found to her dismay that Tot
was laid out on the floor, on a folded blanket, with his sister carefully
loosening his collar and turning his head to one side.

"Oh dear—has he had one of his turns? I am so very sorry. Is there
anything else to be done for him?"

"It is rather cold up here; he would be better for another blanket to
cover him."

"I'll fetch one."

When Alvey returned and the boy had been warmly wrapped, she
said, "What brought that on, do you know?"

"Oh yes," said Nish matter-of-factly. "It was Grandma. She suddenly looked at us and knew us."

"Gracious me! Are you sure? That is wonderful news."

"Yes, quite sure." Nish told the story. "And Tot was so pleased and
excited that he could feel one of his fits coming on. But luckily Duddy
was there by that time. So we came up here—"

"Poor boy, he feels things so keenly. It is too bad—"

She looked down at the small thin shape outlined under the blanket,
only a tuft of black hair visible at one end.

"He will do well enough now," said Nish practically. "We may as
well leave him alone. Shall we go back to Granny? Shall I tell you my
new story?"

Three days later, Mrs. Winship suddenly spoke. Alvey and the children were there at the time. Tot was reciting a list of Latin preposi-
tions, Nish drawing a picture to show her grandmother, while Alvey
gently massaged the old lady's arms, neck, and shoulders.

"*A, ab, absque, coram, de, palam, clam*—"

"*Cum,*" prompted Nish from the table.

"*Cum, ex,* and *e*—"

Alvey was permeated with an extraordinary and completely novel sensation. She felt hollow, estranged, almost light-headed. She had finished her book. What in the world shall I ever do now? she kept asking herself. The book had occupied less than a tenth of her real time, but the idea, the presence of it had been with her so continually, for so long, that she felt unbalanced, as if she had lost a leg. Now I have some conception of how poor James— Resolutely she thrust the thought of James away. I am certainly not going to moon and pine for James just because I have lost Wicked Lord Love. James is not for me. I must just find some other way to employ my mind.

And just at present there was no lack of opportunity.

Nish completed her painting and came to hold it out before Mrs. Winship.

"You see, Grandmother, it's a—"

"Myrtlewood," pronounced the old lady suddenly. "Matchwood. Snow apples."

They all gaped at her, thunderstruck.

"Stubby. Tender. Disguise."

"*Yes*, Grandma! Say some more words! Say lots of words!"

"Briar. Mourn. Goat."

The door opened, and Lady Winship came in. She held an open letter.

"Children I have good news for you. Major Fenway writes to say that your Papa has gone through the operation, and, so far as can be ascertained at this time, it has been successful; his bones are correctly set, and they are straight again."

"Can he walk?" asked Tot, but Nish cried, "Mamma, Granny has spoken! She has said words!"

"She has?"

"Glass. Paper. Wheel. Cascade."

"Good heaven. Does she understand us?" said Lady Winship doubtfully. She approached the bedside, letter in hand. "Ma'am, I am happy to inform you that Aydon—that your son's legs have been reset, in Edinburgh, and he is going on as well as can be expected."

The eyes widened. There was a reflective pause. Then: "Ed—"

"No, ma'am, *Aydon.* Your son Aydon."

"Ed—"

"Edinburgh!" cried Nish. "Edinburgh, Granny!"

"Ed-in-burgh."

Duddy, entering the room at that moment, dropped the basin of warm water she carried. Tears poured unchecked down her weathered cheeks.

"Oh, ma'am," she whispered. "Oh, ma'am!"

"*Can* Papa walk?" persisted Tot.

"No, no, of course he will not be allowed to try, even, for many weeks yet. — Oh, I must write to Aydon directly, to tell him this news about his mother. He will be so very happy—" Lady Winship paused and thought for a moment. Then she said to Alvey in an altered tone, "Or, no, perhaps it would be best if *you* wrote to your father about it."

"Of course I will, ma'am, if you wish me to," said Alvey, rather puzzled.

Some peaceful weeks followed. Little Katie cut a tooth. More snow fell. Over Christmas, however, there came a thaw for several days. Alvey struggled into Hexham with an immense list of household commissions. Invited to accompany her and assist, Parthie refused, curtly. Well, thought Alvey, I have done my best; if she does not wish to help, or enjoy herself, bother her! And she dismissed Parthie from her mind. She bought leather boots for the three children, who had all grown a great deal in the last months, salt fish, lemons, raisins, nutmegs, thread, cloth, embroidery silks, black pepper, and Java rice. She also carried her clean-copied manuscript to Mr. Allgood, who promised to read it at once and advise her as to its potential saleability.

"I would be *very* much obliged, sir, if you would dispatch it to your cousin without delay," said Alvey firmly, "while the roads are temporarily clear and the mail's in transit; for, once the roads become blocked again, I suppose it might be many weeks before the parcel could be sent."

"Ah, you are like all young writers," said Mr. Allgood, smiling, in what Alvey could not help considering a patronising and superior manner. "Anxious for your work to be seen and appreciated as soon as possible. Well, well, I shall convey it on its way as soon as may be, do not fear—"

He glanced down indulgently at the first page, and his eyes widened; he read a few more lines, and his expression changed completely. Looking up at Alvey with a great deal more respect, he added, "It shall go off today, I promise. And that is a great piece of self-sacrifice on my part, for I shall not have time to read it through, and I should dearly like to! Is there any news, Miss Winship, of your sisters?"

"Yes, sir, Meg and Isa are settled in Bath for a month. Meg finds Bath a delightful town."

"And Miss Isa?"

"Well," said Alvey cheerfully, "as you probably know, she hates all cities, and finds Bath a repulsively noisy, dark, and confining town. Also, she says, it rains there every day. But she is bound to admit that the houses are handsome and the libraries excellent. So, for the moment, I think she is resigned to her situation."

"I wonder if she will ever come back to us. Or if she will encounter some eligible young gentleman in Bath—"

All of a sudden, Mr. Allgood looked very wistful.

By New Year's Day—which was celebrated in Birkland village with a bonfire and barrels of blazing tar—the old lady was speaking slow, careful sentences.

Her memory had come back, and Nish was encouraging her to knit on large wooden needles.

"Why do you visit your grandmother so seldom now?" Alvey asked Parthie. "I am sure she would be very glad to see you more."

"Does she ask for me?"

"She never *asks* for anybody. She likes to see everybody. The more different faces, the better she is pleased. And you used to be her favourite."

"That is so no longer," said Parthie sourly. "Nish and Tot are her little angels now. They can do no wrong."

Yes, because they were *there*, helping her when she needed it, Alvey thought, but did not say.

When she herself was in the room with old Grizel, much of their time was spent in a kind of roll call of the family.

"Let me see, now, Meg and Isa, where are they?"

"In Bath, Grandmother, until the end of February."

"And James? Following his studies in Edinburgh."

"Yes, and his friend Major Fenway writes that he is working exceedingly hard and has made an excellent impression on his professors. And that is all thanks to your help."

And his grandmother would be very happy to receive a letter from James, Alvey had written to Major Fenway—but letters to and from Edinburgh were scanty and much delayed, nothing had been heard from James as yet.

"And Aydon—he, too, is in Edinburgh?"

"Yes, until his legs are sufficiently mended to allow him to travel. But Guy—Major Fenway says that he is making steady progress."

Then there were the servants to be enumerated.

"Ellen? Mrs. Slaley? Grace, Janet, Stridge, Surtees, Blackett, Carey?"

"They are all well, Grandmamma, and send their best respects."

"That is well. I must make a list of all these people in case I forget any. Remind me to do that. — And Archie? And Annie Herdman? And wee Geordie?"

"Annie died, Grandmother—do you not remember?" Alvey said gently. "Poor little Geordie was found in the Lion Pool, drowned. And Annie—"

"Ah yes. I do remember. Was it not Charlotte who drowned wee Geordie? Did not somebody tell me that?"

Alvey felt her mouth go dry, her blood turn icy chill. She swallowed and said, "Oh, *no*, Grandmother. No, never. Nobody could have told you such a thing."

"In the Lion Pool," said old Grizel dreamily. "That was where Duddy found Charlotte's ring."

"*Never* say such a thing! It can't be true. You must have dreamed it."

"Perhaps . . . And what about Parthie? Where is she?"

"I am here, Grandma," said Parthie's voice from behind Alvey, who turned round sharply. How long had the girl been standing there? Her face was quite expressionless. She moved forward and politely kissed the old lady's cheek.

XIV

Alvey contrived to waylay Parthie on her emergence from the old lady's room after a half hour's visit.

"You know that it would be terribly wrong to repeat or pass on anything that your grandmother has said to you—in her confused, rambling state?"

"Why in the world should I wish to do so?" said Parthie coldly. "Excuse me—*sister.*" And she walked away to her own room.

Alvey was obliged to be content with this unsatisfactory reply. If only she does not go talking to Mr. Thropton! Furthermore, she reflected, what I said is not true; the old lady is far from confused. She does not ramble. She is slow, but she is clear.

Detachedly Alvey wondered, as the days went by, why Parthie did not go to Lady Winship with the story of her own imposture; and then she supplied herself with the answer: it is because Parthie suspects, probably with reason, that her mother would take very little notice, if any. She would not care, one way or the other. Lady Winship is certainly in a very peculiar frame of mind; *can* that suggestion of the old woman's possibly be true? God help her if it is. But I find it hard—I find it almost impossible—to balance such a suggestion with what I know of the woman that I have wheeled back and forth so many times. — And yet, I do know with what callous lack of consideration she behaved to Annie Herdman, making her shut the child in the stable room; that I know to be true. And what about the ring? We have only Duddy's word that she found it in the pool where the child was drowned; but then, what would she, or Mrs. Winship, have to gain from such a fabrication? Could anybody else have seen it in the pool? How long did it lie there? But, in any case, the ring is returned now. And they need not have done that. And now nothing can be proved about it, one way or the other.

Oh, how can I tell what to believe?

Having no invented romance of her own to engage her thoughts, Alvey's mind was now horribly vulnerable to such speculation and brooding. And it was not helped by a letter from Guy Fenway which presently arrived, rather soiled and battered, having been passed from hand to hand along the way.

Although the roads were, at present, impassable to mail coaches, a few intrepid travellers did still manage to make their way on foot or on horseback. These were for the most part horse copers, tinkers, clock menders, "gaun folk" as the servants called such itinerant waygoers with their packs and pack mules. In the winter months they were always welcome at the Hall for the news and merchandise they brought—gipsies with crockery or baskets, old men with birch brooms, pedlars with thread papers and scissors and herbal remedies. Mr. Allgood had promised that, if he received any news about Alvey's book from his cousin, he would, in default of the proper mails, find some such means of transmitting it to Birkland Hall. An old lady called Mug Lizzie brought the letter from Guy Fenway and was well fee'd for her trouble. But there was no word from Mr. Allgood.

"Sir Aydon goes on well now," Guy wrote, "and has walked a few steps. His progress is slow but definite. And one most positive feature of this is that he can now walk entirely without pain, although the legs are still weak. He himself is quite amazed at this. He was, at first, slow to mend, and spent several days in a state of delirium during which he required continual attention, for he was liable to throw himself out of his bed and do incalculable damage unless constantly supervised and restrained. Fortunately that period was of short duration. But while it lasted either James or Mr. Harle or I myself sat with him continually. During one of these periods he talked to me at great length in a rambling, distraught, incoherent manner; I do not feel it would be right to reveal the precise nature of his communications; but I can tell you that he appears to be harbouring some terrible suspicions against his wife. I hope—I trust—I feel fairly certain that these are unfounded. I do not think he has divulged them to her. But she may well

have guessed what is in his mind. He has kept these ideas to himself
and brooded over them until they entirely occupied his thoughts, and
have wholly eroded the relationship between husband and wife; and, I
am sure, also contributed to his own low state of mental and bodily
health. I hope most profoundly that some means can be found of
dispelling these suspicions . . ."

Sir Aydon believes that his wife murdered wee Geordie, thought
Alvey instantly. At some point he must have picked up that idea. From
his mother, perhaps? Or is it possible that Lady Winship confessed the
deed to Guy Fenway when she recovered from her faint after the
garden was destroyed. Could Sir Aydon have been in the dressing
room next door, listening? Guy does *not* say the suspicions are unfounded. He merely says, "I hope some means can be found of dispelling them." But how, if they are correct? Or even if they are not
correct, even if the wretched woman were to deny them entirely, how
is the truth ever to be discovered?

Of course Sir Aydon believes that she was jealous of his fondness for
wee Geordie. Because she suspected that he was the child's father?

Even if *he* denied *that,* how could the truth ever be proved?

What a wretched, wretched tangle they are in, Alvey thought. I do
not see how it can ever be unravelled. Perhaps it would be better if
they were to remain apart. Yet he must come back to Birkland. Everyone misses him: strange, but true. And she could hardly leave; Birkland has been her entire life. Where else could she go?

Oh, Wicked Lord Love, thought Alvey sadly, what a happy, nonsensical, harmless career yours has been, compared with the dark,
swampy, thickety land that these poor souls inhabit. — Yet when I
came here I thought this place such a haven. And so it has been, for
me.

I must write back to Guy, and try to reassure him.

She could not write back to Guy immediately, however, for Mug
Lizzie had gone on her way, and communication with the world beyond the village was for the time cut off.

And as for the village . . .

One morning Alvey went in search of Lady Winship, having been
applied to by Blackett, the head groom, for some instructions regard-

ing the horses, on which she was wholly incapable of making a pro-
nouncement.

Lady Winnship was discovered in the library, where she often sat
nowadays, wistfully staring out at the Lion Pool. With her was Mrs.
Slaley.

"Ma'am, can you tell me if in the past—" began Alvey, but stopped
in mid-sentence, for neither of the other people there had even noticed her arrival.

Mrs. Slaley, pale as it was possible for anyone of her complexion to
be, was pleating her apron distressfully.

"Aw thowt it best to tell ye, ma'am, what fowk are sayin'. It's not
reet they should say it behind yor back and ye not knaw."

"Thank you, Mrs. Slaley. You did very right to tell me. And it was
courageous of you," said Lady Winship faintly. "They are saying in
the village that I—that I murdered the child—Annie Herdman's
baby?"

"Ay, ma'am. They say 'twas fathered by the maister—and so ye
were angry aboot it, an' did awa' wi' the boy."

"I see. And do you believe that yourself, Mrs. Slaley?"

Mrs. Slaley swallowed, and said firmly, "No, ma'am. Ye *wor* a bit
hard on Annie, now an' now, but ye'd nivver do a thing like yon. That
aw do believe."

"Thank you, Mrs. Slaley. You are a good woman."

"And ye've elwis bin gud to me, ma'am, and I've knawn ye ower
twenty year."

"What about the other servants? Do they believe this of me?"

"Nay, ma'am, nane o' the owder ones, Ellen or Grace or Blackett
or Carey. Nane o' those as knaw ye well."

"I am glad of that," said the faint voice.

"As to the yoonger ones, aw canna say."

"Of course not. I wonder if Mr. Thropton knows—what he thinks."
Lady Winship went on, half to herself.

Mrs. Slaley made an indescribably derisive noise, which conveyed
her opinion that it was of little consequence what Mr. Thropton knew,
or what he thought. Then she curtseyed, with dignity, and turned to
leave.

Alvey had remained all this time motionless, transfixed, halfway between the door and the fireplace; Mrs. Slaley, as she walked by, gave her a little frowning nod, lips pressed together, as if she said, "Now _you_ have to deal with this situation; and rather you than I."

Lady Winship moved to the window and stood there staring out. Alvey followed and stood by her, wondering how she could possibly pierce the loneliness that surrounded this woman like a sepulchre.

"Ma'am . . . the talk will die down. It is idle spite . . . bred of winter conditions, inaction, lack of diversion, lack of other news . . ."

Slowly Lady Winship shook her head.

"It will never die down completely. The stigma will be on me till I die. And the sooner that happens, the better—"

"_No_, ma'am! You _must_ not talk so!" Now Alvey was really terrified. She clasped Lady Winship's arm. It felt like an oak branch. "Such talk, such thinking is wicked—and—and cowardly, too!"

"Oh, don't trouble yourself. I am not the sort to terminate my own existence. Once," said Lady Winship thoughtfully, "once upon a time, I would have been too eager to see how my young walnut tree did, and if the yellow flags throve and the new rose plants; and even now, after my garden has been murdered, I can still look forward to the pussy willows and the first primroses."

"Well, thank God for that. There must," said Alvey angrily, "there _must_ be some means of scotching this talk—silencing those spiteful tongues. If Mr. Thropton knew—he should do something—"

"Mr. Thropton! Now that I come to think about him," said Lady Winship, with one of those streaks of insight which always took Alvey by surprise, "I fancy he is more likely to have started the talk than be instrumental in putting an end to it."

"So what should we do, ma'am?"

"Perhaps the sheriff ought to be informed. If Aydon were here—"

"The sheriff? Who is he? What would he do?" Thank heaven Sir Aydon is _not_ here, thought Alvey.

"Old Lord Linhope, over at Watch. He is Tot's godfather. But I believe he is very ill . . . What could he do? Put me under restraint, I suppose; have me arrested and imprisoned until I can be tried and the matter cleared up."

"_Arrested?_" Suddenly Alvey felt sick. This was like some wicked nightmare. "But there is no evidence. Ma'am, you are taking this all far too seriously. Just because there is evil, spiteful gossip—"

"I wish Aydon were here," said Lady Winship simply. "He would know the proper action to take. I will write to him."

What good will that do? thought Alvey helplessly. He himself believes the tale.

"I have brought this on myself, in a way." Lady Winship frowned and rubbed her forehead. "I did do wrong." She lifted her head and stared at Alvey, still frowning. "I did pretend that I believed James to be the child's father. Which I never did. Let James take the blame, I thought. He is not here, what does he care? I thought they would be gone from the district long before James ever came near us again. I acted a part—that was very wrong. And perhaps this is my punishment."

"Why did you do that, Mother?"

"I was afraid that the tale would spread that the child was Aydon's—"

And was it? Alvey wanted to know, but could not bring herself to put the question.

Grace appeared in the doorway.

"Miss Emmy, could ye come? Aw wuddint trooble ye, but Janet's cut herself in the dairy: a reet nasty cut and they're all frit—"

Ever since she had dealt with the emergency of Stridge's wound, Alvey had been applied to in accidents of this kind, which, in the cold and dark of winter months, were of more frequent occurrence, when tools were slippery and hands were numb with chill.

"Of course, Grace; I'll come directly."

Next day Lady Winship moved herself into the Tower Room.

"Until the matter of Annie's baby is cleared up," she informed Alvey and Mrs. Slaley, "I shall consider myself confined to this room."

"But how can it ever be cleared up? Suppose it never is?"

Lady Winship shrugged, gazing remotely past Alvey and out of the window.

"Then, I suppose, I shall remain here. Unless legal measures are taken to remove me elsewhere. You may give the children their lessons in the library . . ."

Mrs. Slaley and Alvey stared at one another in dismay as the door closed on the mistress of the house.

"Mebbe she'll git the notion awt of her heid, Miss Emmy, by an' by —when spring comes—when she hears the birds callin'—when the maister cooms back—"

Knowing Lady Winship's obstinate, tenacious nature, Alvey doubted this. Besides, closeted up there in the Tower Room, how would she ever know if the talk died down or not?

And what a nuisance it was going to be having Lady Winship in the tower; she would need far more wood and coals carried up than the children, who occupied the room only during a portion of the daylight hours, and were spartan in their disregard of cold; and servants would have to take up meals and washing water and carry down slops. It was hard on the children, too, being deprived of their eyrie.

Martyrdom creates a kind of selfishness, thought Alvey; I must put that down in my notebook—only, to what end? I have no story through which to plait it . . . *How* I wish that the young men would come back with Sir Aydon.

In the meantime, it was at least a considerable relief that the old lady was now sensible enough to be supplied with such information, and even appealed to for occasional advice in household affairs.

"Humph! Charlotte's as stubborn as a mule," said old Mrs. Winship. "It's a fortunate thing that you are here just now to run the household, miss; my daughter-in-law is perfectly capable of remaining up there for twenty years out of sheer pigheadedness. That's where Louisa inherited *her* obstinacy. And Meg has it too; only Meg, as it happens, has never been crossed."

Alvey opened her mouth to speak; then quietly closed it again.

"We'll see what falls out when Aydon gets back. Is there any news of him? How does he go on?"

Happily Alvey was soon able to satisfy the old lady on these points. Another letter had come from Guy Fenway, delivered by Fish Benjie. Sir Aydon was walking more freely within doors, though he had not, as yet, ventured out. No term could yet be set, however, as to his stay in Edinburgh. A long coach ride, with its jolting, bumping, and vibration, was thought very inadvisable for several months to come. But meanwhile the news and lively doings of the city were benefitting Sir

Aydon greatly; various old friends had come to see him; if not *recon-ciled* to his son's new choice of profession, he was at least becoming inured to talk of it, and to seeing James; a kind of truce existed be-tween the two, wrote Guy, which, no doubt, in time, would warm to a better relationship. James, by the by, sent his best regards, hoped that his grandmother was mending, promised to write to her that *very day*, or, at least, the following day; he was most deeply engrossed in his studies.

No word came back about Alvey's novel.

During a slight thaw she struggled to Hexham on horseback es-corted by Surtees. While Surtees bought a few necessities for the house and stable, Alvey went to call on Canon Beaumont and his sister, who had heard rumours of Sir Aydon's removal to Edinburgh and were eager and interested to learn the full facts of the matter. What Alvey really wished to discover was whether any talk about Lady Winship had percolated as far as Hexham; she was relieved to find that this did not seem to be the case—unless the Beaumonts were amaz-ingly discreet. And, remembering Miss Beaumont's lynx-eyed obser-vation and relishing discussion of every tiny gesture at the Assembly, Alvey thought it unlikely that, if such a tale had come to her ears, she would not wish to talk it over.

"You will stay the night, Louisa?" invited Fanny Beaumont wist-fully, but Alvey said no, she had to get back: "My mother is not—is not very well, still deeply distressed by the loss of her garden; and with grandmother only just recovering from her seizure—"

The Beaumont ladies perfectly understood, and entrusted her with all manner of kind messages.

Before starting for home, Alvey went to Mr. Allgood's shop and bought Lord Byron's *Hebrew Melodies*, which she had a faint hope that Parthie might enjoy. The girl had been looking so stifled lately. As on the previous occasion, Alvey had asked her if she would enjoy the ride to Hexham, but Parthie was no horsewoman and curtly refused. Al-vey, despite her dislike, could not help feeling sorry for Parthie, who seemed to have so few pleasures or resources. Perhaps Lord Byron would do the trick . . . Also, of course, Alvey wished to see Mr. Allgood, who, smiling, produced a letter for her.

From Edinburgh? No, it was not. It came from Bath, and was in Isa's handwriting.

"No news from my cousin, I fear," said Mr. Allgood kindly. "But editors, you know, are *very* busy men; they have so many matters to deal with. And indeed, there have been remarkably few mails from the north; only about two in the last six weeks."

"Of course I know I must not be impatient," said Alvey.

But she was bitterly disappointed just the same, as she rejoined Surtees and the horses, having stuffed Isa's letter, unopened, into her reticule. That could wait until she was at home.

The journey back was hideously cold. A ferocious northeast wind seared their faces all the way; the horses jibbed and whinnied and shook their heads angrily as they were forced onwards into the biting blast.

"Slaister on, Miss Emmy! Aw doot there's a hale whack o' snaw on the way."

The snow began, indeed, when they were still an hour's ride away from home, and blew in their faces so savagely that they were obliged to dismount and lead the horses; the one hour's ride lengthened into three, and it was well after dark when, to Alvey's infinite thankfulness, they crawled into the comparative shelter of the pine grove and saw the lights of the house shining down below.

"I'd have been lost for sure without you, Surtees. I'd never have found my way in this."

"Ah, nivver mind it, ye're a right plucked 'un, Miss Emmy."

Alvey was warmed, both physically and in her cautious heart, by the welcome she received from the kitchen staff. Mrs. Slaley sat her down by the fire and made her swallow a bowl of barley gruel with whisky and ginger in it.

"We began to think we'd nivver see ye more, the pair o' ye, when it coom on to snaw se sudden."

"Oh, Mrs. Slaley, this gruel is wonderful. I believe it would bring the children's prickly monster back to life. Now I must run up and see my mother and grandmother; there's a piece of news for them."

She had read Isa's letter while the gruel was preparing.

"Meg is very cross and sick," wrote Isa mournfully. "She is breeding, and has made me promise to return with her to Tinnis Hall in

April, for she cannot bear to be on her own while she feels so down-pin. John, of course, is overjoyed. I think of you often in the winter snow and wonder how you do? Pray, pray send word to York, which will be our next address, if you can. And how does your writing fare?" "Miss Meg's expecting a baby," Alvey told Mrs. Slaley.

"Bliss me! That's grand news. Aa rackon Maister'll be hoping it's a boy."

A boy, a boy, Alvey thought impatiently as she climbed the stairs, why this need, this insistence on having a male child? As far as I can see, women are stronger than men, they are more resilient, they endure better . . .

She had intended to run up the stairs, for she feared the old lady would have been suffering anxiety at her late return. But the long struggle of walking through the snow, leading the reluctant horse, forcing her way against the gale, had rendered her legs so stiff that she could only climb up slowly and painfully, like an old woman herself.

She was greeted with a storm of reproach.

"There you are at last! I wonder you thought it worth returning at all! Why not stay with the Beaumonts?"

"Don't scold," said Alvey, and kissed the cold papery cheek. "There, I brought you a puzzle game. And a novel by Jane Austen, of which Mr. Allgood speaks very highly. — Where are the children?"

"They became so worried about you that I could not endure their company and sent them to bed. They will be asleep by now."

"And Parthie? Has she not been in to sit with you?"

"Haven't laid eyes on her since breakfast time. Considers herself too grand to be bothered with me since I became senile." The old lady sniffed.

Carrying a candle, Alvey visited Lady Winship, who registered her return with a calm lack of interest; then she went to the children's room. Their own candle was still alight, but gave only a small patch of illumination in the big, shadowy room, which, situated on the third storey, was seldom visited by any adult save Grace, who scolded but had no power to make them remove the boxes of birds' eggs, bags of quartz stones, the stag's skull with antlers, the doll's house constructed out of wooden packing cases, the bundle of lapwings' feathers, the bows, arrows, and spears. Picking her way across the floor was a hazardous exercise. The room, at the opposite end of the house from Alvey's, faced north and west; through its two windows the roar of the Hungry Water could be heard, even above the roar of the gale. Despite adult prohibitions, the children's beds had been pulled directly under the windows. Alvey approached that of Tot, which was nearer to the door, and found both children in it, wrapped, cocoon-like, in all their blankets (for the room was icy), clamped tightly, head to tail, like zodiacal fish. Alvey wondered if they were asleep, but Tot said instantly, "What made you so late?"

"The storm. We had to walk the horses from Rievershield."

"You should *not* have gone," he said furiously. "It was very unresponsible behaviour."

If she had not been so tired, Alvey would have smiled, he sounded so like Sir Aydon.

"I know, and I am sorry; but even Surtees did not expect the snow to come on so soon or so hard."

Nish took hold of Alvey's hand, grinding it punishingly between her fingers.

"You ought not to have gone. We thought you would never come back. It was a wicked thing to do!"

And all for nothing, Alvey thought. All for no news from Edinburgh.

She said conciliatingly, "I did do a number of useful errands; bought things for Grandmamma—and for Mamma—I have brought you some new books and crayons—and pictures of animals—"

"We could have managed without them," said Tot.

"Yes, but Surtees needed spermaceti oil—and a deal of other things—"

"You ought not to have gone," said Nish again. She flung Alvey's hand away from her angrily and huddled down again beside her brother. "Go away! We were asleep till you came, disturbing and waking us."

"Is it not too cold for you, right under the window?" said Alvey, and thought she sounded like a fussy grown-up.

"We prefer it," said Tot haughtily.

"Good night, then."

Neither child replied. Nish blew out their candle before she had picked her way back to the door.

Alvey longed for her own bed and the warming pan she had seen Grace preparing. But first she went to Parthie's room and tapped for admission. Receiving no answer, she gently opened the door, and was startled to find the room unoccupied, the bed empty. Could Parthie still be in the drawing room?

But then, on the dressing-table pincushion, she saw a square of white: a letter.

"Since No Body in this house apreciates me," Parthie had written—her spelling was not much better than Nish's, Alvey reflected—"I am leaving and going to Coldstream with Mr. Thropton, where we are to be Married. He loves me dearly and wishes me to be his wife. Then we shall go on our Wedding Jurney and return when Papa is better to claim my Portion. Goodbye! Christian Parthenope Winship (soon to be Thropton)."

Mercy! thought Alvey in horror. Where can they be now? Eloped! And she only fifteen! What a shocking thing! Ought I to tell Lady Winship?

Deciding not to do so immediately, she ran down again to the kitchen, where Mrs. Slaley and Surtees were banking the fires and setting all to rights.

"Miss Parthie's run off with Mr. Thropton."

"Eh, awa', naw," said Mrs. Slaley. "Yon parson was bound to git one o' ye."

She did not seem in the least surprised.

"But in this storm! When did you see her last?"

It appeared that Parthie had left the house, privily, and carrying a large carpetbag, not ten minutes after the departure of Alvey and Surtees for Hexham. So that is why she seemed almost pleased that I was going, reflected Alvey.

"You did not mention the matter to Mrs. Winship—or to Lady Winship?"

"Well—'twas noon of our business, rightly—and we thowt ye might as well rest in ignorance till morn, so weary as ye looked—"

It became plain to Alvey that the servants thought Birkland Hall would be well rid of Parthie, who was fretful, complaining, and required a great deal of attention.

"Yon Thropton's welcome te her! He'll be sorry soon enow."

And as Parthie had started so early, it was reasonable to assume that the pair would have reached their destination long ago.

"How far is Coldstream?"

"Fifteen, twenty mile. The blacksmith there, Sandy Robson, he'll wed folk as canna get wed in their own parish."

Rather a comedown for Thropton, thought Alvey, a clergyman in his own right, to be obliged to have the ceremony performed by a Scottish blacksmith. But apparently he thought the prize worth it.

"She's so young!"

"Lasses gets wed at fourteen," said Mrs. Slaley bluntly.

"Should I tell them tonight?"

"Naw, let the old 'uns sleep. Tomorrow's time enow."

In agreement with this, Alvey retired to her own bed, so warm and welcoming. Yet, unexpectedly, once in its shelter, she found herself prey to a desolation of loneliness and grief. Why in the world? It was not from envy of Parthie—nor of Meg, fretful in her pregnancy. Wretched Parthie, spiteful, unlovable as she was—yet what a fate to be shackled, at such an age, to such a man! Nor was it, entirely, disappointment at the lack of news about her own book. News, recognition, these things would come in the end, they were bound to, they must. Nor was her distress caused by the sharp reception she had received from Mrs. Winship and the children; for that, in some degree, was deserved, and showed at least that she was of use, of value to them. She could still feel the old woman's cold soft cheek, and Nish's little bony fingers angrily clamped on her wrist.

So what makes me so miserable?

Restless, changing her position for the twentieth time, Alvey decided at last on the source of her sense of deprivation and solitude. It was the closeness of those two children, huddled together in their need for comfort. No one, ever, in my whole life, has been as close to me as that, she thought. And very likely no one ever will be.

XV

For several days after the trip to Hexham, Alvey was obliged to keep to her bed. She felt considerable guilt at this, since neither of the older ladies now played much part in the functioning of the household; but she had caught a severe cold; her head ached, her back and limbs ached, she was alternately chilled to the bone or burning with fever.

"It'll pass, it's naught," said Ellen, fomenting with hot flannel and administering spirits of nitre. "Ne'er worry your heid, Miss Emmy, matters'll rin alang weel enaw for a twee, three days."

The children, having evidently agreed to forgive her, were touchingly considerate and brought offerings to her bedside of apples, drawings, and stories they had written. Failing Parthie as a recipient, she gave them the *Hebrew Melodies*. Byron perhaps might not suit them as well as Scott, but still . . . In fact, they discovered "The Assyrian came down like the wolf on the fold," and read it aloud to one an other with shouts of enthusiasm.

The elopement of Parthie was much discussed, of course.

Their view was identical to that of Mrs. Slaley.

"Thropton's welcome to her. She's always peevish and selfish and horrible. I wonder that he wanted her."

"It was because he always wanted to be married to someone in our family," said Nish.

"I wonder he did not ask Emmy."

"I would have said no. But in any case—" Alvey stopped, uncertainly.

Nish went on for her. "Probably Parthie told Mr. Thropton that Emmy was not our real sister. So she would have been no good to

him, not a Winship. Parthie was always going on about you to *us,*" she
told Alvey. "She used to say that you had probably murdered Louisa
and buried her in a hole in the ground. Or had her shut up somewhere in a tower."

Once Alvey would have laughed at such gothick fancies. But now,
thinking of Lady Winship, she shivered. The children, however,
seemed to take their mother's self-imprisonment calmly enough.

"What did you say to Parthie when she told you these things?"

"Oh, we told her that we'd a deal sooner have you than the real
Louisa. So then she gave up troubling us."

"How did you know, so soon, that I was not the real Louisa?"

"Because of the scar."

"Scar?"

"Louisa had quite a bad scar on her wrist, where Tot bit her once,
when she was pinching him . . . Papa made him stay in bed for three
days," said Nish reminiscently. "It was on her right wrist. Did you
never notice it?"

"No, never."

"Where is Louisa now?" Tot inquired, not with any great interest.

"In India, I suppose, being a missionary; where she wanted to be."

"And a good riddance to her too. Perhaps Parthie and Mr.
Thropton will go to India. I hope they don't stay on in Birkland."

Unfortunate Parthie! thought Alvey. I suppose first she tried to tell
the old lady about my fraudulent dissimulation—but Mrs. Winship
had her stroke, so that was no use; then she persuaded Thropton to
tell Sir Aydon, but he waited too long. No doubt he hoped the information would be his passport to favour, to being rewarded with
Parthie's hand in marriage. Failing that, she grew impatient and made
him elope. Somehow Alvey felt certain that the prime mover in this
escapade had been Parthie herself; she could not imagine the placa-
tory, servile Thropton initiating such a risky step. How would Sir
Aydon take the news? He must be written to and informed, of course;
that must be attended to as soon as she was up. She felt certain that
Lady Winship would not have done so; and found that she was right.

"But do you not agree that he ought to be told?" Alvey said rather
diffidently, as soon as she was sufficiently recovered to climb the stair
to the pele tower.

"Oh yes; but if I wrote, it would only increase his anger against me. If you do so, I daresay he will not think much of the matter; he never cared two straws for Parthie. He will only think the worse of Thropton."

Nobody mourned Parthie, poor girl, not even the old lady, whose chief adherent and hanger-on she had used to be. But Mrs. Winship did receive the news of the elopement in a thoughtful, gloomy manner, brooded over it for a while, and at last said gruffly, "He was a fool to take her. I'd have thought Thropton had more sense. Better to have waited for Nish . . . He won't keep Parthie long."

"Ma'am, what can you mean?"

"Those legs . . . Few of the women born in Charlotte's family with that affliction live through their twenties. And Parthie has always been of an unhealthy, sickly habit. Indeed, in my opinion, it will be a marvel if she lives long enough for him to claim her dowry."

"Good God, ma'am!" said Alvey, appalled. She thought about Parthie, her selfishness, her sickliness, her despondent, querulous, unhopeful attitude to life, and asked, "Did *she* know this herself?"

"I do not suppose that anybody *told* her, in so many words; but nobody kept it from her, either."

"Was that, ma'am, why you have always been so kind to Parthie—allowed her the freedom of your chamber—appeared to favour her above the others—because you were sorry for her?"

The old woman appeared to give this question some thought. At length she said, "Perhaps . . . I did somewhat pity her, it is true, poor sickly thing. Nobody paid her any mind. Also, it suited me; she was biddable, she courted my good opinion. When you are old, such things have their value."

But she imposed upon you too, thought Alvey. Tidying out Parthie's room with Grace, packing up her things—"For, nae doot, she'll be wanting 'em gin she cooms back a wedded lady to the rectory," as the maid observed—Alvey discovered many articles that had evidently been purloined from Mrs. Winship's room: pieces of lace, toilet utensils, ornaments, perfumes, washes, even books.

"No wonder I thought I was growing so absentminded," drily observed old Grizel. "The girl was a proper little magpie."

Not all the lost articles were found; some, no doubt, Parthie had taken with her on her nuptial gallop. The cupboard in her room also contained an amazing quantity of Minerva Press romances, of the most lurid character, presumably inherited from the departed Miss Waskerley.

Parthie must have found the adventures of Wicked Lord Love—if she read any of them—sad, tedious stuff after these tales, thought Alvey, leafing through the pages of these sensational works, filled with abduction, rape, duels, disembowelling, fratricide, matricide, patricide, infanticide, and sororicide. "Best use them for lighting fires," she said to Grace, and dropped the whole bundle in the wastepaper basket, lest Nish and Tot acquire a taste for such reading matter.

But then, on second thoughts, she reclaimed them and locked them up in a trunk. What right had she to destroy Parthie's books? And the girl might be glad of them when she came back to inhabit the gloomy rectory with Mr. Thropton. Especially if, as Mrs. Winship prophesied, she were likely to become ill . . .

Alvey felt bitterly remorseful about Parthie. I treated her all wrong, I ignored her obvious need, I blame myself extremely for being odiously thick-skinned, shortsighted, and *superior.* I hope to heaven that repulsive man is treating her reasonably well. Oh, how could I have been such a blind fool?

Fish Benjie presently delivered a letter from Guy Fenway. Sir Aydon, Guy wrote, had been much startled at the tidings of his daughter's elopement—startled, shocked, and entirely disapproving. "But," wrote Major Fenway, "it is a measure of Sir Aydon's recovery that such an event, which would have wholly overthrown him a few months back—very possibly been the cause of a paralytic stroke—at this juncture induced in him no more than a few snorts of displeasure. He is of course far more indignant with Mr. Thropton, but considers him more stupid than wicked; for one thing, as Sir Aydon says, he himself would have thrown no obstacles in the way of Mr. T.'s courtship and marriage to Miss P. in the ordinary manner, if that was what he wished; Miss P., Sir Aydon asseverates, was always a silly, henwitted girl and he personally would not wish her on his most inveterate enemy. 'In my opinion she will drive the parson mad in six months,' he said several times. 'Mr. Thropton will be justly served for his cupidity.' Upon James's inquiry as to whether Sir A. intended to deprive Miss P. of her dowry, Sir A. said no, certainly not, he had no such intention, but he would reduce it to three thousand instead of the promised five, since there should be *some* penalty imposed upon behaviour of such a hotheaded and shameless nature; he did not wish to be the talk of Northumberland because all his daughters ran off, one after the other.

"Sir A. goes on excellently well, and it is our hope to escort him back to you early in April if the roads are then fit for travel. Meanwhile, dear ma'am, I send you my most cordial regards. James transmits his love to his grandmother and hopes she received the letter he dispatched to her some weeks past. — I remain &c."

I do not believe James *ever* wrote to his grandmother, Alvey thought crossly. He has been continually promising to do so ever since they left. I am heartily glad that I am now over my infatuation for him—or, at least, *almost* over it, that it no longer pains me so very greatly—for I can see that he is not to be relied upon, his promises are worth nothing at all. It is fortunate that Guy Fenway is such a good correspondent.

February and March went by, cold, bleak, and confining. Snow fell, and more snow; sometimes the Cheviots sparkled out, spectacularly white, but often they were veiled in cloud for days together. The Hungry Water roared louder and louder; ice formed along the edges, but the current in the middle was too swift to freeze.

When the weather was fine, the children went out tobogganning in the pasture that sloped down to the river. Little Betsey was old enough now to accompany them for a short time, but she quickly became cold, wet, and, when her boots were full of snow, she started to cry and had to be escorted home by Alvey. Whereas Nish and Tot were prepared to continue at this sport for hours on end, returning blue, half frozen, but exhilarated by the tingling air and rapid motion.

"It's lucky that Annie's cousin made us that sled before he went off," Tot said. "It's by far the best we ever had."

"I wish he were here to ride on it with us," Nish said.

"Annie's cousin? Who was he?"

"His name was Sim. He went away . . . It was lucky you bought us those boots too, sister Emmy, otherwise we'd have had to go sledging in our bare feet."

No day since that of the storm had been fine enough for another trip to Hexham; no news had come from Louisa, from Parthie and Mr. Thropton, or from Mr. Allgood's cousin.

Alvey, during this period, found herself in a curious state of limbo; purged of her novel, eager to begin another, yet with no theme very particularly in mind. She longed for the process of writing, which had become an addiction, but no tale was there waiting to be told. Time by no means hung on her hands, however; with Lady Winship still voluntarily confined to her tower, the running of the establishment, indeed of the whole property, devolved almost entirely upon Alvey; by the end of three months she began to have a very fair notion of household economy, the keeping of accounts, and estate management. She spent a good deal of time in the library, reading such works as were there on farm management, forestry, and stock raising; she consulted extensively with the elderly bailiff, Lumley, whom she found to be a well-disposed, sensible man. In any time left over from these occupations and the children's lessons, she read the various memoirs of county worthies and local histories which she found in the library, having long ago exhausted her own stock of reading matter.

"I wish, Miss Emmy, when Sir Aydon comes back, ye'd try and persuade him to raise more sheep and put down less of the land to wheat," Lumley said over and over. "This land's terrible poor for wheat; but, like all o' the other great landowners, Sir Aydon's fair sot on it. Now sheep, I grant you, wouldna bring such a profit, but they'd put the land in wonderful good heart, after twee, three years; and they say the price o' wheat is tumbling fast; when all's said and done it's nowt but a gamble."

"Well, I promise to mention the matter to him, Lumley, but you know Sir Aydon; he's partial to his own way, and not likely to pay heed to any other person's advice, let alone that offered by a mere female."

"I wish he'd such a heid on his shoulders as ye have, Miss Emmy. He's too hasty in his judgments."

This surprised Alvey; she would have said that Sir Aydon was too dilatory and reluctant to reach a decision; but she supposed it came to the same thing in the end. He would think for weeks without coming to any conclusion, and then make a hasty plan without reference to any of his considerations.

"Still, Lumley, Major Fenway says that my father is a changed man now that his legs no longer give him so much pain; he has become calm, collected, and reasonable."

"Well, well, I'll believe that when I see it."

At last the day of return came. The sun had shone for two weeks, snow retreated to the upper slopes of the hills, and down below the grass was greening, the roads had begun to dry out. Birds sang vociferously. Alvey had not the heart to keep the children at their lessons for many hours at a stretch; their longing to make a first exploration up the river and examine their long-unvisited territory was so deep and evident.

"It is always so exciting after the winter, you see, Emmy, because everything is changed; rocks have washed down and sandbanks have shifted and there are new islands and channels—"

"Yes, of course, then, go, but you will be careful, will you not? The river is still very full, and it grows cold long before dusk . . . And since your father is expected sometime during the latter part of the day, it would be a terrible pity if you were not there to greet him."

Nish and Tot plainly felt that their presence or absence would be a very minor feature of Sir Aydon's homecoming, and they skipped off in the middle of further admonitions from Mrs. Slaley about not taking boots off or getting feet wet. Alvey had a deep pang of envy for them and wished that she could have gone along with them, jumping from rock to rock, climbing up beside waterfalls, crossing by stepping-stones, finding treasures in pools, floating sticks down rapids. Absurdly, she wished either one of them had said, "You come too, sister Emmy." Of course she could not have gone; somebody had to be there to welcome Sir Aydon; but still, she wished they had asked her . . .

As the day went by her apprehension grew, and she could not help feeling that it was well founded. Even if Sir Aydon's disposition was so greatly improved as Guy Fenway alleged, he was coming home to a strange and gloomy scene, of which he probably had received little conception from the letters written by Alvey and Lumley. His wife had shut herself in the pele tower, labouring under doubts and guilts, some acknowledged, some still unexpressed. Her feelings towards her husband were far from wifely; she certainly bore a deep grudge against him for all those dead and stillborn children and for the others in whom he had taken so little interest. She suspected him—still?—of having fathered Annie's child. She herself was accused of having done away with the child. And Sir Aydon—did he believe that? How was all this to be resolved? Would Sir Aydon, now that his health was to some extent re-established, be able to grapple with such a knotty situation? Or would he sink back into the lethargy and despair that was paralysing him when Alvey first came to Birkland?

These were not the only questions that made her nervous and despondent. As well as his relation to his wife, there was his relation to herself. Had any tale of her deception reached him? Had Mr. Thropton written from wherever he and Parthie were spending their honeymoon, exposing Alvey's impersonation of Louisa? Had Guy, at any point, thought it proper to inform James, or James's father?

Even if her imposture were not exposed, Alvey felt anxiety enough on her own account. Here she had been, without authority or experience, in virtually sole command of this man's household for the last three months of his absence. No major catastrophes seemed to have occurred, so far as she knew—except, of course, Parthie's elopement—yet how could she tell which of her actions or decisions he might choose to censure?

When the carriage was first seen threading its way through the pine grove, she felt half inclined to creep away and hide herself until the first homecoming should be over. But that would be stupid and childish.

She put on a clean tucker, smoothed her hair, and went to the front hall, where the upper servants, waiting in sober joy to welcome their returning master, parted to let her through.

She would hardly have recognised the man who descended from the coach. He was straight and vigorous, his complexion many shades lighter and clearer, his hair visibly thicker, grey still, but with a reddish burnished look to it, not the ragged wispy fringe that she remembered. He looked round him alertly, with evident deep delight at being home once more.

"Ha! The old copper beech still standing, I perceive; it managed to survive the winter gales, that is capital!"

Then his eye lit on Alvey.

"Ah, there you are, my dear. You, too, look well, I am glad to see."

"Thank you, sir. I, too, have survived the winter gales."

He approached, shook her hand, then gave her a hearty kiss, which took her entirely by surprise. Over his shoulder she met the watchful, amused eyes of Guy Fenway, who had escorted the carriage on horseback, and now, dismounting, came to greet her.

"You are blooming, Miss Winship, I am happy to find. And here is your brother, in much better fettle than when you saw him last."

James also had been on horseback, and Alvey must admire the expertise with which he swung himself out of the saddle, though Surtees was at his bridle immediately to help him. He, too, looked far better; still thin, but not so fine-drawn, still pale, but not so haggard. He greeted Alvey with, she thought, some constraint, and asked immediately after his grandmother.

"She is impatient to see you; can hardly wait. She is in her own room."

Sir Aydon was greeting the little ones, Betsey capering about, Katie now almost at the walking stage but borne at the moment in the arms of Tushie. Alvey was just, in her own mind, beginning to anathematize Nish and Tot, for never being at hand when it would be suitable for them to appear; but now, by great good fortune, they did arrive, having evidently run all the way back from some distant spot. They were scarlet-faced, panting, untidy, and muddy, but at least, Alvey said to herself, no one, *no one,* can say they are weedy, sickly, unpromising children. They looked lively, healthy, even happy to see their father. And he seemed pleased to see them; much struck, indeed, with the improvement in their looks.

"Good Gad, I'd hardly have recognised the pair of ye. I declare, you've shot up like fireweed. Well, sir! Well, miss! Are you sorry to see your bad-tempered old dad home again, eh? Eh?"

Now he's overdoing it, Alvey thought in anxiety, but Tot replied matter-of-factly, "No, sir."

And Nish cried, "Are you better, Papa? Are you quite better?"

"Why, let us hope so, miss! And now I must go in and see your mother and grandmamma."

"Come and walk on the terrace," said Guy Fenway to Alvey.

"Oh, but I—"

"There is nothing that needs your attention, I am sure. Sir Aydon is with his wife. James is with his grandmother—"

"And so he should be," she said with asperity. "He never *once* wrote to her—"

"Is that indeed so? I thought that he had written once."

"She never received a letter from him. And it would have meant so much to her. After all, her money is supporting him."

"Well, I am happy to see that your infatuation has come to its natural end."

"I was never infatuated!"

"No?" he said with a quizzical expression. "But what about Lady Winship? Tell me all about her. — How charming you look. Even more charming than I remembered. And I have thought about you a very great deal."

How strange, Alvey thought. *I* had forgotten *him* almost entirely. Except for those strange inquisitorial eyes. And his voice . . .

"About Lady Winship. They are saying in the village that she murdered the baby who was drowned. And so she has shut herself up in the tower. As a kind of penance."

"Does she confide in you? Did she *confess* to the murder? Is that why she shut herself up?"

"No; not precisely. She seems to feel a deeper guilt for having taxed James with being the father of the child, when, all along, she did not really believe him to be so. It was Sir Aydon whom she really suspected."

"Yes," he said, "that was what she told me."

"Of course. When she talked to you after the garden was destroyed."

"There have been no more incidents of that kind?"

"No; only gossip and slander. But the season has been hard; people have been obliged to keep to their homes. What do you think will happen now?"

"Oh, very likely it will all die away. If Sir Aydon and his lady can only straighten matters out between them. — Tell me about your writing. Did you finish your book?"

"Yes, I did, and sent it off."

"To which publisher?"

She told him the name of Allgood's cousin. "But two months have passed—nearly three—and I have heard nothing," she said forlornly.

"I believe it often takes a devilish long time," he comforted her. "Publishers are invariably aged grey-bearded men. They are very slow. It takes each one weeks and weeks to read a manuscript. And then they pass it to the next; five or six probably have to read it before they reach a decision."

"And you? How does your work go?"

"Admirably. I hope to sail for India during the summer, to rejoin my regiment. By then I shall be very much better informed about tropical diseases."

She felt a slight chill at the thought. "Tropical diseases! How disagreeable. And James? What will he do?"

"Oh, he will remain in Edinburgh. In due course he will be a great man, a member of the Royal Society and so forth. Sooner or later his father will have to reconcile himself to having brought forth a distinguished medical man." Guy added with more gravity, "I fear I also have to inform you that James has fallen in love yet again."

"Oh?" Alvey replied on a carefully lighter note. "Who is the lady?"

"A Miss Jessie McLoughlin, a daughter of the minister in St. Brendan's Church. She is very pretty and has no more brains in her head than that skylark we can hear."

"And will it be serious this time?"

"Oh, who can tell?" he said impatiently. "In any case, James cannot support a wife at present. He knows that. — Now, let us talk about Parthie. Were you very much surprised when she absconded?"

"No, I was not." Alvey related the chain of events that had led up to Parthie's elopement. She ended: "And so, my term of residence here is strictly limited. Any day now, when Mr. Thropton and Parthie return to Birkland rectory, I am bound to be exposed."

"Dear me." Guy sounded quite perturbed. "What will you do then?"

"Take myself off, I suppose. There will be no place for me here any longer."

"You had best come to Edinburgh. Plenty of young ladies there earn their living; you could teach, or find a position in a publishing office. At the very least you could get work reading, or copying."

Alvey had a strong revulsion against anything of the kind. Live on a pittance in the town where James Winship and Guy Fenway were so comfortably and respectably established? Not if she had any alternative!

"I will have to wait and see," was all she said.

After they had taken another couple of turns up and down the terrace, she asked, "How long can you stay this time, you and James?"

"Alas, we must return as soon as the horses are well rested. The day after tomorrow, probably."

"I am sorry for that."

He gave her a hopeful smile. But his tone was ironic as he answered, "It would gratify me if I thought that sorrow was for me. But I know full well it is for James."

"On the contrary! I value your counsel and opinions very highly, Major Fenway. I simply regret that you cannot be here to give them for a longer space of time."

"You do very well as you are. In those children you have certainly wrought a most beneficial change. — Is there any word of the wandering Miss Louisa, by the bye?"

Alvey frowned. "No, there is not; the last letter I had from her was many weeks ago. I hope—I hope that no misadventure has befallen her—"

"Dear me. If she were to perish in a shipwreck—or be murdered by incensed Hindoo or Muhammedan priests who resented her attempts to proselytize—how would you ever learn of the event? You might never hear at all. And that would place you in a grave moral dilemma, would it not, and a most equivocal legal position. In theory you might stay here forever—"

"Oh, but I should not wish to!" she cried out loudly, in denial of that part of herself which asked nothing better in life.

Two days later the young men left to return to Edinburgh. James and Alvey had hardly spoken to each other. From pride, she had kept out of his way as much as she could; feeling Guy's observant eye on her, she did not wish to give him the slightest grounds for thinking that she courted James's company; which indeed was far from being the case. In fact, James had spent a large portion of his time out with the children, they walking, he riding old Phantom; the three were evidently very happy together, and the children showed and felt straightforward sorrow at his departure.

"If only James could live here always," sighed Tot.

"He has to go off and make his way in the world. Boys do. I wonder why," said Nish. "*I* shall never leave Birkland."

"Meg and Isa and Parthie have."

"Isa means to come back."

"And when Papa dies," said Tot matter-of-factly, "James will come back and be squire here, as Papa did when Grandfather died."

"You will have to leave sometime, Tot, and go to school. And earn your living."

"No, I shall not!" cried Tot furiously. "I shall never leave Birkland."

"Someday you will have to." Nish was sad but resigned.

"No, I shall not, because of my fits. I shall stay here always and run the estate for James."

The children were now on far better terms with their father. They talked to him more freely at mealtimes and he even formed the habit of going out with them, as James had done, he on horseback, they on foot, for he still found it hard to walk fast. As these excursions proved highly agreeable to all parties, he soon procured a pair of ponies for the children, so that they could all go farther afield.

Meanwhile Lady Winship remained in her self-imposed confinement. Alvey sometimes went down to wander mournfully about in the wrecked garden; here now, spring flowers, snowdrops, daffodils, crocuses, were beginning to push their way through the tangle of broken bushes and upheaved rocks. Several times Carey had asked Alvey if her leddyship wouldn't like him to begin putting the place to rights, and Sir Aydon had also carried the request to the Tower Room after his return; but a negative answer always came back.

"She feels, so long as she is under suspicion, that she has no right to reclaim the garden," said Sir Aydon.

He had had, Alvey knew, a number of interviews with his wife; what the purport of them had been, Alvey could only guess.

Had Charlotte told him that she believed him to be the dead child's father? And what could he have told her in reply?

It is strange, Alvey thought, how, when I first came to Birkland, all this shroud of woe and suspicion and mystery had but newly entangled the family. And yet I had so little awareness of it. All I thought was: What a comfortable home! Because I was so engrossed in my own tale I had no eyes to look about me. Yet the belief is very commonly held that writers are more observant than ordinary folk! It seems to me just the reverse. I think I must have less perception than anybody else in the household. In the same way I misread Parthie—or, at least, failed to divine the real grounds for her bad nature.

"So long as Mamma is under suspicion! But that is so indefinite!" she said now, helplessly. "How can such a thing ever be proved, or disproved, now that it is all in the past?"

Sir Aydon sighed. Plainly he was not at all happy about the way matters stood; but at least he bore it better than he would have six months ago.

"Can you not talk to her, Louisa? Put her in a better frame? You are such a good, clever girl! Indeed, I am greatly impressed with the manner in which you have taken hold of affairs while I have been away. You are a better daughter than I deserve."

"Oh, sir, don't say so!" cried Alvey, colouring deeply in confusion at his commendation. "I don't deserve your praise, indeed I don't."

"Well," he said, "I think you do. But can you not talk to Madam, persuade her that she is immolating herself all to no purpose?"

Alvey felt that some much more radical conducive factor was called for, but she promised to think about the matter.

"Yes, yes!" he said. "Some time when the children and I are out, you know. You and she could have a good long confabulation . . ."

Alvey sighed. People do not change entirely, she said to herself. That they should do so is too much to expect.

On a day when Sir Aydon and the children had gone out early, and Alvey was wondering if this was the moment when she should at least attempt to carry out his hopeful suggestion in regard to Lady Winship, a note was brought to her, which, said Amble, had been delivered by Whin Bob the clock mender. It was penned in an unfamiliar masculine hand. In formal but civil terms it requested Alvey to go into Hexham and meet "a friend" there at the White Horse Inn.

Perplexed, curious, her head buzzing with conjectures, Alvey asked Surtees to saddle old Phantom. Could this be some business relating to her book? Might it be a message from Mr. Allgood's cousin?

"Would ye wish for me to go with ye, Miss Emmy?"

"No, no, thank you, Surtees, that is not at all necessary. It is a fine warm day, and you have dozens of tasks to perform for Sir Aydon; I shall be very well on my own."

All the way along the road she was filled with hopeful fantasies about her book. And it was a glorious spring day, besides: round white clouds drifted high in a brilliantly clear sky, the distant hills were streaked with lilac and lavender; masses of primroses, washed by last night's rain, sparkled along the roadside.

Arrived in Hexham, Alvey left her horse, as was the family custom, at the Black Bull, then set off on foot to the quieter White Horse, which was situated by the market gatehouse. There she asked for "Mrs. Armstrong," as the note had instructed, and was led upstairs by a waiter.

Really, thought Alvey, this is exactly like one of those Minerva Press romances that Parthie had hoarded. Shall I be abducted and never return to tell my tale at Birkland? Will my drowned corpse be found floating face down in the Tyne?

Half amused, half nervous, she tapped on a door, and entered when a voice inside called, "Come in!" A heavily veiled lady was seated at the window, looking out into the marketplace.

"Well, ma'am," said Alvey, "I am here, as you see, in speedy answer to your summons: in what way can I serve you? — Good God— *Louisa!*"

For the lady had put back her veil and displayed Louisa's well-known features.

"Louisa! I thought you were on the other side of the world! What in heaven's name are you doing here?"

"Did you not get my letter?" said Louisa—so much in her old, rather faultfinding tone that Alvey was instantly transported back to the gatehouse room of the Abbey School.

"Letter? No, the last letter I had was dispatched from Port Elizabeth and said that your voyage was proceeding prosperously. I am—I am quite thunderstruck to find you back in England. What happened? Did the missionary life lose its appeal?"

Alvey spoke almost at random. The whole universe seemed to be wheeling round her in a most disorderly and unbalancing manner.

"No, certainly not!" said Louisa sharply. "It was just that—well, if you did not receive my letter, I see that I shall have to explain."

"Indeed you will!"

"Lieutenant Dunnifage asked me to become his wife. And we were married at Madagascar, Captain Middlemass officiating."

"Oh, were you, indeed," said Alvey slowly. "Now I begin to understand."

"So then—so then we thought it best to return home—by boat from Fort-Dauphin to Djibouti and Suez, and by land to Port Said, and by boat again from there. My husband," Louisa said proudly, "Lieutenant Dunnifage has so many nautical acquaintances that our journey was achieved in the most expeditious manner; it took us no more than ten weeks from the day of our marriage."

"Well, I am very happy to hear that, but I am still more than a little surprised at the suddenness of your decision to return home. Has Lieutenant—has your husband, then, no interest in the missionary life?"

"Oh yes, he has indeed—a very *great* interest," said Louisa quickly. "Only he—we—thought firstly it would be as well to claim my dowry from Papa—"

"Ah—"

"Which it might perhaps be better to do in person than—than by correspondence from such a long distance when things might be misunderstood—"

"Yes; I imagine you are right about that."

Two thousand deducted from Parthie's portion for eloping, thought

Alvey. Will the penalty be the same for Louisa? Or larger, as she went farther afield?

"And then, my husband, Lieutenant Dunnifage"—Louisa glanced fondly at her ring hand, which was covered by a discreet grey kid glove—"my husband pointed out that a missionary life can be lived just as well in this country, if not better; why should we labour to convert the heathen in dirty feckless lands overseas when there are so many of our own labouring classes in need of counsel and direction? In fact, my husband has always cherished plans to create and direct a mission for sailors in Liverpool, which is his city of birth—and I am, of course, very happy to fall in with his wishes, which concur so perfectly with my own—"

"Of course they do. I quite see that."

Except that Liverpool hardly seems the same as the hot sun and palm trees of Serampore, thought Alvey; she had heard descriptions of Liverpool from Amble, who had a cousin there, and thought it sounded a gloomy city; but very likely Louisa paid scant heed to her surroundings. I daresay she will never notice the difference.

"So," Louisa continued, "we thought it would be best to give you prior notice before I returned home; to give you sufficient time, you know, to remove yourself from Birkland. For it would be most singular and embarrassing—and might give rise to all kinds of talk and scandal in the countryside—if we were *both* to be there at the same time. That would never do! So we are staying here, quietly, for a day or two, as Mr. and Mrs. Armstrong—just until you have left—"

"Until I have left," repeated Alvey, rather blankly.

"Well," said Louisa, a note of impatience now finding its way into her voice. "You always did intend to do so—did you not? I most clearly recall how many times you stipulated that your residence at Birkland should be *for a period only*. You were most emphatic on that point! You cannot deny it. Have you not, then, completed your work on—whatever it was, the piece of writing upon which you proposed to embark?"

"Oh yes. I have. I completed a novel."

"Well: there you are, then. You can have no wish, no need, to remain at Birkland any longer."

"But—"

Alvey was silent. Her mind felt curiously blank. To Louisa, she could see, the matter seemed quite simple. Louisa, all too plainly, had not been changed in the slightest degree by her experience of the wider world, or her venture into matrimony with Lieutenant Dunnifage. She was still the self-absorbed, humourless creature of Abbey School days, with but one idea in her head, plunging directly towards her own objective, quite regardless of any other person's interests.

And what could Alvey produce as an argument against her scheme? Yes, I know, I remember, I did stipulate that there should be no binding commitment, that I should be free to leave Birkland at the end of a year. And it is true that I have completed my book. But human affairs cannot always be marshalled so simply into a neat, businesslike pattern, like the pieces in a game of chequers: you return, I depart. I go, you replace me. And the family at Birkland can have no reason to observe any difference. What about your husband? Where does he fit into the pattern? Am I to take him over, in exchange?

She smiled a little, at the thought.

"Why do you smile?" said Louisa sharply.

"Nothing. A foolish thought I had."

How explain to Louisa that, outweighing all careful plans and calculations, a place and its inhabitants could take such a grasp on one's heart as to shift the whole balance of responsibility, and make the idea of suddenly going off and abandoning them seem too painful and heartless to contemplate?

Do I, do they, have no say in the matter?

Louisa had altered considerably, in outward aspect, Alvey noticed, since she left the Abbey School, where her apparel had always been of a Quakerish plainness and austerity. Now her clothes and general appearance were decidedly smart, even stylish; somebody, the Tothills, or more likely Lieutenant Dunnifage, had been encouraging her to make the best of her handsome looks. She wore a silk dress, a gold chain, her hair was carefully arranged in ringlets. She contrived to make Alvey feel countrified and dowdy; and it was evident that this burnished exterior had helped augment her already abundant self-confidence.

With a deliberate air, she examined the watch hanging from her waistband.

"Well? How soon can you make ready to quit Birkland?"

"But, Louisa—this suggestion is quite preposterous! Have you not thought about it at all? How can we simply change over, like—like a pair of puppets?"

"I see no difficulty. Not the slightest. What can you mean? We changed places before; therefore we can change again. No one, it seems, remarked on the original substitution. So why should they now?"

Because I am a better actress than you, and put my intelligence into the role. Because—

Alvey said, "But that was so different. You had been away from home for a long period—"

And furthermore, she was about to add, the substitution *was* remarked—by Tot and Nish, by Parthie, by several other people, I strongly suspect—but at this moment the door was flung open, and, loudly exclaiming, "Well, well? Is it all arranged? Have you settled the matter between you?" a booted and greatcoated young man made his brisk way into the chamber. Alvey had a vague recollection of seeing him downstairs: he was a rather soapy-complexioned individual, with shiny cheeks, fair whiskers, dun-coloured hair, and eyes the colour of weak tea. Louisa surveyed him with all the pride of possession.

"This," she said to Alvey, "is my husband. This is Lieutenant Dun nifage. It was he who wrote you the note to Birkland. So that," she added, with complacence at her husband's skill as a conspirator, "people should not recognise *my* handwriting and be surprised."

"I am happy to meet you, sir," said Alvey, thinking how very far this was from being the case.

"Good G-gad, ma'am, the l-likeness really is quite s-stunning, ain't it?" He had a slight stammer. "S-saw you downstairs, c-could hardly credit—evidence of m'own eyes! M-might be twins, the pair of you." Louisa frowned. Her husband encircled her waist with his arm, and playfully slapped her thigh. "Well, my love? D-do you have it all fixed up between you?"—eyeing Alvey jocosely. "In with A and out with B, eh? Eh? One shoulder of mutton drives another d-down, ha, ha! Well, you can scarcely complain, ma'am, you have had b-board and residence, free and p-plentiful, for any number of months, have you n-not?"

"I am not complaining, sir."

"But, Mr. Dunnifage," said Louisa discontentedly, "Miss Clement is raising difficulties. She seems positively not to wish to take her departure."

"What, ma'am? Why, how can this be? Sure, you c-can't be so un-grateful!"

"I am not ungrateful," said Alvey, stung. "It is not ingratitude. But, do you not understand? The family, the household, have become ac-customed to me. Indeed—during Sir Aydon's absence, while he was undergoing an operation on his legs—they came even, in some sort, to depend on me—"

"Oh, was there something amiss with Papa? But he is better now, you say? And surely my mother was there—"

"That is another problem—"

"But, in any case, it is entirely nonsensical to suggest that they could have depended on *you*—that is ridiculous, you know—"

"Coming it a bit too strong, wh-what?" said Lieutenant Dunnifage. "After all, you are quite an outsider! What can you know of Birk-land affairs?"

"Fine old place," said the lieutenant, nodding his head. "Heard—great deal about it—"

"Well, I—"

"Besides," Louisa went on swiftly, "you say that Papa is back at home? So there can be no need for any further offices on your part. The rest of the family, I suppose, are in good health?"

"Excuse me, Miss Winship—Mrs. Dunnifage"—in response to a look of displeasure on Louisa's countenance—"but do you propose to make your appearance at Birkland as if—as if you had never been away since leaving school? You propose merely to step in and take my place—pretend to be me, in other words?"

"Pretend to be *you?*" The look of displeasure on Louisa's face deep-ened to positive ill-will. "How in the world could I do *that?* Or why should I? You are the intruder, *I* am the rightful in—incumbent. Natu-rally the household must, by degrees, come to understand that a change has been effected; but, since I am the true Louisa, whereas you were merely an outsider, a deceiver, an interloper—"

"Quite, quite. Quite! Shocking, hole-and-corner sort of business," muttered Lieutenant Dunnifage.

"That exchange," continued Louisa, firmly ignoring her husband, "must, self-evidently, be accepted by the whole household as a change for the better. *You* will be gone from Birkland, *I* shall be established, and family affairs will be in their proper train once more."

"But how can they—?"

"For my part," added Lieutenant Dunnifage, "I f-find it hard to c-comprehend, ma'am—always have done—*deuced* hard—how a simple, God-fearing, right-thinking young l-lady—such as m'wife here—could have allowed herself to be b-bamboozled and embroiled in s-such a m-murky, chancy kind of subterfuge—said so, over and over, when I first heard of the b-business, didn't I, Loo, my love?"

"Oh!" gasped Alvey, really outraged. "When it was entirely her own—"

"Fell out very handsomely for *you,* ma'am, I can s-see that part of the affair. Yes, yes—for you it was a honey-fall, no q-question! And I d-daresay you thought to be snugly established at B-birkland for the rest of your n-natural term, what?"

"I certainly did not!" snapped Alvey, doing her best to forget and obliterate the many times she had secretly, guiltily imagined such an outcome. "And, sir, I must inform you that you are totally mistaken! The scheme was conceived, planned, and worked out in every particular by your wife—it required many, many weeks of persuasion—begging, *pleading*—on her part before I would agree to be party to it."

"Oh, ho! Naturally you would say so, now! But I have heard quite a different tale from *her;* and I well know which tale to believe. So, I don't doubt, will Sir Aydon!"

Louisa remained silent. But, observing her expression of smug, impervious self-satisfaction and rectitude, Alvey could understand how she might easily have convinced Dunnifage that the idea for the deception had not been hers, but had come from Alvey, and that Louisa had been a reluctant, conscience-stricken party to the scheme, only falling in with it because it liberated her to follow her vocation. Perhaps she had even convinced herself, also?

"Next time I take part in any conspiracy," said Alvey bitterly, "I can see that I must make certain to have my partner's agreement in writing, signed and sealed—"

"What *can* you mean, Miss Clement?"

"Oh, never mind it! It is all too disgusting and sordid!"

"Indeed, I quite agree with you, ma'am! And what S-sir Aydon will say, when he hears the tale, I s-shudder to contemplate. If I were you, young l-lady, I should take care to be well away from B-birkland before he discovers what a v-viper he has been nurturing."

"You are seriously suggesting," said Alvey, regarding the couple with wonder, "that if I do not agree to leave, Louisa, you intend to present yourself to Sir Aydon as a poor, abused innocent, whose place had been usurped behind her back by an imposter—while she herself just happened to have taken a berth on a ship bound for the Indies—is that what you will say? What about that letter you wrote to your papa, promising future obedience?"

"*You* wrote that!" pounced Louisa triumphantly. "You cannot say that you did not!"

"Very true. So I did. And well I am being punished, now, for my part in the business," Alvey sighed.

"*P-punished?* Good G-gad, ma'am, your punishment has not even c-commenced yet! Only wait until it all comes out. There must be a s-substantial jail sentence for such impersonation—be sure of that!"

"Oh, don't disturb yourselves," said Alvey tiredly. "I will fall in with your proposals—if only in order to terminate this vulgar, humiliating wrangle."

"I should t-think so, indeed. Vulgar and disgusting it certainly is!" pronounced the lieutenant.

Louisa frowned at her husband. Alvey perceived that the history of the deception was a somewhat sore and sensitive area in their conjugal felicity. Despite his satisfaction at having acquired a wife with a handsome portion waiting to be claimed and also (Alvey guessed) one several rungs above him in the social ladder, Lieutenant Dunnifage was honestly scandalised at the means she had taken to escape from her home, and neither of the pair could be comfortable until that escapade, and Louisa's inconvenient partner and accomplice in it, were satisfactorily disposed of, buried, forgotten, and out of mind.

"So what was your intention?" Alvey inquired of Louisa. "When did you wish me to remove myself from Birkland?"

"Oh. Well, I presume that you will require a night to pack up your belongings? Then, I suggest, you return here tomorrow. How did you come here, by the bye? In the carriage?"

"No, I rode here on horseback."

A slight crease appeared between Louisa's brows at this, but she reflected and finally said, "Well, it is no matter. I daresay that would cause less remark. So: you will return here tomorrow. Then what will you do? You most certainly cannot remain in Hexham."

"No indeed," Alvey agreed drily. "Mr. Allgood and the Beaumonts would think it decidedly odd if I were to take up residence in rooms here—"

"You had best take a coach to Newcastle. There used to be one in the afternoon—"

"At half past three," said Alvey absently. She had sometimes observed its departure. And, she thought, perhaps one of the servants can tell me of a small inn, or somebody with apartments to let in Newcastle.

Louisa continued with her plans.

"Then I will ride your horse back to Birkland. After a few days, three or four perhaps, when I have sufficiently established myself with the family, Mr. Dunnifage will join me—"

It must be very singular to have no imagination at all, thought Alvey, regarding Louisa with fascination as she outlined this scheme. Convenient, too, in many ways. How did Louisa propose to account for her acquaintance with the lieutenant? When did she intend to reveal the fact of their marriage? Immediately? Or after a period of time had elapsed?

"So. That is all agreed. You will return at this hour tomorrow?"

"Yes; I can see that is the only thing to do. Birkland Hall would certainly not be large enough to accommodate both of us."

"*Both* of us? Have you taken leave of your wits? *Both of us?* When you have not a shadow of right to be there?"

"No? But I must leave you; I shall have a great deal to do. I wish you both good day."

Alvey made her way down the stairs and across the marketplace to the Black Bull. She had intended visiting the bookshop—she had ordered *Alphonsine, The Female Quixote, Margiana,* and *Ida of Athens,* and hoped to find them ready for her; she wanted to ask Mr. Allgood if there were yet any tidings of her novel—but all these plans had been driven completely out of her head. Finding an ostler, she had Phantom resaddled and set off mechanically on the well-known road across the Tyne bridge and back to Birkland.

The servants must be told, she thought. I cannot bear that they should think me a deceitful interloper who sneaks off without daring to wait for the truth to be discovered. But the family? The children? Old Mrs. Winship? Sir Aydon? How can I bear to tell them—just *now?* It is too sudden. I should have had some warning; some notice.

Well, to do her justice, Louisa did say that she had written me a letter about her change of plan. I wonder what became of that letter.

It was a fortunate circumstance that old Phantom knew every stone and heather clump along the road home, for his rider did little to guide him; she rode with a loose rein and used her handkerchief more than once.

Suppose I never ride this road again? After tomorrow? How shall I be able to bear that?

Through the tight net of her grief, Alvey was acutely conscious, more than ever before, of the beauty that lay about her. Even the road under her horse's hoofs seemed to have acquired a luminosity that she had never previously observed; the specks of granite grit shone like diamonds in the sun's declining rays. As she rode over the high spine of the hills between Hexham and Birkland all that familiar, far-distant landscape, distinct in every detail, it seemed, for over seventy miles, to the mountains of Cumbria and the western ocean, was invested with a mournful clarity and brilliance, like the dream of a prisoner waiting for his execution.

And Louisa did not even *want* to come back! She sets no value on this place. Her only object is the money, in order to found a seamen's mission in Liverpool.

I suppose I should really be grateful, mused Alvey, shaking a couple of tears from her eyes in order not to miss the curved shapes of the pine-tree tops in the Birkland plantation, while Phantom began his careful plod down the steep hill—as a writer I should feel gratitude for the existence of Louisa. What a character! I am quite sorry now that I did not introduce her into the story of Lord Love. She would soon have sent him to the right-about. — I wonder if she did really convince herself that the whole substitution scheme had been my suggestion. I fancy that she might be capable of such a mental transposition; her own intentions are so supremely important to her that any obstacle to them—even her own faulty behaviour—must seem so trifling as to be almost nonexistent. And then, *quite* nonexistent.

Am I a shameful coward not to dig in my heels, refuse to quit Birkland so tamely, remain and face the horrible scene that must take place with the two of us proffering our different versions of the story?

Well, if I am a coward, it is not only for my own sake. It would be too childish and selfish to remain and dispute what is, after all, a point of no ultimate significance. When I am aware that the family have so many other and graver matters to distress them.

I could write to Sir Aydon, she thought wistfully—perhaps when I am established in Newcastle, I could write to him from there, to explain—

The sight of the old grey house through the pine trunks almost undid her. I will take care to remember it like this, she promised herself, with the sun's rays falling sideways on red bark and grey stone. Then, to her considerable surprise, as she came closer, she perceived a whole group of persons, out on the gravel sweep in front of the house. They all seemed to be talking excitedly.

Alvey was reminded, for a brief, nostalgic moment, of her first arrival at Birkland; of how Lady Winship had come with uncharacteristic speed from the front entrance to warn the girls about the fate of poor wee Geordie.

How terrified I was then, Alvey remembered. And oh, how I wish this was that day again!

But what has happened? It must be something of a terrific nature to fetch them all out—Sir Aydon, Amble, Surtees, Blackett—Lumley—the children—who can have arrived?

Then she noticed a stranger—a tanned, weathered young man whom she was sure she had never seen before, though his cast of countenance was in some way familiar. A cousin, a nephew?

"Who is that?" she murmured to Surtees, as he came to help her from the saddle.

" 'Tis young Sim Whittingham, Miss Emmy, poor Annie Herdman's cousin back from the wars. He's been telling Sir Aydon how he was took by the press gang and borne off to sea, eighteen months agone, and only won free from his ship when the peace come, and then he was a plaguy long way from home, in the West Indies, and had to work his passage back, and only come in to the port of Newcassel yesterday—"

"Poor fellow," said Alvey, wondering parenthetically if he had come to Newcastle on the same ship as Louisa and her lieutenant. "That press gang was certainly a shocking, wicked institution."

"You're reet there, Miss Emmy," said Surtees, leading Phantom away to the stables.

Skirting the excited group, Alvey slipped hastily indoors, grateful for the opportunity to make her way upstairs to her own room while everybody's attention was focussed on the newcomer.

In a vague manner it occurred to her that the household seemed unusually stirred by this arrival; had Sim been a groom? a gardener? a house servant? She did not recall his name having been referred to above a couple of times, casually, by the children; what was his connection, apart from his relationship to Annie? Something about a sled . . . ?

Her mind was so tired and bruised from the encounter with Louisa that she could spare little energy for conjecture; the true significance of his return did not come home to her until dinnertime, when the children told her with round eyes, "Sim is here! We were afraid he might be dead, but he's come back. And he's told Papa that *he* was the father of Annie's baby."

"*What?*"

"Well; we knew that all the time, of course," added Nish.

Alvey gazed at the child blankly, in silence, for a moment; finally, finding her voice, said, "You knew *all the time?*"

"Yes; when we met Annie running up to Pike Force that evening, she told us to say goodbye to Sim for her, if ever he came home again. She didn't know where he'd gone. He was her dear lover, she said. And we weren't to tell a soul else."

"And so you have kept quiet about it all this time?"

"Of course," said Tot, and Nish nodded. "She *asked* us to."

And what else, Alvey wondered, may those children know about that they think it better not to reveal? Or about which they have been asked to keep silent?

Sir Aydon said heavily, "He's a good, decent fellow, poor Sim. He took the news like a man, though anybody could see it was a sore blow to him. He was truly attached to Annie. Not like old Amos . . . Sim used to work over at Tinnis, for Chibburn, but I shall offer him a position here, if he wishes; looking after estate matters, under Lumley, perhaps. Lumley's not so young as he used to be. Whittingham's a good, handy lad, and has got a bit of book learning in the navy, he tells me, bettered himself. Ay, ay, it was a bad business, a bad business . . ."

"He looks a little like James," Alvey said absently. "I was trying to think, before dinner, of whom he reminded me. It is James, of course—" Her mind was still principally elsewhere.

Sir Aydon cleared his throat.

"Well, as to that—I daresay you have forgotten—perhaps never knew?—that Sim's mother was said to be my uncle Robert's daughter—"

From what seemed another lifetime, Alvey remembered Isa's voice saying, "Bastards were quite a commonplace in our family during the last century. It is said that our grandfather and great-uncles fathered dozens, about the countryside . . ."

How stupidly frightened I was, on that ride towards happiness.

Well, she told herself robustly, perhaps I shall find happiness in the town of Newcastle. Who knows what is waiting for me there?

"And that naturally accounted," Sir Aydon was explaining laboriously—for whose benefit? Alvey really must pull herself together and attend to him—"that accounted, you see—the likeness transmitted through two generations—accounted for people taking the notion into their heads that wee Geordie must be the child of James—or—or myself—"

And perhaps, poor man, you wished it was so, Alvey thought briefly. How can I take my books? Must I leave them behind? I do not see how I can carry a bundle of books on horseback. I had best leave a

box of things and ask Louisa to see that they are sent on to me when I
have a direction to which they can be forwarded. All that has to be
arranged . . .
   She felt unutterably desolate.
   After dinner she went to visit the old lady, who was greatly brisked
up and full of interest at the news of Sim's return.
   "At least," she said, "that clears up one skein of the mystery. Sim
Whittingham! Well, well, why did I never guess at such a likely solu-
tion? But it is true he was not here very often; working over at Tinnis,
he only revisited Birkland on feast days and holidays . . . Let us
hope, at all events, that Charlotte, now she knows Aydon is free from
imputation, may see fit to issue forth from her seclusion . . ."
   But if it was she who killed the child?
   Suppose that is another secret that Nish and Tot have been asked
not to reveal?
   "I hope she may come out. Oh, I do hope so," said Alvey. "Ma'am,
there's something I must tell you."
   "What is it, child? You look very pale. You have no ill news of
Meg? Or of Parthie?"
   "No, nothing of that kind, no ill news at all. In fact, in a way, I
suppose you could call it *good* news. Ma'am, I believe that you have
always, or almost from the start, been aware that I was not the real
Louisa—have you not?"
   "Humph!" said old Grizel. She regarded Alvey sharply, quirking
up the corners of her pouched mouth into a sceptical twist. "Don't tell
me that you are commencing to have a tender conscience about *that*, at
this late stage? You have played the part of Louisa a great deal better
than she would have played it herself. Yes, yes, of course I knew! Saw
through you from the start. Had received a letter from Louisa—some
long time previously, while she was at that school, presumably before
she had conceived the plan of substitution—describing the extraordinary resemblance between herself and one of her schoolmates—put
two and two together, therefore, when she became, all of a sudden, so
unexpectedly compliant about renouncing her missionary ambitions.
— Well, well, what is it? Louisa has not won a martyr's crown, I trust
—not been put to death by incensed Hindoos?"
   "Oh no—"

"Then what? You're in some predicament, hey? Just as I expected. You're in love with James and wish to marry him, is that it?"

"No, no, ma'am, nothing of that nature." Though Alvey could not help clenching her hands. She took a deep breath and said, "It is simply that the real Louisa has returned."

Later she went to tell the servants. As she had expected, the news came as no surprise to any of them.

"Aabody cud tell ye weren't Miss Lou," said Mrs. Slaley. "We kenned it fra the first. Weel, not preceesely the first, but verra soon; yer ways were that different—"

"Miss Lou always fainted dead away at sight o' blood," said Amble. "I always did ask myself how she'd fare in wild, foreign parts—"

"An' yon cat o' the owd leddy's could never abide her—"

"Aweel, she jist didna have yer nature, Miss Emmy, that's the lang and the short of it."

"And mun ye go? Canna ye bide? There's room for the twain o' ye, and we'd a deal liefer have ye than her. She was a sour-natured body, even when she was a wean in her cradle, was Miss Lou. And that's a fact."

"No, no, Mrs. Slaley, there's no place here for two of us. And she's the rightful child of the house, after all. She wants to come back, she wishes me to leave. I plan to go to Newcastle, I expect I shall be able to earn a living there by teaching French or music—"

"Ye can bide with my sister Bessie," said Mrs. Slaley at once. "She'll be prood to have ye. And that way we'll no' lose touch with ye. She has a bakery in the street called the Side, next to the Collingwood Arms tavern—"

Last, Alvey went to say good night to the children.

"I have hardly seen you all day," she said.

"Well, who chose to go to Hexham? And never brought us back any books! What was the point of going?"

Alvey could not speak, but Tot said kindly, "Well, tomorrow we'll work hard all morning at our lessons. And perhaps we won't even go out with Papa in the afternoon. He'll wish to talk a great deal with poor Sim, I daresay."

Nish was half asleep. She muttered, "I wonder if Sim's coming back will make old Amos feel more friendly towards our family? Now he knows wee Geordie wasn't James's child, or Papa's . . ."

"You should not talk about such things," said Alvey absently. "You are too young."

"Why? When everybody knows about them. And we knew, after all, the whole time," Tot pointed out.

Alvey was sitting on Nish's bed, where both children were curled up. Darkness came late these days; the room was luminous with dusk; it was still possible to see.

Tell them or not? she thought. No. I can't. I'm a coward. It's too hard. It's too complicated. They would argue. And that would be too painful.

She said good night and quietly left the room. How could I dare to sit in judgment on James? I am just as great a coward as he was.

She called back, "Don't stay awake too late talking!"

As for herself, she was up most of the night, packing, and slept not at all, and rose at five in the morning.

Come back tomorrow at this hour, Louisa had said; but Alvey could not bear, now that sentence of banishment had been issued, to remain an extra half hour, an extra five minutes, at Birkland. She would ride to Hexham and wait there, in the abbey church, until it was time for the coach to Newcastle.

"I fair hate to see ye go, Miss Emmy," said Surtees, leading round Phantom.

Alvey nodded, not trusting her voice. Then she thought of something.

"Just a moment, Surtees."

Detaching a crooked pin from her collar, she walked across the sweep and dropped it into the Lion Pool. Several others lay there, slowly rusting. The ferns drooped around the edge of the basin. The clear water gushed down, out of the lion's mouth, and would go on doing so for hundreds of years.

Then Alvey let Surtees help her into the saddle, and rode off along the road to Hexham.

XVI

Mrs. Bessie Robson had a pie-and-cake shop in the Side, Newcastle. The two downstairs rooms of her house were given over to the business, which was a thriving one, and the rooms on the next floor she inhabited herself. But the two attics, with their sloping ceilings, were unoccupied, and Miss Clement was kindly welcome to the use of them, Mrs. Robson said, for so long as she wished to stop. Mrs. Robson was a widow, her husband, a corn chandler, having been carried off by the cholera during a bad epidemic some five years previously.

"And then, at first, I did use to have lodgers, but, the business picking up and going on so prosperously, I reckoned I'd please maself and only take quiet decent folk now and agin, as it'd be no dole to have in the hoose. And I can see that th'art one o' that kind, Miss Clement, let alane coming wi' my sister Fanny's good word."

So Alvey took up residence in the two neat little rooms with white scrubbed board floors, sloping ceilings, a couple of pegs on the wall to accommodate her clothes, a chair, a washstand with jug and basin, and a narrow bed. There was no table, but the sills of the dormer windows were wide and square, and only a foot from the floor; she supposed she could use one of them for a writing desk. Both rooms could have been tucked into her bedchamber at Birkland, and left plenty of space over. At the rear, the window looked across a timber yard. Beyond that could be seen slate roofs, black now in relentless rain; beyond them, higher buildings, church spires, the masts of ships; beyond all that, somewhere to the west, must be the hills she had abandoned.

For the first two weeks of Alvey's sojourn in Newcastle the rain poured down daily, almost continuously.

"I've nivver knawn a June like it," said Mrs. Robson.

At Birkland rain had been bearable—even a pleasure—because of its beauty: layered clouds of it moved up the valley, torn fragments or slanting grey lines obscured the trees, or changed them to silver; hills appeared or vanished, as the clouds parted and then joined again; the river's voice grew louder, the grass grew greener. But here in the city, rain brought only ugliness, dark, and discomfort. Steaming dray horses stamped and shuddered and hung their heads; filthy water poured in torrents along the cobbled thoroughfares; coaly smoke hung in the damp air, thick and gritty; the roofs and chimneys of the gaunt buildings were hidden in murk. To Alvey, accustomed to the immense silence of Birkland, the city's noise seemed shattering; all day every day factory bells rang, steam hissed, voices bawled, wheels and hoofs clattered incessantly over the paving, hammers clanged and saws shrieked. Under the heavy cloud of rain, all such noise seemed doubled in volume. Alvey hated the town, the blackness of every object in it, she hated the row and dirt, the ugly hard shapes of the buildings, the bad smells, above all the sense of being totally enclosed, hemmed in all around, for miles in every direction, by swarming people and houses; she hated the suffocation, the hunger caused by the lack of a single green thing; there was not a branch, a leaf, a blade of grass to be seen. At first she did not even wish for fine weather; where could be the benefit? There were no fields to walk in, no hills to climb; but after she had been soaked through several times over she became desperately weary of the incessant, torrential downpour. Besides, there was nowhere to hang her wet things, except in her small and chilly chamber. At Birkland, returning from a rainy walk, one turned automatically into the great cheerful kitchen, where a couple of ranges always burning kept the flagstones warm underfoot; shoes and outerwear left there would dry overnight, and Ellen or Stridge would have brushed and pressed them by next morning; here, even after several days, garments put on again would be as damp as when they were taken off.

In consequence of which, or perhaps just from general misery, Alvey caught a shocking cold. For two days she continued to drag herself about with heavy, throbbing head, painful throat, and aching back and legs; then she took to her narrow bed and only wished that she might die in it.

"Ee, indeed, 'tis a tirrible damp season," Mrs. Robson said philosophically, bringing Alvey a posset. (She pronounced "season" *seeasson*—it took Alvey a moment or two to grasp her meaning.) "I don't knaw when there's bin sic a wet summer. An' I rackon ye're a yoong lady as is used te comfort, coming fra' Birkland Hall."

Tactfully, Mrs. Robson had never inquired *why* Alvey had felt the need to quit such a stately residence and seek humble accommodation in Newcastle; she was a woman full of natural kindliness and delicacy. To nurse a lodger and bring her invalid fare lay well beyond the obligations of a landlady with her own business to run, and so Alvey hoarsely protested, but the good woman merely said, "Nivver trooble thaself, hinny. Maw sister Fanny'd nivver forgive me if aw let ye dee in maw hoose. There, noo, sup down the dram, 'tis winter caudle cup, brimming wi' limmons an' oranges, an' thur's barley in, too, 'twill slip easy down thi throat."

Next day, however, Alvey declared that she was recovered. Doggedly she got up, dressed, fetched a broom and hot water from the kitchen, tidied her chamber, and would not permit the lame Mrs. Robson to continue cooking for her, or to climb the steep stair with any further delicacies. But still, for longer than a month afterwards, the ill effects of the malady lingered, leaving her thin, haggard, readily fatigued, imbuing her with a deadly lassitude and indifference. During the first week out of bed she could barely manage to drag herself beyond the corner of the street, and was frequently forced, at that point, to creep home again and lie down on her bed. There she passed long, dismal hours, gazing at the slope of the ceiling, deprived even of the will to take up a book and read, paralysed by a weight of depression and grief such as she had experienced only once before in her life.

She did not write to anybody at Birkland. What would be the purpose? Her life in that place was over. There would be no point in trying to explain, to justify, to apologise. A deep shame almost suffocated her when she tried to think about any individual members of the family; she could not endure the pain of their knowledge that she was a sordid imposter. In a note to Mrs. Slaley, asking that her box of books be forwarded, she added: *Please do not tell* ANYBODY *where I am.* Her only wish was to be lost, hidden, forgotten.

Lying, without occupation, in this reduced state, she found that memories of that other time, ten years distant, when she had lost her home, came back in spasms of excruciating clarity. Especially at night, when the clangs and howls of industry abated, and only the sounds of human voices came from the street, drunken, joyful, or merely argumentative, keeping her awake hour after hour, Alvey would toss on her thin pallet, watching lights flicker over the wall, reliving those weeks in sharp detail: those weeks of pain and family division during which Paul and Sarah grimly detached themselves from friends, connections, livelihood, and, finally, from their own child, in order to depart for the distant community in Indiana. Even the word "Indiana" still carried, for Alvey, an ominous ring, an evil vibration.

The decision had been neither easy nor simple. Paul, to be sure, had looked forward with hope to the new life at Unison; but Sarah had been far less confident as to the rightness of their plan. Paul had never cherished particularly warm feelings towards his daughter; the whole bent of his strong character had from youth onward been devoted to religion; he wasted no time on human relationships. Whereas Sarah and her daughter had been bound by close affection. Only in belief did they differ: Alvey from her earliest days had been a humble sceptic, respecting the creeds of others, herself certain of nothing; but Sarah was a devout, straightforward Christian, therefore unquestioningly prepared to obey her husband, in whom she had thorough confidence. She respected his wide intelligence. But his contentious, difficult nature did trouble her; she had seen him quit, in turn, the Society of Friends, the Unitarians, and the splinter group founded by himself.

Sarah must, her daughter had felt dimly then, and with certainty now, have entertained a secret fear that Paul would, in the end, come to differ from the tenets of Herr Müller, and leave Unison as he had left the other sects. Thereby nullifying his wife's sacrifice of herself and her child.

This doubt, deep if unuttered, had made Alvey's mother more and more silent, withdrawn, and tremulous as the weeks drew on and the day of departure came closer. Nothing was stated, but Alvey was acutely aware of her mother's distress.

She was haunted by a particularly sharp memory of short, slight Sarah, who, at thirty-five, had the drawn look of a woman twenty years older, her lips pressed hard together to prevent them from trembling, as she walked about the small empty New Bedford house for the last time, in a pretence of making sure that it was properly clean for the next comers; next, making a careful survey of the miniature yard, where she had grown parsley and lavender. Not a garden in Lady Winship's sense of the word, thought Alvey, but she had loved it and taken a gentle pride in its neatness. Women so easily put down roots; it seems they can't help it. Two young apple trees had been obtained, with the help of a Quaker friend coming out from England. That year, for the first time, one of them had fruited, half a dozen tiny green apples; but they were nowhere near ripe on the day appointed for Paul and Sarah to leave. The month was August. Alvey saw her mother touch one apple with a careful finger, press her lips even harder together, and walk hurriedly back to the house.

Then, at the last, one tight, throttling embrace: "Goodbye, my precious child. Behave thyself well—but that, I know, thee will! We shall surely meet again—in a better world, if not in this—" and Paul had impatiently hustled his wife into the coach that was to take them on the first stage of their journey.

Partings are the worst pain in life, Alvey thought. Is it harder to be the one who leaves or the one who remains behind? Now I begin to understand how Sarah must have felt, going away, relinquishing me to the care of someone who was almost a stranger. Now, for the very first time, I believe I feel a touch of the agony she must have gone through. And I thought that _I_ was suffering at that leave-taking! What I felt then was not a fraction of what I feel now — Yet, she thought (in honesty to that desolate ten-year-old), what I felt then was dreadful pain: home, family, my entire world snatched away—and all in the name of virtue and the worship of God!

Had Paul and Sarah ever left Unison? If they had done so, Alvey thought, Mother would have found some means to reach me; she must have been longing to know what I was doing to support myself, whether I had become a writer as I planned. She was so hopeful for me, so proud of my early essays . . . It was because of that ambition for me, I know, that she accepted my decision not to accompany them.

No, they must still be there. If Sarah is still alive. But, though so hardworking, she was far from robust. There would have been many privations, much physical labour, bleak winters, perhaps even hostile savages to contend with . . .

Alvey had little doubt, in fact, that her mother must have died years ago.

At least, she tried to comfort herself, Nish and Tot are not losing their home. Nothing of that kind. They have the hills, the Hungry Water, the house itself, all that natural beauty, which has more importance for them than human relations. All their accustomed haunts and habits.

But, said the accusing inner voice, the reason why humans had little importance for those children was that no one had ever troubled to befriend them. You had begun to supply part of what they needed. Therefore it was the height of heartless irresponsibility to abandon them without an explanation.

And what about Grandmother? What about Sir Aydon? What about his wretched wife? Having—in some sort—taken on the care of these people, was it the behaviour of a right-thinking adult to go off and leave them again?

Father would say yes; that I suffer from conceit and vainglory in thinking they need me. He would say it is no part of anyone's duty to be a prop to another, or point the way they should go; we are each single souls, and must stand alone in the presence of God. We should work towards our own salvation, and not arrogantly think we are capable of directing anybody else.

Louisa would certainly disagree with Father about that! And, for once, I find myself on the same side as Louisa. I think that Father's views are priggish nonsense—and, very likely, just a cloak for his own selfishness.

Louisa. Will she not take charge of those children—help them, teach them? And—and perhaps talk reason to her mother, give Sir Aydon sensible advice about the estate, befriend the old lady?

You know perfectly well that she will do nothing of the kind. She will collect her jointure as soon as she can extract it from her father, and then be off to pursue her own ends. She will quit Birkland without a day's delay or a second thought.

Well: at least she cannot bully or terrify the children any longer. They are too old to be afraid of her now. And I did play some part in that change.

With a deep, shuddering sigh, Alvey pulled herself off her bed, and moved on stiff legs to the window, where she lowered herself awkwardly to the floor and crouched, leaning her elbows on the wide sill, gazing out across the timber yard. The long hours of another night had crawled slowly past; the rain had abated and a watery sunrise gilded the chimneys; down below, men were taking off their jackets, hoisting a huge log into position so that it might be sawn into ship's timbers.

As she had done for many days, Alvey watched the men with a feeling of dreamy unreality. Who is this *I* who is watching them roll that log? Do I exist? How did I come to be here in Newcastle, in this shadowy little room? Newcastle? Where is that city? Did I dream the life at Birkland Hall? Or the one in New Bedford? Which life was the illusion? Or is it all illusion together?

Mother would say: pull thyself together, child.

Caught unawares by a sudden shock of piled-up emotion, Alvey doubled over, as if she had a physical pain in her heart, laid her head down on her arms, and wept for her mother with the total abandon of a ten-year-old.

After a long while, she swallowed, scrubbed her eyes with a towel, dressed herself neatly, smoothed her hair, and went down to ask Mrs. Robson if she might put up a card in the shop window, offering French tuition and piano lessons. And not before time; her funds saved from teaching at the Abbey School were almost exhausted. Pocket money given her by Sir Aydon she had felt proper to leave behind at Birkland. There would be a small amount of interest accruing to her, in New Bedford, from Cousin Hepzie's modest legacy; soon she must find the energy to write to America about this.

"Ye look a bit better today, hinny," said Mrs. Robson. "I was beginnin' to be troobled aboot ye. Have a hot bap; they're nobbut fresh oot o' the oven."

The fresh bread was delicious; for the first time in weeks, Alvey felt a genuine pang of hunger.

Nish and Tot had gone to ground in the hay barn, as, these days, they frequently did. This summer the hay crop had been late and scanty, because of all the rain in June, but at last, in mid-August, it was cut and stooked and gathered. The children had their annual adventure of riding in from the hay fields, holding on to the chains of the flat, horse-drawn tilting bogies that carried in the big, slippery mounds of hay, one at a time; but the event's enjoyment was deeply flawed by the absence of Alvey; so many times they had told her about it, and promised her that hay making was the best fun of the summer.

Now the barn made a refuge for them, stacked as it was almost to the roof with the springy, sweet-scented crop; they could roll in it, leap from the crossbeams above, practise gymnastics, hide from each other, or just read and think. Lumley, of course, disapproved furiously of the children playing in the hay: "Spoils it for the beasts," he said, "they'll not fancy it after ye've moocked around in it," and menaced them, when he found them, with the untimely end of Rab Artingstall, a shepherd boy of the last century who had taken refuge in a hay shippen one stormy night and been killed by fumes from the half-rotten crop.

"That's naught but an old wives' tale," Tot said scornfully. "And we *have* to have somewhere private from interference."

Their problem these days was not Louisa, who took little notice of them, but Lieutenant Dunnifage, who persisted in hunting them out, whenever bad weather kept them in the house, boring them to excruciation with geography lessons. "Where's Madagascar?" he would shout. "C-come on, now! You young ones have got to be quicker off the m-mark than that!" Or, when the rain slackened, dragging them out to the paddock, where he made them do physical jerks and something he called "Indian drill." "I hate to see such a pair of l-listless, whey-faced young ones about the place," he often said. *"You'd* n-never do for a midshipman about *my* ship, M-master Tot, I can tell you!"

"I wouldn't wish to," muttered Tot.

Lieutenant Dunnifage was heartily bored at Birkland. *Why* Louisa's father couldn't make up his mind and get down to naming a sum for the dowry, sort matters out Bristol-fashion and shipshape, why the old

Put must make such a piece of work about it, and not just shell out the ready and have done, the lieutenant simply could not comprehend; day after day the old fellow mumbled, "Yes, I'll think about it tomorrow," and then shut himself up in his library, leaving orders that he was not to be disturbed. And, oddly enough, nobody, not a soul in the family or about the estate, seemed to value Louisa's husband as he deserved; indeed, sometimes he thought they hardly valued him at all. Sometimes he even found himself wishing for the astringent company of Captain Middlemass, who had not set a particularly high value on him either, but at least the lieutenant had had his appointed place in the ship's hierarchy and felt sure of it. But here he had no function except to harass the children.

Fortunately he had not yet discovered their lair in the hayloft. The hay was piled so high that the door leading into the stable yard was totally blocked; the children's means of ingress was to climb in at the loading window, using fingers and toes to scrabble up the eight-foot wall, in which there were large, handy crevices between the stones. Once inside, they were safe enough, so long as they remembered to keep their voices down lest they be heard by people passing through the yard. A convenient niche in the wall held a few books, green apples, and a bottle of water, for the dust in the hay made them thirsty.

Nish had a secret fear that Surtees or Lumley would some day bolt the front window, not realising that they were inside, imprisoning them; but Tot pointed out that they could always escape through a tiny slit window at the back, which gave on to the orchard; though it was true that would entail a drop of twenty feet, because the ground fell away sharply.

"You could get through, as you are smaller," he said generously. "And then you could come round to the front and let me out."

"Suppose I broke my leg?"

"Why should you suppose any such thing? Now be quiet, I'm reading Marmion."

Nish had no objection to being quiet. She was writing a story about a lord's wilful daughter who ran off to be a sailor, and rescued a prince who had been exiled on a desert island by a usurper. Her tale was heavily influenced by The Tempest, which was the last thing Alvey had been reading them before she left.

Every now and then Nish heaved a deep, frustrated sigh.

"Oh, I *wish* Emmy were here."

"Well," snapped her brother, "she's not, so what's the use of wishing?"

"I can see the *end* of my story, but the start is dull, and I can't do the middle."

"Write something else, then," he said unsympathetically.

"Emmy's so good at helping when I'm stuck—"

"Emmy isn't here!"

Incautiously, he had raised his voice.

They heard the loud nasal tones of Lieutenant Dunnifage, outside in the stable yard.

"Is that you young 'uns? Did I hear your voices? I'm positive I did! Come along out—where are you l-lurking? C-come on—I'm sure I heard you!"

Nish and Tot cowered lower among the hay. They heard the lieutenant move a few steps away, and his voice again.

"D-do you know where those children have got to, Surtees? It's high t-time they did their exercises."

Would Surtees give them away? No, he was saying woodenly, "Aa cuddn't say, sir, aa'm sure; they might be joost anywhere—" But then came Louisa's step, quick and clipped, along the cobbled path, and her impatient voice broke in: "They are almost certainly in the hay barn, Mr. Dunnifage; my brother James used to spend *hours* in there, when he was their age—though why you should feel obliged to trouble yourself with them, I cannot conceive—"

Heavy footsteps began moving purposefully back in their direction.

There were a number of cards in Mrs. Robson's window, offering tuition on the flute, rooms for rent, or apprenticeships in dressmaking. The location, in this well-frequented shop, was an excellent one. In only five days after putting up her notice, Alvey was surprised, but relieved, to acquire four pupils: a young man who wished to learn the piano, an elderly lady who wanted French history read aloud to her, and two little girls, the daughters of an alderman, who required French conversation while being taken for walks. Their combined fees would pay the cost of Mrs. Robson's rooms and leave a small amount over for food and necessities; Alvey could, with relief, feel herself fairly self-supporting.

The alderman's daughters, Edith and Jemima, were spoilt, shrill, stupid little creatures. Confronted by their ignorance and lack of will to learn, Alvey appreciated even more, in retrospect, the eagerness, attentiveness, quick wits, and thirst for knowledge which she had found in Nish and Tot. Teaching them had been like throwing crumbs to hungry birds. Whereas the Grainger girls were interested in little but the endless supply of new frilly dresses their mother had made for them; drilling a few phrases of French into their reluctant minds was harder work, Alvey thought, then building the Roman Wall, and would take about as long. Still, she did not dislike escorting them about the streets of Newcastle. The weather had improved. August was dry, sunless, but temperate enough to make walking a pleasure. And Alvey began at last to find some merit in the city, which, though undeniably black and dirty, was not without architectural interest, and a lively, prosperous place, rich from its profits as a seaport and its coal and shipbuilding industries. Coal and industry were not the only features, Alvey found. The Sandgate region, to be sure, was full of drunken seamen and foul-mouthed navvies, whose language, fortunately, was almost wholly incomprehensible, but there were Norman arches to be seen, and Roman stonework. Newcastle was full of history. There were gateways, flights of steps, and enticing little alleyways known as "chares"; there were handsome new Georgian houses, a ruined castle to admire and explore, fine shops and theatres; even open country, not really so very far away.

Sometimes Alvey went with Edith and Jemima to Jesmond Dene, where the bubbling brook, the grass and trees, made her ache with longing for the Hungry Water; but her favourite excursion was to go down to the banks of the Tyne, and look wistfully westwards along its wide and busy reaches, wondering which drops of the river had come down from Birkland and under Hexham bridge.

On Saturdays she sometimes caught a horse bus to the edge of the city and walked along the Roman Wall, here almost at its easternmost extremity.

Kindly Mrs. Robson often asked Alvey how she did, pressed a singing hinny or piece of gingerbread on her as she passed through the

shop—"Bless ye, lass, ye're as thin as a rail yet, white as a clout"—and
kept a solicitous eye on her lodger; but it was conversation that Alvey
chiefly missed, not food; the gruff good sense of Sir Aydon, the mean-
dering, yet pithy commentaries on life emanating from Tot and Nish,
the servants' shrewd observations, old Mrs. Winship's sudden fierce-
nesses and piercing intuitions.

How are they all doing? Alvey still wondered miserably, a dozen
times a day. How did Louisa contrive to present the matter? How did
they take my departure and her arrival? What happened? Have they
quite accepted her now, and put me out of their minds? Were they *very*
angry? What did Sir Aydon say? Is Louisa still there? How long was it
before she introduced Lieutenant Dunnifage into the household? And
did she reveal that he was her husband? What did Sir Aydon say to
him? Was Lady Winship at all happy to see her true daughter—was she
surprised? Did she even notice the exchange? Can Louisa have managed to persuade her mother to give up that voluntary self-imprisonment?

Oh, how I long to be there, in my room, sitting at the window table,
listening to the silence, which will presently be broken by the thump
of children's feet on the stairs and the thunder of the breakfast
gong . . .

It was like, Alvey thought, beginning to read a book of surpassing
interest, arriving at the last chapter, only to discover that the last hundred pages have been cut away.

Mid-August came, and the Grainger family departed for three
weeks to the seaside, to Alnmouth. Alvey had looked forward to more
leisure in their absence, but acquired another job at this time, translat-
ing French correspondence for a wire- and nail-manufacturing company who exported large quantities of goods to Brussels and Ghent.
She enjoyed her excursions into the manufacturing part of the city and
was kept busy for several days a week, but missed her outings with the
Grainger girls and went once or twice, by herself, to the Roman Wall.
Now, looking northwest towards Whittington and Capheaton, she
imagined the heather in bloom, its fiery plum colour, almost painful to
the eye, under the grey sultry clouds. The hills around Birkland had
just been fading from this barbaric purple when she first arrived. I

prefer them green or brown, she thought. But what is the use of such preferences? I shall never see those hills again.

When the Graingers returned, at the beginning of September, she was sincerely pleased to see the girls, and listened patiently to their tales of rolling down sand dunes and fishing from a coble for whiting and mackerel.

"And what is the French word for 'boat,' Edith?"

"Oh, I've forgotten all that old French, Miss Clement!"

One afternoon, after Alvey had, with the utmost difficulty, managed to insert into their heads the fact that *la canne* meant "the stick" and *la bague* "the ring," and had escorted the girls home to their fond mamma, she found that lady, as was her habit, taking tea in her suffocatingly curtained and flounced and frilled and valanced drawing room.

"There you are, my angels! Did you have a pleasant walk? Come and sit down now, and have your tea. — Ah, thank you, Miss—er— say goodbye now, properly, girls, *au revoir, mademoiselle, merci bien.* Did you learn a great number of French words this afternoon? That is good. Bring your cups here. I have not yet poured the tea because I have been so engrossed in reading this very entertaining new romance that your kind papa brought home for me from Thurstan's." And Mrs. Grainger held up a volume, handsomely bound in red leather with gilded edgings and silken book marker. "*Wicked Lord Love.* Oh, it is the most amusing tale! When you are just a little older, my loves, you shall read it; as soon as you can understand long words."

"Good heavens, ma'am!" exclaimed Alvey. "I mean—pray excuse me—might I just take a glance at that book you have there?"

"Why—I suppose so—yes—if you wish it, Miss Clement," said Mrs. Grainger stiffly, making it plain that she thought the nursery governess was taking a considerable liberty. And she enfolded the book in a sheet of clean writing paper before passing it, with some reluctance, to Alvey, who turned at once to the title page.

WICKED LORD LOVE, By a Lady. In Three Volumes,
    price One Guinea. Published by Seward & Company,
    Publishers, Pleasaunce, Edinburgh.

With trembling fingers she opened the first page and read the opening lines—*her* opening lines.

"Why it is—it *is*—my own book! How very amazing!"

"*Your* book, Miss Clement? Pray, what *can* you mean? Mr. Grainger
just brought it home for me, this very afternoon, from Thurstan's
Library."

"Yes; no; I did not mean that it was my property, Mrs. Grainger,
but that I am the person who wrote it. I am the author."

"*You,* Miss Clement—the author of this book?" Mrs. Grainger
plainly received the statement with total disbelief. She added, after a
moment, as if very kindly giving Alvey a chance to retract and redeem
herself, "I mean, you know, that is so wholly improbable! Are you
quite positive that you do not find yourself mistaken, Miss Clement?
Very few people, after all, are clever enough to write a book and have
it published—especially such an amusing one as this!"

Alvey had been rapidly flipping through the pages, and now collected herself. "No: I am quite sure. And thank you, Mrs. Grainger,
for letting me look at it." She added quietly, "Goodbye, Edith, goodbye, Jemima. I shall see you on Thursday. Don't forget those words
between now and then," and, handing the volume back to Mrs. Grainger, she took her departure.

Before returning to Mrs. Robson's house in the Side, she made her
way with all speed to Thurstan's Circulating Library, the foremost in
Newcastle, which occupied a prominent position near the Bigg Market. And there, in the front of the shop, on a large round table, she
saw a whole red-and-gold pile of *Wicked Lord Love.* Trembling a little,
from sheer excitement, Alvey asked for a copy, handed over her
twenty-one shillings, and saw the three volumes wrapped up. Then,
with her heart beating like a sledgehammer, she hurried back to her
attic to gloat over it. It reads *beautifully* in print, she thought. Oh, what
nonsense it is! And what fun I had writing it!

Tomorrow she must start to ask questions; must write immediately
to Messrs. Seward & Company and demand to know why they had
never been in touch with her, never paid her; but, for now, she was
content just to sit in her stuffy little room, barefoot, on the bare floor-
boards, and gloat; then to lie down, at long last, on Mrs. Robson's

lumpy mattress, not to fall asleep but to think over and over again: I am an author! I have had a real book published! I am an author!

The next morning was devoted to the composition of two letters; one to Mr. Allgood, giving her direction in Newcastle, "whither she had removed, owing to family differences, and was living under the name of Miss Clement"; the second, and this a highly indignant one, to Seward the publishers, demanding to know why they had published her book without even doing her the courtesy of apprising her as to their intentions, or offering terms.

In the course of the following week she had replies from both.

Mr. Allgood wrote:

> My dear Miss Clement: I am more than happy and relieved to hear that you are safely settled in Newcastle, for some wild rumours have been flying about the countryside regarding mysterious duplications and replacements; and I am credibly informed that a *second* Miss Louisa Winship, an exact likeness of the first, is now in residence at Birkland Hall. As to *which* has the right to reside at Birkland, I would not pretend to judge, but to which one my loyalty is owing there is no question, and it is to the author of *Wicked Lord Love* that I pen these lines.
>
> I learn with great dismay from my cousin Jamie that there has been some hiatus in communication; it appears that during February storms a mail coach went off the Great North Road and many letters were destroyed or dispersed and never reached their destinations; it seems all too probable that his to you, offering terms for the book, was among their number.

Perhaps I did James an injustice, thought Alvey; perhaps he did write to his grandmother and that letter was lost too. Letters do go astray, I suppose . . .

"Suffice it to say," continued Mr. Allgood,

> that my cousin was entirely delighted with your manuscript and commenced work on its publication without a day's de-

lay; so anxious was he to put the work before the public that, failing to receive a reply from you, he neglected to wait until he had your authority to proceed. He informs me, moreover, that the first subscription was exhausted before publication, and another edition is already in preparation. But you will be hearing from him directly regarding these matters. He sent me a copy of the work for myself and my chief purpose in writing is to inform you of the immense pleasure and entertainment it has given me; if I may so put it, the experience was precisely like dancing through a daisy field on a warm day in May!

Good gracious, thought Alvey, and tried to imagine Mr. Allgood performing such an activity.

> My great hope is that you will in the course of time return to Hexham to inscribe the copy of
> your devoted admirer and well-wisher, etc., etc.
> Cyril Allgood.

James Seward wrote:

My dear Miss Clement, I am overjoyed to have your new direction from my cousin Allgood and write in haste to tender my most sincere apologies. I understand that the first letter I wrote you in February offering terms for your novel never reached you. I ought of course to have written again, but assumed that you were perhaps away travelling and would reply at a later date. My excuse for immediately proceeding without further consultation must be my extreme eagerness to put this delightful Work before the public; an eagerness which, I am happy to say, has been amply justified, for the first imprint is already sold and a second in preparation; I have hopes of even a third or a fourth. My Accounting is appended herewith and it is with great pleasure that I enclose my draft for £221.6.4 being the monies owing to you at this time (if you agree to my terms).

I need hardly tell you, Miss Clement, that I shall await the next Product of your pen with the most hopeful and confident impatience; perhaps a sequel, a further instalment of the escapades of Wicked Lord Love? I understand there is already talk of a possible dramatic representation of the piece at Covent Garden with Kean in the title role; Mr. Siddons is at work on one at this present time & is hoping to persuade his wife to emerge from retirement; so you can see that a second instalment would reach the Public at a wholly propitious moment—

Good God, thought Alvey dazedly, my fortune is made. She looked at the account sheet: "By Commission to Author of 10%: 2,000 copies sold, WICKED LORD LOVE 21/. To Author: £221.6.4."

I could live for a year on that alone—with care; but then he says that another edition is in preparation; perhaps a third and fourth. And also a dramatic version—how are the profits from dramatic representations divided I wonder?

Life had suddenly changed colour in the most astonishing manner. She was still in a state of wretched homesickness for Birkland; but at least she had plenty, now, with which to occupy her mind: hopeful, forward-looking thoughts, prospects of new ventures, new vistas.

Mr. Allgood had, with his letter, enclosed two other papers. One proved to be the missing letter from Louisa; doubtless it had followed a different route from Madagascar and arrived on the heels of its sender. This described her happy marriage to Lieutenant Dunnifage and announced her intention of returning home forthwith to claim her dowry; "and so that Papa can have the pleasure of meeting my Husband for himself and seeing with his own eyes the interesting Sensibility & amiable Sympathy which characterise my beloved Spouse." That's as may be, thought Alvey, who had formed no very favourable impression of Lieutenant Dunnifage.

You will, naturally, upon receipt of this, wish to procure yourself some other Domicile to which you may remove upon (or, preferably, *before*) our arrival at Birkland, so that there need be no embarrassing Juxtapositions. I leave the arrangements for this to yourself.
Yours &c Louisa Winship Dunnifage.

The second letter was from Isa, posted in Durham. She had written:

My dear Alvey,
Here we are staying with Major Fenway's uncle the Bishop, in whose house we are treated with the most Distinguishing Kindness and introduced to all that is interesting and amiable among the local society; in other words, we are very snug. But I need not tell you, dear Alvey, how acutely impatient I am to complete the last stage of our journey and arrive at Tinnis; not Birkland itself, alas, but at least in my beloved Northumberland. I have so *much* to tell you, and even more, I am certain, to hear. How does my father go on? And has poor Mamma recovered from the brutal destruction of her garden? And what is the word of James and his friend? I am really wild to see you, and shall hope to ride over for a day's visit as soon as we are safely installed among the Chibburns.
With best affection, Isa.

This letter gave Alvey a decided pang. How much I should like to see Isa, she thought; Isa is a real friend, perhaps the only one I have made in my life. With the possible exception of Guy Fenway?

Since the discovery that she had become a published author, Alvey felt herself to be an entirely different person. I have grown to be an adult, she decided; and looked back with wonder at that stricken creature who huddled against the window, day after day, lacking the energy to creep beyond the corner of the street. Now, too, she was afflicted less often by those painful assaults of childhood memory—though she did feel a deep, deep sadness at the thought of what pride and pleasure her mother would have taken in this visible, tangible evidence of achievement. But in her heart of hearts Alvey had no doubt at all that Sarah must be dead. "So I must feel all the pride on her behalf, since my success is thanks entirely to her early teaching, and her example of hardworking persistence; any credit is due to her and I needn't give myself airs."

She did not give herself airs, but this new self-confidence made her think long and hard about her relationship with the family at Birkland.

I did help them. I know I did. And I think I could continue to do so.

But it would be impossible to return there without invitation. And certainly not if Louisa and her husband were still in residence. Oh, how I long to hear from somebody there—just to know how they feel about me.

I'll write to Isa at Tinnis Hall. She and Meg must be there by now. That is my best course.

She did so directly, but had received no reply when she next went to conduct the young Misses Grainger for their educational ramble. Returning from this promenade on which she had, with considerable difficulty, taught her two charges the phrases *"je ne sais quoi"* and *"je ne sais pas,"* she found herself invited to take tea with Mrs. Grainger, and was amused to discover that her status had, during the passage of a week, been subject to a complete revision. She was received (like Isa and the Chibburns) with most distinguishing kindness. Evidently her pretensions to having written *Wicked Lord Love* had been canvassed and accepted; indeed Mr. Grainger himself presently arrived from his place of business and congratulated her upon her success.

"They are talking aboot it all over the town, Miss Clement, all over the coontry, I oonderstand, indeed they are; ye've got a right money-spinner on yer hands there, I tell ye straight! Ay, it's real laughable stuff, so it is; I'm amazed a female could write anything so humorous." He was a red-faced man with a pompous air and self-satisfied expression; he looked at Alvey with real astonishment and respect.

"Thank you, sir."

"And we'd be pleased if ye'd coom to an evening party my good lady is giving next week, Miss Clement; Saturday evening; an evening party with wine and refreshments. The cream o' the town will be there, so ye may dress as fine as ye please," he added, looking with some disparagement at the grey dress which Alvey thought appropriate for her rambles with Miss Edith and Miss Jemima.

"Why, thank you," she said doubtfully, "I should be very happy, but—"

"Now, now; we won't take any 'buts,' will we, Mrs. Grainger? We'll look to see you then. And—ahem—"

Having written a novel that received public acclaim, Alvey now discovered, entitled her to a substantial increase in the emolument she was receiving for her French teaching; in fact her fees were to be more

than doubled; perhaps Mr. Grainger feared that if Alvey were to become well acquainted with the cream of the town, she might inadver-
tently reveal to some of those persons the rather small payment which
had previously been thought sufficient for her services.

It was with no little dread that Alvey looked forward to the Graingers' evening party; but she was not destined to attend it. On the
previous day, when she returned from reading Fénelon to old Mrs.
Morley, she was told that a gentleman had come to visit her.

"A real fine, well-spoken gentleman," said Mrs. Robson, big-eyed.
"He were a mite lame, like, so I wouldn't wish to make him climb all
the way up. Ye'll find him in my front parlour, hinny; Winship, the
name was."

James! Alvey's heart bounded so violently that she was obliged to
stop and rest halfway up the stairs; it was with a shaking hand that she
lifted the latch of Mrs. Robson's front-parlour door.

And the person waiting inside was not James, but his father.

Without a word he walked across the room and folded her in a
strong embrace. Then he held her at arm's length and scolded her.

"Wretched, wicked girl! How could you dare to play such a trick on
us? Hussy! Minx! I do not know how you have the gall to look me in
the face! Of all the outrageous—abominable—barefaced—*intolera-
ble*—"

"Stop, stop! Oh, I deserve it, I know I do; I deserve all that you
say—"

Alvey found herself crying with positively enjoyable abandonment;
tears cascaded down her cheeks. "I do deserve your displeasure," she
gulped, "but, after all, it *was* your daughter Louisa who planned and
initiated the scheme; without her insistence it would never have come
about—"

"I am not talking about *that,* you silly besom, I'm talking about
running off and abandoning us in that extravagant, nonsensical way.
How could you *do* it? Just because *Louisa* had come back? As if I cared
the snap of a straw whether Louisa were there or not—"

"But she *is* there, is she not, Sir Aydon?"

"Oh, ay, she's there, with that rhubarb stick of a husband of hers;
she's there right enow. But she won't be for long, now I've found you,

about it—very much. Should have acted sooner in the matter of Louisa's jointure. To tell you the truth—a kind of lethargy came over me after you left us—found myself very down in the dumps—"

"Oh, sir—I am so very sorry—"

"And so you should be, my girl! There we were, left high and dry— with no one but Louisa for cheer and comfort—and *she's* about as much comfort as the prophet Jeremiah; in fact, of the two, I'd sooner have him—and that *devilish* bore of a husband of hers. Tallow-faced, stuttering puppy! To see him drinking my port, night after night, was almost more than flesh and blood could bear. — So why didn't I pack off the pair of them, you may ask? Well—in a way—I hardly know myself—"

Alvey felt that she could easily guess. The combination of Louisa and her husband—their complete self-satisfaction coupled with determination to pursue their own ends—made a tremendously strong negative force. She could imagine the stunning impact of their presence on the household at Birkland. And how Sir Aydon might have turned stubborn in protest.

"To tell truth," he confessed, "I did let myself fall into a despondency. I know I should have given the wretched girl her portion and sent her off directly with a flea in her ear—which was all she deserved after that precious scheme she hatched. Oh, she spun a fine tale about how it was entirely your idea—but I could tell *that* was a Banbury story as soon as she opened her mouth. Knowing the two of you as well as I do. And so I told her. No, it just went against the grain with me to give her her dowry so easily. I kept putting it off. She'd got us into this sorry state, I told myself; let her kick her heels for a while at Birkland. Why should she think she could just walk home, turn us all topsy-turvy, and then clear out again as soon as she had got what she came for?"

"I daresay I should have felt the same," said Alvey.

"Understand my position, do you? Good girl. Thought you might. But it led to harm. For there was this wretched husband of hers, at a loose end, with time on his hands, all set to make mischief."

"Oh, good God! What can he have done!" asked Alvey with foreboding.

"For a start, made those poor children's lives a burden. So Nish told

not if I have any say in the matter. Why in the world, you silly girl, d
you let her talk you into leaving?"

Why indeed? How to convey that it had seemed, at the time, er
tirely inevitable?

"Now," he said, "you must pack up your traps and make ready to
ride back with me; start packing directly."

"But, sir, consider! Now that everybody knows I am an imposter—
that I have no shadow of right to be at Birkland—how can I—?"

"How can you?" he thundered. "How can you? Because *I* bid you,
that's why! I am the master of the house, damn it! For that matter,
everybody except myself and Charlotte seems to have been well aware
for months before you left that you were an imposter, and precious
little difference did it make to them. No, you must come," he went on
in a different voice, "for my mother's taken another of her queer turns
—I'll tell you the cause presently, another bad thing that happened—
she's uncommonly low—can't seem to get her breath and she keeps
asking for you. So, if you're a Christian lass, as I don't doubt you are,
you must come back. Setting aside the fact that the children were fair
broken-hearted—"

"Oh!" she cried. "Parting from them was the hardest thing I ever
did!"

"Well then, don't make any more pother about it, but just pack your
traps, like a good girl. I'm dining at the Castle Hotel—to give the
horses a bit of a rest—ordered dinner for six. We should leave directly
after, and be home by sunrise. So come along to dinner as soon as you
are packed."

As soon as she sat down to dinner, Alvey said anxiously, "Sir, you
spoke of something else bad that had happened at home—at Birkland.
Please do not keep me in suspense any longer." She studied his face,
which did look exceedingly tired and drawn. "Is it—does it relate to
Lady Winship?"

"Hey? Oh, no. No, Charlotte's much as she was. Not any better,
but no worse, I'm glad to say. No, the matter relates to Tot."

"To *Tot?*" Alvey's heart jolted horribly. "Why—what has happened
to him?"

"Well—" Sir Aydon frowned, crumbling a roll. "I blame myself me afterwards. Always hounding them about, under pretext of giving them lessons, in navigation and so forth; chivvied them and teased them, obliged them to do exercises, and kept on, particularly at the boy, telling him that he was a milksop and a mollycoddle, nothing but a baby."

"Odious, hateful man!" Alvey clenched her hands. "I *knew* I was right to dislike him the moment I laid eyes on him. Oh, *poor* Tot! So, what happened?"

"That mad, wild old fellow, Amos Herdman—you know whom I mean?"

"Annie's father, yes. The children are rather afraid of him. The one who did the damage to Lady Winship's garden."

"Well—it's thought so—yes. And he has uttered other threats since. But nothing of a definite nature."

"What did he do?"

"It seems he came past the paddock one day, when Dunnifage was making the children run races—or some such thing—and shouted a whole string of abuse at them over the wall—and young Tot was upset by it and turned very white. So Dunnifage had to taunt him about that, and tell him that he was a puling little coward, to be so frightened of an old man. Said something about you—your teaching being only fit for girls—"

"Oh! Oh, what a monster! So what happened?"

"Tot went off and was not seen all day. That was yesterday. In the evening Nish came to me, half drowned with crying, and told me he'd meant to show Dunnifage that he was *not* a coward, so he had gone up to the old man's hut, where he lives all summer, to—to beard him in his den.

"Nish had an idea that Tot was going to do this. He wouldn't let her go, but she followed, at a distance.

"He went to the door, she told me, and called something; the old man wasn't inside, Nish said, but somewhere close by. She saw him steal up behind Tot and hit him with a club. And then dragged him into the hut. Nish ran to the door, and shouted, and banged on it, but it was fastened, the old man paid no heed. So then she ran all the way home."

"How *dreadful*. Poor child! What happened?"

"I sent up all the men from the house, Stridge and Blackett and Carey—they shouted and threatened to break the door, but Amos said if they did he'd cut the boy's throat."

"Oh *no*—then what?"

"That was when my mother had her attack. Duddy—*idiot* woman—had to go and let it out—old lady turned blue directly—at first we thought she was done for. Surtees went off hell-for-leather for the sawbones—Cunningham—knew he was in the neighbourhood, visiting old Lady Burnacres—came directly—bled her, and she recovered consciousness. Asked for you. So," Sir Aydon said simply, "I came for you. Mrs. Slaley gave me your direction. Seems she knew it all along."

"But Tot? What of him?"

"Still in the old man's cabin—so far as I know—with the men outside. Unless by this time they have succeeded in effecting an entry. Of course," said Sir Aydon, "I hope that is the case."

Alvey stared at him in consternation.

"You mean to say—you left home—not knowing, with Tot still at the mercy of that madman? Oh, why are we sitting here? Let us go *at once*—how could you bear to come away?"

"Well—" he mumbled, "it was life or death for m'mother too—and whom could I send? Do you see? Sufficient men up at Amos's hut—Lumley in charge—nothing *I* could do better—"

Yet it was plain to her how it had wrung him to come away.

"Let us go—please let us go—indeed I could not touch another crumb—"

She pushed away her half-full plate.

"Well, we had to bait the horses and give you time to pack," said Sir Aydon. "But I'll be glad to set out, and that's a fact."

"Glad to see ye, Miss Emmy, hinny," said Archie the coachman, stowing Alvey's box in the boot.

"I wonder how in the world I can ever persuade anyone in the house to use my real name?" Alvey murmured, as they were bowling westwards out of Newcastle. "Perhaps I had best continue as Emmy."

The point was a trifling one, but any topic, anything had value that might possibly distract Sir Aydon, who fell, at the shortest pause, into a grim, anxious silence, tapping his fingers restlessly on the strap.

"What is your real name?" he asked, and when she told him: "Alvey, Alvey? Hm, it seems to me there were cousins of that name on my father's side, half a century back or more—that would account for the singular resemblance, I daresay."

"That comforts me a little—makes me feel less of an outsider."

"Of course you must be connected with the family; any fool can see that. Tell me about your parents."

So she told him, with much greater ease and fluency than when she had told Guy, and he listened and exclaimed, and said it was the damnedest thing he had ever heard in his whole life. "And they are still here? Living in that devilish settlement, what's its name—Simony, Sanctimony?"

"Unison. Yes; so far as I know. If they are still alive. Supposing they had left, I am sure my mother would have been in touch with me."

"But how would she be able to find ye?"

"I left my direction with a bank in New Bedford."

"Well, well, all that was deuced bad luck for you, my dear, but it was a piece of good fortune for us, I can tell you. Now you must never run away from us again."

"Well, sir—we shall see. If—if—" She abandoned that beginning, and said, "I would be very happy to stay until—until the children are a little older, at least. But then, later—supposing, for instance, that James should marry, should bring home a wife—"

"I *had* thought how handily it would fall out if you were to marry James."

His tone was wistful; but, over the pang it gave her, Alvey replied firmly, "No, sir, I'm afraid that idea won't wash. James prefers—a different type of female. I am sure that, by and by, he will choose a charming wife, and you will love her very much, as much as your own daughters."

"Wouldn't be difficult. Curious thing how I never cottoned to any of my daughters," he muttered. "Isa's well enough, I suppose, but Parthie and Louisa are both antidotes. And Meg selfish as they come—"

"Nish is a darling—"

"Well, she's improving, I grant. The one I had a *real* soft spot for—died before you came, you never knew her. Maria, that was—had a look of m' sister who also died . . . Curious, when you first arrived at Birkland—thought for a moment you were she—remember it well—"

Alvey, too, remembered that curious moment.

"What a long time ago that seems."

They talked about Lady Winship.

"Does she improve at all, sir, since I left? Has having the real Louisa at home helped her?"

"Not in the least. Why should it? Never cared a rap for Louisa— stubborn, priggish girl. Louisa ain't at home now, by the bye. Went over to visit her sisters at Tinnis, before all this trouble came on us. No, Charlotte's still under a cloud, poor thing; kinder to me, since she heard the news about Sim Whittingham; but she still vows that, if it's believed about the countryside that she did away with wee Geordie, up in that place she will stay till her dying day."

With great trepidation Alvey asked, "Do *you* believe she did that dreadful thing, sir?"

After a moment or two he replied, "No. No, I don't. I did have the notion in my mind at one time, I must confess—when I was so low myself—but no; I can't believe Charlotte would be capable of such an act. She is not a particularly *kind* woman, mark you; thoughts too far away, engaged with that garden of hers; but she'd not be wicked, she'd never be spiteful. No; I think she must have visited the pool, perhaps, early in the morning—found the child drowned already— tried to move him, perhaps, then grew frightened and desisted, when she found it was too late—"

"How can she ever be persuaded to return to normal living?"

"I had hoped the summer would bring it about," he said gruffly. "But that didn't come to pass. Perhaps your intervention, my dear?"

"It had no effect before . . ."

They talked of Tot, tacitly agreeing to ignore the present crisis, to assume that it would, it must end well.

"I see such an improvement in the boy," Sir Aydon said. "He is so much more open, fearless in his dealings with me—it is a shocking pity about his disability—"

"He may grow out of it in time, Major Fenway thinks. And even if he does not, it has no bearing, you know, upon his intelligence, which is considerable. After all," said Alvey gently, "some of the world's greatest men have been of an epileptic habit."

Sir Aydon flinched at the word, but said, "What do you think, then? School would be too much for him, hm?"

"Why not a tutor? Some sensible, active young man? And then, later, university, where he can mix with minds of his own calibre?"

"Odd that both my sons should turn out so bookish!"

"But Tot spends all his days in the open air."

"Oh well, you know what I mean."

More and more, as the carriage hurried towards home, Alvey and Sir Aydon talked about the estate. Anything, she thought, to keep his mind away from what might await him at home. And in estate matters he was always ready to be engaged.

"If, as Lumley suggests, you put down some of those wheat fields to pasture—wheat prices, he tells me, have fallen from a hundred twenty shillings three years ago to fifty-three shillings sixpence—wheat can no longer be said to be a profitable crop—"

"Are you a Whig, girl?"

"No, sir, I am an American. I have no English politics. But I can see a practical course when it is laid under my nose."

For the first time, he actually laughed. "American! Gad, I suppose you are. Well, no doubt, in the end, I'll have to let you and Lumley persuade me."

"Lumley says that in a hundred years Northumberland will be covered with sheep."

"Perhaps if I bought more sheep that might do something to appease old Herdman," he murmured.

"But—good heavens—will you not arrest him? Put him under restraint? After what he has done now?"

"We must wait and see," he said heavily. "Wait and see what he *has* done. Look: now you can see Cheviot; we are nearly home. Morning is coming."

It was a different homecoming from any of her previous returns. Established now as necessary and wanted, even if not belonging by birth, Alvey felt more certain of her welcome than she had done before. — The joy as they rolled down the last hill was very profound

—even accompanied, as it was, by such acute anxiety and suspense. She looked about her alertly at the signs of summer's end—the fading heather, the vermilion berries on the rowan trees, rose hips and heart's-ease and purple knapweed.

Nish and Tot had taught her all their names.

Amble met the carriage with a grave face.

"What's to do?" demanded Sir Aydon. "My mother? Is she still—?"

"Yes, sir, the old lady's still with us—thank the Lord—though I'm feared she's still parlous—"

"And Master Tot?"

"No change in that affair, sir; the men are up there yet; seems there's no way o' flushing the owd devil out, short o' setting fire to the hut. — Grand to see ye home, Miss Emmy," he said warmly to Alvey, who felt tears spring into her eyes at what, in these distressing circumstances, she felt was undeserved kindness. And this feeling was enhanced when Mrs. Slaley came out, cap strings flying, and enveloped her in a voluminous hug.

"Eh, Miss Emmy, hinny, ye're a sight for sore eyes!"

Into the middle of this scene rode Louisa, coming round the corner of the house on Phantom; she seemed profoundly startled at the sight of Alvey, and her surprised look deepened into one of strong displeasure. It seemed that she had just returned from Tinnis Hall and still knew nothing of the disturbance that had sent her father off to Newcastle.

"*Miss Clement!* Why, pray, are *you* here?"

Tersely, her father told Louisa the story of Tot and old Amos.

"I will go and talk to the old man," announced Louisa. "I will remind him of the Gospels, and reason with him. I shall very soon be able to bring him to a better state of mind."

"Fiddlestick, girl!" Sir Aydon moved away from her impatiently. "What use in the wide world do you think *you* can be? You will only do more harm than good."

Amble was heard to mutter, "Words is dirt cheap, hinny."

Nish came out of the front door. At the sight of Alvey her face went blank. She turned, as if to re-enter the house, without speaking. But, at that moment, Stridge came running through the trees, crying, "Oh, quick, come quick! He've stabbed Surtees wi' a gurt knife—and he's dragging Master Tot up on the crag, an' he says he'll throw him off Pike Force. He's mad as a loon!"

"Amble—fetch my pistols! Bring them up there!" called Sir Aydon, and started after Stridge. Then he remembered Alvey, and turned.

"I'll go to your mother, sir," she said quickly.

"Yes, do that, good girl. I must go—see what I can do—"

Alvey nodded, swallowed convulsively, and walked into the house. Passing close to Nish, who still stood, irresolute, on the doorstep, Alvey touched her hand, and said, "Will you come to your grandmother with me?"

But Nish angrily jerked her hand away.

"No, I won't. I hate you. You went off and left us, and *now* see what has come of it. I *hate* you!"

"I am sorry," Alvey said helplessly, and then she went up to the old woman's room. There would be not the slightest point in my accompanying Sir Aydon to Pike Force, she thought. I would only be in the way. And I was brought back, after all, because of Mrs. Winship—

Duddy was there, in the room, sitting by the old lady's bed. For once the maid was not mending. Her hands lay idle. And her face was drawn and seamed with sadness; it looked like a grey rock on the fells, Alvey thought, and, with a shiver, remembered the crags and the sheer drop of Pike Force.

"Eh; ye're back then, Miss Emmy," Duddy said in a lifeless voice. "How is she?"

"Badly; I doubt she'll no' come out o' this one."

The old lady's breathing was slow, painful, and rasping; each longdrawn harsh sound filled the silent room.

"Shall I sit by her for a while?"

"If ye wish," said Duddy ungraciously; she moved away as if she hardly knew what to do with herself, but finally left the room. Alvey sat down and watched the still figure, which was propped against a pile of pillows. She took one of the cold hands, and, as the children had been used to, gently manipulated and rubbed it.

Half an hour went by; Alvey had the feeling that there were three presences in the room: herself, the patient, and something else, something shadowy and enormous, which was gradually overmastering the old woman—like a great fibrous forest, growing and growing, sucking up the air and light, sucking life out of the aged body. If only she could battle against it—

I wish I could pray, Alvey thought. But not that kind of prayer, petition; no, I just cannot.

All of a sudden the closed eyes opened and looked straight into hers.

"How are you, Grandmamma?" Alvey asked quietly.

The eyes flashed with fury.

"What do you think? Not at all well. Stupid thing to ask! Ought to have more sense." Mrs. Winship brought these words out in separate gasps.

"I'm glad, at least, that you have strength to scold me."

"Shouldn't—have gone away—" the pale lips enunciated.

"No, and I am very sorry for it. But what was I to do? Louisa had come back; there was hardly room for us both."

"Odious creature. As for that husband of hers, he's a dolt, an oaf, a blockhead—has no more faculty than a soused herring."

Alvey burst out laughing.

"Oh, Grandmother—I do love you."

Mrs. Winship's face worked. "A fine way you have of showing it—running off in that Drury Lane fashion."

"Well, I promise I will stay here now. Till—till—"

"Till what?" The brilliant, shortsighted eyes stared into hers ironically. "Till I'm gone? And then run away again? And what about Tot? Have they got him away from the madman?"

Alvey drew a shaky breath. "Not yet."

"What's happening?"

"Sir Aydon has gone up there." Alvey said nothing about the waterfall.

"Well, if all those fools can't get my grandson away from that lunatic—"

"Don't tire yourself. Just waiting takes a lot of strength."

"You're young to know that."

They went on waiting, in silence. Once Mrs. Winship asked, "Where were you? All this time?"

"In Newcastle. Teaching French."

She heard a sniff that might have been a laugh. But the old woman had no strength to spare, and was not really interested in Newcastle. I won't distract her with red herrings, Alvey thought. She has to keep all her energy for the one thing.

Much later, when dusk was beginning to gather in the corners of the room, Nish came stealing round the door and crept across the room to the bed. Opposite Alvey she dropped to her knees and buried her face in the coverlet, holding her grandmother's hand against her cheek. There she stayed, motionless, as if she had run out of motive power.

Mrs. Winship's other hand patted her head.

"There, there," said the deep, hoarse voice. "Don't take on, child. The worst doesn't always come about. And if it does, we learn to face it."

After another immensely long time they heard the sound of voices downstairs, doors banging, commotion.

"Something's happened," said the old woman.

"Shall I go and find out?"

"Don't stir yourself. Somebody's bound to come up here and tell me. That's one advantage"—another sniff—"of dying. For once, you are treated with proper consideration."

The door opened. Tot came in, carrying a candle.

"Who is it? Who has come in? I can't see. Come closer, whoever you are."

"It's *Tot!*" said Nish in a voice of pure astonishment. "*Is* it really you? Not your ghost?"

"It's me," said Tot. He sounded weary, but, somehow, remarkably *adult*, Alvey thought; almost amused. "Me, not my ghost."

"So what *happened?*" demanded the old woman. "Did the madman let you go?"

"Louisa came and read the Bible to him. And lectured him a great deal. All *kinds* of bits of the Bible she read aloud—some of the Prophets, and Revelation, and the book of Job—she went on and on and on—and in the end he began to cry and said he was a poor old man. And just let me go."

"Well!" said Alvey weakly. "How—how very capable of Louisa! So I suppose she really is right to want to be a missionary."

"You won't die; will you, Grandmother?" said Tot.

"Well; soon," she said. "But not just yet. The news is too interesting."

XVII

Strangely, Louisa was not at all puffed up about what she had done. Her husband, Lieutenant Dunnifage, was odiously puffed up; he behaves, thought Alvey, as if he, personally, had organised the whole rescue, instead of remaining behind, quietly drinking sherry in the library of Birkland Hall.

And it was Louisa who petitioned that old Herdman be allowed to go free, not charged with abduction, or assault, or trespass and damage. Or murder.

"He truly repents," she kept saying. "You cannot wish to transport somebody who *truly* repents of their sins, Papa."

"I certainly can. The murdering old blackguard."

For old Herdman had admitted, both to Louisa, and to Tot in the course of that long thirty-six hours in the shepherd's hut, that it was he who had drowned wee Geordie in the Lion Pool.

"He kept saying that he was going to drown me too; that he'd drown all the Winship boys until there wasn't one of that name left in the country. He said it was a pity James wasn't killed at Waterloo," said Tot.

"But Geordie wasn't a Winship boy; Sim Whittingham was his father."

"But Annie had put it about that he was James's child. Old Amos said our family deserved to have everything taken away; he told me about smashing up Mamma's garden too."

"Weren't you frightened?"

"Yes," said Tot judicially. "I was, when I first came to and found myself tied up in his hut. If he hadn't hit me on the head with something he'd never have got me in there. Yes; then I was frightened. But part of the time he wasn't *very* mad; not altogether. He talked about when he was a boy; on and on. Sometimes he was quite sensible. I told him the poem about the Assyrian coming down like a wolf, and he liked that. I could have got away then if he hadn't tied my hands behind my back, because he was walking about the hut, shouting 'Purple and gold, purple and gold.' Then, when the men outside began shouting, he turned wild again and got out his knife. I thought he would cut my throat. — How is poor Surtees?"

"Oh, it is only a flesh wound on his ribs," Alvey said. "He will mend fast enough."

She could not help smiling at the thought of Tot reciting "The Destruction of Sennacherib" to the old madman. What a boy he is, she thought proudly. Sir Aydon caught her eye and smiled also.

"Well, well, perhaps I will not take proceedings against the old devil. Perhaps, if his brother at Riding Mill will undertake the care of him— What do you say, Charlotte?"

"Yes, that will be best," faintly agreed Lady Winship. "We want no more anger and destruction."

"I am bound to say, Louisa," pronounced her father, "that you did very well; very well indeed. Must confess I didn't think you had it in you."

Louisa smiled at him with calm self-approbation.

Lieutenant Dunnifage and his wife left next day, greatly to Alvey's relief. The lieutenant regarded Alvey, if ever he was obliged to notice her existence, in a most singular fashion, with disapproval, almost with detestation, as if he were trying, with all his power, to make her disappear from his line of vision. Well, it must be strange and disagreeable, thought Alvey, to know that your spouse has a duplicate; that you had the ill luck to pick, not a unique object, but one of a pair. And, furthermore, that she hatched that discreditable plot; it must tend to devalue what you have chosen.

The couple had, however, been finally successful, she gathered, in wheedling Louisa's full dowry out of her father.

"I reckon she earned it, at the last," said Sir Aydon. "To begin with, I won't deny, I had been minded to halve it, as I had planned to for

Parthie; but then, when Louisa came up to the mark so over old Herdman, I thought: Well, why not let her have the whole? But that's the
very last penny you'll have from me, my girl, I told her; don't think
you can come soft-soaping me to pay out for that mission of yours, for
I don't hold with such things; a decent lodging house is all that
sailormen need, not a plaguy mission."

"Thank the Lord they have left again," said old Mrs. Winship. "I
couldn't die in peace and comfort with that Dunce-Face in the house;
nor with Mrs. Saintly-Airs Louisa. Now that it's just the family again,
I'll take myself off."

And she did, on the following night.

"Don't you go blaming Alvey, now, miss," she said to Nish, "for
I'm due to go, and glad to. You'll see, by and by; when it's your own
turn. And I leave you my cat Maudge, and mind you comb him properly, and see that he gets plenty of yeast; you know how fond he is of
yeast."

"Yes, Granny."

"Parthie ran off with my best Paisley shawl. When she comes back
—if she comes back—with that Thropton—you can tell her she may as
well keep it. That's all."

And Mrs. Winship died.

All the family were grouped around her bed, and Duddy; and she
went off so collectedly that no one could regard it as a tragic event, it
was simply a happening, the end of a period.

Though I shall miss her horribly, Alvey thought; Charlotte is no
substitute at all; especially now that she has begun planning for her
renovated garden.

"What's this I hear? Is Mr. Thropton back in the rectory?" Sir
Aydon asked Amble next day at breakfast.

"Yes, sir. He returned yesterday, it's said. But I reckon he's scared
to come and see you."

"Eh? How so?"

"Poor Miss Parthie—"

"What about poor Miss Parthie?"

"Seems she passed away on their wedding journey, sir. Word just came. She caught a low fever and died at Greenlaw, two months agone. Mr. Thropton stayed away till now."

"Good God. What a—oh well, no use going into that, I suppose. Wretched man," said Sir Aydon at length, gruffly. "How will he ever find the courage to look me in the face?"

Everybody was startled and shocked. But no one could pretend to feel great grief.

"It's not as if it were Grandma," said Nish.

"I wonder where he buried her," said Tot.

"I suppose I'd best go down and call on the poor devil," said Sir Aydon. "In the circumstances, I can hardly summon him here to discuss arrangements for Mamma's funeral."

He had, however, underestimated Mr. Thropton, who came up to the Hall shortly after breakfast. Red-faced, with an appropriately lugubrious expression, twisting his black gloves about—had he a supply of black gloves always at hand, wondered Alvey, or did he buy them on the journey?—he was there almost before the cloth had been removed from the table.

"Ah, my dear Sir Aydon—doubly dear to me now—we must endeavour to console one another in our mutual loss; I speak now, Sir Aydon, not only as your pastor and minister of God, but as your son, and, may I say it, as the grandson of the dear and venerable lady who has left us—"

"No, you mayn't say it," barked Sir Aydon irascibly. "Mrs. Winship would have seen you further before she'd have permitted you to address her as Grandmother. Nor do I regard you as a son. I'm amazed at your impudence, sir, indeed I am!"

Mr. Thropton opened his eyes wide. He seemed sincerely grieved and astonished.

"I am surprised at you, Sir Aydon! But I make allowances. This is a time of sorrow and mourning for you. Your beloved daughter, your cherished mother, in one grievous swoop! — For myself, I do not repine. The Lord has chastened me, and because of this, I know He loves me. I know it well, and I rejoice in my chastening—I am happier, I may say with truth, than I have ever been." He looked it indeed. His fish-mouth smiled benignly, opening and shutting as if it took in plankton from the atmosphere. Had Parthie become such a trial to him already? wondered Alvey unkindly. He went on: "My beloved Parthenope has left me, but I know she is in a better place, interceding for me there. And I am rejoiced at this evidence of my great Father's care for me—He goes before and behind me, He watches over me at all times, never for one moment forgets me. In this chastisement I am reminded of His great love—"

Alvey thought: He hardly seems to look at the matter from Parthie's point of view; and she resolved to record his words in her notebook as soon as she could find the opportunity to do so.

Only, for what purpose?

Sir Aydon looked as if he might explode, but restrained himself. "Humph! As to that—but what's the use of talking? My daughter, I understand, is interred at Greenlaw?"

"Alas, sir, she is. An appropriate headstone is in preparation—humble, as befits her scanty years."

And I wager I know who will have to pay for it, Alvey thought.

Arrangements were discussed and devised for the old lady's funeral; then Mr. Thropton's protruding eye allowed itself to rest on Alvey.

He said, "It gives me great concern, Sir Aydon, to perceive that you still retain under your roof a person who, as I learned from incontrovertible evidence shown me by my late, dear wife, has no shadow of a right to be here, eating your crumb, drinking of your cup—"

"Odds fish, sir!" burst out Sir Aydon, unable to contain himself any longer. "Will you stop preaching on at me like some wretched dissenting hedge orator? I will have whom I choose under my own roof. And Emmy ain't drinking out of my cup but out of her own, and so she shall continue to do. I bid you good day, Mr. Thropton."

Red with indignation, he stamped out of the breakfast parlour, leaving Mr. Thropton to cast up his eyes in a forgiving manner, and then favour Alvey and the children with pitying glances, as if regretting the fact that there was no chance of their rescue from eternal fire. Then he took his own dignified departure.

"If he thinks he'll ever get a penny out of me for Parthie's portion, he's mightily mistaken," said Sir Aydon at dinner.

Old Mrs. Winship's funeral was held next week. James and Major Fenway returned for it from Edinburgh, and Isa came over from Tinnis Hall; Meg was too near her time to be able to venture.

Alvey was delighted to see Isa, and was interested to observe that, though basically she remained wholly unchanged—still as round-shouldered, stooping, shortsighted, and untidy as ever—yet she had somehow, during the course of her travels, contrived to become distinguished. The untidy clothes were of excellent quality and cut, the untidy hair dressed in a careless, but fashionable, mode, and when Isa wished to peer away into the distance, she balanced a tortoise-shell lorgnette on the eagle's beak of a nose inherited from her grandmother, and squinted through the glass with an air of absentminded haughtiness which was entirely accidental but impressive in effect.

She greeted Alvey with warm affection.

"*How* delighted I am to see you! I was so cast down when I heard you had left Birkland, and so happy to receive your letter from Newcastle. I have a thousand things to tell you. And, fortunately, I am able to remain for a week or so; Louisa has come to quarter herself at Tinnis Hall." She gave a sniff, reminiscent of her grandmother. "It seems that Liverpool is not a very comfortable town; so until Lieutenant Dunnifage can prepare a suitable abode for his bride, Louisa prefers to avail herself of the Chibburns' hospitality. But now, come, tell me about yourself. Poor Grandmother! I am sorry not to see her again. Though she always put me in a fright. And Parthie! *There* is a thing! She was always so devouringly anxious to grow up and enjoy adult privileges; and look what it has led to. I hope, at least, that she did so on her wedding journey; that Mr. Thropton indulged her and gave her a few treats."

"I very much doubt it," said Alvey, who found it desperately painful and guilt-inducing to contemplate Parthie's wedding journey—in that bleak weather, with no comforts, escorted by that repulsive man —staying at second- or third-rate country inns, with no female to aid or advise her. Parthie, who had always been accustomed to spoiling and self-indulgence. Imagination faltered at the details. "Wretched girl," Alvey said. "I feel hideously remorseful, now, that I did not take any pains to befriend her. If I had realised that her disagreeable nature was due to ill health—that her span was to be so short—"

Isa said firmly, "Just because people are unfortunate cannot make us love them," And, as so often, Alvey was impressed by her rock-bottom common sense, which made her own guilty self-questionings appear little better than false sentimentality.

James, informed by his father that Alvey was *not* his sister, indeed no relation at all, seemed, during the first day of his return to Birkland, utterly aghast and appalled at this bizarre situation. He eyed Alvey as if she were a basilisk, liable to strike him blind if provoked.

Alvey endured this in patience for twenty-four hours; then, seizing the chance of a moment when they were alone together in the drawing room, she said, "Come, brother James! You cannot treat me as if I were a monster forever. Do you not think it would be best to behave as if we were, in reality, brother and sister?"

He mumbled, "Yes, I suppose so," with an utter lack of conviction.

Alvey looked at him sadly. She could see his beauty; she could still be charmed and bedazzled by it. But she could understand, also, that her love for James had been a kind of mirage, a condensation of her feelings about the place, the country, the family; what she had seen was an image of him, floating up in the air, dangling in radiance, out of touch with the earth. The real young man, down below, was quite another matter; good-natured enough, hardworking, intelligent, even brave, even idealistic, in his way, but perhaps rather shallow, rather slow-witted when it came to human relations. Not unlike his father, but with less experience. Not connected in any way with the picture of him she had carried in her head.

"There! Never mind it!" she said kindly. "I am very happy to see that you have learned to manage so well on your artificial leg—" and received from him a cross, embarrassed smile.

And I would so much have liked to talk to him on so many subjects, she thought sadly. About the dreadfulness and uselessness of war—on which I am sure that we have similar ideas; and about his medical ambitions—but what is the use? I am irrevocably classified for him as a scheming woman, a kind of sister, only worse; not at all the kind of female with whom he wishes to have any dealings.

After the funeral was over, Guy Fenway said to Alvey, "I have
hardly had a chance to talk to you as yet. May we stroll on the terrace,
or can we take a longer walk?"

"Isa would be glad to take you for a longer walk; she is longing to
revisit her old haunts. For myself—I do have a number of household
duties; but I should enjoy a walk on the terrace, for half an hour."

"So," he said, when they were walking side by side, looking out at
the greening valley, "you ran away, and now you have been drawn
back again. Was that really a sensible course of action?"

"To go, or to come back?"

"To come back."

"Oh, but I had to! The children needed me—matters were all at
sixes and sevens—and the old lady—and Sir Aydon—"

"But cannot Isa now take care of all that? She was born here, after
all."

"Her mind is always somewhere else; she is like her mother."

"But don't you see!" exclaimed Guy impatiently. "You have let
yourself be caught in a trap! Louisa has escaped, but now *you* are a
prisoner in her place—snared in the web of family life."

"But I enjoy it."

"You will never be able to do your own work. They will make a
drudge of you."

"But I did manage to work—"

"Marry me!" he interrupted, without listening to what she said.
"Dear, dearest Alvey, marry me, and come with me to India. Escape
from all this! As my wife, in Hyderabad, you will have such a different, more interesting, more fulfilled life—"

"Go to *India?*" She was utterly taken aback; she could not have
been more startled if he had recommended that she marry the Duke
of Wellington and remove herself to Patagonia. "Marry *you,* Guy?"

"I love you," he said stiffly. "It may have escaped your notice—"

Looking back, she supposed she had noticed that he seemed to take
pleasure in her company. But love? She said hastily, "Oh, I am sorry,
Major Fenway, I am truly sorry. Indeed, I am—am deeply sensible of
the honour you do me—but no, no, it is not to be thought of, it is
quite out of the question. I am very sorry—very sorry indeed—you

are a good, a worthy, an intelligent man—it is not that I do not appreciate what you have to offer—"

Go to India, when I have just regained all this?

"What in the world would I do in India?"

"As my wife—there would be many— But you can't, you *can't* refuse me! I *love* you!"

"I am afraid you must learn to do without me." As I learned to manage without James, she thought. "I am probably not in the least what you imagine," she added consolingly. "We none of us are, really, are we?"

"If it is a case of your writing, you could do that just as well in India. Many ladies keep journals, I understand. There would be ample leisure— After all, you will never get much done here, with everybody pressing for your attention all the time."

"But I have. I did. I had a book published."

"*I* did not hear of this? Nobody informed me."

"Nobody knows. It came out under a nom de plume."

"Indeed? It did? What was the title?" he asked in a disbelieving tone.

"*Wicked Lord Love.*"

"Oh, come, my dear girl! You could not have written that. How could you possibly? I have heard of the book. I have even read it. What could you, situated as you are, know about such things?"

"I invented them."

"You are not seriously intending to tell me that *you* wrote *Wicked Lord Love?*"

"I am not intending to tell you. I have told you."

"But that book has been—is—a staggering success! Everybody in Edinburgh has been reading it—everybody in the country!"

"Yes, I know," said Alvey cheerfully. "I believe it is going to make my fortune. They are going to do a dramatic representation at Covent Garden."

Now he turned and looked at her, almost indignant with astonishment.

"*You* really wrote *Wicked Lord Love?*"

"Well, there is no need to show *quite* such surprise," said Alvey, now beginning to feel a little affronted on her own account.

For she could see that in some way his feeling towards her had subtly changed; he was not altogether pleased at the news; it had somewhat upset him. Perhaps he was already beginning to feel relief that she had declined his proposal? For what kind of a wife would she have been to introduce into regimental headquarters?

"Well, I was never so astonished in my life," he said at last in a quenched tone. "And I confess I do not at all see how you are to continue writing that kind of tale at Birkland Hall. Here, in this rural spot? In the depths of the country?"

Alvey hesitated, then said, "Nevertheless, here was where I wrote it."

"What makes you wish to write such stuff?"

"Oh, how can I tell? It just comes out."

She glanced at the watch on her waistband. "I am so sorry. I fear that I must leave you now; a number of people are coming to dinner and I have to consult with Mrs. Slaley. But I think you will find Isa in the drawing room—"

"Never mind, thank you," he said. "I have no wish to talk to Isa," and he strode off across the stable yard.

When the funeral guests were departed and the household reduced again to its normal quota, Isa said to Alvey, "I am sure you will be wishing to get back to your writing. I have not seen you retire to your room *once* since I have been at home. You must be longing to get to work. Just tell me what to say to Mrs. Slaley and I will say it."

"Oh, thank you. How kind you are! But I have not yet resolved on what my next book is to be about. And I find it does not help to sit at my desk and chew my pen."

"You did finish a book, then?"

"Yes, I completed one. I even had it published," said Alvey, beginning to feel that this was a rather too familiar conversation, and might become even more so. "It was called *Wicked Lord Love.*"

Isa said kindly, "I am sure it was very good. I hardly ever read novels, as you know. I prefer biography and memoirs. And, of course, we have been travelling . . . Was it well received?"

"Yes."

"So, now you will write another. What will it be about?"

I just told you—
Alvey said, "I am still waiting to decide."
And here was her problem. For, despite Mr. Seward's encouragement, the hideous suspicion was beginning to overtake her that she would never in her life be able to produce a sequel to *Wicked Lord Love*. That extravagant creature had leapt fully accoutred from her imagination and he was, if not an only child, at least the only one of his kind; she began to realise that there would be no successor to him.

"If I do write another novel," she said hesitantly, "it will, I think, be of a different kind. Perhaps the story of a family—a family such as this one."

For how could she write about the pasteboard gallivantings of another Lord Love when, after all these months, she had been feeling her way, like a person groping out of darkness into light, among real, solid forms? And a good half of them, she was now beginning to apprehend, she had never properly seen or understood—

It would be an entirely different kind of writing. One that she had never learned. It would mean starting all over again, from the very beginning.

"A family such as this?" Isa was puzzled. "But that would not be at all interesting. Our family is nothing out of the common. Just like any other."

"I daresay, when you get to know them, that all families are different from one another."

Isa sighed. "In my opinion, ours is decidedly dull . . . By the bye, did Major Fenway ever speak of me to you? He is such a clever, interesting man. And very kind, too, I think." She looked up hopefully and went on: "I have sometimes wondered what he thought of me." Did a tear sparkle in those shortsighted eyes? "I hope that he comes back to Birkland," she said simply.

Alvey answered quickly, "No: I fear he did not speak of you. But that means nothing."

She could not bear to quench the hope in those eyes. Not just yet. A loves B, she thought. B loves C. Oh, what sad geometry! She added, "You would hardly wish to travel to India, though, would you? He goes there in six months' time."

"No-o. That is true. I would not." Isa sighed again. "Well—if you do not need me—I shall get my sketchbook; I will be up on Blinkbonny Height, if anyone should ask where I am—"

Alvey went in search of the children, and found them just about to set off on an adventure.

"Making more islands?"

"No, we have found a Wilderness. It is a piece of land that seems to belong to no one—"

"Shaped like a triangle—" eagerly put in Nish.

"In a bend of the Hungry Water, and it is all covered over with brambles and whin and sloe bushes, so we are turning it into a Maze. With tunnels. It will take weeks and weeks and weeks," said Tot with satisfaction.

"Can I come too?"

"Not just yet. It would be too prickly for you. When it is all done we shall invite you to come and see it," Nish said kindly, and then the pair dashed away, carrying packets of food put up for them by Mrs. Slaley.

Alvey stood looking after them for a moment or two.

Presently she went up to her room and flung open the casement. Last night had brought the first autumn gale, with wind and pouring rain. The Hungry Water roared a new and louder welcome. And she could hear the subdued, conspiratorial chirpings of autumn birds— lapwing, stonechat, water ouzel, kestrel, curlew, and, up among the pines, a pheasant.

Now I have got to choose, she thought. I am going to be obliged to make a horrible choice: between my own imagination and the real world . . . .